HELLFIRE

VOLUME #1

A WHISPER OF ARMAGEDDON

Dedicated to Sensei Alan Smith, 6th Dan Aikido

A special thanks to the finest sensei I have known,
who taught me how to handle conflict, both in combat and in life:

"If he wants to go that way; let him go that way."

1

It was barely dawn, but it was mid-August in Helmand Province, Afghanistan, and the temperature was already climbing towards sweltering. Harry Thorne took a sip of water from his flask and wiped a trickle of sweat off his eyebrow. He didn't need to be in this dump, his father was a wealthy barrister, so he could have had a privileged upbringing and a cushy life, but he hadn't, he'd fought authority all his young life and bounced from one school to the next until he'd burned out his welcome. Which made his decision to join the marines all the more surprising, but it had been the making of him. He'd been a fat kid, but now at twenty-eight he was as fit and lean as a marathon runner and tanned to mahogany by the desert sun. The same blazing sun that had put thin streaks of white in his dark brown hair and given his hazel eyes squint wrinkles that would have driven a vain person nuts, but bothered him not at all. With his light frame and lack of height, he could have been a jockey — except he couldn't ride. His build was ideal for his chosen profession of sniper, where a light frame and compact height meant he could get into firing positions that a bigger man would have to pass up for second best. But his wiry build and lack of inches wasn't the only reason he was an expert in his trade; it was the punishing training, the constant practice, and his God-given talent, for which he was eternally ungrateful.

He took off his non-regulation camouflaged boonie hat and wiped the sweat off his brow, even though it would be replaced within a few minutes. He'd been watching the compound for four hours and was getting really sick of the view, the bugs, the discomfort, and the whole bloody thing. This had all the hallmarks of a total standard-issue screw-up.

The spooks had received a tip-off from the locals that this dump was being used by the Taliban for some nefarious purpose — bomb making, training, or some shit like that. So here goes 3 Commando Recon again to check the place out for unfriendlies, which is how come he was sitting in the sparse cover of a bunch of scraggy fruit trees on a hill overlooking the tumbled-down mud-brick buildings. Nothing, precisely nothing, was moving down there, or had moved in the whole time he'd been sitting there. And just to make sure, he squinted through the scope of his suppressed L115 sniper rifle suspended from a branch by a cord and pointed steadily at the front door of the largest building in the compound.

He heard the rustle of twigs and a tired sigh off to his left. That was Tom Daley, whose job, along with Big Jack Howe off to his right, was to prevent any ne'er-do-wells strolling in and finding Harry in an embarrassing position, so to speak. Everyone called him BJ, it being quicker to say in an emergency.

Harry was still fed up, but what do you want, Harry? Work in a bank? Yeah, right, like that was ever an option. It was just like his ol' mom always said — the sudden crackle in his earpiece stopped the ritual grumble before it got properly started, which was a pity because this one was going to be a classic.

A disembodied voice told him the choppers were inbound. Captain Ian Campbell — a fine Welshman, as Harry would point out to any press-types nosing around — was telling them not to do anything. Now what did the little prick expect them to do? Jump up and shout "Boo!"? You know, inbreeding has a lot to answer for. No, to be fair, Scotty was okay, a bit stiff, but a good guy. He'd crawled out onto the open road to pull that squaddie back into cover when they'd walked into an ambush a few months back. True, they shouldn't have walked into the ambush, but that's the nature of ambushes, they tend to be surprises.

As ordered, Harry did nothing. After a couple of minutes of doing that, he felt the beat of the Chinook's rotors as they swooped in to deposit the main assault team into the grey dust, and a few seconds later he heard the unmistakable sound of Kalashnikovs laying down heavy fire on the troops disembarking from the helicopters. He continued to do nothing. The crack of a Lee-Enfield sniper rifle came from forward and to his right, and he waited for the order to say hello to the insurgent sniper.

"God One. Go," Scotty said calmly in his earpiece. Tom and BJ heard the order too, and the three of them moved quietly out through the back of the copse, keeping the gnarled trees between them and the compound.

Tom Daley was as ginger as it is possible to be without being Scottish and took any ribbing about it really well, by decking anybody stupid enough to try. He was the human equivalent of a giraffe, with stick legs and a thin, ramrod-straight body. Ginger and over-tall, a perfect target, and many had tried, only to find this giraffe was a carnivore. He bent low, like a folded pipe cleaner, and led the way out of the trees, his HK MP5 sub-machine gun scanning right and left ahead of them.

BJ was on Harry's six, holding a C7 assault rifle fitted with an under-barrel AG-C grenade launcher and EC97 sight, an awesome fire support weapon he called Santa's Little Helper, in honour of Bart Simpson's unappreciated mutt. It wasn't through some squaddie-inverted humour that the lads called him Big Jack; he was a bear of a man, but like any friendly grizzly, he was as easy going as a jolly giant, until someone crossed the line, and then he tended to break them in half.

Between them, Tom and BJ could lay down 1400 rounds per minute, while Harry's L115 could castrate a gnat at a mile and a half. Some insurgent sniper was about to see how many virgins there are left in heaven — and that was likely to be a disappointing discovery, with the competition Harry had sent up there recently.

They moved as quickly as they could without drawing attention and getting themselves killed to death, which meant it took nine minutes to move out of the trees, slide down into the wadi without raising dust, and creep round to the top of the bare and sun-baked hill overlooking the compound, where the Enfield was still cracking away.

Harry was hot and sun-baked, and a swarm of flies had decided they liked the sweat running down his face. Probably the high alcohol content, he guessed. He spotted the place he'd been looking for and signalled his two watchers to flank him as he crawled up the dusty slope and looked through the scattered rocks that would be his fire position — if he didn't get his head blown off in the next two seconds, that is. He inched back from the ridge, careful not to raise even a whiff of dust. So far so good and his head was still intact.

He glanced left and right at BJ and Tom and saw they'd positioned themselves below the ridge, but in a good position to lay covering fire down his side of the slope. Okay then, show time.

He took out his Tigger handkerchief and wiped his face left to right and up and down, twice. Then, ritual complete, he unslung the L115, slid the dust sock off the suppresser, pulled the bolt, and chambered a .338 lapua round, his favourite load for its awesome stopping power. Okay, enough pratting around, time to pay the piper.

Normally Tom would be acting as his spotter, ranging the target and calculating windage and elevation, but at only twelve hundred yards, Harry could have hit the compound with a rock... well, almost. So Tom focussed on making sure nobody stumbled on their little camp-out.

Harry slid the rifle through the small rocks, rested it gently on its bipod next to a larger boulder, and squinted through the scope at the compound below. He'd doped the scope for the estimated distance to the compound, intending to use the mil dots to fine-tune the shot. And right there, in the middle of the mil dots circle, was the sniper, lying on a roof between piles of rubble and taking shots at the boys in the LZ a half mile away to the west.

As he started his slow breathing, he saw the sniper setting up for another shot, but didn't change his pace or rush the highly practiced action, as missing wouldn't save the intended target and would just give the guy a chance to move someplace else and get back to killing marines.

The sniper lifted his head to take a peek before firing. Harry squeezed the trigger, and a moment later, bits of the peeking head sprayed over the rubble around the ex-sniper. Harry had never favoured head shots, they were for the flash lads, but that guy had just stuck his up like a prairie dog, so bugger it. He slid back down the hill without worrying about dust, as the kick of the super magnum had put up a plume that would mark their position well enough.

"Playtime's over, lads," he said and set off down the slope towards the LZ and the relative safety of the eighty or so marines dug in behind the rocks, wadis, and in any handy itsy-bitsy rabbit hole.

Tom led the way, and BJ brought up the rear. Harry's rifle, having done its job, was now near useless if they had to fight their way out, so was slung over his shoulder. Normally he would be carrying his C8 CQB carbine for close up get-going work, but in this terrain, it would have been too much, too heavy, and just too many guns.

Without a word, Tom turned and fired up the hill back towards their little shooting spot. His sub-machine gun on full automatic was capable of hosing the hilltop at 800 rounds per minute from the hundred-round Bet C-Mag drum magazine he favoured, but common sense dictated that emptying the mag might be spectacular, but it would probably be fatal when the rest of the insurgents turned up, so he settled for dropping the four guys who'd suddenly appeared on the ridge, with a short and acceptably accurate burst. He grinned back at Harry.

"Take a bow later, flake," Harry said, and they set off at a steady run that would cover ground, but without risking a broken leg or a twisted ankle that right now would be a terminal disorder. He saw the dust kick up around him before he heard the crack of Kalashnikovs, but he didn't need a diagram to tell him what was next if they didn't get to cover in the next few seconds.

Just for a change, Fate was playing fair, and they slid backside first behind a tumble of boulders, just as a machine gun opened up, its lace of 50 calibre rounds tracking them. Harry squinted through the dust and spitting rock chips to see BJ and Tom face down behind the tiny, tiny cover.

"For Chrissakes, shoot a few of them!" Harry shouted above the scream and whine of rounds looking for their little pink hides.

Easier said than done, but one thing was a racing certainty, if they just lay there, that's where they were going to die. The sniper rifle was just too long to get into action without getting Harry's head blown off, so it was down to BJ and Tom.

Oh, lucky them.

Tom disobeyed his common sense and looked up through the gap in the rocks to see the insurgents swarming over the rise. Word had clearly got out that three sun-crazy marines had got themselves cornered, and every mother's son had grabbed a weapon and headed over for the turkey shoot. Jesus, there were hundreds of them.

He rested the MP5 on the rock, swore loud and hard, and squeezed off a five-second burst that sprayed fifty nine-millimetre rounds into the mass of bodies spilling over the ridge, dropping them in rows as if they'd suddenly lost the use of their legs, which strictly speaking, they had.

The insurgents took cover from the sudden and unexpected slap from the cornered invaders and gave BJ the space he needed to get the under-slung grenade launcher into operation, with devastating effect, as dust and body parts blasting across the hillside proved.

Okay, cool. Harry swung the sniper rifle round and up. At a hundred yards, it was like shooting tiddlers in a small barrel. Sure, he was limited by the five-round mag and bolt-action single shot, but every shot blew an insurgent's head clean off. Not as effective a mass-killing machine as the sub-machine gun or the assault rifle, but the shock value of seeing the guy in front of you lose most of his head had a lot going for it.

Outstanding, boys. Except the shock stopped the mob for only a moment and mostly pissed them off. A few seconds later, they'd rallied and were on the move again, almost oblivious to Tom and BJ mowing them down and Harry blowing bits off anyone who looked to be in charge.

Harry looked at the hilltop and had a sudden flash from the movie, *Zulu*, when the braves chugged up like a train. It looked for all the world like some sad padre would be paying the folks a visit.

A dust storm blew up. Well, thank you, Lord. Then he heard and felt the familiar thud of rotors beating the air, followed by the unmistakable rattle of a 30 mm chain-gun pouring 625 rounds a minute into the mass of bodies on the hillside.

He closed his eyes against the dust and sand blasting into his face, smiled, and said a silent thanks to the God he didn't believe in. Adding a request that the Apache pilot didn't get carried away and start firing the Hellfire missiles, or they'd all be toast.

The gunship roared over the hilltop in pursuit of the insurgents, who'd suddenly realised they had other pressing business elsewhere.

"Let's get the hell out of here," Harry said, to the backs of the other two, who were already heading south for the winter. "Hold up," he shouted after them. "What about protecting your principal, here?"

Tom shouted something that sounded like "rock you", but the Apache is a noisy beast.

Harry looked back at the hillside littered with sprawled bodies and unrecognisable bits of flesh that had looked for a while like being their final resting place. Not a bad result, then, though it could be said that orders to stay under the radar might now be a thing of the past, and Scotty would almost certainly say that, or something similar and a bit more colourful. Still, at least Harry would get to hear it. So yeah, a result.

By the time they'd covered the half mile to the compound that was the target of the dawn raid, they were in full sun and sweating again, and Harry raised his arm and smelled his armpit to prove it.

"Oh, very attractive," Tom said with a slow shake of his head.

"His mother would be so proud," BJ added with his customary grin.

"Leave my mother out of this," Harry said, feigning hurt feelings. "You know what my ol' mom always said—"

"Who are you? Get out of here. I'm calling the police!" The other two recited together.

"Oh, I've mentioned that before, then?"

"Once or twice," Tom said, pushing the big wooden doors open and stepping into the shade of the compound. "Once or twice a day, that is."

Harry stepped into the compound and backed up to the mud-brick walls. The other marines were already in there, going from house to house in search of bomb factories, drug labs, or stacks of 'how to be a good Taliban' magazines, but one thing he didn't do was rush in where wise men fear to tread.

BJ and Tom had forgotten their banter and were crouched low in the hard shadow of the high walls, scanning the interior for any sign of hostiles. The place was probably crawling with them, but they were keeping their heads down. Wise boys — except for the dead ones lying sprawled in the dust as breakfast for the swarms of flies. It looked like a half-dozen insurgents had won the chance to stand and fight the company of highly trained marines storming the compound, to give their bosses the chance to get the hell out of Dodge. Idiots.

Harry signalled BJ to go left and Tom right, while he walked straight down the middle of the narrow alley leading up to the square, twenty yards or so ahead.

A noise from up ahead saw the three of them move further into the deep shadows along the side of the alley and take up kneeling firing positions. Harry signalled them to hold and crept forward, scouring the shuttered doors and windows and peering at the rooftops silhouetted against a blazing sky.

He bent down without taking his eyes off the buildings and scooped up one of the Kalashnikovs from the valiant rearguard, who hadn't fired a shot before being blasted to bloody rags. The recycled weapon was much better suited to the alleys and flat-roofed buildings than his L115. That delay saved his life. He'd advanced maybe another fifteen feet when something or somebody detonated the IED.

Weirdest thing, in the microsecond after the flash and before the shockwave hit, he replayed the lecture from that boring little man who'd explained how an explosion kills you, as if anyone really wanted to know. The first thing that would hit him would be the highly compressed air particles travelling faster than sound, and it was this that would cause the most damage and kill him. He was pleased to know he'd be dead before the shockwave, white-hot shrapnel, and searing heat hit him. Always thinking positively, that's Harry, he should be called Pollyanna — but only once.

That was as much as the slow-motion explosion allowed. The blast hit him. He felt it for an instant, felt his body leaving the ground, and then crimson shards cut off his thinking.

BJ and Tom were twenty feet away, but the shockwave tossed them up against the building like rag dolls before the blast-wind sucking back into the vacuum pulled them off the walls and hurled them towards the blackened hole in the wall. By the time they hit the ground, they were unconscious, which shows God can have kind moments.

Well, that's it, then, Harry thought in the blackness. *I'm dead*. And he probably was, except that being able to think it kinda negated that possibility. He opened his eyes, but nothing happened to the blackness, except maybe it swirled a bit in counterpoint to the roaring in his ears and pounding in his head. A symphony of agony.

He told himself to move, and his body told him to go to hell. Beyond the roaring, he thought he could hear something, high-pitched and rising and falling. Probably his eardrums giving up the ghost, although behind all the roaring sound, it sounded like a child crying. Now that was just nuts, what would a child be doing... in a compound of houses and families. Shit.

He squeezed his eyes shut and open again, and this time was rewarded by seeing the blinding sun just clearing the rooftop enough to get to him. He took a breath and felt a broken rib play let's stab the lung. Staying still is good; he'd do that, except there was that screaming again. He wished it would just shut up and let him die in peace. No such luck. The screaming got louder, and he knew that he was going to live for at least long enough to suffer the agony of traumatic amputation of various limbs.

Somebody groaned, and he strained to hear above the roaring. There it was again, and he realised it was him. My hero. He risked puncturing his lung and pushed himself up slowly on his elbows. The pain crashed in his brain like a Hawaiian breaker, and he lay back down. The hell with this; he wasn't going to die chewing dirt. He sat up, closed his eyes, and fought the inclination to fall flat on his face. Okay, up — well, sitting at least, which was better than lying down and much better than being dead. His body reminded him of the error of that assertion.

Okay, he was going to do something, but what? Rescue the lads? He heard the scream again and looked across the alley that he'd flown across just a few seconds before. The mud-brick house was on fire, which was nuts. He shook his head slowly, and his brain bounced against the broken bones of his head, or at least that was the picture his mind painted. Thanks a bunch. Mud-brick houses don't burn. He didn't get it, must be shock or shit like that. No, dummy, mud don't burn, but the stuff inside does. Crap.

He leaned forward onto his hands and knees. Now that wasn't very bright, and his body tried to fall back into the dust to rest, just for a moment or two, but he resisted it by cranking up his will to breaking point. Okay, he stayed up. Now the hard bit. He pushed himself up into a kneeling position and felt the world spin, but he was up and was staying up. He put his hand against the wall to steady himself and saw it red with blood, but that he could worry about later. He put the other hand on the wall and pushed. The pain was beyond agony, and he heard his cry, as if from a distance. He opened his eyes and was amazed to find he was on his feet. Okay, he was leaning against the wall with his head hanging down like a three-day drunk, but up. He was going to do something, what? Oh, right, the kid, but it'd be dead now, so just let it be. He needed to rest. He'd rest when he was dead.

He staggered two steps across the fifteen-foot alley and stopped, waiting to either throw up or get over it. He went with option one. The screaming kid focused his attention, and he looked up to see a little girl, maybe seven or eight, standing in great big hole in the building's first floor, with flames cracking and jumping behind her. Ten seconds, twenty tops, and the kid would be in the flames.

"Jump!" someone shouted up at her, and he realised it was him. Stupid on two counts: she was Afghan so wouldn't understand him, and who the hell was going to catch her?

She jumped.

He caught her. God above knows how, and he wasn't telling. One second she was plummeting to her death — okay, probably not death from ten feet, but a bit of a mashing, which come to think of it, is the same thing out here in the middle of shitville, anyway—the next she was in his arms. And man, it hurt like crazy, but was a fair trade.

"Pappa!" she shouted in a kind of English that explained her jumping as instructed. What? What was she going on about? Oh shit, Pappa was under the rubble with all that fire heading his way. He put the kid down and started pulling at the mud-brick blocks covering a grey-robed body. There was no way he was going to be able to move them, not all busted up like he was, but the slab moved. What the hell? BJ stared at him with blank eyes showing extra white against his blackened face. Harry nodded and tried to say something, but gave up and leaned back against the wall to stop himself falling over.

An insurgent leaned over the roof edge opposite and shot him.

This time there was no slow-mo realisation of what was happening or descent into unconsciousness. One instant he was leaning against the wall, the next he was dead.

Tom opened up with the sub-machine gun and just held the trigger and screamed with shock and fury. The shooter came apart under the blizzard of bullets, but there were others, lots of others. Suddenly the rooftops were alive with Taliban intent on finishing the job.

Tom and BJ dived into the partially collapsed building, indifferent to the fact that it was still burning. Bit of a blister or shot to bits? No contest there. They shot everything that moved. BJ fired grenade after grenade onto the rooftops, snatching up the reloads without looking, while Tom laid down a withering blitz of bullets at anyone stupid enough to look over or get himself blown over. But it couldn't last; at eight hundred rounds a minute, it took only seven seconds for Tom to expend all the ammunition in the drum magazine.

On cue, the insurgents appeared across the skyline and began spraying the alley with automatic fire. Tom saw Harry's leg jump as a bullet tore through it and began to climb over the rubble, but BJ pulled him back and screamed at him not to be stupid. He was right, of course, because he wouldn't last two seconds out there. He swore and pulled out the last magazine for the sub-machine gun. Somebody was going to pay.

BJ tapped his arm, and he looked up to see the craziest sight he'd seen since he came to this insane place. The old man they'd pulled from the rubble was out there in the alley, dragging Harry by his blood-soaked webbing, while bullets kicked up the dirt around him like hailstones on a pond.

"Christ!" Tom shouted and swung the sub-machine gun up and round, firing short bursts at the insurgents leaning over the rooftops to get a shot at the madman. The throaty crack of the grenade launcher told him BJ was on the case. The insurgents shifted their attention away from the old man and to the two men who were killing them faster than it seemed possible.

They both knew it was just a matter of seconds before all their ammunition was gone, and then the insurgents would be all over them like flies on a rotting dog. What they needed desperately was—

The Apache gunship roared overhead at roof height, its chain-gun raking the rooftops and killing everyone up there, friend or foe. Mostly foe, because who's going to be stupid enough to be up there when all this hot metal is flying around?

Tom slapped BJ on the shoulder and grinned like an idiot. Suddenly the smile vanished, and he jumped to his feet and clambered over the rubble, but the old Afghan was gone, along with Harry.

BJ followed him through the broken bricks and into the narrow recess leading to a tall wooden door. Harry's body was leaning limply against the mud wall with the old man sitting next to him, his head in his hands, exhausted.

BJ knelt next to Harry's body and put his hand on the old man's shoulder without thinking. Okay, Harry was gone, but the old guy had stopped him getting all chopped up by those bastards.

Tom stood over them and felt the life drain out of him. He felt old, old and tired. What was the point of all this? The Brits had done this before, back in the 1800s, and got creamed. Those who fail to learn from history...

And thousands of men like Harry — no, not like Harry. Tom sat down next to his friend's body and hung his head.

Harry opened his eyes.

2

Harvey Thorne was a barrister, and even coming from the East End, and so the wrong side of the tracks, he was a scarily successful one, but he was having a bad day, and it was barely nine thirty. His day was about to get a lot worse. He was sitting behind an oversized leather-topped desk in an oversized office. The black leather chair creaked as it bore his weight — weight which would soon return to normal, as soon as the expensive exercise equipment did its thing, that is, as soon as he started using it. No one could suggest he was fat, no one would ever say that; in fact, he was almost the perfect weight, for a man a few inches taller than his five eleven.

His dark jacket hung on the curved coat stand by the window, below the motorcycle crash helmet with smoked visor, a signal to anyone who cared to read it that Harvey was having a mid-life crisis, a signal repeated by the shocking neon-pink tie with the lightening motif, and the red and yellow striped socks, which in some cultures would be a hanging offence.

He looked up from a close-typed report and out at the Thames flowing grey in the summer rain. Some people would kill for the location his chambers occupied, overlooking the river and in easy walking distance to The Strand, but Harvey had done that, been there, got the— well, not actually the T-shirt, he wouldn't have been seen dead in one, but he'd done the prestige bit, and... yes, he was bored. He wanted to do something else, instead of having to deal with rogues and villains, thieves and crooks, but politicians are the same the world over.

He wished something would happen to break the monotony. Someone should have told him to be careful what he wished for.

The office door opened silently, and a young woman with shoulder-length auburn hair and ink-dark eyes came in, stopped for a second, and brushed a speck off her immaculate dark business suit. She looked out at the river. One day.

"Something I can do for you, Laura?" Harvey asked, slightly irritated at having his brooding moment interrupted.

"Morning, Harvey," Laura said with a smile that lit up her face.

He sighed. "You know I like to be addressed as Mr Thorne in the office."

She shrugged. "Course you do, and I'd like a barman to ask for my ID, but neither is going to happen, is it?"

Which was true.

She continued to look out of the window distractedly. Harvey coughed, and she sighed and came back to this planet.

"That chap from the MOD is waiting."

Harvey frowned and waited.

"You know," Laura said, but obviously, he didn't. "The grumpy one with the moustache." She shook her head. "Who wears a moustache, since Mafeking was relieved?"

Harvey sighed. "All those nice, respectful young people, how did I get you as junior counsel?"

"Like winning the lottery, Harvey. Just plain luck."

"Quite. Are you going to show Sir Richard in any time soon?"

"Why," she asked, "doesn't he know the way?"

Harvey raised his eyebrows and was about to say something witty, but looked past her as a tall and very thin man in a wrinkled pinstripe suit ducked and entered the office. He did indeed have a moustache, not a handlebar, but one of those walrus things that usually had bits of whatever was eaten last stuck in it. At least he managed to avoid that, so it wasn't all bad.

Sir Richard stepped past Laura without a glance, as if she was one of those subalterns who had made his life so bothersome. He didn't look happy, but then he never did. He sat in the chair opposite Harvey, composed himself for a moment, and then told him. "Your eldest boy," he began, but Harvey was ahead of him.

"Something has happened to Harry?" Harvey's voice shook with the urgency of the question, and his soul seemed to fall out of him.

Sir Richard raised a long, slender hand. "No... well, yes." He waved the hand. "He's not... well, you know dead, well, not yet. Injured, I'm afraid, but I'm told he will probably recover." He was clearly a loss to the church of tact and compassion.

Harvey picked the good news out of that and breathed out slowly.

"I thought I'd better come and tell you myself," Sir Richard said a little pompously. "Rather than one of those dreadful people from the ministry, or God forbid, the regiment."

Harvey hadn't heard any of that. "Thank you, Richard," he said, in case he needed to. "What happened?"

Sir Richard frowned for a moment. "Got shot, I understand." As if that was enough.

"God!" Harvey said, with the confirmation of what he already knew still hitting him like a fist.

"Wounded twice, I believe," Sir Richard added, getting into the compassion role. "Chest and leg." He thought about it for a moment and nodded confirmation.

"But is he all right?" Bit of a dumb question, but Harvey was stunned and, for the first time in his life, struggling for words.

"Oh, I believe so," Sir Richard said. "On his way back to the UK. Fixed up in Camp Bastion and put on a transport home. Selly Oak Hospital first, I'm told." He waved his thin hand and smiled. "Back on his feet in no time, you'll see."

If that was his attempt at reassurance, he probably shouldn't give up his day job.

Harvey stood up, and Sir Richard frowned. "Are you going somewhere, Harvey?"

"Of course, I'm going to Birmingham."

Sir Richard frowned again. "Why?"

Harvey stared at him while his brain tried to reconcile the lunacy of the question.

Sir Richard caught up. "Oh, he's not there yet," he said, waving his hand again dismissively. "On his way. It's not a five-minute flight, you know."

Harvey sat down slowly and put his head in his hands as it whirled with shock. He'd objected loudly when he'd been told the boy was joining the marines, throwing his life away, almost literally it would appear, but he'd been wrong, it turned him from a timid, overweight teenager into a man any father would be proud of. One day he would tell him so and just hoped he'd get the chance.

"Harvey," Sir Richard said gently, "he's a tough boy. He'll be fine."

Laura strode in and crossed to the coat stand without speaking, unhooked Harvey's jacket, and came back to the desk, ignoring their puzzled expressions.

"Alan will have the car out front by the time you get down there," she said, holding the jacket for Harvey to put on. "You have a helicopter at Docklands that will get you to Birmingham in forty-five minutes."

Harvey's mouth opened and closed slowly, like a hooked fish, but no words came out — for a change.

Laura waved him up, thrust his jacket on, and pushed him gently towards the door. "What?" she said in response to his puzzled look. "I left the door open, couldn't help but overhear." She threw what could have been a smile at Sir Richard. "And it isn't such a long flight after all. He arrived at Selly Oak this morning, so that's good."

Harvey nodded, grateful for once that he hadn't chosen one of those nice respectful young people as a junior. "And Margaret?" he asked, struggling into his jacket.

"I think she can fly there herself," Laura said under her breath, "I'm sure she has her own broomstick." She saw how tired Harvey suddenly looked and nodded. "It's done, Harvey. Now you get out of here and go see your son."

Harvey and Margaret were standing at the foot of Harry's bed, both remembering him as a small child asleep on his Tigger pillow.

"Well, it certainly wasn't me who encouraged him to join the damned marines!" Margaret was shouting in a whisper, a technique she had mastered when the children were very young and shouting quietly was a necessity. "It'll make a man of him, you said. Get him away from all those layabouts, you said. Give him a sense of responsibility, you—"

"Did I say that?" Harvey said, having a completely different memory of the row with his son when he'd told him of his plans.

"You said I'd get myself killed," Harry said, in a voice that sounded like he'd had his larynx sandpapered.

Harvey and Margaret stopped discussing his imminent demise and turned as one — the first time they'd done anything as one for the past five years.

"He's awake!" Margaret said with a grin that would have surely scared the horses.

"Do you think so?" Harvey said, displaying the quick wit that had got him the separation he so regretted.

"So," Harry said, his voice a little less painful, "not dead, then?"

"Not for the want of trying," Margaret said stiffly. "What were you thinking, getting yourself shot like that?"

As questions go, it was right up there in the top ten most stupid.

"Dunno," Harry said with a shrug that paid him back ten-fold. He recovered from the daggers stabbing him in the chest and forced a thin smile.

"Don't ask stupid questions," Harvey said, taking the water cup and putting the plastic straw in Harry's mouth.

"Should you be giving him that?" Margaret said quickly. "I don't think you're supposed to give sick people water."

Harry and Harvey exchanged that old familiar look.

"That's only people you don't like," Harvey said and held the cup while Harry slurped tepid water that tasted as good as an ice cold in Alex.

At that moment, the men in white coats arrived. In fact, one man in a white coat with no name tag and nothing in the pockets. A consultant, then.

"Are you a doctor?" Margaret demanded, stepping up way too close to the man.

"No, madam," the doctor said, body-swerving past her and approaching Harry from the other side of the bed. "I am an accountant, here to help this man with his annual return."

Margaret blinked to clear the misfire, giving Harvey a rare opportunity to get in first.

"How is he?" he said, asking the question required at such times.

"Very lucky," the consultant said.

"Lucky would've been not getting shot," Harry said.

"Quite," the consultant said. "It would appear the bullet glanced off something in your pack, scored a deep groove in your chest, and clipped a rib, but it could have been a lot, lot worse."

"Good to hear, Doc," Harry said with a smile that was mostly morphine high. "A hero's wound, then?"

The doctor tutted, as doctors do. "There is nothing heroic about being blown up and shot, regardless of where."

"So he is going to be all right?" Margaret asked, sounding almost worried.

"Oh yes," the doctor said. "The chest wound will heal well enough." He picked up the chart and looked at it, because that's what it was there for. "But it's the trauma to your gluteus medius that causes me most concern."

Harry frowned.

"Buttocks," the doctor said, noticing — surprisingly — the looks of confusion.

Harry blew out a breath. "I got shot in the arse?"

The doctor watched him without speaking. He'd already said that, hadn't he?

"Okay," Harry said. "It's just my arse. So I'll be fit for duty in no time, right, Doc?"

"Harry!" Margaret said sharply.

"Oh no, no," the doctor said, adding another "no" in case there was any doubt. "The leg wound, although not life-threatening, is very serious. It will take a long time and a great deal of work for you to walk again."

"But I will get the full use back?" Harry asked, though he could already see the answer in the doctor's frown.

"There is no reason why you should not recover almost all of your mobility."

"Almost all?" Harry asked slowly.

"Oh, you won't be able to run far or..."

"Be a marine?" Harry helped out.

"Well, no. I'm afraid your military days are almost certainly over." The good news given, the consultant walked away, perhaps to share his great bedside manner with the other broken soldiers in his care.

"Well, I for one—"

"Shut up, Margaret!" Harvey snapped.

"Well, I never—"

"I seem to remember you did," Harvey added, "but I can't vouch for the last year."

Margaret spluttered and thought of a choice retort, but let it go unretorted when she saw the look of dismay on Harry's face.

"Don't worry," she said in what she thought was a soothing tone, "I'm sure everything will be just fine."

Harvey put his hand on his son's shoulder and ignored the heart-felt reassurance from Margaret. "Let's do this one step at a time," he said softly, completely missing the pun. "Get over the next few weeks, and let's see."

Harry was watching him the way he used to look at him when he was a little boy and missed an easy goal, waiting for the familiar look that said it was all okay.

"Doctors have been wrong before," Harvey said and smiled. Okay then.

Harry closed his eyes. His father was right, doctors have been wrong, and this one was wrong now. Count on it.

3

Laura tried not to stare at Bob, the young man sitting across the desk, but he was just so hot. Not helpful, him being a burglar and a client. Still, you can't ignore nature.

"So, what do you think?" Bob asked with a big grin.

Laura had no idea what she was supposed to be thinking about, except the X-rated movie that had just been running in her head. She was going to have to get out more. "I think," she said with a firm nod of conviction, "that you have a very strong case."

Bob frowned, tilted his head, frowned some more. "But the cops said they'd got me red-handed."

"They can say what they wish," Laura said, "but it will be up to the court to decide your guilt or innocence. And that's why you are here, with the experts."

"Ah, right, like those lawyers on the telly who always get their man off?"

Hot and brains, what a combination. Okay, slightly weighted on the hot side, but hey, who's keeping score?

"Yes," Laura said, flashing her best 'get over here' smile. "We will need to do some work, of course."

Bob smiled back, his blue eyes crinkled and bright. "Okay, can I help?"

Only if you like warm body oil.

Laura made an 'I'm thinking' face, which was mostly achieved by nibbling her bottom lip and frowning just enough. "I will probably have to debrief you properly," she said without the slightest tell.

"Okay," Bob said brightly. "Any time, you just say the word."

Count on it. "I'll check my diary and let you know when I can get you in."

Bob got up, smiled the Smile, and headed for the door, with Laura making sure he was walking okay after the long sit. Yes, everything seemed to be firm... err, fine.

She watched the door close behind him and took a moment to regain her composure. "For God's sake, girl, you're losing it," she said, sighed, and turned the laptop round to see her diary. Drat, no free time during the day, so that would mean an evening meeting, a late discussion, a protracted intercourse, get to the bottom of it. All the facts would need to be brought out into the open—

"Laura?"

She returned to earth to see Harvey standing in the open doorway. "Ah, oh," she said and coughed — that'll cover it. "Harvey, you're back."

"Not much gets past you, does it?"

"I was just, err..."

"Yes," Harvey said, glancing pointedly over his shoulder, "I believe I saw, just err... in the hall."

The air-con was clearly faulty. "How is Harry?" she asked quickly.

Harvey let out his breath slowly. "He's going to be okay," he said, but his tone said otherwise.

"Getting shot in the butt might be a joke in films, but in reality..." Laura shrugged. "He'll be retired from the marines on medical grounds?"

Harvey nodded. "Apparently he'll be almost as good as new, but not good enough to be a marine." He looked at the window without seeing it. "It was his life, you know?"

"Yes, but he'll adjust, other people have come home in body bags." Oh, great going, girl, full marks for tact. She closed her eyes and wished she could press the recall button.

Harvey smiled a tired smile. "It's okay, I know what you mean."

"What's he going to do now?"

Harvey watched her for a moment whilst he thought about it. "He'll come and work for us."

"We don't have much call for snipers." Sometimes stupid comes in sets of three.

Harvey laughed, which was just so unexpected, Laura chuckled too.

"Sometimes I think we could do with one," Harvey said, turning to leave, but stopped and looked back. "The young man?"

"New client," Laura said.

"Oh," Harvey said, "anything interesting?"

"They say he burgled some woman." She looked down at her pad. "Lady Lucinda Druce-White, whoever she is."

Harvey stepped up to her desk, picked up the brief and scanned the bullet point summary. "That will be the Druce-White horsey friend of the Princess Royal."

"Oh," Laura said.

"Oh, indeed. And Margaret's friend, as it happens." He shook his head at the thought. "I trust he didn't do it." Harvey waited for the confirmation.

"Guilty as sin."

Bugger.

"Did you know Margaret has a new man friend?" Laura asked, in an effort to lighten the mood, and to cause a little mischief.

"How do you know that?" Harvey asked, surprised and doing a poor job hiding it.

"Grace told me."

Harvey attempted glaring, but did a poor job. "I do hope you don't discuss my affairs with Grace."

"No," Laura said, checking that her nails were... well, nails. "Not that you have any affairs to discuss. Except that one time, of course."

Harvey looked around before he could stop himself. "Let's not go into that again."

"Yes, I can see how you'd want to let that disappear down the plug hole." She raised her eyebrows. "And anyway, Grace is your partner's junior, so of course we discuss things."

"Things yes, me no."

Laura raised her eyebrows. "Trust me, Harvey, life's too short." She ignored the look. "Anyway, doesn't it bother you that your ex is off on the razzle?"

"She's not my ex, and she is free to do whatever she wishes," Harvey said haughtily and a little miffed. "And please try not to use such base terms."

"Wouldn't hurt you to get a bit razzled," she said with a quick smile.

"I'll have you know I have many female friends," Harvey said — at the worst possible moment.

"Really?" Margaret said, coming into the office perfectly on cue. "That'll be a first."

"I hear that," Laura said half under her breath.

"Good day, Laura," Margaret said, her face smiling, but her tone icy. "You look tired, dear. Did you go to bed too early?"

Laura mirrored the warm, sincere smile. "It's the burden of youth, I suppose."

Margaret's lips tightened to their usual line, and she turned her attention back to Harvey, who was trying to edge to the door without appearing to move. "I understand you have taken the Robert Doyle brief?"

Harvey glanced past her at Laura, who gave him a big nod. "Yes, it would appear so."

"Am I to understand that you have taken this on a pro bono basis?"

Again the glance and the nod. "Yes, I have decided that the facts of the case warrant—"

"So, once again you have taken a pro bono brief without discussing it with me."

True, but nobody was going to say it.

"We take pro bono work," Harvey said quietly. "At least this part of the chambers does."

"You are aware, are you not, that I am prosecuting this case?"

No, not a hint.

"Yes," Harvey lied, "but I don't think—"

"No, Harvey, you don't," Margaret said, beginning her usual stamp up and down the office. "That's always been your trouble, you don't think. Well, can you bring yourself to think about the obvious conflict of interest this raises for the chambers?"

Harvey put his hand on his chin and rubbed it to signify deep thought. "I must say that I can't see one, dear."

Ooops.

"Don't call me dear," Margaret hissed through clenched teeth. "You lost that right when you were caught with that... that tart!" She cut him with a practiced look. "Very well," she said, making a visible effort to control her temper, "let us proceed, and may the best man win. Who, in this case, is a woman." She swept out of the office, reached for the door handle to give it a good pull, missed, tripped, and disappeared out of sight.

Laura checked her nails again, but her shoulders were rising and falling as she stifled her laughter until eventually it subsided enough for her to speak. "Note, she was very specific about being caught with the tart," she said without looking up. "Implying that, had you not been caught at it, you may both still be together."

Harvey sighed. Yes, he'd been with that... err... okay, that tart, but nothing had happened, it was just a silly prank at the club, that was all. Too much drink, and too many dares — which at his age was a bit... well, sad.

He looked at Laura, who looked back with a 'told you so' expression, that being mostly raised eyebrows and puckered lips, but familiar, oh so familiar. What on earth had possessed him to employ a female junior so that he was now surrounded by them. They didn't think like ordinary people.

"Allow me to interpret semantics," he said at last. "I'm the QC here?"

"Better start interpreting, then," she said, tidying up the Robert Doyle paperwork. "Because it looks like you're going head to head with Margaret on the Bob the Burglar case."

"Please do not refer to our client as Bob the Burglar." Harvey was tired; it had been a long helicopter flight to the hospital. Forty minutes, true, but forty minutes in a confined space with Margaret was enough to exhaust anyone, leaving aside the trauma of seeing his son connected to tubes and machines.

"Why not?" Laura asked with a shrug. "They have him banged to rights."

"And in which law book did you read that precise definition?"

"Fact. He did it. He's going down."

Harvey looked upwards. Why me, Lord? But the Lord was playing golf with a chap from Wales. He looked at Laura and decided it could be worse. He just couldn't think how just then. "We shall see,' he said, just to end the conversation politely.

"Ah, right, you think you can get him off?" Laura said with a sarcastic chuckle.

Harvey shrugged.

"Okay then," Laura said. "Let's look at the facts, shall we?" She stood up and leaned on the desk as if addressing the jury. "One." She began counting off on her fingers. "Bob was caught with property from a half-a-million jewellery heist."

"Perhaps he found it and was returning it to its rightful owner." Now, not even Harvey could make that one sound plausible.

"Two," Laura continued, with a look of contempt at Harvey's opening defence. "He's a known criminal with a rap sheet as long as an Andrex toilet roll." Which wasn't entirely true, but she wasn't about to let truth get in the way of a good prosecution.

"Irrelevant and inadmissible."

"And his fingerprints are all over Lady LDW's belongings."

Harvey avoided the obvious and went for the non-committal shrug.

"Not to mention that Lady LDW is next to royalty."

"She sits next to one, if that's what you mean," Harvey said, happy to have pulled it back to forty-fifteen.

"And," Laura said, followed by a long pause, "you say Lady LDW happens to be one of your ex's coven."

"Her relationship with..." He caught himself before he called Margaret his ex, but it was already out there, flapping about like a fish on the desk. "That Margaret knows Lady LDW is irrelevant and has no bearing on the case. And remind me, what property was Bob... Robert Doyle found in possession of, and on which his fingerprints were allegedly found?"

Laura sat down again, having addressed the jury, and waited.

"It was a dog, wasn't it?"

"True," Laura said innocently, "but it was Lady LDW's dog."

"That remains to be seen."

"It has been seen," Laura said, pointing at the photograph half visible in the file. "It's a shitzu."

"Bless you," Harvey said with a smile, the first real one of the day.

Laura frowned an exaggerated frown and then snapped her fingers. "That was a joke, wasn't it?" She shook her head. "Tell me next time, so I'll know when to laugh."

"The point is," Harvey continued, a bit disappointed at the response to what he thought was actually a rather funny pun, "one shitzu looks very much like another."

"Perhaps, but have you ever heard of a burglar owning a fluffy white doggy named Puccini?"

"Just because we haven't heard of it, doesn't mean it hasn't happened."

A reasonable argument.

"Right. That would go down well at the Cut Throat Tavern. They'd throw him out of the burglars' union."

"There could be a perfectly reasonable explanation."

"Yeah," Laura said, "that being, he nicked the pooch with the jewels."

"Nice to see my junior council has such an open mind," Harvey said, walking to the door.

"Fifty says he'll be banged up before you can say M'Lud."

"Hardly ethical to be wagering on the outcome of our own case." He opened the door. "Fifty it is, then." He waited a few seconds, clearly thinking. "Do you actually have fifty pounds?"

4

The hotel room was freezing, which struck the Russian sitting with his feet on the low table as odd. Odd because this was Kabul, and since the Americans and the British smashed everything in sight to get to the Taliban, nothing worked anymore, least of all the air-conditioning. It was odd, too, that the quiet Arab who was watching him from across the table would want to be cold, but Arabs aren't very bright. He'd learned that as a major in the Soviet army of occupation; what he hadn't bothered to learn was that Afghans are not Arabs. And now he wouldn't learn it because the not-very-bright Afghans had kicked him and the rest of his army out. But some things are important, others less so.

Valentin took his feet off the table and stood up stiffly. He was old, even though he resisted the idea, and a cold room plays havoc with aging joints. He was sure he used to be taller, but now he seemed a little bent, barely five foot eight, with hair that had long since passed the greying at the temples stage and was now white and thin. But what he disliked most about getting old was his eyes, which were once sparkling and clear, but now were yellowish and bloodshot. And peeing... well, don't even go there.

"Then we have an understanding?" he said, trying to ignore the clicking sounds from his knees as he stood.

The quiet Arab stood up in a single fluid move that clearly irritated the Russian. "We do," he said in perfect Oxbridge English that jarred with his traditional thawb robe and black-checked keffiyeh headdress. "And I shall ensure that all goes well."

The Russian nodded. He wanted to get outside into the sunshine; he'd been in the cold too long. "Timing is everything."

The Arab nodded slowly. "It always is, Major, it always is."

5

The first time Harry swung his legs off the bed and stood up between the crutches, he almost fainted, which would have given the boys in the squad a hooting fit, but he gritted his teeth and waited for the room to stop spinning.

"You may feel a little dizzy at first, Harry," the nice young physiotherapist said helpfully, if a bit late.

"No, I'm fine," he lied. "Now how do these work?"

The physio stepped closer and adjusted the crutch under his left arm. "There. Now push them forward and swing your right leg." She smiled, close up to his face. "That's the good one."

Oh, that was a joke. Harry grimaced, which was as near to a smile as anyone was going to get while he was pratting around on these things. Okay, you can do this. Like there was an alternative. He put the crutches forward a foot or so and stepped his good leg up between them, his shot leg he held up and back. Later for the heroics.

Okay, one giant step for mankind. He overdid the next step, too eager to just get this bloody daftness over with and start running again.

Lucy, the cute physio, caught him as he started to fall backwards. "Not so fast, Harry, give yourself time."

Yeah, as if he was ever going to do that.

He took a breath, ignored the screaming pain in his chest as the gouged rib protested, and set off. Three more steps and he had it. Out into the corridor, down past the bog and shower room, back up the corridor and into his room. Five minutes flat.

"Okay," he said a little breathlessly as he sat on the edge of the leather physio couch. "What's next?"

Lucy frowned. "Nothing, this is all the next you're going to get, at least for two more weeks."

"Bollocks to that," Harry said, standing. He steadied himself and then put down his left foot.

"Harry!" Lucy took his arm. "What on earth are you doing?"

"Soonest started, soonest finished," he said through clenched teeth.

"No, no, this isn't the way." Lucy pushed and manhandled him back onto the couch. "You idiot! You're not ready for that. You'll tear the stitches and be back in theatre." She actually wagged her finger at him. "Now, you listen to me."

He listened, the pain in his thigh telling him she spoke not with forked tongue.

"First, we get your strength back, while we let nature and medical science heal you. Then you sign up for the marathon. Deal?"

He nodded. "Deal." God, he could do with a drink.

"Very well, one more time."

He sighed. This was going to be a hell of a lot harder than fighting the Taliban.

Amen to that.

6

Harvey's apartment was huge, belying the axiom that crime doesn't pay — except when other people commit it, that is.

He sat on the long leather sofa with his feet on the inlaid wooden coffee table and looked out through the window wall at the Thames traffic passing below. He poured himself another coffee from the tray next to his feet and sighed a tired sigh. The doorbell rang, dragging him back from the edge of what was promising to be a nice quiet rest.

He opened the door, prepared to tell the hawker that he didn't want one, and there stood Ashley, a sultry brunette of Latino descent. His mouth formed a perfect O. He looked her over. He just couldn't help himself. She was in her early twenties, with long straight hair over her shoulders and dark eyes that glistened and flashed sensual mischief. She wore a tight, brown vest under a khaki military-style jacket. The vest was short, and her tanned and firm stomach peeked out between it and the top of her beltless blue jeans. Nobody should be that beautiful; she made the rest of the world look drab.

She smiled a white and beautifully even smile. "Is Rocky in?"

Harvey blinked, closed his mouth, and blinked again, and then pulled himself together with a shake of his head. "Rocky? I'm sorry, you have the wrong apartment." Which was a pity.

"Ashley?"

Harvey's son stepped between him and the door, took the girl's hand, and led her into the living room and immediately towards his room.

"Rocky?" Harvey said to his departing son.

"Yeah," the boy said. "Can't have a name like Warrington if you're a serious musician."

"I hate to break it to you... Rocky, but you're tone deaf." Harvey gave a quick shake of his head. "Do you remember your piano teacher? She was in tears when we came to collect you."

Rocky shrugged and followed Ashley into his room. "Don't worry, Pops, don't play the piano. Cheers."

Harvey watched him go and wondered if he should say something about him going to his room with a stunning young woman. He decided against it, what was he going to say, anyway, that wouldn't make him look like an idiot or a prude?

Rocky put his head back round the door. "Hey, what's this I hear about Mom going on a date?" He nodded approvingly. "Good for her."

"Thanks for your support."

"Hey, Pops, I was just saying."

"And," Harvey said sternly, "I'm just saying, you call me Pops again, you'll be looking for somewhere more in keeping with your struggling musician persona."

"Gotcha, Pop... Dad. But I'm not going to be struggling for long, we made a demo and sent it to the record companies." He winked. "Phone'll be ringing any minute. Want to hear the demo?"

Harvey almost cricked his neck with the speed of the shake. "No. No. No, thank you." He could've added a few more no's, but didn't want to seem too negative.

"Sex, drugs, and rock 'n' roll." Rocky winked again. A tic perhaps. "Didn't they do that when you were a kid, back in the olden days?"

"No," Harvey said firmly, "we did not. We studied hard and lived clean lives." Well, there was someone who wasn't going to heaven.

Rocky stared at him for several seconds, lost for words, before closing the door quietly.

Harvey watched the door for a moment, thinking about his youth, and all that, err... rock 'n' roll. God, was it that long ago?

Rocky pushed the door closed with the heel of his foot and smiled broadly at Ashley bending over the computer desk in the corner, rummaging in the bottom drawer for nothing in particular. Her blue jeans were stretched tight across buttocks that told of long workouts in the gym. He stepped closer and patted her behind firmly, with the denim creating a muffled slap. She giggled and waggled just a little.

She continued to rummage in the bottom drawer for something she wasn't looking for as Rocky reached around her waist and undid the top button of her jeans, then slowly unzipped them. He hooked his fingers into the waist and pulled them down slowly, careful not to move the white lace panties. They were for later.

Rocky smiled, turned her to face him, and kissed her hard. He unfastened her bra and tossed it onto the bed, stepped back and looked her over very slowly, starting at her feet, working up her legs, lingering for a moment where they met her body, then on up to her small breasts that stood out firm and tanned.

She shuddered from the tingle the slow look gave her, reached down, and pulled off his T-shirt. Later... had arrived. He stepped out of his jeans and took a step, stopped, and took off his socks.

Ashley jumped onto the bed, pulled down the pillows and made a pile for his back. She patted them, and her breasts bounced. This wasn't going to take long. He glanced at the clock. Luckily reinforcements were on the way. And Ashley and Amanda loved each other, so all he'd have to do is watch. Well, at least for a while.

Harvey glanced at Rocky's door and shook his head slowly at the loud music. Though, if he wasn't mistaken, that was Neil Young. So things hadn't changed that much since he was a kid. He poured himself another coffee, sat back into the big chair, and got ready for a well-deserved rest. The doorbell rang as soon as he put his feet up, and he sighed heavily, a new and increasingly frequent mannerism. He got up heavily, crossed the big room, and opened the door.

"Evening, son," Frank said, the scruffy old man standing behind a battered suitcase.

"Dad!" Harvey said and instinctively looked both ways down the short corridor, as if he expected to see others there. He expected to see the police.

Frank leaned back and followed his look. "Don't worry, son," he said with a cheeky smile, "nobody saw me come in. I used the back door."

"No, that wasn't—"

"Yes, it was," Frank said, still smiling, "but that don't matter. Can't blame you."

Harvey was about to ask how he managed to use the locked back door, but some things are best left unknown.

Frank picked up his case, walked into the apartment, and looked around appreciatively. "Like what you've done to the place."

Harvey had his frown again. "It hasn't changed since the last time you were here."

"My point exactly." Frank's smile widened. "Margaret was here then, wasn't she?"

Harvey ignored that. "What can I do for you, Dad?" As if he didn't know.

"What makes you think you need to do anything? Can't I just visit?"

"Yes, yes, of course you can. You're always welcome, you know that." And any lingering chance of heaven popped out like a faulty fairy light.

"Yeah, I suppose," Frank said with a slow shake of his head. "Just as long as I don't stay."

"No, not at all," Harvey said hurriedly, slipping his head into the noose. "You can stay as long as you like."

Snick.

"Thank you, son," Frank said, picking up the battered suitcase. "I'll take this to my room, then." He strolled over to the door next to the one used by Rocky and the Latino lovely.

"No, wait," Harvey said, with a hint of desperation. "When I said you could stay as long as you like, I meant—"

Frank looked over his shoulder. "Oh, then you don't mind me living on the streets?"

Harvey was confused, which for a barrister was a terminal affliction. "Why would you be living on the streets? What's happened to your house?"

"Nothing," Frank said. "Oh, your mother threw me out."

"What?" Harvey sat on the back of the sofa, suddenly feeling the need for support. "What on earth for?"

"She found out about the barmaid from the Bush."

Harvey frowned. "The Bush? You mean that brassy blonde girl with the big—"

"The very one," Frank said, his smile back, but bigger.

"But she's only about thirty years old!"

"Twenty-seven, actually," Frank corrected.

"That is a very disturbing image."

"Depends on your point of view," Frank said with a wink.

"Well, no wonder Mom threw you out."

"Oh, it was all getting a bit strained anyway, what with the drinking and gambling."

Harvey waved him towards the bedroom door, admitting defeat. "The barmaid, gambling and drinking? I'm surprised Mom didn't just kill you."

Frank opened the bedroom door and peered into the immaculate room, a state soon to change. "It wasn't me with the drinking and gambling." He pushed the door. "It was your mother."

Harvey did a double take as the door started to close behind Frank. He was joking, right?

The door opened again. "If you still have those blokes in waiter suits bring your meals, get them to bring me a nice rare steak with everything on." He started to close the door and then stopped. "Oh, and a bottle of single malt." He pulled a face. "That stuff you drink gives me terrible gas." He closed the door.

Harvey looked up. "Thank you, God, that makes my life complete."

Harry was walking, if that's what they call the slow stagger he was using to get out of the hospital. Two weeks of agonizing exercise, punctuated by agonising rest, but he was bloody well determined not to be a victim. Sod the sympathy, that and a buck would buy a coffee. He was out of there.

"Okay, Harry," Lucy said, still fussing, "we can't make you stay, but you have to be careful." She put a hand on his shoulder, and he stopped. "Promise me you'll be careful."

Harry flashed a smile that lit up his lined face. "I promise I'll be careful."

Lucy shook her head. "I wouldn't buy a used car from you if that's the best you can do."

Harry chuckled and raised his hand to touch her, but quickly put it back on the elbow crutch that was the main reason he was still upright. "Okay, I promise I will stick with the exercises and the medication, and the ice, and the—"

"Okay, I believe you," she said, stepping past him and triggering the electronic door. "But you must continue your rehab and visit the physio I have recommended."

He nodded. "Deal," he said, resuming the slow walk to freedom, and then stopped and looked back. "Hey, thanks, Lucy, I couldn't have done it without you."

"Bloody right you couldn't!" She smiled and ushered him on. "Now get out of my sight, I have a busy day."

He winked and walked back into his life, with no intention whatsoever of visiting any more torturers masquerading as physiotherapists. What he did intend to do, though, was to get the hell out of there, go home, and go to the pub.

He climbed awkwardly into the taxi, glanced at the crutch for a moment, tossed it onto the neatly trimmed grass, and slammed the door. The taxi started off, stopped, and he leaned out the window to ask a kid on a small scooter to please pass the crutch he'd accidentally dropped.

7

Valentin Tal stood quietly in line in front of the immigration desk and watched his fellow travellers shuffling slowly towards the grim-faced officials. He was smiling, but he had plenty to smile about. He was alive for the first time since '91, before his beloved Soviet Republic had been brought to its knees by lust for Western materialism. It still didn't seem possible that such an unshakable world power had simply imploded. It was Gorbachev's blind drive for modernisation that had turned the USSR into a laughing stock, compounded by the oligarchs flashing the obscene fortunes they had made off the backs of the ordinary man.

Valentin handed his passport to the official.

But the days of rolling over for the Americans were gone, and a new dawn was rising over the world, a dawn that would dazzle everyone. And he almost believed it.

The grim immigration officer behind the desk asked if the purpose of his visit was business or pleasure.

"My business is my pleasure," Valentin replied with a little nod. He could say that sort of thing openly now, nobody would remember him, not after more than twenty years.

The officer gave him a long, hard look, and just for a moment, Valentin wondered if he'd been too smug, but then the officer handed him his passport and invited him into the UK with a nod.

Had it been a week later, the grey border agency officer behind the one-way glass would be retired and Valentin would have passed through anonymously. But on such straws of bad luck, whole campaigns have been known to trip. Mike Taft did a double take as Valentin walked past the immigration desk and stepped closer to the glass. Even with the evidence scant feet away, he could barely believe it. Valentin Tal. He was sure he'd died years ago, and probably not from natural causes. He reached for the phone.

Valentin stepped out into London Heathrow's polluted air and took a breath. All those years he'd been buried in the counterintelligence division of the former KGB they'd rebranded as the Federal Security Service, but now he had a real mission, and he wasn't going to screw it up. Soon Russia would be back, and the world would see how she dealt with the gangsters who had made a fool of her.

And that he did believe.

8

Harry stepped out of the lift on Harvey's floor and waited for his breath to settle down. No point looking all weakly and girlie for the old man. Okay. He steadied himself on the lightweight crutch that was to be his constant companion and set off for the apartment.

Harvey was out, which was no surprise, it being a working day, but Frank was home and opened the door with a glass of single malt in his hand, and pulled the door all the way open when he saw Harry. "Hey," he said with a big grin. "You should've said they were chucking you out, and I'd have come to get you."

Harry clunked into the apartment and sat at the round table still littered with Frank's breakfast that had been incrementally delivered by several waiters. He breathed a long sigh of relief now the nightmare journey was finally over. Maybe Lucy had been right, maybe it was a bit early. Bollocks, a man could die just lying about in hospital, and in fact, he'd seen some of the wounded do just that. A sobering thought. And speaking of sober...

"It's a bit early for that, isn't it, Gramps?" He pointed at the glass in Frank's hand.

"I think it's a bit late, really."

It was a joke about his age, Harry had heard it before, and it still wasn't funny.

Frank saw the look, put down the glass, and changed the subject. "So, what're you going to do now the marines have chucked you out?"

Sensitive, caring, thoughtful, tactful — all words that didn't fit what he'd just said.

"Not chucked out," Harry said. "Yet."

"Right," Frank said, unconvinced.

Harry rested his head in his hands, more tired now than he could remember ever being, and on patrol in Helmand he'd been totally shagged most of the time, but that had been different. Being that close to a sniper's round or an IED does something to a man's perception of what he can endure.

"Let me get you something," Frank said, the smile gone. "You look done in."

Harry lifted his head and forced a weak smile. "Nah, I just need to rest."

"I think your room is still pretty much as you left it."

"Oh, shit. Then it'll look like a small hurricane hit it."

Frank chuckled. "Do you think your mom and your sis would just leave your room in a mess?"

That was a fine example of a redundant question, and Harry smiled. He started to get up and waved away Frank's offer to help. "Old bugger like you," Harry said with a chuckle, "you'll have us both over."

He slept like a dead person, perhaps experiencing what he'd narrowly missed, and didn't wake up until eight thirty the next day, way past his usual reveille.

Harvey was already up, sitting at the round table eating a breakfast of toast and boiled eggs and reading a fawning article discussing the dubious benefits of the UK forming an alliance with the United States and Germany — which to some might have seemed ironic — to rape the Arctic of its resources. A treaty to be signed soon. *We're all going to be rich*, he thought, with a slow shake of his head. He looked up in surprise when Harry clanked into the room on his crutches.

"Harry?" he said and put down the toast. "Nobody told me you were coming."

Harry smiled. "Hi, Pop. Nobody told you because nobody knew." The smile widened. "Not even the doctors."

Harvey stood up and pulled out a chair in time for Harry to crash into it. "Sorry, not used to walking wounded in the place."

Harry worked his way round the chair and sat down heavily. "No probs."

Frank came in from his room looking like the morning after a bender, which was appropriate. He crossed to the table, sat down, and helped himself to Harvey's toast without acknowledging either of them. Eventually he looked up, but only to ask if there was another cup. "Not to worry," he added, slurping Harvey's coffee.

Harvey and Harry exchanged glances. "Would you like breakfast?" Harvey asked.

"Yeah, but just toast and coffee."

Harvey picked up the phone hiding on a little shelf under the table and tapped a number. "Yes, thank you," he said to the unseen speaker. "Can you bring coffee and toast for two, please. Thank you. No, that's all."

Frank picked up Harvey's newspaper before he could reach it, pulled off the front page, and handed it to its previous owner.

"How can you get marmalade on the paper when we don't even have marmalade?" Harvey asked, holding it as if it had been used as a dog loo.

Frank shrugged without lowering the newspaper. "It's a gift."

Harvey had a smart answer ready for delivery, but Ashley walked past, wearing nothing but one of Rocky's shirts.

"Bathroom's through here?" she said sleepily. "Oh, morning."

"Morrr..." Harvey said.

Frank chuckled. "Yes, more would be nice, but I can't see how that could be possible and still be legal." He shook Harvey's newspaper open and went back to reading the sports pages.

Rocky's door opened, and another girl appeared, this one blonde and also wearing one of Rocky's shirts — a T-shirt with some rock band's logo on the front — and padded sleepily into the room. "Do I smell coffee?"

Nobody moved.

The doorbell ringing saved the day. Harvey regained his wits and started to stand, but Frank, showing surprising sprightliness for his age and his condition, got up. "That'll be breakfast. I'm starving."

Harvey was about to remind him whose breakfast it was, but the girl smiled, and he forgot.

"I'm Amanda," she said softly.

"Course you are," Harry said, before the old man's blood pressure ran into the red. "Come and sit down." He pointed at Frank's vacant chair. "And tell us more about Amanda." Which wasn't what he was thinking.

Frank glanced over his shoulder and tutted. Kids, they have no idea how to behave.

"Bonjour," said the little man in the white uniform, "I am Serge, and this is your petit dejeuner." He pointed unnecessarily at the trolley and the domed silver serving tray.

"I'm going to like it here," Frank said, looking from the tray to the half-naked blonde girl, and stepped aside to let Serge enter.

Serge trundled the trolley past and transferred the breakfast to the table, without even glancing at the girl in the tiny T-shirt.

As he rolled the empty trolley back out the door, Frank put his hand on his shoulder. "Don't tell me, let me guess," he said, pulling a thinking face. "I'm good with accents."

"M'sieur?" Serge said, clearly puzzled.

"It's Basildon, isn't it?" Frank said with a smile. "Go on, I'm right, aren't I?"

Serge looked like a startled rabbit caught in headlights.

"Don't worry, son," Frank said, patting Serge's shoulder, "I won't tell anybody."

Serge looked around quickly. "Cheers," he said, losing the French accent. "It's just that they only employ exotics here, and I need the job."

Frank smiled and put his arm round Serge's shoulders. "Don't worry, Sergey-boy, your secret is safe with me."

"Ta," Serge said quietly. "Appreciate it."

"No probs," Frank said, leaning a little closer. "Just keep me topped up with single malt without His Nibs over there knowing about it and we'll be like brothers."

"I can do that," Serge said, shaking Frank's outstretched hand.

"And for God's sake, bring some decent grub, 'cus that stuff in the fridge would stop up an elephant."

"Done," Serge said, rattling his trolley away down the corridor.

Frank went back to the table, to find the girl had returned to Rocky's room with one of the coffee pots, Harvey had rescued his newspaper and was heading for the door and probably his office, and Harry had eaten the toast.

Ashley padded back across the room, things moving as things should. Frank smiled. Yes, he was going to like it here.

Harvey arrived at his office early, it being barely nine fifteen, but the apartment was getting crowded — and the girls didn't seem in too much of a hurry to get dressed. He leaned back in his oversized chair and looked out the windows at the tops of the trees along the river showing the first gold of autumn. He sighed, not looking forward to another winter in London, now that his bones had started to complain about the damp. Getting old, how sad is that?

The door opened, and Laura came in, accompanied by a young man who could get a job flashing his pecs to sell man-perfume, except this young man had chosen a different profession — thank God, because man-perfume, how weird is that? Harvey put the thought aside and let the young man's choice of career stay with its owner.

He watched Laura watching the young man's butt as he came forward with his hand extended. "Robert Doyle, I presume," Harvey said, a little pompously, even by his standards, particularly as he'd seen the man before.

Laura continued to watch Bob's sitting gear until Harvey gave her a long look. She shrugged, took one more look, and sauntered out, almost closing the door behind her.

Harvey scanned the documents on his desk, while Bob examined the crash helmet hanging on the coat rack and smiled.

"Well," Harvey said, looking up from the documents he hadn't needed to read, "it appears the police consider you a low flight risk and have set police bail. Good."

"Lord luv 'em, g'vnor, they know'd I never desert me ol' mom," Bob said in a God-awful Dick Van Dyke cockney accent.

Harvey felt his jaw drop open and snapped it shut with a click. A moment later he'd regained his composure. "Call this a wild guess," he said at last, "but you're not a cockney, are you?"

Bob shook his head. "No, I'm from Barnet. Laura told me to do East End on account of that's where your old man comes from, and so you'd do me a better job."

Harvey looked past him to the open door and promised dire retribution. "Remind me to fire that girl," he said almost to himself.

"I'll tell her tonight," Bob said brightly. "We've got a date."

Harvey put his hand on his brow, but it didn't help, so turned his attention back to the papers on the desk. "On the face of it, it appears to be a rather flimsy case against you, Mr Doyle." He turned over a couple more papers. "They didn't find any stolen jewellery in your possession, which is good."

"Didn't have any," Bob said helpfully.

"So," Harvey said, ignoring the help. "Why did they arrest you?" He raised his hand before Bob could help any more. "Ah," he said, picking up a page and studying it carefully.

"The dog," Bob said helpfully. "A shitzu."

Harvey didn't bother trying the joke again. "Where did you acquire the... dog?"

"Found it," Bob said with a smile. Nice chap, all this smiling.

Harvey watched him steadily for a few moments. "And that's what you told the police?"

Bob nodded. "Yeah. They didn't believe me."

"No," Harvey said quietly, "I can see how they wouldn't."

Bob looked hurt. "I did find it. It was floating in the lake in Saint James' Park. Poor thing was almost in doggy heaven."

He was kidding, right? "Perhaps it was trying to cool off," Harvey suggested without much conviction. "Was it a hot day?"

"No, it was night," Bob said, perking up now. "It was drowning in a sack."

Harvey frowned. "Are you saying you rescued the dog?"

"Yeah, like I said, it was drowning in a sack." He frowned for a moment. "In the lake, really, but in a sack. If you follow me."

Harvey blinked slowly and waited for a punch line. None came. He pulled himself together before he disappeared into the other universe. "And did you tell the police this... this sad story?"

"No, they was in a hurry. There was a big match on the telly, I think. They threw me in a cell and buggered off."

Harvey nodded. "So the police have the... shitzu?"

Bob shrugged. "Dunno, they threw me in a cell."

"Quite. So are you saying you didn't break into Lady Druce-Wright's house?"

"No, I didn't break in."

There was more, and Harvey waited patiently for it.

"Door was open," Bob said with a shrug.

"But you are a burglar, are you not?"

"Yeah, and a good one," Bob said, puffing out his already puffed chest. "Only got caught once," he added proudly.

"Mmmm..." Harvey said, glancing at the papers. "Three years in Belmarsh, wasn't it?"

"Yeah," Bob said with a sigh. "Judge said he wanted to make an example of me." He shook his head sadly. "I wish he'd made a bloody model aeroplane instead."

"So," Harvey said, relieved to be wrapping it up. "The whole case appears to hinge on your possession of Lady LDW's dog. Very good."

"Yeah," Bob said. "Can I go now? I'm meeting the lads in the pub."

Harvey glanced pointedly at the antique clock on the false fireplace.

Bob headed for the door, stopped, and looked again at the crash helmet. "You got a bike?"

"I beg your pardon," Harvey said. "A bike?"

Bob pointed at the crash helmet, and Harvey nodded. "I've got a friend who specialises in, err..." Bob frowned while the little gears engaged. "In picking up superbikes. If you're interested."

"No, no, thank you," Harvey said quickly. The other universe was beckoning again.

Bob frowned. "Do you, y'know, like, ride it?"

"Yes, of course I ride it, what else would I do with it?"

"Dunno," Bob said with a shrug. "It's just that you're a bit... y'know?"

Harvey didn't know, and his expression said so.

"You're just a bit, well, stuck up to be a born-again biker, is all."

"Thank you, Mr Doyle, I'm sure Laura will show you the way out." Among other things.

Bob waved cheerily and left, for the pub, at half nine in the morning, but right about then, Harvey envied him. It had been a long day.

9

It had also been a long day for Sergeant Shaun O'Conner, and it was now turning into a long night. His eyes ached, and waves of pain crashed in his head like breakers onto jagged rocks. How long had he been there, watching the warehouse that did nothing but watch right back? It was too dark to see the time, and checking the dash clock would mean switching on the ignition, and to do that he would have to move, and that was a price too high. He closed his eyes and listened to the pain in his skull.

Anybody who bothered to look at him would have known at once that he was Irish. He was small, standing no more than five foot eight, but had been handsome once, was witty with an easy Irish charm and eyes that flashed with mischief, but he was forty now and looking every day of it. His dark hair was fading to grey and thinning, while his body was doing the opposite, as if to compensate, and his once soft eyes looked tired. But hard living and too much booze will do that to a man.

He thought about the hipflask in his pocket, and for a moment, he almost moved, but tilted his head back against the seat instead. He'd sworn a hundred times that he would not drink on the job, and mostly he made it stick. He sighed and felt the world shift slightly as his tired body finally relaxed.

His father spoke to him, and the part of his mind not yet asleep knew he was dreaming, but he also knew he wouldn't wake up, not until the nightmare had run all its reels. His fifteenth birthday, and the day his life broke.

"You're wasting your time there, boy," his father said, putting a hand on his shoulder briefly as he passed. "He won't come. He's too high and mighty for the likes of us."

But Shaun watched the dark street anyway, guilty at the kick of anger he felt at his father's words. Patrick would come, he always did, except for sometimes. He looked across the small room at the single birthday card wedged between the porcelain horse and the gaudy cockerel on the mantelpiece above the smoking coal fire. It didn't mean anything, Patrick was busy, he was The Man, and one day Shaun would be right there at his side, one day.

Patrick was his older brother by twelve years and was everything he wanted to be, rich, famous, and yeah, feared. In Belfast these days, it was easy to be feared, all you needed was a gun, but people feared Patrick for who he was, not because of some brash swagger and black hood. He'd been wild, but what else was there to do when you're a kid in a country at war with itself? Now he was respectable, in a perverse way, but he was still so close to crazy, you wouldn't want to bet your life on the difference.

Shaun looked back through the rain-streaked windows just as the car's lights went out, and it coasted to a stop in front of the broken gate, where it sat for several minutes, black and silent. He ran to the front door, pulled it open, and stared at the car through slanting rain, but there was no movement inside as the occupants searched the dark terraces for something that didn't fit.

The passenger door opened, and Patrick stepped out, took a long look around, and then came down the path in four long strides. He was tall and had extra-long legs that made him look as though he was walking on short stilts, a fact that had won him the nickname Lucky Legs when he was a kid — lucky they didn't snap off and shoot up his arse. Nobody called him Lucky Legs anymore; they called him Mr O'Conner.

"Hello, kid," Patrick said with a grin as he stepped past him out of the rain.

Shaun was about to close the door when he saw two men get out of the car and start down the path. They were the Boys, the Bogeymen, and he held the door open for them without thinking. They stepped in, nodded, and closed the door and leaned back against it, to stop people getting in, or perhaps to stop people getting out.

"Hey, don't mind Paddy and Mick," Patrick said as he steered his kid brother into the front room.

Shaun saw the room again vividly in his dream, just as he always did, a faded flower-patterned three-piece suite, his father's winged chair and the TV on but silent. He glanced back at the two men with the fat jackets that did nothing to hide the bulges under their left arms. They probably weren't called Paddy or Mick, but he wasn't going to ask.

A moment later, his father came out of the kitchen, walked past the Boys and into the front room, slamming the door behind him. "I see you brought your dogs with you," he snarled, waving his thumb back over his shoulder. "I want them out, now!"

"No need to get stressed out, Da," Patrick said with a shrug. "They'll be going as soon as I've given Shauny here his present."

Shaun took the box, shook it gently, and put it on the table.

"Aren't you going to open it?" Patrick asked.

“In a minute,” Shaun replied, not wanting to miss a moment of this time with his big brother. It was a Celestron telescope, but Shaun didn’t find that out until he opened the present two years later, and then only to smash it to pieces.

He was grinning like an idiot. He knew he was doing it, but couldn’t help it. Patrick was here.

By the time he’d reached Shaun’s age, Patrick was already well on the road to prison, or worse, when the Provos recruited him, recognising courage and a talent for ducking and diving they could use. It saved him from himself, or so it seemed at the time. So for five years Patrick almost vanished from Shaun’s life, turning up unexpectedly, usually late at night, but always with a present for his kid brother. But every time he came home, he would row with his father.

Shamus O’Conner was a staunch Irish nationalist and proud of it, but he would have no truck with the IRA and had made it clear to his sons from the moment they were old enough to know the difference, but Patrick made up his own mind, always had. So they fought, and Patrick stayed away. And it hurt like hell.

The part of Shaun’s mind that knew it was a dream felt his heart begin to thump in his chest, and he knew it was coming.

Shamus turned back from the door. “You’ll be going now.”

“I’ve come to see my brother on his birthday.”

“So, you’ve seen him, now get out.” Shamus held the door open. “And take your thugs with you.”

Patrick gave the Boys in the hall a tiny shake of his head, and Shaun knew for the first time what it meant.

Shamus stepped up so close to Patrick they were almost touching. “As long as you’re with this... this...” He pointed at the Boys. “This scum, you’re not welcome in this house.”

“Patriots, old man,” Patrick’s words came through clenched teeth, “they’re called patriots.”

“Not by me, they’re bloody not!” Shamus pushed past him and leaned on the fireplace for support. “If your mother was alive today, she’d turn in her grave!”

“She supported the cause, and you know it.” His breath was coming in short gasps. “And so should every true Irishman!”

“Cause? Cause?” Shamus roared, “It’s just a bloody cover for gangsters and thugs!”

“The British are the thugs here,” Patrick’s eyes blazed, “and we’re going to drive them out of our bloody country once and for all!”

“And how are you going to do that by killing your own? You forget that I fought with those boys in the war, a real war, not cowards bombing and murdering innocent women and kids.”

"Yes, I remember you fought for the English, and I'm ashamed of it every waking day. You're a bloody traitor to—"

Shamus hit him, not a little slap, but a left hook that spun him and dropped him onto the fire, with china ornaments and cups smashing around him.

Shaun's dream slipped into slow motion as Patrick rolled onto his back and, in blind fury, pulled his gun and pointed it at his father. Shamus reacted as he'd been trained to do all those years before and stamped down on the gun arm, pinning it to the floor. Patrick's hand clenched and pulled the trigger, the gunshot cracking deafeningly and the bullet imploding the TV like a small bomb.

Shaun's head was spinning in shock, and he didn't hear the second shot, so was stunned when his father fell to his knees and then onto his back beside his son, a patch of red spreading over his shirt front. Shaun blinked slowly and looked at the man standing in the doorway, the gun still pointing at the old man. His legs failed, and he fell forward onto his hands and knees next to his father, unable to take his eyes off the crimson bubble fixed on his lips.

Patrick got to his feet, wiped his bloody face on his sleeve, and put his hand on Shaun's shoulder. "It was an accident, Shaun, you saw it. It was an accident!"

Shaun looked up, and Patrick recoiled from the hate in his eyes.

Shaun woke up with his heart pounding and wiped his damp face on the back of his hand. He frowned and wound down the window. He could still hear the gunfire, but this was no dream, the sound of shooting was coming from the warehouse he'd been watching. He stepped out of the car into the cold night, pulled his SIG P230 from its belt holster, and stepped into the shadows. An idea formed in his mind, and he started to move towards the warehouse, heard a muffled sound behind him, and spoke without looking round. "Did you bring the coffee?"

"Left it by the car. Didn't think you'd want it right now," a voice said in the darkness. "What have we got here?"

Shaun stopped and looked back over his shoulder. "I think the girl guides are having a jamboree." He looked at the darker outline in the shadows. "You're the detective, Danny boy, what do you think is going on?"

"Action! And it'll soon be over." Danny crowded Shaun forward, and when Danny crowded, it was big time. Danny Fouillade was a six foot four French-Angolan and built like the proverbial shit-house.

Shaun bristled at the shove. "Hey, back off." He shook Danny's hand off his shoulder. "You can shoot the survivors."

"Cool."

"Jesus, man." Shaun stepped away. "Look, why don't you go that way and ingress via the side door?"

"Ingress?" Danny sniffed. "Have you been reading those American cop manuals again?"

"All the bad men will have shot each other by the time you're finished chatting," Shaun said helpfully.

"Okay, I'm off to ingress."

Shaun watched him go, smiled, and walked across the open yard towards the big double doors at the back of the warehouse. The shooting had stopped after the initial fusillade, and he sighed genuine regret as he opened the small personnel door and stepped into the light. Shooting a few villains might take the edge off his hangover, and who knows? They might have shot back, and that would have been okay too.

The warehouse was mostly empty, except for a couple of cars, and the bodies bleeding out onto the concrete floor in front of the wide-open roller door leading out on the opposite side of the building. Ah well, you can't watch them all from one car. But yeah, that was a bit careless, but in his defence, it had been dark when they arrived. True, but a walk round the building wouldn't have been too tiring.

A movement caught his eye, and he pointed his gun casually at Danny, who stepped in through the metal side door. Harry shook his head sadly and resumed checking the shadows and the small glass office for any movement, but they were alone.

Danny walked up to one of the cars, looked in cautiously, and drew his finger across his throat.

"Why are you doing commando signals? I don't think the dead guys care, and the shooters are long gone."

Danny shrugged, walked up to the bodies on the floor, and rolled one over with his foot.

"Hey, SOCO are going to be well pissed off if you start messing with their crime scene," Shaun said, sounding almost like he gave a shit.

"It's my crime scene right now," Danny said, opened the boot of the nearest car, peered in, and said something that was too muffled for Shaun to catch.

Shaun looked at the spreading pools of blood, put his gun away, stepped over the blood, and joined his partner. It took him about two seconds to see what had gone down. "Drug deal gone bad."

"Wow, did you work that out?" Danny said with mock awe.

"Yeah, you can tell that from the dead guys and the drugs."

"That'll be why you're a detective, then?"

Shaun crossed to the second car and opened the boot. "This one had the money."

"Any left in there?"

"No, some crook has had it all away."

"Pity, my rent's due." Danny strode up to the little glass office and shaded the glass with his hand.

"Don't bother," Shaun said. "If there was anybody in there, they'd have shot you when you fell into the building."

"Why wouldn't they have shot you? Is it a black thing?"

"Who's black?" Shaun said with a puzzled expression.

"Hey, Baxter's going to be well pissed off when he finds out we were sitting outside while the bad men all shot each other to death and drove away through the other door."

"You were fetching coffee," Shaun pointed out helpfully.

"Hey, I was on a break, union rules say I have to have a break."

"Oh, okay, that'll satisfy Mr Baxter, sir, dickhead and asshole."

"Yeah? That's good, then," Danny said, returning to crouch down by the bodies. "I was a bit worried there."

Shaun waited patiently for two seconds. "You see anything odd about these bodies?"

Danny stood up and surveyed the dead. He frowned, pulled his chin, tut-tutted, then nodded. "Ah, one of them is wearing high heels." He pointed at the little guy wearing thin red shoes, calf-length white trousers and a silver ankle bracelet. Tasteful.

"Oh, steady me," Shaun sighed, "detective genius at work."

Danny took a bow.

"Not the one with high heels, Sherlock." Shaun pointed at the nearest body. "That."

Danny followed his finger to the other body with two neat holes in the chest. "He's been shot."

"Damn, you're good!" Shaun pointed at the other bodies one by one. "Every one of them got it in the chest, double tap."

"Military?"

"Yeah, or a pro at least." Shaun looked up at the sound of approaching sirens. "Our troubles are over."

Danny crossed to the open roller door. "Blood here. Looks like one of the poor buggers got a shot off." He looked back at the high heels and ankle bracelet. "Or two shots."

Shaun pointed at the body holding an automatic. "That'll be our shooter, looks like he was a bit quicker than the rest." He frowned. "Odd, though, that none of the others had time to get to their guns."

Danny came back and bent down to examine the dead man's gun. "Smith and Wesson forty. Nice piece."

Shaun closed his eyes and willed his headache away. That didn't work. "We should go meet our brave armed response boys."

"Yeah, they'll just start shooting if we're still in here." Danny stopped for a moment in the open doorway and looked again at the blood on the steel runners. "At least there's some good news."

Shaun nodded and walked out of the building just as the storm troopers arrived and started screaming and shouting at them to lie on the floor.

"Yeah, right," Shaun said. "This is my only suit."

Danny pitched in before he got them both killed. "Hey, we're SOCA!" he shouted, but they just kept screaming anyway. "Come on, think about it, would we still be here if we were bad guys?"

"On the floor, now!" the same agitated voice said.

"He sounds upset," Shaun said loud enough for the marksman to hear. "I thought CO19 boys were all cool and stuff."

"Don't antagonise them, man, they've got big guns." Danny looked over at Shaun with a worried expression. "We should do like they say."

"You can if you like, but I'm not getting down there, there's dog shit and stuff."

A uniformed officer walked out from behind the car headlights and made a show of checking them out. "Oh, great," he said and waved a hand to calm the shooters down. "It's O'Conner. I'd recognise that suit anywhere. Same one you had five years ago, isn't it?"

"Detective Chief Inspector Gardener, sir, how are you, sir? And how are your darling children, sir? And your lovely— "

"Shut up, O'Conner, or I'll let Babbler here shoot you anyway. God knows I'd be doing everybody a service."

"Thank you, DCI Gardner, sir," Shaun said, standing to attention.

"Shoot him, Babbler."

"Whoa! Hang on!" Danny stepped forward waving his hands, realised he was between Shaun and the shooter, and stepped out of line.

"Cheers," Shaun said and tutted. "My friend."

"Think about it, sir," Danny said, ignoring Shaun. "You could shoot him, and many people would be grateful..." He could see the DI was thinking about it. "But if you do, you'll have to buy another bullet, and you know what a pain that can be."

DCI Gardner was weighing up the pros and cons. Decision made, he waved his hand at the firing squad hidden behind the glare of the headlights. "Okay, but next time..."

Shaun shrugged and trudged tiredly to the side of the building and back across the yard.

"Hey, where do you think you're going?" DCI Gardner's voice showed genuine surprise.

Shaun spoke without turning. "I'm going home. It's been a big day."

The DCI sighed heavily and gave up — some cases are just hopeless. "I want a full report in writing, on my desk, tomorrow morning. Do you hear me?"

"Yes sir. Report. Desk. Morning."

Danny caught up. "You're not going to write the report, are you?"

Shaun shrugged. "What is there to say? Five guys got shot—"

"Six."

Shaun slowed and glanced at Danny.

"One in the car, remember? Commando signals?"

Shaun nodded. "Six guys got themselves shot. They were bad men."

"Ever wonder why you're still a sergeant after twenty years?"

They reached the car, and Shaun opened the driver's door. "They hate me because I'm Irish."

"Yeah, right, that'll be it." Danny opened the passenger door, groaned, and brushed the junk off the seat into the yard. "You're a slob, you know that?"

"Hey! There was half a burger in there!"

"Why me, God? Haven't I always been a good Christian? Don't I love children and my fellow man? No, don't answer that." He took out a perfectly ironed handkerchief and wiped the seat before climbing in reluctantly, as if sitting on a doss-house toilet. Shaun started the car and put on the lights.

"What the hell have you got to smile about?" Danny asked as he tried to fasten the seat belt using just his thumb and index finger.

"I was just thinking about Baxter."

"And that's funny?"

"No, but me getting that award tomorrow is going to get right up his nose, and that's funny."

"True."

10

Harry sat on the edge of his bed and massaged his rock-hard thigh muscle. Maybe it was wishful thinking, but it did feel less raw this morning, though that could be the deadening effects of the whisky Frank had poured into him the night before. He lifted his lower leg slowly and was sure the fire blazing in his thigh was less. One of the benefits of getting the hell out of hospital, he supposed. Soon be running up Kilimanjaro. Yeah, right. Okay, maybe not, but one thing was for certain, he'd be thanking that Afghan who'd saved his life some time soon, he swore to that.

To hell with all this sitting around acting like a pussy. He stood up. He sat down. Well, that wasn't the roaring success it had played out in his head. He stood up very slowly, swayed this way and that, probably because he was mostly standing on one leg, but he was up and took a slow step forward on the shot leg, clenched his teeth, and closed his eyes until the crimson wave had washed over him. Pussy. He took another step and was relieved to find this one was marginally less agonising than the last. A few minutes later, he was walking across the bedroom, like a constipated robot, true, but under his own steam and no damned crutch.

Harvey was the first to look up from the breakfast table as Harry lurched out of his bedroom. Frank and Rocky were preoccupied with a squabble over Harvey's newspaper and took a moment to register the great event. When they did, all three froze and stared open mouthed.

Frank recovered first. "You're walking!"

"You're really old, but you haven't lost any of your sharps, have you?" Harry said through clenched teeth.

"Cheeky git!"

Full marks for tea and sympathy.

Harvey got up and strode across the big room, took Harry's arm, and pointed to the chair at the breakfast table. "Come on, for God's sake, before you fall down."

"Not planning to do any more falling," Harry said, quietly grateful to be holding onto something, or someone. Turns out, not being a pussy hurts like hell.

Rocky pulled a grimace. "Err… sorry I wasn't around when you got in."

Harry raised a hand. "No probs." He smiled as he sat down. "I saw the distraction."

Rocky smiled. "Yeah."

"Both of them," Harry added.

"Yeah." Rocky's smile widened. "Ain't being a rock star a bitch?"

Harry raised his eyebrows. "Rock star?" He shook his head slowly. "Pop tells me you just sent in one demo."

Harvey started to say "don't call me Pop", but let it slide, what the hell.

"What's the plan, then?" Frank asked, piling bacon and eggs onto a plate and handing it to Harry, along with enough toast to choke a horse. "Bit of a jog after breakfast, is it?"

Harry took the coffee from Harvey and drank it in one slurp. "Whew, I needed that," he said, wiping his mouth on the back of his hand and brushing the toast off his breakfast so he could at least see the food. "Planning," he said, munching crispy bacon, "to take a little trip."

Harvey frowned, already ahead of him. A barrister doesn't get far unless he can read the writing on the wall, particularly if the writing is a foot high. "Afghanistan?"

Frank snorted and choked on his coffee. "What? Don't be bloody daft!" He wiped his face with an immaculately folded napkin. "He'll be lucky to get out of the building, the state he's in."

"Cheers, gramps," Harry said with a grin.

"You know what I mean," Frank said, raising his hand.

"Yeah, I'm knackered."

"No, no," Frank said. "Well, okay, a bit knackered."

"When are you leaving?" Harvey asked quietly, already giving up on any opposition to the plan. Sometimes you've just lost before the first bell rings.

Frank glared at Harvey. "Don't be—"

"Tomorrow, Wednesday at the latest," Harry said quietly.

"Bro, I think you got shot in the brain too," Rocky said, before returning to the newspaper's celeb section.

"Harvey!" Frank said. "He's your son, you talk him out of this daftness."

Harvey waved him on. "Be my guest."

"Like father, like son. I don't know where you get it," Frank said. "Your mother, I expect."

Harvey and Harry exchanged glances and smiled. Yeah, from Mom. Right.

11

At the same time as Harry swung into the ticket agency on his crutches, Shaun was slipping quietly into the conference room in the town hall, not because he was shy of the publicity or anything like that, he just wanted to see what the turnout was like so that he could pitch his speech at the right level. Yeah, right.

The chief constable had sent his deputy — the miserable sod; there must have been a better media event somewhere else. There were a half dozen journalists hanging around looking bored, and a local new team called Good News, Bad News or No News, or something like that. Okay then, that was cool, he could manage that. What he didn't want was some up-himself prat out to show the public that he was a serious, investigative reporter with stupid questions like "was it necessary to beat the poor, disabled suspect with a fire extinguisher?", or something deep and incisive along those lines. Okay, he had hit the suspect with a fire extinguisher, but he wasn't disabled. In fact, he'd been carrying a sawn-off shotgun, but the prat would probably say it was for the charity clay pigeon shoot in aid of sick orphans. Arsehole. It occurred to him that he was getting wound up by a reporter he'd just invented and kicked it into touch before he fell off the planet completely.

The irony didn't escape him that he was getting a bravery award for capturing an armed robber by accident. Said robber had shoved a shotgun in a bank cashier's face, grabbed a bagful of money and run, right into a couple of bobbies who just happened to be in the way, as they tend to be. He'd shot one of the poor sods and hit the other with the shotgun, but it served them right for being in the wrong place.

And Shaun? He'd been staking out a couple of lowlifes and had just stepped into a doorway for a spike from his hipflask when the guy exited the bank. He could've just shot him, it would have been all legal and stuff, but he couldn't be arsed with all the paperwork, so picked up a fire extinguisher from the shop doorway — one of those CO2 things with the black horn and a big yellow instruction sticker — anyway, the cop-shooter came running by, and he hit him in the face with it, a big swinging arc and a very satisfying crunch. No paperwork required.

And now here he was at the town hall, getting a Well Done badge. Okay, it was all a BS publicity gimmick in support of the chief's political aspirations, but it got him off the street, and there was a bar that drew him in like a magnet.

Two uniforms were also part of the Cops-Doing-Good parade, and they looked up nervously at the thud-thud of the deputy chief tapping the microphone. The thud and the following feedback screech woke up the half-dozen hacks lounging around the bar, and they strolled over to the wooden seats, fishing out their recorders or notepads, as they were supposed to.

"Ladies and gentlemen." That was a laugh. "It gives me great pleasure to present these fine officers with the Bravery Award for their... err... bravery."

Poetry. Was that a tear? Shaun shook his head, downed his whiskey, and strolled over to the podium to watch the uniforms squirm. An overweight copper and a WPC, a woman woodentop — he recalled the gender awareness course he'd been made to attend after a few misunderstood comments along those lines, and woman police constable was on the list, as indeed was woodentop. It was stressed that the lovely little things should be called female police officers. Okay then. He checked this one out. Yeah, cute, filled out her uniform in the right places and had a nice little hat.

The deputy chief was still wittering on about how proud he was that these officers had nearly got themselves killed doing stupid things. It seems the overweight copper had seen a guy with a gun at a street party, shoulder-charged him into a fountain, and knocked over a hot-potato stand. He'd taken that action, apparently, to prevent panic. Well, that worked out just fine.

The cute PC had dived into the Thames when she saw a woman jump off a bridge and held the woman's head above water for twenty minutes. He shook his head. She must be nuts, it had been in February, and hadn't the stupid woman jumped in on her own? Yeah? Then she should bloody well get out on her own. God, that water must have been cold. Good job she was a woman woodentop or—

"Sergeant Shaun O'Conner!"

Applause. Bugger, it was his turn to be paraded. He sighed and climbed up the three steps to the podium as the applause spluttered away, but you don't get much from a few hacks, the barman and a couple of shanghaied passers-by.

He smiled at the cute PC, and she smiled back. Now that was a bit confusing. Did she smile back because she liked him or because she was just glad he was in the barrel now instead of her? Face it, man, it's box number two.

He shook the deputy chief's hand, took the award, smiled, leaned into the mike, said, "Ta", and legged it back to the bar.

"Bit early for that, isn't it?" the cute PC said, coming up behind him as he downed another Irish whiskey.

"You know what they say?" Which of course she didn't. "It's never too early for a Jameson's."

"That right?"

"Dunno." He smiled and looked at her body. "Just made it up."

She looked him up and down in retaliation. "Okay, I'll have the same."

He nodded at the barman, pointed at his glass and the ... female police officer. "I didn't catch your name."

She raised her eyebrows and glanced back at the podium and the deputy chief commissioner politicking for all he was worth. "Police Constable Cooper. I think the deputy chief might have mentioned it."

Shaun shrugged, he'd been checking out her ass so missed all that stuff. "I was thinking about my speech."

She nodded. "Yes, I could see you'd worked on that."

The barman put the two drinks on the bar, and Shaun handed one to her. "You got a shorter name than Police Constable Cooper?"

"Yes." She sipped the whiskey.

"And?" He downed half his drink.

"Kaitlin."

Cute name too. "Okay, but I'll call you Kate," he said and put out his hand.

She shook his hand once. "No, you won't."

"Fair enough." He flashed his Irish smile. "Was it cold?"

She glanced questioningly at the drink, then got it. "Of course it was cold, bloody cold." She shrugged. "Had to be done, though."

"Why?" He caught her frown. "Why did jumping into the Thames on a freezing night have to be done?"

She seemed genuinely puzzled. "The woman would have drowned.

Shaun shrugged. "Her choice."

Kaitlin put her drink down, looked him in the eyes, and shook her head slowly.

Nice one, boy, he thought, *you're in there.*

She walked back to her hero colleague without a second glance.

Yeah, you're in there all right.

"Thought I'd find you here."

Shaun turned at the sound of the familiar voice. "Danny." He smiled. "Get you something?"

Danny looked immaculate, as always, and his usual smile was doing a poor job of hiding in the shadows as he looked at the glasses on the bar. "No, thanks, looks like you've celebrated for us both." He looked over at the deputy chief trying to block the exit and keep the hacks trapped. "How'd it go, then?"

"Lights, action, camera," Shaun said. "Brought the house down."

"Yeah, I bet. Come on, we've got work."

"Hey, hero here." Shaun patted his chest. "Never have to work again."

"Yeah, right. Come on, hero." Danny crossed the function room, smiled politely at the deputy chief, and got the hell out of there.

Shaun started to follow, caught Kaitlin watching him, and winked mischievously. She shook her head sadly, but there was a smile, just a little one. A distant light on a stormy ocean. Yeah, probably marking rocks.

It is a pity, though, he told himself, but look at her man; she's way out of your league. And she was — way out.

12

Bob the burglar was thinking he could get used to this. He was lying on an oversized bed, naked as a naturist holidaymaker and watching the bathroom door and smiling like the cat with a milk moustache.

"Ready?" he called. Then said to himself, "Because I am."

"Almost," Laura said from the bathroom. A moment later she emerged, wearing a judge's black robe, which billowed open as she moved, revealing flashes of firm, young breasts.

"Yes, Your Honour," Bob said with a big smile, "I'm guilty."

From the folds of her robe, Laura produced a riding crop with an extra-wide pink leather spanking keeper, which was guaranteed to provide more slap and less sting. We'll see. "Then," she said, tapping her naked leg with the crop, "you must be punished."

She crossed to the bed, reached under the pillow, and brought out two sets of pink fur handcuffs, which she used to secure Bob's wrists to the brass headboard. She flicked her robe over her shoulders and placed the flap of riding crop on Bob's thigh.

"This is going to hurt you more than it hurts me," she said with a smile.

13

Harry was nine hours into the seven and a half hour flight promised by the airline and was ruing his self-destructive decision to return to Helmand. His leg had started off by simply throbbing steadily, moved up to aching, and then to pounding, and was now working up to the big finale and screaming at him to cut it off. He closed his eyes and tried not to think about it, which anyone who has had any sort of pain knows is just hopeless.

The plane slammed down onto the tarmac, squeezing his leg against the thinly upholstered seat. Great, just when things were looking peachy.

Tom and BJ were waiting for him as he limped between his crutches out of security and into the small arrivals.

"You look like shit," Tom said, smiling and relieving him of his backpack.

"Cheers," Harry said, releasing the pack without protest. "Nice to know you care."

"Who said I care? I just said you look like shit."

"And you do," BJ added, as if confirmation was necessary.

"Love you too," Harry said.

"Shhh," BJ said, looking around. "My boyfriend's the jealous sort."

"Camels don't get jealous," Harry said.

They set off for the domestic flight booking, although it would be more accurate to say Harry set off for the booking, Tom and BJ having gone the other way without a backward glance.

"Hey!" Harry shouted at the departing pair. "Where are you going? The flights are this way."

"True," Tom said without turning. "But the helicopter is this way. You carry on, though, next flight to Kandahar leaves in..." He looked at his watch. "Oh, seven hours and change." He pointed at the exit sign. "Or if you like, you can go by truck, a nice twelve-hour trip on happy roads with nice people, that'll sort your leg right out."

Harry executed the best turn he'd managed since he got the crutches and ran after them — well, swung after them — as quickly as he could.

"Helicopter?" he said, catching them up as they waited for him. "Where did you get a helicopter? You haven't been promoted to generals while I've been away?"

"No bloody chance," BJ said. "Lucky to still be sergeants, without your calming influence."

"Do you spell bollocks with an X?" Tom asked.

"Ah, you stole it," Harry said with a grin. "That's all right, then."

"Nah," Tom said, "nice American gentleman offered us a ride."

"Yeah, right," Harry said. "What did you do, kidnap his sister?"

"Nah, she came right along after one look at the ol' tadger. Said she'd never seen nothing like it," Tom said, with an exaggerated swagger.

"Yeah, so I hear," Harry said, starting to feel a little euphoric now the pain had subsided, and he didn't have to sit in a damned truck for a day.

There were four choppers parked on the concrete pad behind the terminal, but only one had its rotors moving slowly, and as they approached it, Harry planned how he was going to negotiate the Sea King's step. He hesitated for a moment, but that was all it took. Tom on one side and BJ the other picked him up under his arms and put him into the helo, as if he was hanging from a pole in a cornfield. To hell with dignity.

There were four other passengers on board, two US generals and a couple of majors as aides. Great. They watched the Brits lift the civilian on board with an indifference that showed they'd pretty much seen it all. Harry and his supporters sat opposite and tried not to make eye contact or say anything disrespectful. Heaven forbid they should be disrespectful to officers — when they could be overheard.

The big helicopter lifted off with barely more than a deafening roar and swept out over the desert that looked like a rolling red ocean, not that any of them gave a stuff, having seen the spectacular sight so many times, it was now just sand.

An hour later, they touched down at Camp Bastion and waited politely for the generals and their aides to deplane. Tom and BJ repeated the transportation of a civilian exercise, and they were on the scorching tarmac.

"Home sweet home," Tom screamed above the howl of jet engines and rotors from every direction.

"Great," Harry said and headed off across the tarmac.

"Hey!" BJ shouted. "Aren't you going to check in?"

"Nah," Harry said, grumpy now and tired, "I'm just going to find a crib and crash."

BJ and Tom caught up with him, which wasn't difficult, Harry being on crutches. "Drink first," Tom said, "then crash."

The others nodded and headed for Heroes bar. "Maybe a quick viz to Pizza Hut?" BJ suggested, hungry as usual.

"You know they don't sell booze here?" Tom said, with a quick glance at Harry. Maybe he was jet-lagged or brain-damaged.

Harry shrugged. "Yeah, I know, but I've brought enough duty-free vodka in my backpack to drown a Russian."

"Cool," Tom said, picking up the pace, but slowing it down again as he left the limping Harry behind.

"You!" a harsh voice said from somewhere behind them. Only MPs talk like that.

"He doesn't mean me," Harry said, walking on.

"You, you with the bionic legs!"

Ah.

They stopped and turned round slowly. Life can get tedious.

"Where do you think you're going?" The MP looked like a regular squaddie, wearing pale desert camouflage combats with rolled-up sleeves and sand-coloured boots, but the scarlet cap and MP flash on his shoulder said what he was — except that his demeanour and voice had already said all there was to say.

"You will report to the duty officer!" the MP shouted, even though he was now only five feet away. Perhaps his volume control was broken.

"Yes, Sarg," Tom said with a sigh of resignation.

"Do you think my name is Sarg?" the MP shouted.

"No, Sarg... Sergeant," Tom said, seeing the prospect of the pizza and spiked coke fading into the distance.

"Why are you still standing here making my landing strip untidy?" the MP said, his voice rising in pitch.

They headed off to the right as quickly as Harry's crutches would allow.

"Where the hell are you going?" the MP screamed.

This bloke was seriously getting on Harry's tits, and he was about to express his feelings in plain, straightforward speech that avoided ambiguity and repetition, but the MP pointing the other way took the wind out of his sail.

"The Duty Office is that way, you... newly arrived British citizen."

Harry was truly impressed by how the man could make citizenship sound so shitty.

The MP stood with hands on hips, as per the training manual, and watched them go. Tom looked back, waved, and walked on. He looked again and saw the mouth-on-legs striding away. They executed a perfect right wheel and headed for the bar.

Harry had the best night's sleep since the day he'd left this place, the constant roar of aircraft and the thwump of rotor blades a soothing symphony to his jet-lagged brain. He woke up at six thirty as usual and got up slowly. He was sitting on the side of his cot in the accommodation tents and looked up as Tom groaned and sat up slowly.

"That coke was off," Tom said and rubbed his temples.

"Nothing to do with the half bottle of vodka you poured into it, then?" Harry asked, overlooking what had happened to the other half bottle.

"Nah," Tom said, swinging his legs off the cot, "it was the coke."

Harry pointed at the unmoving form of BJ curled up under his blanket and sparked out. "We could just bugger off and leave him to talk to that nice MP."

"Only if you want to get shot in the arse agen," BJ said in a muffled voice.

"Awake, then?" Tom said, standing up stark naked, stretching out, and displaying his porcelain-white junk — definitely not a spectator sport.

"No," BJ said.

"Please yourself," Harry said, "we're off to get a good fried breakfast with— "

BJ was out of bed and collecting his uniform from the floor where he'd stored it before Harry could even mention the fried bread and coffee.

Harry smiled. Okay, he was home. Now, just a little trip out into bandit country, and back in time for din-dins. No probs.

14

The battered white van rolled silently across the market square and came to a gentle halt, while the driver and front seat passenger scanned the sandstone buildings for any sign of life, but there was nothing, not even the obligatory mangy dog. Even in this godforsaken place, pre-dawn was for sleeping, not skulking about, but the four boys in the van searched the perimeter anyway because as Master Sergeant Ethan Gill would say, frequently, "There are two kinds of marines out here, son, the careful and the dead." Okay, a bit Hollywood, but you couldn't fault the logic.

Master Sergeant Gill was exercising the same caution that had kept him alive in more hot zones than a NBC combat reporter on the shit-list. He was getting too old for this crap, and frequently said so, but showed no signs of giving it up. Forty-something — a lot of something — six two and built like a man who'd spent his life in the marine corps should be built. His hair was longer than it had ever been, and he needed a shave, but nothing says marine like a high and tight, and saying that in this part of the world was like marching down Taliban Street singing the Star Spangled Banner.

This flyblown little village was in Afghanistan's Paktika Province in the Hindu Kush Mountains, a stone's throw from Pakistan and one of the most beautiful places on God's earth, but if Helmand was tough, then Paktika was where the tough travelled in convoy.

Ethan climbed between the seats into the back of the van, leaving Sergeant "Al" Caponetto to watch the square. Two other marines sat in the back, watching two young Afghans secured by cable ties and gagged with grey duct tape.

"They been any trouble?" Ethan asked.

Eddie Elward sniffed and patted one of the Afghans on the head. "No, Top, they've been very good. Shall I give them a cookie?"

Ethan closed his eyes and shook his head in despair. "Let's roll."

The Afghans began desperately trying to break the unbreakable bonds, so clearly understood what was being said.

"Hey, hey," Ethan said soothingly, "no need to fret."

Manuel Alvarez opened a trunk and pulled out a crossover bomb vest on which half a dozen blocks of explosives were fastened with greasy cord.

So, there was reason to fret after all.

The Afghans got the message and writhed and bounced against the side of the van.

Ethan made "shhh" noises and put his finger to his lips, while Alvarez put the vest over the shoulders of the nearest Afghan and snapped the buckle shut on the boy's chest.

Elward opened the van's back door and then moved aside to give Alvarez room to throw the boy out onto the square. He hit the hard-packed earth, bounced once, rolled onto his back, and stared up in terror at the Americans.

Caponetto felt the van bounce, looked back, and started it moving slowly across the square and onto the paved road, where he brought it to a gentle halt.

Ethan winked at the remaining Afghan, and as they watched the other boy trying desperately to wriggle out of the bomb vest, he fired a single round from his automatic. That did the trick.

Within seconds, people were peering from windows and doorways all around the square at the madman rolling about in the dust, and a minute later the square was full of men, women and kids out for a closer look. Ethan reached into his pocket and pulled out a small remote detonator, ignored the Afghan's frantic grunting, and pressed the button.

He let the Afghan get a long look at the carnage and then closed the doors and signalled Caponetto to roll.

When they were far enough away from the village, the van picked up speed on the half-decent road. Nobody spoke, but the Afghan looked as though somebody had kicked him in the gut, which was just fine with the Americans sitting and watching him suffer.

Five miles down the road, Caponetto pulled the van over, and Alvarez took another bomb vest from the box. The boy stopped squirming and glared at Ethan.

"Hey, don't blame me," Ethan said, "they're your bombs." He snapped his fingers. "I know what you're thinking." He gave the boy a big smile. "You're thinking about the seventy-two virgins waiting for you in heaven, right?"

The boy just glared.

"Yeah, I can see how that would excite a young man." He gave the boy time to think about it. "Trouble is, as I see it." He raised his hands in mock surrender. "And hey, I'm no cleric, so what do I know? But I reckon you only get the virgins if you suicide yourself blowing up infidels. That being Americans. Right?"

The boy couldn't answer, even if he'd wanted to, but he continued to do the glaring thing.

"So I'll take that as a yes." Ethan pulled an exaggerated puzzled expression. "So, blowing up a bunch of your own women and kids probably won't qualify you for the girls."

The boy stopped glaring as his gears meshed and the implication of what the American was saying clunked home.

"That's right, your pal there," Ethan said, nodding at the back of the van, "just splattered most of the innocents in that village." He shrugged. "So I guess he's burning in hell right now." He frowned. "Hey, you've got a hell, right?" He smiled at the Afghan, reached over, and ripped the duct tape off his mouth. "What do you say, son?"

The boy licked his lips and breathed heavily, but said nothing.

Ethan sat down against the side of the van. "Look, son," he said softly, "we don't want to hurt you." No, of course not, blowing up the other kid was us just being playful. "Look, tell you what..." He smiled warmly. "You tell us something, and I'll tell my superiors you cooperated, and I let you go. What do you say?"

The boy said nothing. Ethan shrugged and nodded at Alvarez, who reached forward, wrapped the bomb vest round the boy's shoulders and clipped the buckle. The boy's tongue flicked over dry lips, and he stared in stunned silence at the explosive blocks on his chest.

"Look, son," Ethan said in the same soft voice, "I don't want to tell my man there to drive to the next village so you can blow the kids to pieces, truth I don't."

The boy was trembling.

"I know you believe in what you're doing and that martyrdom is a big thing for you people. But blowing up your own women and kids?" Ethan shook his head. "You don't want that, and I sure as hell don't want it. I'd like to let you go, so you can go home to your mom and your sisters. You got sisters, right?" Like every Afghan had sisters. "So, what do you say? You tell me something I can pass on to my boss, and you're free to go."

The boy tore his eyes off the explosives and stared hopelessly at each of the Americans in turn. And they smiled back at him. They could see he was thinking about it.

Ethan shrugged and nodded at Caponetto to start the van.

"Wait!" The boy's voice was shaking. "If I tell you something, you will let me go free?"

Ethan nodded. "That's the deal, son."

The boy thought about it. No virgins. "I can tell you only what I know. Perhaps this will not be enough."

Ethan shrugged. "Don't fret, son. You tell me and let me judge, okay?"

The boy sank back against the side of the van as his defiance melted away. "I have heard that there is to be a bomb in Eilat, to bring down a hotel."

Ethan raised his hand. "That's Israel, son."

The boy's mouth hung open, and he shook his head dumbly.

"You see, son, I don't give a rat's ass about the Israelis." He gave him time to translate. "I just want to know about attacks on Americans." He raised his eyebrows and smiled.

The boy began licking his lips again. Ethan nodded at Caponetto. "He doesn't know anything, Al, how far's the next village?"

"Ten clicks, about," Caponetto said and deliberately crunched the gears.

"Wait! Wait!" The boy was bouncing up and down.

Ethan made a big play of waving Caponetto to stop the van that wasn't moving.

The boy took a slow breath. "I do not know of any attacks in America. I am just a soldier."

Ethan shrugged and started to get up.

"But do I know of an attack here," the boy gasped quickly. "And there are many Americans there."

Ethan sat down against the side of the van and tilted his head.

"Do you know a village called Agha Dal?" the boy said.

Ethan shook his head, "Never heard of it. But you say there are Americans there? Where is it?"

"It is in Khanashin District, but I do not know where."

"That's no use to me, son." Ethan sighed and shuffled in preparation to calling it off, which he had no intention of doing; this op had been weeks in the planning.

"Al Qaeda is there."

"So what? Al Qaeda is everywhere," Elward said and shrugged. "Wouldn't mind killing a few of the bastards, though."

"Okay, son," Ethan said, showing interest again, and the Afghan almost relaxed a little. "Tell me about Al Qaeda."

"What's to know, boss, we hide out and shoot the bastards when they turn up," Elward said eagerly.

Ethan glared at him and shut him up. "What do you know about this..." He glanced at Elward. "This Agha Dal place?"

The boy took a long breath, seeing his life expectancy improve. "I do not know very much. There was a door open when it should not have been. I do not know what is to happen," He caught the look and continued quickly. "Except that it is to be big and will be soon."

"Is that all you know, son?" Of course it wasn't.

"I also heard a name." He became very agitated, looking this way and that, more afraid to say the name than he was of the American with the soft voice.

Ethan leaned over and patted his shoulder reassuringly. "You're doing just fine, son. You tell me the rest now."

"The name I heard was... was Mohammed Rahman Ali." He breathed out slowly, relieved that he had said it and it was done.

Ethan, Alvarez and Elward exchanged looks that would have spoken volumes to anyone watching.

"You sure about the name, son?" Ethan never doubted it for a moment.

The boy nodded. "Yes, Mohammed Rahman Ali. He is a great freedom fighter."

"My ass," Alvarez said with a snarl. "He's a stinkin' terrorist."

"That's enough, Manuel," Ethan said quietly and turned slowly back to the boy. "But he's right, son. We call this man Lupus, which means wolf, because he is a killer of children."

The boy's head snapped up, and he looked slowly back at the van doors. They all knew what he was thinking and wondered if he'd say it, without much interest in whether he did or not.

"What else do you know about an attack in Agha Dal, son?"

The boy frowned deeply. "I have told you all I know. There will be an attack sometime soon, but I do not know when." He was getting jumpy again and thought he needed to add more to get out of this hell. "Many Americans will die. This I do know." He couldn't keep the note of pride out of his voice.

Ethan eased himself as upright as the van would allow.

"You said I would go free if I told you what I knew." The boy's voice was thin and breathless. "This I have done. I know nothing more."

Ethan nodded at Alvarez, who opened the van doors after a long questioning look at Ethan.

"Okay, son, you can go." Ethan reached into his pocket, and the Afghan jumped. "It's just a knife." Ethan showed him the switchblade, leaned over, and cut the cable ties.

The boy rubbed his wrists and looked at his captors suspiciously.

Ethan pointed at the open doors. The boy got the message and climbed out onto the dusty road without taking his eyes off the soft-spoken American.

The van pulled away slowly, leaving the Afghan struggling to unfasten the bomb vest with numb fingers.

"Is that it, boss?" Alvarez was frowning.

"Guess so," Ethan said, climbing back into the front passenger seat.

"You're just gonna let him go so he can blow up some jarheads someplace?"

"That was the deal," Ethan said, leaning back into the seat. He flinched, put his hand in his back pocket, pulled out the remote detonator, and tutted. "I think I busted it," he said, tossing it to Alvarez. "Check it out."

Alvarez made a show of examining the detonator, pressed the button, and looked out through the dirty back window. "Seems to be working just fine, boss."

Ethan settled back and closed his eyes. Man, it had been a long night.

15

"So what's the big job?" Shaun said, catching up with Danny as he strode away from the big award ceremony.

"Well, let's see." Danny made a show of thinking. "Splatting that guy with the fire extinguisher kinda blew your cover on the surveillance."

Shaun shrugged. "He was a very bad man. Just doing my duty."

"Oh, that'll be a first, then."

Shaun held up the little case with the bravery medal. "Ahem!" He jiggled the gong out of the case. "Who's the hero here?"

Danny took the medal off him and examined it carefully. "Very nice," he said and tossed it in a rubbish bin.

Shaun chuckled and walked on, and Danny took three steps to test him, confirmed he really was going to leave it, and went back to retrieve it from the old burgers and chips, ketchup and mayo. Gross. He put it into Shaun's breast pocket without wiping it, but that would have messed up his handkerchief.

Shaun put his fingers into his pocket, withdrew them, looked at the sticky mess, gave Danny a dirty look, and wiped his hand on a bus stop window. Stylish.

"Okay, work to do, remember?"

Danny glanced at the smeared glass. "That nice Mr Baxter," he said, with a sad shake of his head, "your lord and master who you worship with every breath—"

"Asshole."

"Yes, I could see how you might want to use that affectionate sobriquet," Danny said with a smile. "Mr... Asshole, says we're to proceed — yes, we're to *proceed*, to Bethnal Green and interview a young gentleman name of Tweetie Pie."

"You're taking the piss. Tweetie Pie?" Shaun said.

"True as I'm sitting here. Tweetie Pie. And you know what's really interesting?"

Shaun's raised eyebrow was the only response Danny was going to get.

Danny sighed, as once again his big reveal fell flat. "He wears high heels."

"Now that is interesting."

Danny cheered up. "Yes, I think so. And do you know what else?"

No response.
"He's been shot."
No surprise, no exclamation. In fact, nothing, Shaun just strolled off.
"Hey, where're you going?"
"Proceeding," Shaun said over his shoulder.
"Please yourself, but the car's down this way."

16

Harry had dumped one of his crutches and was dressed in his desert combats, had a SIG P226 in its belt holster, and his L115 rifle resting in the footwell against his leg. His hangover was reminding him never to touch another drop, and he leaned against the door of the Land Rover as Tom manoeuvred it through the traffic out of Camp Bastion and onto the perimeter road. He turned right onto the A1, apparently oblivious to oncoming traffic, and ignored the blaring horns and shouts of welcome.

"For Christ's sake!" BJ growled from the seat behind Tom. "I'd like to go home not in a body bag."

"You've got no chance," Harry said, easing his head off the side window where it was bouncing with every bump.

"Cheers," BJ said, reversing Harry's move and settling back against the side of the Land Rover with his eyes closed.

An hour later, they turned right off the Kandahar-Herat Highway and, hugging the Helmand River, headed south out into the desert. The dust rolled up and out like a mini sandstorm, marking their progress with a cloud that could be seen ten miles away.

They rounded a bend and almost ran into the US Marine patrol waiting less than patiently for them from behind rocks and stunted and broken trees, though it was the M16s pointing their way that got their attention. Tom stopped the Land Rover, and they all stayed very still. After a few seconds, there was a rap on the driver's window, and a lieutenant signalled for them to get out of the vehicle. They kept their hands in plain sight and stood beside the truck, no point spooking their allies into shooting them a few hundred times.

"Morning, sir," Harry said with a friendly smile. Worth a try.

"Who are you, and what are you doing here?" the lieutenant said stiffly.

The three men avoided looking at each other, in case it set one of them off, and with the nervous — and very young — US Marines watching them down their rifle sights, going off on one was not a sound move.

Nobody was going to be that stupid.

"Well," Harry said softly, "I'm Mother Teresa, and these are my followers."

Tom glared at him, but Harry was grumpy, and that was a bad state when coupled with a size eight hangover.

"We are here to save all these people," Harry continued, sweeping his arm round to cover the barren and empty desert. "We can save you too, if—"

"If you speak again," the lieutenant said slowly, "I will have my sergeant here shoot you."

"Been shot before," Harry said and tapped his crutch.

"Sir," Tom said quickly, "as you can see, we are British Marines out on recon."

The lieutenant watched him steadily for a few moments before continuing in that same easy drawl. "I have received no intel about British army—"

"Marines," Harry corrected.

The lieutenant gave him a hard stare, though it lost its punch a little as it was delivered through silly, metallic-tinted sunglasses only fit for a teenage girlie. Harry kept his thoughts to himself, for a change, though calling a US Marine lieutenant a girlie was probably pushing it too far even for him.

"Or to put it another way," the lieutenant said, stepping closer. "What the hell are you doing in my war zone?"

"Ah," Tom said quickly, before Harry could open his big mouth. "Now that we can understand, sir."

"And stop calling me sir," the lieutenant said irritably. "Do I look like a sir to you?" Well, that didn't come out right and was followed by an embarrassed silence.

"No," Harry said.

"You look like an officer in the US Marines to me," Tom said quickly. "Just like we're in the British Marines. Makes us brothers in arms, don't you think?"

Surprisingly, the young lieutenant did think and nodded slowly. "Okay, you're marines. But it doesn't explain what you're doing in my patrol area."

Harry decided to stop being a prat and come clean. He tapped the crutch. "This is a souvenir from a little village a few klicks south of here, but it could have been a bloody sight worse if an old Afghan hadn't pulled me out of the open." He saw the marine nod once, knowingly. "I'm here to say thanks."

"Okay," the lieutenant said, smiling, which caught them all by surprise. "I can copy that." He stepped back and waved them on. "Watch out for the bad guys," he said as he walked back up the hill to his men, who had now lowered their weapons and were watching the Brits with only mild interest.

"Let's get the hell outa here," BJ said in a stage whisper, when the other two hadn't moved.

Harry waved at the young lieutenant from the Land Rover as they bounced away up the rutted track. "Snotty nosed kid," he said with a shake of his head. "Probably get himself killed by some raghead sometime soon."

"Nah," Tom said, concentrating on keeping the Land Rover out of the deep wadi at the side of the track, "I've been to Quantico and seen these boys. Bit green, but I wouldn't say no to one of them watching my six."

Harry's mouth was open, and he was staring at Tom in mock astonishment. He looked back at BJ, who was smiling broadly. "He means it, doesn't he?"

"Yeah," BJ said. Apparently they sent him over as some sort of exchange bitch, and he got treated great by the Yanks."

"I bet he did," Harry said. "Pretty boy like him, what's not to like? And they'd just lurve his cute accent."

"Fuck off," Tom said eloquently.

17

Tweetie Pie was a stick-thin young man wearing an off-white NHS sling over his left arm and a dangly gold earring. *What the hell is the world coming to*, Shaun thought as he closed the door to the interview room and sat at the chipped wooden table. Danny walked behind Tweetie, leaned on the wall, and made pouting faces at Shaun.

"So, why are you here, Tweetie?" Shaun asked.

That floored the poor boy. "What do ya mean? Don't you know?"

You shot six guys between the eyes, Shaun thought. He looked at the thin little blond with his silk shirt and over-tight trousers. *I doubt that.* "So you see, I know, Tweetie." He couldn't help saying his name. Tweetie, for God's sake! "The question is, do you know?"

"Yeah, course. You fink I'm bloody fick or somethink?"

Mostly somethink, Shaun thought. "Go on, then, impress me." No, he's not getting it. "Then why are you here?"

"Got nicked, didn't I."

There, proves he isn't fick. "Don't do the crime if you can't do the time," Shaun said helpfully.

Tweetie turned in the seat and stared at Danny. "Is he nuts?"

Danny nodded. Of course he's nuts. He said nothing, letting him sweat. Yeah, like that was working.

Shaun pointed at the sling. "Get that in the shootout?"

"Yeah." Tweetie raised his arm, flinched extravagantly, and lowered it again. "But I weren't there."

Shaun glanced at Danny, who'd discovered some interesting writing on the wall that required his complete attention.

Shaun closed his eyes, but that didn't help, it was still looney tunes. He decided it was better to let it go, for the sake of his sanity. "So, this OK Corral you weren't at—"

Tweetie turned to Danny again, but there was no help there. "I don't know no OK Corral, is it a diving club?

"It was a wild west shoot-out, like the one you were in," Danny prompted.

Tweetie started to deny it, but Shaun leaned forward and patted his sling, raising a very satisfying scream from the boy.

"Yeah, I know," Shaun said, sympathy dripping from his voice. "Bullet wounds hurt like buggery, don't they?" Not a great simile, on this occasion.

Tweetie was rocking back and forth, clutching his arm and moaning.

Shaun leaned back to give the boy room to sob, displaying enough consideration and compassion to fill a good-sized bucket.

"I got shot," Tweetie whimpered.

"He got shot." Shaun pointed out to Danny, who raised his eyebrows in surprise.

"That'll be what caused the bullet wound," Danny explained helpfully. Hey, detective detecting.

"Some other guys at the scene weren't so lucky," Shaun said. "If you're the only one not face down on the concrete, then you shot them. That's murder for sure. Probably hang you."

Tweetie gasped and put his good hand to his mouth. "I didn't murder nobody!" He was rocking back and forth in the chair. "They was shooting at me!" He raised his bandaged arm to emphasise the point. "And they shot little Talcum." He fought back tears. "A dear little thing she was, too."

Shaun frowned. "Talcum?" Then he got it. "Calf-length white trousers, red high heels?"

Tweetie nodded slowly and looked as though he might start blubbering.

"How many bodies did they pull out of there?" Shaun said with a frown, as if he'd lost count.

Danny screwed up his face and counted slowly on his fingers. "Six," he said at last and glanced at Tweetie. "Including the... Talcum." He nodded sagely. "Drug deal gone bad, I believe."

Shaun was having much too much fun to quit. "Maybe you'll just get twenty years." He leaned forward, looked around to make sure nobody in the empty room could overhear, and whispered, "Pretty boy like you with all those lonely cons, all pumped up muscles and... swollen." He waited for Tweetie to get the picture.

Tweetie got the picture, his jaw doing an impression of a cartoon character in shock, and he almost became a deceased birdie right there. "Twenty years! But I didn't murder nobody!" He stood up. Danny put his hands on his shoulders and helped him to sit down again. He whimpered and put his good hand over his eyes. That made everything better. "I was there, yeah, but I was only along as the muscle."

Danny snorted a laugh that was unstoppable, and Shaun's shoulders shook visibly.

"What?" Tweetie looked hurt. "Don't you fink I could be scary?"

"You scare the shit outa me," Shaun said in a voice that still shook from suppressed laughter.

"Anyway, I only had a little gun, and it weren't even mine!"

That was it; Danny lost it and almost made it out through the door before he erupted with laughter.

Shaun shook his head in mock reproach. "Excuse my colleague, Mr Tweetie, he doesn't know how to behave."

Tweetie nodded deep understanding. "It's the black blood. You know?" He leaned forward a little. "And do you know what they say?"

Shaun thought he must have finally been transported completely into Daffy Duck land. "This gun... the little one that weren't... wasn't yours..." Shaun caught himself before his brain grew gossamer wings and fluttered away. "Whose was it?"

"I want a brief," Tweetie said, with sudden truculent confidence, a totally unconvincing aggressive pose and a squeaky voice.

"You'll get my fist in your pearly white teeth if you don't tell me exactly what was going on in that warehouse!"

He meant it; Tweetie knew he meant it. He was going to damage his New Smile. Four hundred bleedin' quid, and he was going to—

"Any time today will be fine with me," Shaun prompted.

"I told you, I was along as—"

"The muscle. Yeah, you said."

That wasn't going to save his teeth; he could see that from the nutter's expression. "Why the hell should I take the fall for them?" No reason. "I was there with Big Betty and Curly Sue." Clearly still not enough. "For the delivery."

Danny, apparently recovered, came back into the room. "Big Betty and Curly Sue?" he said, walking behind Tweetie and resuming his position against the wall.

"Yeah, you know?" Tweetie's voice had lost its bravado and was now thin with a hint of a lisp. They didn't know, he could see that, so he would tell them. He was already in it up to his neck, so why the hell should he get himself banged up for those two? Pumped up cons... swollen. Jesus! But you know, it painted a bit of a picture. Then the sudden thought of twenty years banged up smudged the paint. "All right, say I tell you? What's in it for me?"

Danny shrugged. "Well, Mad Max O'Conner here won't beat you to a pulp for a start."

Tweetie's jaw dropped again, and he stared at Shaun. Why'd they call him Mad Max? But look at him, he really did look like a right nutter. What the hell? "I tell you, you let me walk, right?"

Shaun and Danny exchanged glances. "Okay," Danny said, "deal."

Tweetie nodded, swallowed, nodded. "It was Curly Sue's idea. She said that we could make a load of easy money supplying a shit-load of H for one of those rich blokes over in Mayfair."

"Easy money?" Danny said.

"Yeah," Tweetie said, twisting in his chair. This black guy was all right, not a nutter like the other one. He warmed to his story. "Curly Sue reckoned we could make one big score and be on the up. Maybe move upmarket or somethink, and be in the money."

Shaun leaned forward across the table. "So what happened?"

Tweetie wiped his mouth on the palm of his hand. "It was just a con."

"How come?" Danny prompted.

"Turns out Curly Sue owed somebody big time and was going to get her nuts chopped off unless she did this gig." He stared at them with a pleading look that went floating past. "So we thought we was going to this easy drug buy... 'cept nothink's easy with these black guys." He turned quickly in the chair. "No offence."

Danny shrugged.

"Couldn't have been that easy," Shaun pointed out. "You had a gun." He frowned. "A machine gun, for Christ's sake."

"Yeah, but it was only a little machine gun."

Oh, that's all right, then.

"A mini Uzi," Danny added for completeness.

"So what went wrong?" Shaun prompted.

"The Jamaicans had the drugs all fair and square, and Big Betty handed over the bag of cash. One of those sports bag things full of money. I've never seen so much foldings in me life, there must—"

"So Big Betty handed over the money?" Shaun prompted.

Tweetie shook his head. "No... well, yes." He let his brain spin up to working speed. "She was going to, when Curly shot them all. Bam-bam, bam-bam." He pointed at his chest. "I never seen nothing like it. She put two shots in their chests before they even got time to think about it. Big Betty dropped the money, and she got a gun and popped the others." Tweetie swallowed hard. "You got any water?"

Shaun nodded. There was water somewhere. "So how many did you shoot... with your little machine gun?"

Tweetie shook his head. "No, no way." He swallowed again. "I pulled the trigger thing, but nothing happened. And by the time I worked out where the little safety thing was, it was all over." He raised his arm. "I didn't even know I'd been shot, not until it started to hurt." He flinched. "And it really hurt. You ever been shot?"

"Few times," Shaun said. "So, Big Sue?"

"Curly Sue," Tweetie corrected. "It's Big Betty."

Shaun watched him steadily, wondering if slapping him a few times would help. It would certainly help him. "Okay, Curly Sue, then, she ripped off the drugs and kept the money?"

"Yeah, that was the plan all along. Only way she could pay off the Man."

"Man's going to be pleased," Danny said quietly. "Doubt the Yardies are going to be too chuffed, though."

18

Harry climbed out of the Land Rover onto the dusty village square very slowly and tried to minimise the pain, but only managed to get it down to feeling like a broken leg. He looked around slowly, and his neck hairs rose as he pictured the gunmen on the rooftops of the narrow alley leading off the square where Tom had parked the Land Rover. He reached into the vehicle and pulled out the L115, leaned on his crutch more than usual and limped down the alley to the burned-out building that had come so close to being his last place on Earth.

"Okay," Tom said, retrieving his sub-machine gun and the assault rifle, which he tossed to BJ. He strode past Harry to the door where the old man had dragged Harry's body. "So you got us here, AWOL I might add." He blew out his breath in an exaggerated sigh of resignation. "How do you figure to find the old chap?"

Harry tried to look relaxed about it, like he'd worked it out. He hadn't, and the others knew it. "We could ask," he suggested lamely.

"Oh, yeah right, that'll work," BJ mocked. "'Scuse me, Afghan person, but have you seen an old bloke with a little kid who isn't dead?"

Harry had to admit he had a point and wished he'd thought a bit more about it, on the plane perhaps, but he'd been too busy hurting and cursing. "Dunno," he said, seizing control of the moment. "We could split up and look around."

Tom and BJ stared at him like he'd had too much sun.

"No, wait!" Tom said enthusiastically. "We could go house to house!"

"You're a hoot, you know that?" Harry was hot and getting fed up again.

"Or you could ask me."

They turned quickly to find the old Afghan standing at the entrance to the street with the girl whose life Harry had saved.

"Well, there you go," Harry said, hobbling back down the alley. "Just as I planned."

"Bollocks!" Tom and BJ said together.

And it truly was.

The happy reunion of saviours lasted five seconds. Harry had just reached the old man when the Land Rover's windows blew out, followed an instant later by the doors and roof as the RPG exploded in the cab.

Tom pushed the old man into the same doorway he had pulled Harry into, while BJ scooped up the kid and followed them.

Harry watched them push the civilians to the back and take up defensive positions, and then turned to look back up the alley at the blazing Land Rover. "Looks like they're still mad at us," he said and walked surprisingly easily to the doorway and his crouching friends, but adrenalin will do that. "Are you planning to have a sleepover down here, then?"

They looked up at him and then at the Land Rover.

"If they could have shot us, would they have blown up the vehicle?" he asked, with a questioning tilt of his head. "But that situation isn't going to last long." Nobody moved. "Oh, unless you want to hang around and ask for their insurance details?"

They stood up, looking a little guilty, and now that Harry could see the old man, he put out his hand and helped him up.

"We need to get out of the village," he said with a smile of reassurance that didn't work. "Do you know where there is any transport?"

The old man looked confused for a moment, then got it together. "No transport."

Bugger.

"Only a truck," he said and started off down the alley with the little girl holding onto his robe as if her life depended on it.

The three marines looked at each other, and then Tom shrugged and set off after the departing raggedy pair. BJ scooped Harry up with one arm and half carried, half dragged him after the others. Harry formed the swear words, but then saw the little dust mushrooms sprouting along the alley and decided to hell with dignity.

The truck was an ancient 80's Toyota 4Runner, but right then, with bullets zipping past their ears, a horse and buggy would have been welcome.

"Does it run?" Tom said, seriously doubting it.

The old man opened the driver's door and waved him in. Tom obeyed, got in and, saying a quick prayer in case there was a god, turned the key. The engine should have turned over very tiredly, spluttered, or not turned at all, but it didn't, it just fired right up, and he made a note to thank whichever wizard mechanic had delayed their moment of death.

"Get in!" he shouted at the other two.

BJ jumped in and slid over to the edge of the passenger seat, but not so close to the gear stick that Tom would have to touch his arse.

Harry started to follow, stopped, and called to the old man over the back of the truck. "Come on! Let's get out of here!"

The old man waved at him and ducked down a tiny alley with the little girl still hanging on.

"For Christ's sake, Harry, let's go!" Tom crunched the gears in his hurry to do just that, and Harry slid in as the truck took off.

There was a wooden gate, and then there wasn't. Then they were out of the village and onto good rolling sand hills, with holes and rocks and wadis and lots of bullets. The truck was taking fire from what could only be a heavy machine gun, probably mounted on a pickup like the one they were in. They heard the stunk-stunk as the rounds ripped through the side of the truck right behind their seats. This could only end one way.

"Stop!" Harry shouted, and Tom stood on the brakes. Harry jumped out of the truck onto one leg, caught his balance, and shouted back at BJ. "Spot for me, now!"

BJ rolled out of the truck, pulled out a sniper spotter scope, and scanned the walls and windows of the mud-brick buildings, while Harry walked calmly round the truck and set up the L115, its bipod resting on the truck's hood.

"Eleven o'clock, next to the house with the red paint." BJ ran round the back of the truck out of Harry's line of fire and stood behind him so that he could see the bullet's vapour trail and make any corrections.

Harry saw the 50-cal machine gun on the pickup. He snapped back the L115's bolt, steadied his breathing, and fired. The machine gunner left the truck like he'd been hit by a rocket, but another insurgent jumped up and started to get the thing back into action. Harry killed him before he could do the same to them. And the next guy, and the one after that. The fifth insurgent on the rota ran behind the building, showing the good sense his comrades had been missing.

"Okay," Harry said, folding the bipod and putting a sock back over the muzzle to keep out the dust.

BJ clapped him on the back and laughed. "Okay indeed!" He took Harry's arm and steadied him as he made his way back round the truck.

While Harry waited for him to climb into the truck, he put three fingers into one of the holes made by the bullets that had passed behind his seat. Close, but no cigar. He took a long breath and let it out slowly. It had been close, real close, and he wondered how many more lives he'd got left. Not many, was his guess.

19

Tweetie Pie was biting his lip and thinking, Shaun and Danny could tell that from the pained expression.

"What is it, Mr Tweetie?" Shaun prompted. "You can tell us. We're all friends here, aren't we?"

Tweetie smiled, feeling better now he was among friends. "It was Curly."

"What about Curly?" Shaun asked. God, it was like talking to a toddler.

"She didn't seem too bovered by the drugs." He frowned even harder, cracking his thick makeup. "Only interested in the big boxes."

Now it was Shaun's turn to frown, but without the damage to trowel-layered foundation. "Big boxes? What sort of big boxes?"

Tweetie's makeup cracked even more with the effort of thinking. "Long, thin, err... boxes. Heavy. Two of them." More thinking. "Foot square maybe, and this long." He extended his arms as if showing how big the one that got away was. "Or longer," he added helpfully.

Shaun and Danny exchanged glances.

"Like rifle cases?" Shaun asked, but already knew the answer.

Tweetie cheered up. "Yeah, that's right. How'd you know what was in them? I only saw the one. Big, you know?" He put out his arms again, but still too short.

Shaun nodded and looked over at Danny. "Yeah, I know. Question is— "

"Who is buying rifles?" Danny finished.

"The real question is," Shaun said, tapping the table with his fingertips, "*why* is someone buying two sniper rifles."

Danny frowned. "Why do you think they're sniper rifles?"

"Because," Shaun said, "you can buy regular rifles from bloody Tesco these days, but sniper rifles..." He shook his head. "They're special order. So question still is, why?"

"Ah!" Tweetie said. "That's obvious." He waited for them to ask, or even acknowledge that he'd spoken. Wait on. "Somebody wants somebody dead." He nodded sagely. "Twice."

Danny closed his eyes, but it didn't help. "Looks like we've got a turf war coming, and it's going to be high-tech and bloody."

Shaun thought it through. "We should just sit back, let them kill each other, and arrest the survivors."

"Yeah, like Baxter's going to buy that," Danny said with contempt. "When he can be the hero."

"At our funerals," Shaun added.

"Hey, don't say that," Danny said. "You don't want to get his hopes up."

20

They were missing a paddle and up shit creek. Harry saw them first, about a microsecond before Tom spotted the two pickups full of gunmen blocking the narrow, elevated track. He stood on the brakes and brought the truck to a sliding halt in a cloud of dust. The men in the trucks all started firing their AK-47s, but at a thousand yards, they might as well have been throwing rocks, but for the truck-mounted 50-cal machine gun, they were well within range. A fact that became all too obvious when the bullets started kicking up the track on both sides. It was only a matter of time.

"Get us outa here!" Harry screamed.

Tom was already on it and slammed the Toyota into gear, ripped the steering wheel to the right, and floored the gas, sending the truck over the edge of the track and hurtling almost vertically down through the rocks and scrub, losing itself in a choking cloud of dust.

Harry hung on to the seat and the door, trying to keep his leg from flailing around, and failing. He was screaming and cursing, but it was as if it was coming from someone else. Tom joined in the cursing as the truck hit a boulder, bounced to the right, and climbed onto two wheels. He wrenched the wheel and got the truck back down on all fours, but just in time to slam into anther boulder the size of a tank. The left wing of the truck disintegrated like tin foil, but they were still moving, even if they didn't know where to.

"Oh shit!" Tom said and stood on the brakes again.

Harry's eyes were tight shut as the pain blazed through him, but he opened them in time to see the line where the desert ended. Deserts don't just end, his brain reasoned through the pain. Yes, they do, it answered, when they get to a cliff. "Shit!" he shouted, joining in.

They were going too fast and bouncing around too much for the brakes to have a hope in hell of stopping them, and they went over the edge, followed by an avalanche of rocks and shrubs down their crash dive descent.

Master Sergeant Ethan Gill was resting his eyes and leaning back in the passenger seat of the Humvee as it bounced along the rutted track that was probably a freeway to these people. Manuel Alvarez was driving, and Eddie Elward and Al Caponetto were in the rear trying to catch some Z's. Ethan eased his back and tried to ignore the tuneless crap coming from the radio station Manuel favoured.

"Yeehar, fuckin' ariba!" Ethan said without opening his eyes.

"What was that, boss?" Manuel asked, knowing damn well what it was.

"Can't you get anything decent on that thing?"

"No, boss. Don't you like mambo? Good for the soul." Manuel chuckled quietly.

Ethan was about to tell him exactly what mambo was good for, but Al leaned forward and pointed up the almost vertical slope stretching up into the hills. "Please, boss, can we play sliding down the mountain as well?"

Ethan opened his eyes and followed Al's pointing finger to the Toyota heading straight down the hill, bouncing over boulders and bucking like a fairground bull. Manuel pulled the Humvee over, and they waited for the truck to flip and explode, like in the movies. Cool.

Tom was far from cool, fighting the steering wheel as it snapped left and right, and hoping to God that they didn't hit anything bigger than that last boulder, or they'd flip and breakfast would be milk and honey on a cloud. Heaven? I don't think so.

He felt the truck slew left and tip to an impossible angle, giving him a panoramic view of the desert and the boulders waiting to mash them. A teeth-rattling collision with another house-sized rock and the view changed to take in the upside of the cliff as the truck ran backwards for a bit of a change. They slammed into what used to be a tree before it got depressed and died. The impact crushed them back into the seats, but at least they had stopped. Safe. The truck creaked and complained and rocked from the impact.

"Shit! Shit! Shit!" BJ said.

The others let their breath out slowly, and Tom pulled a stupid grin. "Christ, that was—"

The Toyota slid right, and the depressed stump climbed out of the sand and joined them on their little trip downhill to mangled mush. Tom pulled the steering wheel full right, and for a second the wheels found purchase enough to get the nose round and pointing down the incline, but then nothing.

Great, Harry thought, *now they'd be able to see what was going to squash them.*

The front of the truck crashed down into a gulley, sending the back climbing into the air. An instant before the laws of physics flipped the truck onto its roof, it dropped back down with a bone-crunching shock that flipped the wheels out of the gulley and sent them on their way again. Luck doesn't get any better than that.

The Americans were out of the Humvee now, to get a better look at the idiots in the truck getting squished.

"Twenty says they're buzzard lunch," Eddie said, squinting up against the bright sky.

"I'll take your money," Al said, but still thought it was a long shot.

"Those are people in that vehicle," Ethan chided. "But I'll take that action."

The Toyota had now slewed forty-five degrees to the left and was bouncing over a long bump that rose out of the sand like a buried tree. The truck lifted onto its right front wheel, pirouetted almost gracefully, and crashed down onto its side, tipping Tom and BJ onto Harry — just in case the pain in his leg wasn't excruciating enough. It slid, bounced, and screamed for another twenty feet, the rocks shattering the windows and filling the interior with broken glass and dust. Then it stopped. They were alive. God, it was a miracle.

They were perched on the edge of a sheer drop that the kind and bountiful Lord had put there to make sure the last stretch was a doozy. The truck creaked and rocked slowly back and forth as the occupants tried to untangle their bodies.

Tom spat out dust, opened his eyes, and looked straight down onto the track fifteen feet or so below. "Don't move!" he shouted.

Harry and BJ turned their heads slowly, thinking the worst, but there were no gunmen there, just the drop and the rocks. Great.

"Don't move," Tom repeated.

"You know," Harry whispered, "this reminds me of *The Italian Job*."

"Oh, for Christ's sake!" BJ growled.

"How'd that end?" Tom said without moving.

"Hang on a minute, lads. I've got a great idea," Harry said through gritted teeth.

The truck groaned and rocked sideways towards the drop.

"Okay," BJ said quietly, "what was the great idea?"

Harry shrugged and was going to say the movie ended there, but his movement tipped the balance, and the truck groaned like the death cry of a redwood coming down and went over the edge.

The Americans barely flinched as the Toyota crunched in a mangled heap onto the track and rocked slowly on its roof.

"Pay up," Eddie said, putting out his hand.

Al groaned and fished about in his pocked for the money that wasn't there.

Never one to part with cash unless absolutely necessary, Ethan strode off towards the wrecked truck. "It ain't over till the fat lady sings," he said over his shoulder.

"Those hajjis are dog meat," Eddie said with a shrug and reached for his water flask. It was hot, and he was getting a bit bored now the action was over.

Ethan crouched down beside the truck and looked in through the shattered window to see if anybody had survived enough to save his twenty dollars. "Shit!" he said and began pulling at the passenger door, but it was fused into the crushed bodywork.

Eddie and Al exchanged a quick glance and ran over to see why Ethan was so keen to get into the truck. Contraband maybe. It took a single look to recognise the desert camouflage in the heap of bodies.

Al Caponetto was a cruiserweight boxer for the corps, and his 200 pounds was all muscle, so when he pulled on the truck door, it knew better than to resist. With a grinding scream like a living thing, the door came away along with the hinges, and the Toyota gave up the bodies so the Americans could pull them out into the dust. Not elegant, but there were no first responders hiding in the bushes — and no bushes.

"They dead?" Eddie said, leaning over Ethan and Al as they untangled the Brits, "cus if they are, I still win the bet."

Such deep human kindness just tugs at the heartstrings, and Ethan gave him a long, unpleasant look by way of thanks. "You really are a piece of work, Eddie. You know that?" He rolled Harry over and put his fingers on his neck in search of a pulse.

"This one's alive," Al said, feeling Tom's carotid artery. He turned to BJ and repeated the pressure on his neck. "This one too."

"Make that a triple," Ethan said and checked Harry over slowly for broken bones or bleeding, but found nothing. "You lose your bet, Eddie," he said and dripped water from his flask into Harry's open mouth.

"Funny," Eddie said with a shrug, "but I don't seem to mind much."

"Well, ain't that big of you," Al said, grasping BJ under the arms and dragging him away from the truck.

"Yeah," Eddie said, repeating the move with Tom, "my mom used to say I'm all heart."

"How is your mom?" Al said, checking BJ over for breaks. "Tell her Lover Boy says hi."

"No probs," Eddie said. "And tell your sister I said—"

"If you two boneheads have finished," Ethan said, "shall we get these boys out of here. We've got company."

Al and Eddie straightened up, looked up the hill, and heard the sound of engines rolling down to meet them. A moment later came the unmistakable thump of a 50 cal opening up.

"Shit! Eddie said and stepped closer to the Toyota.

"That won't save you from a 50 cal," Ethan pointed out. "Okay though, they can't depress the gun enough to tag us here."

"Oh, that's reassuring," Al said, "but their truck has wheels, so they can come on down, and I bet they have AK—"

AK-47 rounds zipped past, kicking up dust between the upturned Toyota and the Humvee. The three Americans grabbed one Brit each by their webbing and dragged them up against the vertical drop the truck had crashed down and hoped they were out of the firing line.

Harry opened his eyes and then closed them again against the painful sunlight. "Shit!" he groaned.

"Yeah, man, and we're all in it up to here," Ethan said, risking a lean forward and a quick look up the hill and being rewarded by a blizzard of small arms' fire.

Maybe it was timing, or the familiar sound of AK-47s, but both Tom and BJ came round and sat up slowly against the cliff. Neither man spoke, but it was clear from their expressions that they knew what it was they were in and how deep it was.

Harry looked over at the Toyota where their weapons still lay and stood up shakily, gripping his leg with his left hand for support and to try to suppress the pain. He edged along, keeping his back to the rock until he was level with the upturned truck.

Ethan watched him with a slow shake of his head. "Your buddy seems to have hit his head in the fall," he said to Tom, who was now also on his feet.

"No," Tom said, following his friend slowly, "he was crazy before the fall."

"Shall we give them covering fire?" Eddie asked, unslinging his M16.

Ethan looked at him steadily. "Sure. You go first." He pointed at the clearing and the dust from the barrage of bullets.

"We've gotta do something, boss," Al said, licking his dry lips. "Those insurgents'll be rolling down the road with their 50 cal any second now."

Ethan knew that, but the question was, what was the something they gotta do? Running out into the open and firing blind up that hill was a one-way ticket to a full military send-off in Arlington, but staying put was, as Al pointed out, going to get them just as dead.

Harry ended the analysis by taking two steps out into the open and diving under the truck's upturned flatbed. Bullets whined off the bodywork and ripped into the tyres, sending them spinning, but the flatbed had been reinforced to carry something heavy — and almost certainly illegal. He crawled up to the cab, forcing his leg to push him, and fumbled inside through the shattered rear window. He found what he was looking for, pulled out the L115, and kissed its stock. He rolled out from under the truck, keeping the reinforced flatbed between him and the hill, crouched behind the front wheel, rested the rifle on the underside of the engine, and waited.

He didn't have to wait long. A few seconds later they all heard the sound of approaching vehicles and knew it was the truck with the 50 cal and the other pickup carrying the rest of the insurgents. The first truck rounded the bend five hundred yards up the road. Harry killed the driver with a single shot through the chest. The truck seemed to wobble and then dipped and flipped, spewing a dozen gunmen into the desert.

Harry swore noisily, and Eddie frowned at Ethan. "Wrong truck," Ethan explained without taking his eyes off the second vehicle carrying the 50 cal as it slewed to a stop next to the wrecked truck and its troops scattered in the dust.
The 50 cal opened up, tearing chunks of sandstone from the rock face a few feet above the Americans' heads as the operator found the range. Harry put a round into his heart as he stood wide open behind the pedestal mount. With a feeling of deja vu, he dropped the next man to take the weapon's stock, and the next. It was beginning to look like he was going to stop this on his own. Some of the scattered gunmen recovered their wits and started running towards him, joined by six more from the truck with the working but unmanned 50 cal, all firing wildly as they came. There was no way he was going to stop them, not with a sniper rifle.

Tom appeared behind him, having retrieved his sub-machine gun from the truck using Harry's technique. "Any left?"

Being hit by fire from the running gunmen would have been just bad luck, but the rounds coming from the gunmen up the hill were well aimed and punched into the truck's bodywork, and it was a racing certainty that one of them was going to get hit real soon.

BJ arrived with the first part of the solution in the form of his C7 assault rifle. Harry jabbed his finger up the hill and then at the under-barrel grenade launcher.

BJ looked up the steep slope and grimaced. "That's a hell of a long shot at this angle and blind."

Harry shrugged. "Don't need you to hit them," he said, snapping the bolt back on his rifle. "Just make some dust and some noise."

BJ slid the grenade launcher barrel forward, pushed in a high explosive round, snapped the launcher back, and reached into his pack for the next round. "Say when."

"When," Harry said and stepped forward, with Tom moving in behind him and taking up covering position against the rapidly closing gunmen.

Harry sighted up the hill as the first grenade exploded among the rocks, with exactly the desired result. The gunmen ducked behind any handy cover and waited for the other grenades. Harry counted silently and breathed out very slowly. "Three," he said, and right on cue, the gunmen started to put their heads up to see if it was over. And it was for them. Moving with the smooth action of a machine, Harry shot one in the head, snapped back the bolt, shifted his aim, and put an 8.6 mm round into the next gunman's chest. Again the bolt clicked back, but before he could fire, his target sprayed blood, spun, and went down. Harry didn't look, he knew the sound of M16s on full automatic, and letting the Americans do what they were doing real well, he stepped back up to the side of the Toyota.

The eighteen or so gunmen were now less than fifty yards away, and their firing was getting a hell of a lot more accurate. Tom got to work with the sub-machine gun, and BJ with his assault rifle on automatic, but it wasn't going to be enough. The Americans ran up the slight rise to the truck, threw themselves onto the sand and opened up with their M16s. Better. The gunmen were being blown backwards, sideways, and apart, and showing good sense, dived to the ground behind the boulders Mother Nature had rolled down the hillside over a million years ago just to provide them with some cover. So, it was going to be a protracted shootout. Seriously bad news, with ammunition for the good guys being pretty much what they had in their webbing or stowed away in the Humvee.

Harry looked around for a way out, but saw only flat killing ground and the sheer rock face. So, it looked like he was going to get killed again, and this time for real.

One of the Taliban touched his ear, and Harry knew he was receiving instructions, probably the best way to slice open an infidel. The gunman shouted something, and the rest of them hightailed it back to the remaining truck.

Not going to die, then, that's always a good result.

"What the hell?" Tom said, lowering the sub-machine gun with its empty mag.

"They're leaving," Eddie said, standing up for a better look.

"Ya think?" Ethan said, pulling Eddie's legs and crashing him to the sand. "Let's wait for them to go before we start waving, shall we?"

The truck fired up as the gunmen piled into the back, spun its wheels in the dust, and headed on out.

"They're in a hurry," Tom said quietly. "What just happened here?"

Harry shrugged. "Looks like somebody pulled the plug on this little fracas. But why they quit is beyond me. They had us dead to rights."

"Not quite," Eddie said, standing up again. "I think there would've been a few more funerals in the old Bedouin camp if they'd tried it on with old Eddie Elward."

Harry and Ethan exchanged a long look, and Ethan shrugged. "Inbreeding."

Harry nodded — he'd seen *Deliverance*. "Any chance of a lift?" He pointed towards the Humvee. "I'd rather be somewhere else when they change their minds."

Ethan smiled. "Grab your gear."

Harry looked back at Tom, and he climbed into the upturned truck and passed their packs out to BJ.

Ethan did a double take when BJ handed Harry the elbow crutch. "What in God's name are you doing in a war zone with one of those?"

Harry smiled. "It stops me falling over."

Ethan looked at him for a long time, as though considering his sanity, and then headed for the Humvee. "Y'know, these Brits are all nuts," he said to himself.

Harry looked at BJ with an expression of surprise and pointed at himself.

BJ nodded slowly. He'd never had any doubts about Harry's sanity. The man was totally crazy. So what did that make him? Because it was a certainty that he and Tom would have followed Harry into a burning building — or hell, if that was hotter.

The question the gods on their mountaintop might have been asking was, would he have still followed him knowing that he and Tom would never see another morning.

21

"So who the hell is this Curly Sue?" Shaun asked, trying and failing to connect the drug rip-off and the rifles.

"Everybody knows Curly Sue," Tweety said, but clearly not. "Runs Oscar's Pussy Club." No response. "You know, *the* Oscar's Pussy Club?" As if saying it twice would make everything crystal.

"Yeah, okay, Oscar's Pussy," Shaun said. "So, Curly Sue gets into some sort of trouble, and she—"

"He."

"What?"

"Curly Sue is a he," Tweetie explained.

"Oh, right," Shaun said. "So *he* agrees to pay off this guy by ripping off the Jamaicans?" Nod received. "So who is he?"

"Who's who?" Tweetie asked, frowning.

Shaun needed a drink. "This man, the man who Curly owed big time, the man who was going to cut off her nuts."

Tweetie nodded slowly, buying time for dots to join up. "An evil mastermind," he said with gravitas. "The brains behind heists too big for Crimewatch."

"Oh, please," Danny said, but then caught Shaun's hard look. "Nothing's too big for Crimewatch," he said quietly.

Shaun wanted to go home, to a bar, anywhere. Tweetie was wearing some disgustingly sweet aftershave, or more likely, perfume. It was musk or some crap like that, and it was getting to his stomach. And he still needed a drink. "This Mr Big, the criminal mastermind?" he said, trying to put the thought of a drink out of his head.

Tweetie looked puzzled.

"Who... is... he...?" Shaun said slowly.

Tweetie nodded again. Still no sign of the glass of water was there, and here he was being all helpful and citizenish, but do they show him any respect? Course not, to them he was just a—

Danny coughed, and Tweetie glanced back to see him pointing at Shaun.

"Oh, you want to know who he is?" He tried a smile, but it was like smiling at a grizzly bear fresh from its winter sleep — with the same result. Shaun leaned forward, took a handful of the long blond locks, and banged his head on the table.

Tweetie screamed and grabbed his hair as Shaun let it go. "Ow! Bloody hell! Ow! You've broken my nowsh."

"Not yet," Shaun said quietly, "but in about five seconds I'll sort that."

"What's he want?" Tweetie pleaded with Danny.

"Think he wants to know who set up the bloodbath in the warehouse."

"Then why didn't he just bloody ask, instead of smackin' me about?" He put his hand on the growing bump on his forehead. "You could've caused brain damage doing that."

Shaun glanced at Danny, but said nothing. After a second he stood up.

Tweetie's jaw dropped, then snapped back shut. "It was an Irish bloke, like yourself," he said in a rush.

Shaun sat down and nodded. See, all it needed was the right word, the right gesture, an act of kindness. Pure police interview technique in practice. His trainer would be so proud.

"Irish?" he said, leaning forward.

"Yeah," Tweetie said quickly, "a really nasty bloke, you wouldn't like him."

"I'll let you know," Shaun said with a smile. "Has this nasty Irishman got a name?"

Tweetie frowned. Of course he'd got a name, what sort of question was that? Oh, bugger it. "Yeah, his name is Patrick somefink... O'Conner, I fink."

Shaun clenched his fists, turning his knuckles white. "Patrick O'Conner? Are you sure?" He spoke very slowly, as though his jaw wasn't working properly.

"Yeah, Curly Sue said he supplied the guns for the drug buy, reckons he supplies guns and stuff to... well, anybody who'll pay."

Shaun turned and walked out of the interview room, turned right down the corridor, and stood by a dirty frosted window, but it didn't matter, he wasn't looking at anything except Patrick's bloody face as he stepped over his father's body.

Danny watched his friend go, waited a few seconds, then followed. He strode down the corridor and put a hand on Shaun's shoulder. "Hold up, man. I know what you're thinking."

Shaun turned to him with a look he'd seen before, every time somebody mentioned his brother.

Danny took a small involuntary step back. "Come on, man, you know what Baxter said would happen if any of us went off book again."

"He's been holed up in Ireland for twenty years," Shaun said, struggling to contain his anger. "Totally untouchable, with the Boys watching out for him. Well, now he's out of his hidey-hole, and that little poof in there can give me a reason to go get him." He shook Danny's hand off. "What do you want me to do, walk away? Well, it's not going to happen."

"But Baxter—"

"Screw Baxter! The Troubles are over, and Patrick's here, without his Provo minders to protect his ass." He started to walk away. "Call it a peace dividend."

Danny had been Shaun's partner for five years and knew when arguing was a waste of breath. He strode after his friend. "Okay then, but we do it by the book."

And that would be a first, but it made him feel better.

This time Valentin Tal was hot and wishing he was back in Baghdad, except the hotel had been freezing, so he was caught both ways. He'd been to London many times, but those visits had mostly been legitimate, and he'd been able to stay in at least moderately decent hotels with British air-con that almost worked some of the time, but this visit was... how did the Americans put it? Ah yes, under the radar. So, because he was... under the radar, he was staying in a grubby little hotel in Shepherd's Bush. No air-con, and no anything else — except unseen vermin.

He was sitting on the grubby bed with his single travel bag unopened beside him. If things went well, he wouldn't have to stay in this place at all. If things went well, which they rarely did. He stood up slowly and crossed to the wardrobe, slid open the flimsy door, and looked in. Inside was a large khaki canvas bag leaning against the woodwork. He would have preferred something a little quieter about its contents, but he'd had to acquire the weapon in-country, from a common dealer, as shipping it through the normal diplomatic bag route had been ruled out. Too many people involved, and too many opportunities for a leak, now or later.

Someone knocked on the locked door, and he opened it without any of that sneaking about or peering through the peephole — which would have been tough anyway, as there wasn't one. He nodded at the man standing in the corridor and stepped back to let him in.

"You're late," he said as the man brushed past and looked around.

"Didn't know I was still in the army," the visitor said in a heavy German accent.

"That would be good," Valentin said. "Then we could throw you out again."

The man laughed a deep laugh and put out his hand. "Still the same old Valentin, no?"

Valentin shook the offered hand. "I wish that were so, Branislav, but the great days of the German Democratic Republic are behind me."

Branislav nodded slowly. "They are behind us all, my dear friend." He smiled. "But one last throw of the dice, for the comrades of the Nationale Volksarmee, yes?"

"Enshallah," Valentin said, mirroring Branislav's smile.

"You, my friend, have spent too many years with those heathens," Branislav said. He looked around the shabby room and smiled broadly when he saw the vodka on the dresser. He picked up the bottle, filled two tumblers, and handed one to Valentin. "Budem zdorovy," he said, raising his glass and clinking it against Valentin's. "To the good old days."

"Good old days that were perhaps not as good as our memories paint them, eh?"

Branislav emptied the glass and nodded slowly. "Oligarch scum sold us out for money."

Valentin nodded. "A lot of money."

Branislav glared at him for a moment and then laughed his big laugh and filled their glasses again. "So, do you have it?"

Valentin put his glass down untouched and crossed to the wardrobe, sliding the stiff door open again, reached inside, and brought out a battered attaché case of the sort much favoured by wannabe execs in the seventies.

"You are showing your age," Branislav said, smiling and shaking his head slowly.

Valentin dropped the attaché case onto the bed, opened it, and dropped the photographs onto the dirty sheets. Branislav stopped smiling.

"These are the targets?" It was a redundant question. He drew his breath in sharply. "The hornets will be buzzing." He picked up the photo of the US President. "You have arranged a speedy exit for us?"

"No need," Valentin said. "We will almost certainly be killed."

Branislav nodded without emotion. "It is a good time to die, as it was once before."

Valentin nodded. "Ah, Berlin. It was... how do the movies say? Hot. It was hot."

"One minute," Branislav said, picking up his vodka. "One minute was all that saved us from the CIA death squad." He raised his glass. "Cheers!" He smiled.

Valentin clinked his glass against Branislav's. "To staying ahead of the death squads."

Branislav nodded and downed the vodka and looked across at the open wardrobe. "I see you have the tools." He stood. "Let me see."

"No, my friend," Valentin said, crossing and closing the creaking door. "We will meet at a more appropriate venue, and there you will choose your bride."

"And Jurgen?" Branislav asked. "This is a job for the Brothers Vogel, yes?"

Valentin glanced at his watch, a reflex action, since he knew exactly what time it was, he always did, a habit from in his days in the field. "He will be here," he said quietly, and that was enough for both men. He picked up the tumbler of vodka, raised it, and drained it in one swallow.

They were back in the game.

22

Harry sat back against the side of the Humvee and closed his eyes as it rocked and bounced its way from wherever they had been to wherever they were going. His leg hurt, his head hurt, and just about everything between hurt, but that's what'll happen when you fall off a mountain in a crappy pickup truck.

"Where we going, Master Sergeant?" he called between bumps

Ethan spoke without turning. "Somewhere that ain't here," he said, watching the desert for any sign of an ambush. There wasn't any, and that was worrying. Those boys just giving up like that when they had them cold, well, it just wasn't natural. He didn't like it, though he admitted to himself that he would have liked the alternative a whole lot less.

Harry leaned forward and watched the grey desert bounce past through the small side window. Like Ethan, he couldn't understand why the insurgents hadn't finished them off when they had the chance, and they definitely had more than a chance back there. Maybe they didn't want to lose any more people because between them, the boys had taken a heavy toll. Truth was, though, these fanatics didn't care about being dead, you only had to see those nutters who blew themselves up to kill women and kids in a market someplace — he didn't know, and probably wouldn't have cared, that his travelling companions had instigated just such a nutter-blast in a village not that far from where he was right then. *Something isn't right*, he thought and watched the desert more closely.

The Humvee stopped, and everybody instinctively checked their weapons and tensed, ready for a firefight.

"Village," Ethan said.

The men in the back leaned forward and saw a stone village at the bottom of the long hill on which they'd stopped. Nothing moved down there, but that wasn't news, it was near midday, and sensible people stayed in the shade. But nothing moved, not even a bird or a scraggy dog.

"That Agha Dal?" Eddie asked and then shut up under Ethan's icy stare.

"I don't like it," Harry said quietly.

"Ya think?" Ethan said, signalling Al to go forward. "Slowly," he added, unnecessarily.

Al took the Humvee down the long slope at near walking speed, everybody inside ready for whatever it was that was spooking them. The vehicle was moving so slowly they could hear the scrunch of gravel beneath its huge tyres and the steady thump of the engine barely turning over. The men in the back craned forward and watched the surrounding slopes for the ambush that was almost certainly waiting for them, but there was still nothing, not a hint of life. It was eerie and, yeah, a little scary.

Harry carefully slung his rifle over his shoulder and took one of the M16s from the rack without asking, or even thinking of asking. The L115 could give a chicken a new arsehole at a thousand yards, but in the close confines of a village, it was only slightly better than a big stick. Eddie glanced at him and grinned maniacally. He was teetering on the edge of crazy, and Harry made a mental note to make sure he was behind this guy's rifle if things turned dramatic.

Al took the Humvee past the high walls surrounding the first houses in the village, up to the square in the middle, and stopped, keeping the engine running and his foot covering the gas pedal.

There was a market in the square, a couple of dozen ramshackle stalls selling farm-type produce of every kind. There were tented stalls selling clothes and sandals, fixed table stalls heavy with vegetables, and glorified wheelbarrows loaded high with the produce from a single crop. And between the stalls were the corpses.

The men in the Humvee had seen it all, been there, done that, but this was worse than anything they'd ever seen. Old men, women, and little kids sprawled out in the unmistakable posture of agonising death.

Harry opened the side door and dismounted, keeping the M16 pointing where he was looking as he scanned the surrounding buildings for signs of life, but there was no life in this village, even the dogs were dead in the dust.

He didn't need to be an expert on WMD to recognise a bio-weapon attack when he saw one — and he saw one right here.

The rest of the men climbed out of the Humvee, cautiously sniffing the air and searching the harsh shadows for anything that needed killing. Caponetto stayed in the vehicle, his foot still hovering over the gas pedal and his eyes scanning the buildings.

It was utterly silent, without even a breath of wind to disturb the scene from hell. They instinctively formed a skirmish line, five or six feet apart, and advanced slowly into the market and onto the clear circle in the middle.

And there lay the bodies of sixteen marines, a whole patrol scattered like broken toys.

Ethan tore his eyes off the marines and searched the surrounding buildings for any sign of the bastards who'd killed these boys. The bodies were bait, he was sure of it. He signalled urgently for the others to move forward, but it took several seconds for the signal to register through the shock. Then one by one they recovered, spread out again, and moved ahead. Nobody asked what they were looking for, they'd already found that, but they moved on anyway almost on autopilot, through the sprawl of dead marines.

"I don't get this?" Tom said to nobody in particular. "Patrol like this in a village like this one, they wouldn't have stood a chance against those 50 cals, so why use chemicals?"

"I can guess," Harry said, his borrowed M16 tracking across the tops of the surrounding buildings. "Now we know why they took off in such a hurry back there."

BJ gave him a questioning look and then nodded. "Yeah, they wanted us to see this." He stopped and looked around quickly. "And they wanted us here!"

On the flat roof of the most prestigious building overlooking the market square, a sniper watched the infidels through the scope of his rifle. He put the cross hairs on Harry as he was carrying a sniper rifle of his own, but then switched it to the American nearest the buildings. Eddie. This one first, and in the chaos that would follow, he would kill the sniper. He breathed out slowly and squeezed the trigger.

The bullet was probably on its way when Eddie stopped to look down at a little girl holding a grubby rag-doll.

They all heard the bullet pass, but instead of the expected panic and chaos, they moved like a machine, dropping onto one knee and swinging their weapons in the direction of the shot. In the stillness, the recoil had raised a tiny puff of dust that hung in the air like a Google map pointer. They opened up on that spot.

One of the hornet swarm of bullets hit the sniper, barely skinning his cheek. Normally that would have been his lucky day, normally. The shock lifted him, just a little. The next two rounds hit him in the forehead. Strike one insurgent shootist.

At the first sign of trouble, Caponetto floored the pedal, and the Humvee jumped forward faster than it seemed possible for a monster like that, dust and grit spraying from its tyres. Without a word, the rest of the men turned and ran round the stalls to meet it, piling in through the open doors, as the square suddenly came alive with automatic fire from every window.

Caponetto hung a U right through the market stalls and across the open area in the middle, but even in the reckless dash, he instinctively slowed to avoid the bodies of his fallen comrades, and then floored it again and took off at maximum acceleration in the direction they'd arrived, reasoning that since they'd come in that way, the truck should fit the road on the way out. A reasonable assumption, except for the pickup truck blocking the end of the narrow street. Caponetto took an instant to recognise the truck and the 50-calibre machine gun on its flatbed.

"Shit! Shit! Shit!" he hissed and turned right, even though there was no right turn, just a mud-brick wall. The Humvee went through it like it wasn't there, just as the 50 cal opened up and punched fist-sized holes in the remaining bricks. The Humvee came out through another wall, and Caponetto pulled the wheel left, bounced the truck off a building, and floored it again, heading west and the hell out of there. Bricks, washing lines, and crap of every kind bounced off the hood, and the mirrors gouged out the walls as the Humvee tore down the narrow alley.

It was a good thing all the villagers are dead, Harry thought, or this crazy marine would have done the job himself. The thought ended abruptly as the Humvee slewed into a wider street, skidded, and did the ploughing through buildings trick again as another 50 cal on another pickup opened up. *Bugger, these machine guns are like gold dust, but these guys seem to have an arsenal of them*, he thought, between being bounced off the sides of the truck. Seatbelts, now why didn't he clunk-click? Ah, that'll be because of all the bullets he was dodging at the time. One thing was as clear as crystal to him right then, they were bottled up in the village, and all the crazy driving in the world wasn't going to get them out. Only dead.

"The mosque!" he shouted above the thunder of mud-bricks bouncing off every side. "Get us into the mosque."

Caponetto glanced at Ethan and got the go-ahead. A right turn through the downstairs rooms of somebody's pride and joy and they were back into the market square, bouncing over the bodies and ploughing in through the front door of the mosque where the sniper had made the fatal mistake of sitting up after being clipped.

Caponetto stood on the brakes, killed the engine, grabbed his weapon, and dived out of the vehicle in two seconds flat, followed in close order by the rest of the occupants. The horde of insurgents would have been real scared to see the determination on the faces of the six men alone in the great big building.

Ethan, Caponetto and Eddie took up firing positions in the small windows facing the square, and Ethan glanced back quickly to see BJ and Tom bound up the stone stairs to the roof, with Harry following one stair at a time, though he lost sight of him in seconds in the swirling dust from their crashing entry. *Okay, good*, he thought, at least these Brits weren't completely inept. He looked around as the dust thinned and nodded. Good choice, thick walls, no other windows or doors beside the big wooden ones where Caponetto had parked the Humvee. If they were going to hole up someplace, this was as good as it was going to get. A stream of 50-cal rounds screaming in through the window changed his focus. He swung back against the wall and hoped to God the Brit sniper could shoot and the last outing hadn't been just luck, because if he couldn't, they were dead as dog meat, with the little M16s as much use as slingshots against the 50 cal. If they'd even get a shot off among all the

AK rounds that were pouring in with the big stuff. Shit, there must be hundreds of them out there!

Harry could shoot, no doubt about that, but right then a 35 mm machinegun in a building across the square was making the parapet bricks he was hiding behind look like they were in a hailstorm. He signalled to BJ and Tom, and they nodded their understanding.

Tom counted down on his fingers to BJ, swung the sub-machine gun over the parapet meant to stop devout worshippers meeting their god too early, and sprayed the building with nine-millimetre rounds without any real expectation of hitting anyone, but it did the trick. For a moment, the stream of incoming bullets stopped, as the machine-gunner reacted as any sane man would and ducked. A moment later, the reflex was countermanded, but BJ's grenade launcher had already pitched two 40 mm grenades at the machine gun's position. The first one hit the wall below the gunner's rooftop cover and exploded harmlessly, but the second dropped right between his knees — a grenade launcher's hole-in-one.

As most of the machine-gunner sprayed out across the square, Harry was already placing the L115's bipod on the parapet and snapping back the bolt. He swung right, knelt, steadied himself for an instant, and then fired. As usual, the 50 cal hadn't got a shield since the gunner had never needed one before, and he didn't need one now... well, not any more.

The instant the heavy machine gun stopped firing, the three Americans swung into action, their M16s knocking men off the building opposite like shooting clay pigeons. Too bad these pigeons shot back, and Ethan ducked back just as a whole bunch of angry shooters sent a blizzard of bullets at his favourite head.

The driver of the pickup with the 50 cal had clearly been at the last engagement, slammed the truck into reverse, and disappeared behind the houses before Harry could do his knocking over the gunners one by one thing, which was a pity.

Harry scanned the building through his scope and whistled. It looked like there was a gun sticking out of every window, but that might have been fear upping the count, except in the heat of the action, fear was hiding in a safe place, and all he felt was his heart thumping in his chest. He traversed right, looking for a target among all the targets. On the roof of a low building, an insurgent was hitting and shoving a bunch of guys into setting up a mortar tube. Two targets of opportunity, then. First, the officer, or the nearest these guys had to an officer, then the men. No wind, not too steep an angle from this roof to where they were making a dog's breakfast out of setting up the mortar. Should've been an easy shot over a couple of hundred feet, but all that annoying incoming fire was making dust. Harry sighed, put the sound of the bullets ripping into the mud-brick out of his mind, and took the shot without even thinking about it. The hitting and kicking officer slammed back like he'd been hit by a truck. The three men setting up the mortar stood up. They stood up! At that range, even Tom's sub-machine gun could do the biz. Unlike Harry's single-shot L115, the MP5 didn't need a bolt pulled back, and even on semi-automatic it made short work of the idiots standing in plain sight.

Harry looked around the square at the men behind the parapets or firing out of the upper windows of almost every house, and at the two pickups creeping back into view, and did the maths. A hundred bad guys versus six good guys — if you count the man on crutches. He swung the rifle a few degrees left on its bipod, sighted and fired, pulled back the bolt, and fired again in a single move. Okay, still a hundred to six, but the pickups weren't going anywhere soon, unless they could find some very brave drivers, and taking the 50 cals out of the game at least meant the mud-brick wasn't just tissue paper. Out of the corner of his eye, he caught a glint of sunlight. "Down!" he barked, and the other two dropped behind the parapet and watched him hugging his rifle in his lap, his back against the low wall. "Sniper," he said and signalled them to keep down.

Okay, this was going to be hairy. He'd made the sniper's position, but only approximately, and he would need time to get the L115 into action, time he wouldn't get. Asking the guys to run a diversion would work fine, right up to the point where they were dead, and that didn't appeal much. He shook his head at BJ, who was patting the grenade launcher beneath his rifle. The sniper would have seen where they ducked and would most likely be lined up on their position, if he was any good, and he had to assume he was.

He made a crawling gesture with his fingers for Tom to go to the right corner and keep the hell down. Tom started his manoeuvre, and Harry patted his rifle and signalled BJ to make his visible above the wall so the sniper would see they were still where they were supposed to be. Tom reached the corner and sat back against the wall and waited. Harry fed a round into the chamber, took a breath, and signalled the direction of the sniper to Tom with the flat of his hand.

Tom snapped the sub-machine gun on auto, stuck his head above the parapet and squeezed off a stream of bullets towards the sniper. To his friend's horror, Harry stood up. BJ swung round and up and emptied his clip at the roof across the square and then pumped a grenade.

Through the scope, Harry saw the sniper up close and big, as though he was checking his brow for zits. He saw the look of surprise on his face and the desperate swing as he tried to sight on the madman standing in plain sight. Harry squeezed off the shot, saw the sniper's head come apart up close and in full colour. Cool. He had a moment of clarity and dropped back down behind the parapet before he got his ass shot off by the AK-47s all pointing his way.

"You crazy shit!" Tom shouted across the roof and received a nod and a grin in response.

On the ground floor, the Americans were having their own war story, and hoping it wouldn't be cancelled after the pilot.

Ethan snapped the third 30-round clip into his M16 and checked his pack and found he had only two left. "How much ammo you got?" he called, and Al and Eddie held up two fingers. Shit. He looked over at the Humvee wedged in the doorway. Plenty of ammo in there, but with the big wooden doors smashed to matchwood, getting to it would put him in plain sight of everybody with a gun, so not cool. They would have to do what they say in the movies and make every shot count. He recalled the highly experienced and battle-hardened officer who'd spent his entire career in training, telling the class that two percent of expended rounds actually hit an enemy. Now that was total BS, and every marine in the classroom knew it, but they just let the idiot ramble on about suppressive fire to target hit statistics because it kept him busy feeling important and they got to rest. Truth was, unless they got the ammo out of the Humvee, they were toast, and even if they did, same thing probably.

He looked the Humvee over. It was half in and half out of the wide doorway, with splintered wood scattered all around and a gap of maybe three feet from the sides to the walls. Every few seconds a plume of dust would erupt by the Humvee, and nobody was even near the thing, so he knew what would happen if he—

He got up and walked to the vehicle as calmly as if it was waiting outside the bar ready to take him home. The sheer insanity of it must have stunned the insurgents because not a single round came his way. Going back would be a different story; he was going to get creamed.

He closed the driver's door behind him, reached over, started the engine and drove the thing right into the middle of the holy mosque. Well, that solved that problem. It also infuriated the insurgents, who expressed their anger by throwing everything they had at the open doorway. Bullets screamed and whined off the polished stone floor, slammed into the back of the Humvee, or drilled the interior walls. Al and Eddie dived under the Humvee to get out of the way of the rounds shucking through the room like hornets with sunstroke.

"Man, that was close," Al said, whistling his breath out. Eddie didn't answer with his usual wisecrack, and Al shuffled round on his back to where he could see his friend. "Shit, boss, Eddie's hit!"

Ethan opened the Humvee's door, threw the ammunition packs to the side of the doorway, pulled out the MOLLE medical bag from behind the seat, then stepped out and walked round to the front of the vehicle away from the door, completely ignoring the incoming rounds. He bent down, saw Eddie's foot, and pulled him out. He'd taken a round in the stomach, which, as anybody who's seen a John Wayne movie knows, is really bad. Eddie was clutching his stomach, his face contorted, and his eyes clamped shut. Ethan took out a syringe from the medical bag and injected 5 mg of morphine into Eddie's neck. He waited five seconds, which he reckoned was long enough to watch your friend suffer, and repeated the morphine hit.

Eddie's breathing eased, and he opened his eyes. "Cool, boss. Can I take some home?"

"Yeah, sure you can, son," Ethan said, opening Eddie's combats to apply a field dressing to the wound. A field dressing was woefully inadequate; he could see that. What Eddie needed was a medivac to a full surgical hospital, and even then...

Al slid from beneath the Humvee, took one look at Eddie, and walked back to the window without speaking. A few seconds later, Ethan heard his M16 shouting his fury at the men who had killed his friend. He put the medical bag under Eddie's head and wiped the dust from his face with a tenderness that no one would ever know about. "Hey," he said softly, and Eddie opened his eyes. "I'm gonna shoot a few bad men. You hang on in there for a while, right?"

Eddie smiled a microsecond smile. "Go," he said in a hoarse whisper. "I'm gonna be just fine."

"Yeah, son," Ethan said, getting to his feet. "You're gonna be just fine." He stepped out to the right side of the Humvee, but instantly stepped back and ran to the wall on the left as bullets churned up the ground he had vacated on both sides of the vehicle. He looked out through the narrow window and saw them coming out of the houses across the square, like ants pouring out of a nest. Jesus! He killed them, Al killed them, and on the roof, the Brits poured a torrent of fire and grenades onto them, but they just kept coming. It was totally insane.

"Out!" Ethan shouted and bolted for the stairs with Al a pace behind him. He stopped for a moment on the stone steps and looked back at Eddie, who was holding his M16 between his knees and pointing it at the door. Okay, that's how he'd want to go if it came to it – yeah right, more like when. He took the steps three at time.

Tom almost shot the Americans when they burst onto the rooftop, smiled, and returned to firing over the parapet.

"We gotta move," Ethan said. "Now!"

Harry slung his L115, picked up the M16, and staggered in an agonising crouch towards the far side of the roof without a word. Some things are self-evident, and the insurgents pouring into the ground floor was one of those things. He caught the packs Ethan tossed him and handed one off to Tom as he ran past doubled over to keep the parapet between him and the rooftops below. BJ lifted the other pack as he passed him on the right, grunting something that could have been anything from "clips in my vest will fit yours" to "chips are best with red sauce", but Harry chose not to have a discourse on his friend's enunciation on the top of the mosque, under fire, outnumbered, and really, really in the shit, and limped and stumbled for the far side of the roof with the others.

Ethan waved them over the parapet, and it said a lot for their faith in him that they jumped off the roof without looking, to land in a heap on the adjacent roof five feet below. Tom put his hand on the wall to vault, heard the commotion behind, and turned. The insurgents were spilling out of the stairwell onto the roof and would have his friends under their guns before they got to cover. He knelt on one knee and calmly switched the sub-machine gun to fully automatic, waited for the bandits to work out that the infidels had fled, and squeezed the trigger as they turned in his direction. Nobody could live in front of the MP5 under those conditions, and no one did. As the insurgents poured onto the roof under their own impetus, Tom mowed them down. They fell over each other, bits of them spraying across the brick roof, while others tried to run, but there was no cover in that killing zone.

Harry heard the distinctive rattle of the MP5 and turned to give his friend covering fire, but the mosque roof was too high for him to see anything at all. He started to run back, but Ethan grabbed his arm. He snatched it away angrily and took a step before he realised the American was right. He wouldn't be able to do anything except get himself killed. He stood for a second and then turned and ran after the others as they jumped the three-foot gap to the next building. He stopped at the edge. It might only be three feet, but his leg was already buggered from jumping off the mosque, and all it was going to do now was drop him into the alley, which some folks would think was a bad thing. He unslung the M16 from his shoulder, turned, and knelt on his good knee.

The slaughter on the mosque lasted a long, long ten seconds before Tom's magazine was spent. He reached into his pack and pulled out the last one, but it snagged on something, only for a moment, but in a firefight, that's all it takes. A 7.62 mm round hit him in the right forearm, not a fatal wound by any measure, but it killed his arm, and he dropped the MP5. And that was the fatal.

Harry heard the sub-machine stop and the short but intense burst of AK-47 fire and waited for the bandits to come pouring over the wall. But this wasn't his big moment to be a hero — deceased. He stared up in surprise as BJ landed next to him, hooked him under his arms, and tossed him over the gap like a sack of coal. Not dignified, but effective. He would have executed an excellent forward roll, but the sniper rifle slung across his back was his best friend and he wasn't going to damage that, so he landed hard and skidded on his ass. A moment later, BJ followed him, scooped him up in the same way, and bundled him across the roof and over another parapet, this one chest-high and requiring another undignified assisted Fosbury flop.

"Jesus, man," Harry grunted as he hit the stone floor and BJ landed on him. "What the hell have I done to piss you off?"

BJ shrugged and handed him his M16, which he'd included in the stylish rescue. "Tom's down," he said, turning and firing his assault rifle at the insurgents clambering over the mosque parapet.

"Yeah," Harry said, closing his eyes for a moment and seeing his friend's face.

"You going to sit there and sulk?" BJ said, squeezing off another round. "Or are you going to help kill ragheads?"

"Dunno," Harry said, "I like it down here, it's quiet, and it's—"

BJ kicked him in the butt, which pretty much did the trick. He stood up stiffly and looked along the wall to see Ethan and Al firing steadily at the mob streaming over the mosque. They were calm and looked for all the world like they were shooting tin ducks at a fairground stall. Fire, change aim, fire, change aim. Steady and deadly. He looked back across the rooftop at the insurgents, high on bloodlust and climbing over their comrades to get to them. Man, they could use Tom's sub-machine gun right then.

"Move!" Ethan shouted, and he and Al headed for the rooftop doorway.

"You've got to be kidding me!" Harry growled, reached over, and rapped BJ's shoulder. "Hey, we're leaving."

BJ sighted, fired, and ducked behind the wall. "So soon, I was just getting started." He hooked Harry's arm, and they ran and stumbled to the doorway.

Ethan and Al gave them covering fire from either side of the doorway before following them in and slamming the door.

"Oh, good," Harry said, catching his breath from the pain. "We're safe now, then."

Ethan gave him a dirty look and led the way down the stone stairs past the first floor room that was the main living area for the family with the kid's toys that would never be played with again. He stopped for a second at the door to the street, checked both ways, and when the others caught up, pointed across a wide, dusty wasteland at a small building inside a compound with low walls. "There," he said. "That's defensible on all sides."

Harry shook his head. "We go in there," he said, "we're never coming out again."

Ethan shrugged. "I'm open to other offers."

"We have to circle round back to the Humvee and call in air support," Harry said.

Ethan shook his head. "Tried that, the radio's dead. Must have taken a round or something."

"Shit!" Harry said, summing up everyone's thoughts on that. "Then it's the Alamo over there, then."

"What about circling back to the Humvee and just getting the hell outa town?" BJ said.

For a second they thought about it, but then Harry reminded them about the trucks and the 50 cals. "We wouldn't get a hundred yards before those guns turned the Humvee into scrap metal." He was about to expand on the full-of-holes theory when they heard the sound of many feet coming down the stairs. "Shall we go, gentlemen?" he said and lifted his arm before BJ did it for him.

They left the house at a run and were halfway across the wasteland, heading for the compound, when the insurgents rounded the corner of the buildings at the end of the street. They stalled for a second of indecision, surprised to see the infidels out in the open, but then opened up. Bullets zipped past on all sides and kicked up the old familiar toadstools of dust around their feet. They weren't going to make it unless they did something. And BJ did the something. He dropped Harry, pumped three grenades into the group of fighters, and a second later they lost interest in the attack amid the shrapnel and body parts.

Somebody should have shouted, "Go! Go!", but that somebody was as eager as everyone else to get the hell out of the open ground and into cover. BJ hooked Harry under the arms again, and they ran. Al hit the wooden front door at a dead run, smashing into it with his shoulders. Either the door was going to give, or his collarbone was. The door crashed inwards, followed by Al, who executed a forward roll and came back to his feet in the middle of the room. He ran back to the door and covered the others as they half fell half ran inside.

Harry would have applauded, but the sound of AK rounds slapping into the brickwork kinda broke the moment. He pushed the door closed, mostly to spoil the view for the insurgents spilling out of the house they'd just vacated, and those running into the street from both ends. *Here we go again*, he thought as he checked his ammo. You'd think they'd stop for afternoon prayer and give us a nice rest. The wooden door was splintering, and rounds smacked into the walls opposite.

"Hey, did anybody see any RPGs out there?" Harry said. "Because if there are, we are in deep shit."

Good point, well put.

"Harry, for Christ's sake!" BJ said and muttered obscenities.

Ethan and Al gave him a long questioning look, but he ignored it and pointed at the stone steps leading to the upper floors. "We'd better get the hell out of here."

The Americans were confused, that much was clear from their expressions.

"Go!" Harry said, limping across the small room and heading up the stairs. "Before they fire the bloody RPG I just wished on us."

The Brits were crazy, the exchanged looks said that, but they got the hell out of the room anyway, not because of the superstition or any of that shit, but just because the rounds coming in through the door were annoying.

They fell behind the parapet surrounding the wide roof and took a careful look over. The RPG operator was just finishing aiming the weapon and pulled the trigger, sending the grenade screaming across the wasteland and into the ground floor room they had just exited — for non-superstitious reasons. The explosion blew out the damaged door and the three windows, but the thick mud-brick was too much for it, and the house stayed built.

Harry had already started bringing his M16 into line the moment he looked over the parapet and fired a burst at the RPG operator readying the weapon for another shot, dropping him onto his weapon. The man behind him rolled him off and bent to pick it up, which was plenty of time for Harry to take more careful aim. *Time to play knock over the idiots again*, he thought as he squeezed off the shot.

Everybody on the road below saw where the shots were coming from and opened up, and those who didn't see, pretty soon got the idea. Harry sat back against the thick wall and grinned at the others, confirming his mental status, but that didn't bother him because they'd all be dead pretty soon, and the state of his mind wouldn't really count.

"Take a look what's happening," he said to BJ with a grin.

"Yeah, right," BJ said as bullets slammed into the brickwork and whined off into the bright sky. "I like this pretty face, and so does the missus."

"You guys are totally crazy, you know that?" Al said, shaking his head to emphasise the point, and then grunted sharply and bounced back off the parapet.

"Sniper! Sniper!" Harry shouted, and they moved.

Harry dropped the M16, hugged the L115 to his chest, and rolled forward, coming to his feet and running in a single painful move. He hit the stone dome above the stairwell and pressed against it just as BJ arrived and sat down. "Cheers," he said with a stern look. "I carried you through no-man's land, through thick and thin and mostly thin. And what do you do?" He shook his head. "You take off at the first little istsy-bitsy drama and leave me to it. My superhero."

Ethan looked back across the roof at the crumpled body of his friend and knew this was what awaited them all, even the Brit making jokes to cover his fear. "Did anybody make the sniper's position?"

"No," Harry said, "but to get the angle over the parapet, he has to be higher than us, and I don't see any—"

"There's a water tower past the end of the road," BJ said. "Saw it when I was carrying your ass across no-man's land."

Harry nodded. "Okay, then that has to be it." He put his head round the end of the dome and took a quick look, and a bullet took a chunk of brick out of the wall just above his head. *Not bad for a snapshot*, he thought as he pulled his head back into relative safety. "Yeah, he's in the water tower." Which was a serious bugger, as the only way to get a shot from this side of the building was to step out into the open, and nowhere in the manual did it say that was a good idea in a firefight.

"We are seriously in the smelly stuff," BJ pointed out helpfully. "They're going to be all over us if we don't get back to the wall and stop them crossing the yard."

"Off you go, then," Harry suggested.

"I was thinking," Ethan said, interrupting their banter. "Somebody killed everybody in this village, right?"

They nodded, good deduction, what with all those bodies.

"And my bet is it's these boys here."

Another nod, same deduction.

"Then how come they don't hightail it out and just chemical us to death, then?"

Harry and BJ exchanged looks. "Got any other thoughts?" Harry asked and then raised his hand. "Cus if you have, you just keep them to yourself, okay? I'm having trouble keeping my shit together as it is."

Ethan shrugged. "Just thinking, that's all." He tilted his head questioningly. "So, got any sniper-ass ideas on how to get rid of the guy in the tower?"

Harry thought about it some more and then pulled a slender dagger from his belt and began testing the sand between the blocks forming the battered dome. It took a second for the other two to work out what he was doing, then Ethan nodded. "Hey, it could work, the mortar looks crappy enough."

Ethan stepped back through the roof door into the dome and began scraping the mud-brick mortar from around one of the blocks. It was basically just sand, and in a couple of minutes, the foot-square brick moved and wobbled. "Okay," he called over his shoulder as he worked the brick out. "New window conversion complete."

Harry edged up to the hole and took a fast look through before pulling his head back. The tower was twelve hundred metres away, so the insurgent sniper was no dunce to have hit Al with one shot, but he would have to be a superstar to put a round through the foot-square hole, so Harry took another long look.

The sniper was on the tower, sure enough, but the thing was built on a plinth made of the good old mud-brick, and all Harry could see through his spotter scope was the shadow of his rifle protruding through a gap in the top of the low wall. What he needed was one of those M82 Special App 50-cal sniper rifles he'd fired on the range, with that and a Raufoss 50-cal round it would be a done deal. The round would have hit the wall and made a little hole, but on the other side, it would have become a shotgun blast, killing everything in its path, but that beast was a tank killer, and he always favoured the lighter L115; it was his baby, and he knew its every mood and idiosyncrasy, but even so, this was going to be a tough shot.

"Don't want to rush you," Ethan said quietly, interrupting his wishful thinking, "but the Indians are off the reservation and strolling across the road and will be up here any minute to kill our asses."

Harry nodded without really listening, taking the time to estimate the distance to the target and to confirm there was no wind. He continued to watch the shadow of the sniper's rifle while he doped the scope on the L115 to 1200 plus 2 and smiled. Twelve hundred metres plus two minutes of angle to give it the trajectory, it was an estimate, but one he'd done a thousand times, so now it was just instinctive. The L115 may not have the shotgun blast potential of the M82, but the mud-brick wall for a water tower would be thin, just enough to stop idiots falling off, so it should be no problem. The trick was to put the bullet where the sniper was, and since he was behind a wall, that wasn't an easy shot.

He took slow tactical breaths to steady himself and calm down, fired, and saw the puff of dust as the round penetrated the mud-brick, and then the sniper's head appear above the wall as his body was blown up and back.

"Okay," he said and slung the rifle, "we can say hi to the visitors now."

They crouched and ran back to the parapet and knelt beside Al's body. The insurgents were on the wrong side of the building to see their sniper go down, but the bodies of their comrades scattered across the road and onto the waste ground had given them good reason to think twice before rushing the compound. They assumed that the enemy was just waiting for them to run out into the open, and right when they decided they were mistaken, the enemy was in fact behind the wall waiting for them to rush out into the open. They obliged.

Two or three at first, running out into the road, stopping and bolting back for cover to draw the defenders. Ethan was watching them from the corner of the roof where a stump had been nailed up for a washing line, giving him the little cover he needed not to get his head blown off. He waited. Then they came en masse.

"Showtime," he said as he swung up his M16, aimed, and fired rapid single shots. A less experienced marine might have set his weapon to full auto to knock down as many of the charging insurgents as possible in the shortest time, but that would have burned his ammo that was already in short supply. So he killed them one at a time. By the time he'd dropped the second man, the two Brits were in action also on semi-auto, either following his lead or because they'd been around the block a few times too.

The insurgents were determined to put an end to it once and for all and just kept coming. Something needed to be done before they got close enough to the house to be out of the kill zone, and BJ did the something. He stood up, leaned over the parapet, and fired the first grenade from the launcher into the dozen insurgents racing for the door, elated they'd made it alive. There's a saying about counting chickens from unhatched eggs that would have summed it up for them, if they'd known it, or been alive to consider it. He unlocked the breach and swung it out, fed in another grenade, snapped it shut, aimed, and fired again in less than four seconds. And repeated the move, again, and again.

The effects of a rain of high explosives on the insurgents would have been amusing if it hadn't also been deadly. They stopped in their tracks as the grenades exploded amongst them. Some running right, some left, some just standing and staring up at the building in disbelief. A few raised their weapons, but Harry and Ethan stopped that nonsense before it began. After a minute of carnage, the wasteland was littered with bits of humans and wrecked weapons.

They had broken the charge, but the price was high. BJ slumped to his knees, groaned once, and fell forward, his head resting against the wall keeping him on his knees.

Harry dropped down beside him, turned him, and sat him down, but it was clear from the rag-doll way he flopped to his left that he was gone, and Harry reached over and closed his eyes with his fingers. "Thanks, BJ," he said softly and sat back against the wall, all the strength draining out of him. He put his hands over his eyes and tried to shut out the world for a moment, to keep his sanity.

Ethan glanced down at him, moved over to the corner of the roof, and scanned the empty street and the buildings, which were probably teeming with insurgents. He looked up at the sky and then at his watch. Almost seven, so it would be dark soon, so no snipers, which was good, but the insurgents would be able to stroll on over and kill them, which was bad, probably. He looked over at Harry and was relieved to see he had put aside the loss of his friends and was scanning the buildings through his spotter scope. Okay then.

Harry could see them in the shadows and in the alleyways, just waiting like predators for nightfall. He shifted his weight off his leg in a vain effort to ease the stiffness that had replaced the pain. "Ethan," he hissed and waited for the marine to look his way and then signalled him to come closer.

"I've been thinking," he said to the American now sitting with his back to the low wall. "In about half an hour, they're going to be scuttling over us like cockroaches on a jam sandwich."

Ethan nodded and looked over at the dome and the door to the stairs. They'd come that way, they'd pay a high price, but the end result would be the same.

"So," Harry said, following his gaze. "I think you should get the hell out of here."

Ethan jumped a little in surprise and opened his mouth to speak, but Harry waved him silent.

"Let me finish," he said firmly. "We're dead here, I know it and so do you." He tapped his leg. "I'm not going anywhere, but you could get out of here if you tried, right?"

No doubt about it.

"Then you go." Once again he waved Ethan silent. "I'll cover you and make a bit of a fuss." He could see by the way Ethan looked around that he was weighing it up. He was going to say no, that was a certainty. "Somebody has to tell the brass about the chemical attack here. This wasn't some accident or reprisal, this was a test."

Ethan knew that too, he could tell. "Can you imagine what this would do to the boys at Camp Bastion?"

Ethan sucked his teeth. "It would be a massacre," he said almost to himself. "They're supposed to be prepared, but that's bullshit, nobody could be prepared for this."

"Then you have to get out and tell them about it," Harry said.

Ethan looked at him for a long time, knowing he would be leaving him to die, but staying just doubled the number and did nothing to shorten the odds. He looked up at the sun sinking in a brilliant colour show on the horizon. If he was going, he needed to go now. He put out his hand.

"Okay then," Harry said, shaking the hand of the man he'd known only a few hours, but already felt like an old friend. He looked around quickly. "Help me get the weapons up onto the wall. Say five feet apart."

Ethan chuckled. "Like *Beau Geste*, right?' Nod received. 'Okay, but can you move enough to make it work?"

"What do I have to worry about? If I bugger my leg up, what difference is it going to make?"

Ethan picked up BJ's assault rifle and Al's M16 and placed them on the wall, their barrels extending out far enough to be seen, but not so far as to be obvious. Then he put his own M16 on Harry's right and waved down Harry's protest. "Hey, if I need it when I'm out there, I'm dead anyway. It'll do more good here."

Harry watched him move quickly to the stairwell at a crouching run, stop at the top, and nod a quick goodbye. Okay then, just me and a hundred Taliban, what's wrong with those odds? Not much. He watched the night shadows race across the rooftop and climbed up to an excruciating crouch behind his M16 wedged on the wall.

At the first sign of men coming out of the buildings, he opened up on full auto, spraying the doors and the windows, and when the clip was empty, he moved to Ethan's M16 and fired that, and then onto Al's, firing up and down the street and at the buildings and hoping they would think the boys were all still in town.

He left BJ's C7 on semi-automatic, picking targets that showed up as darker shadows against the pale mud buildings. He thought about getting any remaining grenades from BJ's pack, but the thought of kneeling down and having to get up again put the idea to bed. Pretty soon they would suss that there was only one rifle firing, then—

They rushed the compound again. Harry fired down at them without bothering to aim, emptied the C7, and slid down to sit against the parapet. He reached over and pulled his sniper rifle onto his lap, snapped back the bolt to chamber a round, and pointed it more or less at the stairway.

Funny, really, way things turned out, he thought. He'd come back to thank the old guy for saving his life and got himself killed doing it. And his friends, and that was the hardest thing to swallow. Tom Daley, consummate soldier and nutter. He smiled. And BJ. He looked down at his friend almost lost in the dark shadows. A giant of a man in more ways than just physical strength. Both gone now, and for what? This shithole? He closed his eyes and said thanks to his friends. His eyes snapped open at the sound of men on the stone stairs. Well, if I knew any prayers, or could think of anyone to say them to, now would be a good time.

The first insurgent ran up the last of the stairs and out through the open door. Harry shot him in the head, just for the bloody hell of it. He swung the rifle and rapped the barrel hard against the edge of the wall, no point giving these bastards a perfectly good weapon. He hoped they wouldn't notice it was bent and one of them would try firing it, and then it would either blow his head off, or drive him nuts by missing by a mile. A small victory, but hey. He put the rifle down at his side and waited to die. And he thought about his father and mother and how they would be well pissed that he'd got himself killed when he was on medical leave.

He heard barked orders echoing from the stairs and closed his eyes. The hell with them, they're not going to see me give a shit. He thought about whistling a tune, but couldn't think of one, and anyway, his lips were bone dry. If he had a guitar, he could play a tune, if he could play that was. *Drums*, he thought, *anybody can play drums, what's hard about beating a stick on a pig's skin? Now the piano—*

"So," a soft voice said in a perfect English accent, "you are one of the infidels who have been causing me such a headache."

Harry opened his eyes. Okay, not dead yet, that's a plus. He looked up at the speaker and saw a guy in a dirty dish-dash like everybody else in this country, but he was pale, almost white. So, a man who kept out of the sun, either by choice or through location. "Who's asking?" he said, conscious that his voice was a bit strangled from the tension of waiting to be killed.

"That is not really important, is it?" the man said in that same soft voice. "I see you are a marine too, as are your American friends." He waved a hand at Al's body. He looked around and frowned. "Ah, we seem to be missing one." He nodded slowly. "That would be the big American sergeant. Gone to warn the authorities, I assume."

"Nah," Harry said, "he's just gone for a piss. He'll be back in a bit."

The man smiled to reveal perfect white teeth. Western white teeth. "No matter." He sat down next to Harry, which was a bit of a stunner.

"Got any cigarettes?" Harry asked, mostly to mask his surprise.

"I do not smoke," the man said.

"Nah, me neither," Harry said, "disgusting habit and bad for your health."

The man raised his eyebrows and then smiled. "Oh, I see. Very good." The smile vanished. "I expect you are wondering why you are still alive."

Harry shrugged. "Crossed my mind, but hey, it's your party."

"Yes, isn't it?" The smile again. "You are alive, Sergeant, because I wish you to do something for me."

Harry looked him in the eyes. "If you want me to end your misery," he said with a little shrug, "then I'm your man."

"You cope with fear well, for an infidel."

"There you go again, calling me names. You're going to hurt my feelings."

The man smiled without humour. "So, Sergeant," he said, the smile vanishing again, "I'm curious about what you are doing here in this... Godforsaken place."

Harry shrugged. "We thought we'd do a bit of sightseeing, it's a nice day."

"We could torture it out of you," the man said, but he lacked conviction, and Harry picked it up.

"I doubt that."

"We could kill you." The man went for option two.

Harry shrugged again. "Been there. It's overrated."

The man nodded, as though he actually understood, and maybe he did, there was a whole mess of killing going on.

"Do you have a name?" the man asked.

Harry fixed him with a look for a moment, to let him know what he thought of that stupid question. "Harry," he said. What the hell?

"Well, Harry," the man said, getting to his feet with an easy grace that made Harry feel even more like an invalid. "It's been nice talking with you." He walked away across the rooftop to the door and stopped.

This is it, Harry thought. Ah well, I've had a good innings. Which was a lie.

The man turned, and Harry expected to see a weapon, but even in the fading light, he could see his hands were empty.

"This thing I wish you to do for me," he said and waited for a response that didn't come. "Do you know a man named Valentin Tal? He is a Russian."

Of course not, stupid question. "No, can't say I do. Does he arrange sightseeing tours?"

The man laughed, but cut it off quickly, betraying that it was involuntary. "No," he said, stepping onto the stairs. "Get to know him. You will be surprised."

The man left. They all left. And Harry was still alive.

He sat there for half an hour, just waiting for them to come back and say, "Oops, sorry, we forgot to kill you," but nothing, after the sound of them leaving. It made no sense.

This unknown Russian, this Valentin Tal, was the reason they hadn't been chemicaled to death and why Harry was still alive. The soft-spoken Taliban had sacrificed all those insurgents just to say that name. Valentin Tal the Russian. Harry frowned; it still made no sense. Why was he alive? Well, you've got a choice here, mate. You can sit and ponder the meaning of life, now that you still have one, or you can get the hell out of this cesspit before some less forgiving mooj comes along and finishes the job.

He took option one and climbed stiffly and painfully to his feet. Pity he'd broken the rifle, though, he liked that weapon. He limped slowly across the roof and listened at the stairs, half expecting the man to jump out and shout, "Fooled you!" before blowing his head off.

The stairs hurt like hell, but it showed he wasn't dead, which was a serious plus. Last part of the puzzle was how the hell was he going to get back to civilization? A thought popped into his tired mind. They wouldn't, would they? He changed direction and limped up the dark street to the mosque and stood in the shattered doorway. The Humvee was still right where Al had left it. And that is what he called a result.

23

Jimmy Detroit came from Chicago. Which could have just been a quirk or a bit clever, but his choice of professional name wasn't smart-ass, he needed a handle for secure communications with his clients and never overlooked an opportunity for misdirection, even if it lacked true finesse. What is it they say about there not being such a thing as an old bold hit man? Whatever, but Jimmy would have taken exception to two things: first off, he wasn't a hit man, he was a cleaner, and second, he wasn't old — okay not a wet-behind-the-ears kid, but not old; these days fifty is the new thirty, all the magazines say that. And okay, third, who says he wasn't bold?

He wheeled his suitcase out through the ground floor doors of Heathrow's terminal five and looked around for a taxi. There was a bunch of them at the taxi rank, which seemed reasonable. It was almost nine o'clock, dark — as it should be — and cold, but not as bitterly cold as it had been in New York that morning, but somehow it was depressing, though that was probably coloured by his opinion of this God-awful country. Warm beer, bad teeth, and driving on the wrong side of the road — whose dumb idea was that? Okay, he was going to be here for a few weeks, so suck it up. Yeah, like that was going to happen. First thing was to get to the hotel, take a long shower, and order some room service and bourbon, a whole lot of bourbon. Hell, he could do this, easy. God, he hated this place, and he hadn't even arrived yet.

He climbed into the taxi and waited for the driver to get his luggage, climbed out again, and put his case on the back seat. "Radisson Edwardian. You know that one?"

The taxi driver said something unintelligible, maybe in a foreign accent, but everybody here was going to have a foreign accent. Shit, doesn't anybody speak American?

He spent the hour's travel time going over the details of the contract. First, it was short notice, much shorter than he would usually have accepted. He always returned to Chicago after a gig, to pull his life out of the gutter that was his working day. Listen to good music, dine on fine food, and practice Taoism with Master Chen to continue his search for enlightenment and immortality of his soul — until he was ready to go and kill somebody else.

This contract was different, so he forwent his usual period of respite. This was to be his last, his swansong, after which he would buy the boat and head on down to Hawaii and just... He hadn't got past that point yet.

Part of him hoped this gig was going to be something special, something to remember as the last and the best. Sometimes wishes have wings.

24

Ethan saw the Humvee coming up the dirt road, but then a Humvee isn't the sort of profile that's easy to disguise, but he stayed down behind the boulders, with all those creepy, bitey things that live under boulders, and watched it approach. It struck him as suicidally nuts that the insurgents would take the vehicle because any passing A10 Thunderbolt was going to turn it to scrap metal as soon as word got out that it was no longer in friendly hands. He squinted and tried to look past the headlights, and when he saw the Brit as the vehicle drew level with his position, he jumped up and ran to the road.

Harry had seen him hiding behind the boulders, mostly, it's true, because he expected him to have made it about this far and be skulking in the rocks. He smiled and watched him through the rear-view as he ran into the road and waved his arms about like a demented orang-utan. He let him curse and jump up and down a bit and then brought the Humvee to a gentle stop.

Ethan ran the fifty yards or so Harry had covered since he'd seen him and climbed in through the passenger door.

"Lucky you jumped out into the road and did that rain dance," Harry said, chuckling.

"You knew I was there, you bastard," Ethan said, but his voice betrayed his relief at not having to walk fifty miles through bandit territory back to Camp Bastion. Okay, he could have done it, but not by choice. He watched Harry for a while before he asked the question that hung in the air like the punch line to a crappy joke. "They let you go?"

Harry shook his head. "Nah, fought my way out using a mooj's severed limb." He swaggered his shoulders. "It was a mighty fight, but they were outgunned."

Ethan continued to watch him without a flicker of expression. At some point the prick would tell him what the hell happened, but when that point would come was anybody's guess.

The silence did what silence does. "This Taliban guy, who by the way, spoke English better than I do, just sat on the roof with me and passed the time of day talking about politics and the weather, like we were friends sitting in the park. Then he got up and left, saying I was free to go. Maybe he took a shine to me." Harry shrugged. "People do, you know, I'm a nice bloke." Before Ethan could make the obvious comment, he continued, "Then he asked me about this Russian."

Ethan glanced at him. "What Russian?"

Harry shook his head. "He said a name, but I'm buggered if I can remember it," he lied. "I was bricking it at the time," he lied again.

Ethan shook his head. The Brit was speaking a sort of English, but he wasn't getting it. "Why would this Taliban guy just talk and then walk, why not kill you?"

"Don't know," Harry said, "but I'm not sorry."

"No, I can see how you'd feel that way." Ethan rested his head against the seat and closed his eyes. Half an hour later, he opened his eyes and sat up. "Russian!"

"Where?" Harry said, startled out of a little zombie driving.

"No, not where," Ethan said, "who?"

"Oh, okay, that clears that up, mate."

"Think about it," Ethan said, his voice animated. "What's the only reason this Taliban would let you live?"

"Maybe he had the hots for me?"

"No," Ethan said, "well, maybe, but that's not it."

"Oh, shame."

"It can only be that he hates this Russian guy—"

Harry knew he was waiting for him to remember, but found an obstacle in the road to hold his attention.

Ethan decided he didn't know his name, or he would have told him. Why not? "He hates this... Russian guy, more than you."

"Stop it. I'm getting all teary eyed."

Ethan smiled, finally starting to warm to this weird Brit. "Russians were here first, right?"

"Not really," Harry said. "Persians invaded first, then the Greeks, then Huns, then the Arabs, then Mongols—"

"Yeah, okay," Ethan said a little irritably.

"Then the British for the first time. Got our asses kicked good and proper."

"Not much changing, then," Ethan said. "Point is the Soviets beat this place up pretty bad. Killed and imprisoned a lot of ordinary people."

"Mostly just killed them," Harry added.

"That's it, then," Ethan said, resting his head back against the seat.

"What is?"

Ethan opened his eyes. "This Taliban commander wants you to kill the Russian, that's why he spared your life."

"Tough titty," Harry said. "He wants him dead, let him do it his bloody self."

"Yeah," Ethan said, closing his eyes again, "I don't get it, makes no kinda sense."

Harry nodded. "That's what I said, but hey, nothing in this stinkin' country makes any sense." But he was talking to a sleeping man.

It was three a.m. when Harry stopped the Humvee at the gates of Camp Bastion, and the shit storm commenced.

25

Shaun walked back into the interview room and leaned on the table, and Tweetie Pie leaned back, the chair creaking and threatening to tip. "I want to meet Curly Sue," Shaun said flatly.

Tweetie jumped, and the chair lost its battle with gravity, dumping the birdie onto the dirty floor. He screamed, clutched his arm, and rolled over so that his face was scant inches from the scuffed vinyl with non-specific stains. He looked at the dried bits, cried out again, and scrambled to his feet, finally standing in front of the chair Danny was holding for him, as a gentleman would for a lady. Tweetie smiled at him. Danny rammed the chair into his legs, and he sat down with a yelp.

Shaun was still leaning on the table, watching the performance with little interest, and Tweetie watched him back for several seconds before the wheels started whirring and he remembered why he'd been on the floor, the one with all that... stuff. "No way!" he said at last, raising both his hands as if to ward off evil. "No way. Are you crazy?" He thought about it for a moment and then lightened up as he deduced the big plan. "I could tell you where she is, and you go and see her." He looked on hopefully.

"That would be rude," Shaun said, dashing his hopes. "I need you to introduce us, all formal like."

Tweetie's jaw dropped. "But she'll rip my bloody balls off!" Okay, man up. "No. And you can't make me do it." So there.

Shaun stood up. "You're choice. They'll love a pretty boy like you inside." He frowned at Danny. "Do we have guys named Bubba in our prisons?"

"Big hairy blokes who like to play mommies and daddies?" Danny nodded. "Yeah."

"Wait! Wait!" Tweetie was having trouble breathing. Oh God, it was a nightmare. "All right, all right," he said at last, his voice fading to a whisper.

"There's a good boy," Shaun said. "Sit. Stay!" he ordered and left the room.

Danny caught up with him as he strode down the corridor. "By the book, man, remember?"

Shaun looked at him steadily for a few seconds, then nodded. "By the book. Yeah, that'll work, this being an illegal op. But yeah, okay, but if the book gets in the way..."

"Deal," Danny said, "Now let's get the Tweetie out of his cage."

The custody sergeant examined their identification for the third time. "So you think that you can just waltz in here and take one of my prisoners?"

Danny nodded and even managed a friendly smile. "It's a perk of being the Serious Organised Crime Agency," he said slowly, enjoying the sergeant's look of annoyance.

The custody sergeant looked at the IDs again, just in case they were bogus. "Prima donnas," he said under his breath. "I'll have to speak to my superior," he added pompously.

Danny shrugged and glanced at Shaun, but he was in a world of his own, and from his grey expression, a world of pain.

The sergeant put down the phone. "Okay, you can have him."

Danny turned to leave, but the sergeant rapped his pen on his desk.

"Not so fast." He opened a drawer and pulled out a stack of forms. "Paperwork first."

He's loving it, the dickhead. Danny took the forms, wrote 'SOCA' on every page, signed the last one, handed them back to the scowling sergeant, and went to fetch Tweetie.

Shaun stood by the door, staring out into the street, but seeing a sitting room with worn furniture and an old man's crumpled body.

26

Margaret tossed the black dress onto the bed to join the others in a heap. She didn't remember it being this hard to get ready for a date... no, of course it wasn't a date, it was just a meal and pleasant conversation with a dear friend.

Okay, if that makes you feel better.

She rummaged in the over-stuffed wardrobe and pulled out a pearl silk strappy dress and held it up. She'd worn this at Rebecca and Steve's dinner on the Strand, with Harvey. She sighed and ran her hand over the material. You know, it hadn't been so bad then. Why did he have to go with that—

"So, does Dad know you're out on the tiles tonight?"

She turned and glared at Annie standing in the bedroom doorway. Annie was nineteen and as confident as any attractive young woman would be. Real blonde hair, deep blue eyes like midnight sapphire and a giggle that would make a zombie smile. People could hate her for being so damned lovely, but charisma came with the package that just drew everyone to her like a siren song.

Who said life has to be fair?

"I am not going out on the tiles," Margaret said, tutting quietly, knowing that this was exactly what she was doing, albeit put rather crudely. "And," she added with a flick of her long, once-blonde hair, "I don't care if your father does know. We're separated, remember?"

"Yeah, like how could I forget," Annie said with a little pout. "You moping around all the time."

"I do not mope!" Margaret turned back to the wardrobe and resumed her rummaging. "And don't say yeah, it sounds so... so..."

"Common?"

"I was going to say crude, but yes, common will suffice."

"You're such a snob, you know that?"

Well... yeah, she did — except she never said yeah.

"Would you, you know?" Annie asked.

Her mother looked up, frowning. "Would I what?"

"You know, go back to Dad."

Margaret was about to squash the very idea, but stopped and took a slow breath. "Depends."

Annie saw a glimmer of hope for the old couple. "Depends on what?" Whatever it was, she would make damned sure it happened.

Margaret sat on the pile of dresses on the bed. "I suppose it depends on whether or not he's sorry."

"Oh, he's sorry," Annie enthused. "I know he is."

Margaret tilted her head questioningly. "Did he say something to you?"

"No, he didn't need to, I can tell."

"Oh, suddenly you're psychic?"

"So," Annie said, pulling the fading hope back out of the tubes. "If he says sorry for... well..."

"Going off with that tart," Margaret helped out.

"We don't know that he actually... you know?"

"There aren't any pictures, if that's what you mean," Margaret said bitterly. She stood up slowly and began rummaging in the wardrobe again.

Strike one hope.

A rather plain-looking girl about Annie's age appeared in the doorway behind her. "How's it going?"

"Slowly," Annie said over her shoulder. "Mother wants to look old and haggard."

Margaret half turned and glared. "I beg your pardon!"

Annie smiled at the plain girl and raised her hand to signal five. The girl flashed a quick smile and strolled off.

"That's Penny Thing, isn't it?" Margaret said distractedly as she continued to rummage.

"Trainer," Annie corrected.

"Oh, is she?"

"Is she what?" Annie asked with a frown and then shook her head. "No, she's Penny Trainer, not my trainer... well, not in that sense, anyway."

Margaret looked back over her shoulder. "You should be a little careful there, dear."

Annie's frown deepened.

"I believe she is... well, you know?"

"Know what? Is she rabid or carrying bubonic plague?"

"No, of course not, don't be silly. I simply meant she is... she likes... she doesn't like men."

Annie shrugged. "What's to like?"

"Quite," Margaret said, returning to her distracted hunt for just the right dress.

"So what's the plan? Quick din-dins, then back to his place for a bed wreck?"

"What?" Margaret said, her mouth saying more, but no sounds coming forth. "I'm your mother."

"Well, doh! What has that got to do with anything? Get in there."

"I'm sure I don't know what you are talking about."

Annie smiled a smile that a celeb would sell their mother for. "Oh, come on. Don't tell me you haven't seen the guys checking out your ass?"

Margaret's jaw dropped, but her eyes joined in with a smile.

"They can tell you're back on the market, you know. It must be a scent thing."

"Oh, for heaven's sake," Margaret said, but the rebuke lacked conviction. "I can't say I've noticed."

"Then get noticing, you'll like it."

"What, at my age? I doubt that I'll get much practice." Margaret smiled to herself at the truly weird conversation with her little girl and at the memory of the glances she'd noticed all too clearly.

"What is that supposed to mean?" Annie said, taking her mother's shoulder and turning her slightly. "Forty-something, and in pretty good shape, if I'm any judge."

Margaret checked herself out in the wardrobe mirror. Not too bad, perhaps. "A bit too much here and there, and not enough elsewhere."

"Rubbish," Annie said, taking the dress Margaret was holding. "Unless you wear this, of course."

"What's the matter with it? I think it's—"

"A very sensible dress," Annie continued with a sniff. "Trust me, Mom, you'll never get to crease any sheets wearing that granny dress." She hustled Margaret out of the way. "Let me see what you have in this time-warp box." A few minutes later, and a pile of dresses on the floor, she held up a tiny, one-shoulder-tie black dress, the material for which wouldn't have made a large handkerchief.

Margaret's jaw dropped. "I can't wear that! Anyway, I'd never get into it."

Which was really the same as saying, I wish I could get into it.

Annie held it against her. "Yes, you will." She smiled and winked. "And it won't be for long anyway. Not once Mr Wonderful sees you in it."

"I don't think so."

"Breathe in and don't eat anything."

"I'll faint from lack of oxygen."

"The plan," Annie said, pulling open drawers in search of something suitable for beneath the dress, "is for Mr Wonderful to faint from lack of oxygen. Put it on."

She pushed the drawer closed and held up a thong that was no more than a string. "And something for dessert."

She left her mother holding the thong between her thumb and finger and examining it at arm's length. But she would be wearing it, the glint in her eye said that.

Annie closed the bedroom door quietly, and Penny swept past and caught her arm, pulling her urgently along the short corridor.

"Whoa, what's the hurry?" Annie asked with a grin, knowing damn well what the hurry was.

Penny pulled her into the bedroom, closed the door, and switched on her MP3 player station. Justin Bieber's "Believe". Which goes to show, being gay doesn't mean you can't like good boy singers.

Annie leaned on the door, smiling as she watched Penny hopping on one leg while she pulled off her jeans. She pulled off her T-shirt and just dropped it on the floor. Cool. Annie liked this girl. Okay, a little bit plain, if plain means her hair was just brown and a bit short, and she wore wire-rimmed glasses, but she had personality to spare and a sense of humour that would make a bouncer laugh. The other things she liked about Penny became apparent when she pulled off her purple bra. She had huge, magnificent breasts, with deep auburn nipples.

Penny slapped her bottom and scampered off into the en-suite shower room. Annie shook her head slowly, bent down, and put the discarded clothes on the dresser, with a smile. Penny was always in such a hurry. Sometimes you have to make time to enjoy the moment.

She took off her clothes, folded them, and put them next to Penny's on the dresser, then padded into the shower room.

27

Harry had been kicked out of the marines... well, pretty much, with just the formality of a court martial, the boot up the backside, and a firing squad to come. But they'd let him come home while they got their ducks in a row, which was very sweet of them. Nobody had wanted to know about the village or the ambush, all they wanted to hear was why the Taliban commander had let him go without even slapping his wrist.

Harry had never been so insulted in all his life — well, okay he had, many times, but he wasn't going to let these jumped-up shits treat him like a traitor. Well, they could get stuffed and their shitty regiment too. Except the last part was a lie, and he knew it. He hadn't got a snowball's chance in hell of convincing the guys in the red berets that the Taliban had just had a little chat with him and sent him on his way. They believed he'd given them something, something valuable — and who could blame them? Yeah, true, but stuff them anyway.

He paid the cabbie and stood in front of Harvey's apartment building and wondered what he was going to say to his father. Shit, he'd be spitting blood. Nah, Harvey wasn't like that; he was always calm, just the sort of man you need in a serious crisis. And, Harry boy, crises don't come more serious than this one. Dishonourable discharge, life in prison, and firing squad, and his pay would probably be stopped. Not a rosy future, then.

He wondered how the American was faring and felt a twinge of guilt for getting him into this. But hang on, who got who into what? The yanks had driven into the village, and he, Tom and BJ had just been passengers, remember? Yeah, so quit the guilt trip.

The automatic doors opened, so somebody must have recognised him. He crossed the marble foyer and nodded at the concierge. What was his name? Eric? No, Ernie, yeah, like Morecambe and Wise, easy mistake. He envied him his nice, simple life. Self-pity is seductive, warm and welcoming. And for pussies, so he quit that too.

Okay, Pops, let's get this over with.

Harvey was reading about the treaty negotiations with the US in the evening paper, but not really taking in the details. His head was replaying the telephone call from Sir Richard, telling him what a damned mess Harry was in. He looked up as the door opened and Harry entered. He put down the newspaper, crossed the room, and took Harry's pack, put a hand on his son's shoulder and nodded once. Fatherly reassurance done. Tick box.

"Thanks, Dad," Harry said sincerely. "I needed that." And that was true too. It was almost as reassuring and loving as a punch on the shoulder from a friend.

"Drink?" Harvey asked.

"Does the Pope shit in the woods?"

Harvey poured him a drink, looked at it for a moment, and then splashed a whole lot more into the glass and handed it to Harry.

"Rough trip?" Harvey asked, as much to get over the awkward moment as to elicit information he already knew.

Harry nodded. "You heard about Tom and BJ, then?"

"Yes, Sir Richard brought me up to speed."

"Big of him," Harry said bitterly.

"It's not like that, Harry, Richard has your best interests at heart."

Harry watched him for several moments, waiting for the punch line.

"Sit down, Harry," Harvey said, pointing at the couch. "Before you fall down. You look awful."

"Thanks," Harry said, but lowered himself onto the soft couch with a sigh.

"Tell you what," Harvey said cheerfully. "I'm going out to dinner this evening, to your mother's favourite restaurant as it happens." He smiled at a little private joke. "You come along too, just the two of us. It will help get you back into the swing of not being shot at."

Harry was about to decline and then thought, *what the hell*? "Okay, but I need some rest and a shower first."

"Yes, please," Harvey said, and Harry bunched his shirt and sniffed it. "Right, it is a bit ripe, but it's been a big twenty-four hours."

"Yes, so I hear."

Harry frowned, but let it go. A shower and a sleep were calling. Home sweet home, and he'd better start getting used to it because this was it from now on.

He was sparked out when Harvey came to wake him, and he started to wonder if he'd need to go to the fridge for a flat fish to smack him with, when he finally groaned and opened his eyes.

"I was having a great dream," he said grumpily. "About these twins, belly dancers." He shook his head. "Never mind, it's gone now."

"Don't kid yourself," Harvey said, heading for the door, "it would have been gone even if it wasn't a dream."

"Cheers, Pop, you really know how to lift the spirits of your poor wounded hero son."

"Get dressed, hero, and wear something presentable," Harvey said, stopping at the open door. "We're going somewhere smart, so it will be a culture shock for you."

Harry sat up. "The doomed man's last meal."

Harvey turned. "And that's something I need to talk to you about."

"What? The meal or the doomed part?"

"The meal can sort itself out," Harvey said. "The doomed part is less certain." He closed the door behind him, leaving Harry none the wiser for the enigmatic comment.

They arrived at Restaurant D'Amore by taxi, which was a bit of a surprise to Harry, as his father was entitled to a car and a driver. Maybe he'd given the old chap the night off. Odd though.

Mario opened the door and greeted Harvey like a long-lost brother, and with a sincerity that would have won an Oscar. "Mr Thorne!" he gushed, as if Harvey arriving for the table he'd reserved was a big surprise. "How nice to see you again." Still, it's nice to be welcome. "Please, I have your table all prepared."

Right, straightening a napkin is a big deal.

"And who is this?"

Harry, you plonker. But Harry just smiled nicely.

"Is this your son? Oh, I don't see him since he used to sit under the table."

Gush, gush. The food better be good.

They entered the up-market Italian restaurant selling bog-standard Italian food at up-market prices. Not bad if you can get away with it, and looking at all the occupied tables, Mario was doing just that. Harry followed his father, who was following Mario to a table tucked away in the corner. Harvey sat against the wall with Harry facing him.

Mario fiddled with things on the table that didn't need any attention. "And will Mrs Thorne be joining you tonight?"

Harvey shook his head. "I'm afraid not, Mario, just me and Harry."

Mario looked confused for a moment, but covered it by snapping his fingers to call over one of the harassed waiters. Rude, but effective. "This is Aberto." He indicated the poor boy who was to be their slave for the night by twitching his thumb in his direction. "Anything you wish. Nothing is too much trouble."

Aberto stared around at the sea of occupied tables, with the look of a man with a broom after a hurricane.

A couple arrived at the door, and Mario swept off to gush all over them, much to Harry's relief. He took pity on the poor boy standing, frozen in indecision. "Hey,

Aberto, you go and do waiter things. We'll work out what we want and give you a whistle."

If that was supposed to be reassuring, it failed big time. Aberto shook his head so hard, it was in danger of bouncing off down the restaurant. "No! No! No whistle."

Harry smiled, nodded, smiled some more. "Okay. Bugger off now."

Aberto fled.

Harvey studied the menu, in fact, he studied the small print on the menu, and in order to do this, he had to hold it up in front of his face. Harry was seriously perplexed because for all the world, it looked as if he was hiding from something. He turned in his seat to see who Mario had gone to fuss over, and all became clear. He leaned across the table and pulled the menu down to reveal Harvey.

"You knew she was coming here, you old gumshoe you."

Harvey looked past him at Margaret and her date, who was helping her off with her coat to reveal the little black dress Annie had chosen for her.

This time she saw the men notice her, all of them, in fact, and Annie was right, she did like it. She didn't see Harvey notice her because he was hiding behind the menu again.

Harry leaned forward and spoke to the menu in a whisper. "So this is why you were so keen to come to dinner at this particular restaurant, on this particular night." He looked back over his shoulder at his mother sitting with her back to him, and smiled. "So what do you intend to do? Duke it out with him on the car park." He chuckled. "That should be worth seeing."

"A coincidence, I assure you," Harvey said, his eyes appearing above the menu now the coast was clear.

"Right. Of all the gin joints in all the towns in all the world, she walks into this one." Harry tutted. "Coincidence, my arse. You're stalking her."

Which was undeniable.

"No, I'm not," Harvey denied. "I admit that I know Margaret frequents this restaurant, and I may have idly wondered if I might see her, but that's as far as it goes."

"Yeah, right," Harry said. "Warrington... aka Rocky... mentioned that Margaret had a date tonight. Funny that, don't you think?"

"Order your food," Harvey said irritably.

"You have all the menus."

Harvey handed him the one that had been his hide, but his eyes remained on Margaret's back, a whole lot of Margaret's back at that. She could be a pain, true, okay, very true, but he did miss her. And she'd never shown that much skin when they'd been together, unless she had, and he hadn't noticed. He swore he'd notice if things ever righted themselves.

He watched her date — for date he clearly was — scan the wine list and order for them both. Margaret won't like that. He saw her head nod distinctly, and he shook his sadly. But then the Date ordered the main course for them both. Now that really was a fatal male chauvinist mistake. Ah!

Margaret did the nodding again. This was clearly a doppelganger, replacing the real angry Margaret with a friendly, happy version. It wouldn't last.

Harry put down the menu he hadn't looked at, having too much fun watching the expressions war on his father's face. There was expectation again, oh, and surprise, and ha, disappointment. He smiled, pleased to see he loved her so much because with that much love, anything was possible. Cue soppy music, full moon and cherubs. Pity life isn't the movies because in this life they would probably never tell each other how they really feel, for fear of painful and humiliating rejection, so they would go on being lonely into a sad old age. Then Annie's face appeared in his mind, and he grinned broadly. Right, like that would be allowed to happen with his little sister on the case.

Aberto came back, and Harry ordered tomatoes on toast with an Italian name for two to start, and for main course, fettuccine carbonara, once again for two, as Harvey was out of it. He was going to order the same wine the Date had, Chateau Margaux 95, because it sounded good, but then he saw the price and ordered a bottle of used house white. But hey, Harvey wouldn't notice in his present state.

Then the game was afoot. The Date excused himself and headed for the toilet. Harvey got up quickly, rattling the glasses on the table, and sat down again to check the fine print on the menu, but nobody noticed, or more accurately, Margaret didn't notice, so he stood up again, slowly, and sidled over to the toilet door, where he lurked.

Mario came out of the kitchen, gave Harvey a puzzled look, and swung over to where he was standing. "You would like a drink?"

Harvey stared at him for several seconds. "Why would I want to have a drink, standing outside the toilet?"

"I do not know, sir," Mario said, "tonight is very confusing." He mumbled something under his breath and continued on his mission to deliver pasta to one of the tables, but continued to cast suspicious glances at Harvey, who was still lurking.

"Oh, sorry," the Date said, coming out of the washroom and almost colliding with Harvey.

"That's perfectly all right," Harvey said, making no attempt to get out of his way. "You're with that woman over there, aren't you?" He indicated Margaret's bare back, and the Date nodded, but gave him a questioning look. "You should know that fellow over there..." He pointed at Harry. "Is a private detective who appears to be watching you and your woman friend. I believe he has one of those... what do they call them?" He frowned deeply. "A hidden camera. Yes, I am sure I saw him fiddling with a hidden camera behind a menu."

The Date stared first at Harry, then at Margaret, his mouth making O shapes.

"I do hope you don't mind your face being all over the tabloids tomorrow, connecting you to that... that woman."

He clearly did and began looking around as if there might also be a television crew on hand to capture him and... that woman. The colour drained from the poor man's face as he warred with his desire to flee, against his sense of chivalry. Desire won, and he fled, snatching up his coat from Margaret's chair, but careful to keep his face turned from Harry and his hidden camera. He headed for the door, stopped, and strode back across the restaurant to stand in front of Harry's table with his hands on his hips, all macho.

"You should be ashamed of yourself! You're a disgrace, man. This is no way to make a living."

Not bad as introductions go, but the closing was better. He started to leave, but his anger got in the way. "You should be flogged!" he said through gritted teeth.

Harry stopped reading the label of the bottle of recycled wine and looked up slowly. "Are you speaking to me?" he said softly.

"Yes, I'm bloody well speaking to you!" the Date snapped.

"I'm sorry," Harry said in the same soft voice, "I don't speak English."

The Date's mouth was moving, but no words were coming out. His face screwed up as he tried to compute what the man had just said, failed, and spun on his heels and stamped out, without even glancing at Margaret.

Harvey returned to the table, clearly very pleased with himself and at the outcome of his plan, while Harry gave him a long, slow look of rebuke.

Harvey watched Margaret speaking to Mario, who nodded and went back to the bar. Harvey winked at Harry as she asked to relocate to his table. He nodded towards Margaret standing up slowly and coming over.

"Margaret," Harvey said, standing. "What a surprise. I didn't know you still used our restaurant." He smiled and pointed at a vacant chair at their table. "Please, join us." He looked past her. "Your friend seems to have remembered important business."

Margaret smiled and was about to speak when Mario returned, gave her a slip of paper, and walked away, but kept watching, as pretty well everyone in the restaurant was now doing. "No, thank you, Harvey," she said with a smile, "but please, have this on me."

She dropped the paper on the table, said goodnight to Mario and Harry, and walked out with dignity, and a cute ass.

Harry picked up the paper, chuckled, and handed it to Harvey. Aberto passed with a silver ice bucket, stopped, and stared at the now vacant table.

"Bloody hell!" Harvey said, holding the bill like it was burning his fingers. "What were they drinking?"

Harry's reflexes had been honed by years of combat training and real firefights, so for him, to think was to act. He stood up, tapped Aberto on the shoulder, took the bottle of wine out of the ice bucket, and put it on his table next to the recycled house white in a single fluent move. Aberto looked from one to the other, gave up, and went back to the kitchen, mumbling something in Italian.

Mario came over and stood with an air of irritation that his magnifico restaurant should be the scene of such a... well, a scene. He was going to tell them, to explain to them that such behaviour is not—

Harry patted his arm and got his attention. "Got a doggy bag?"

Mario was way past confused by now, but of course he was, he was in a domestic feud.

"You know?" Harry said, waggling the bill between his thumb and finger at the stunned man. "A bag for the grub we... Dad is paying for."

Mario wanted to say something, but the silence in the restaurant was too deafening. "I do not know... sir... but I will ask," he said stiffly and walked away. "Tonight is very confusing," he repeated to himself, and his shoulders sagged.

28

When not on an op, everyone called Ethan 'Spike' because of his long hair. It was almost like humour. Others called him something else, but those that do, do, those that can't, teach — and those who are too stupid to do either, throw rocks and hope nobody notices they're crap.

He was muttering quietly as he read the contents of the folder that had magicked itself onto the desk they'd allocated him at his new and hopefully temporary posting to Navy Seal HQ in Virginia. It transpired that his experience in that damned village was vital to military intelligence, may God bless them all. He swore, and it turned out his Arabic vocabulary was far wider than just business use.

A red folder was always bad news, and this one seemed redder than usual. He closed it and tossed it across the desk. Shit, every crappy assignment that comes down the tube. Wasn't it enough that he'd got the intel on the chemical attack? No, of course not. And what a cluster-fuck that turned out to be. The navy had sent in one of their drones, a Silver Fox, to take air samples and check for chemical residue before the marines could go in and get the bodies of their comrades, and they lost it. How the hell do you lose a sensor drone? He read on. There was some sort of radio interference, and it just vanished, but not before it told them the place was clear, the chemical weapon having died of boredom, or some such shit. Losing a drone in a war zone was seriously embarrassing, but not too much, if you don't tell anyone.

So the question was, who'd stolen it? And the answer, even a five-year-old could have worked out, was the Taliban leader who'd waxed their asses. Now he was supposed to go get the son of a bitch. He picked up the file and read his name, even though it was committed to memory. Lupus, they called him — The Wolf. Now why was that? Well, that was because they liked to give these guys grandiose names, so it could be bigged up when they caught him. Problem was, nobody could catch this one, yet here they go, passing the buck down the chain of command and saying, "Go get him." Outstanding.

He rolled his chair back, got up, and walked to the window overlooking the scrub brush and the Potomac River beyond the car park, and let his mind do its thing.

Every fact he'd read or heard about Lupus was stored in his human filing cabinet, catalogued, indexed and on-line. Not a free gift from God, it was just like the rest of his skills, down to discipline, hard work and practice. The men under his command looked to him to keep them alive, and he did his damndest to do just that. He thought about Al and Eddie and shook his head sadly. "Well, you did a great job there," he said to the tired face reflected in the window.

He forced his attention back to the job at hand. Mohammed Rahman Ali, AKA Lupus, forty-four years old, born into a rich and influential family in Riyadh. But he'd tossed the good life to go out and kill Americans, and he was real good at it. He'd first surfaced with the bombing of the US embassies in Tanzania and Nairobi, and followed those with a list of atrocities right up to Nine Eleven.

Ethan tapped the windowsill with his fingers and thought about tactics. Lupus was shrewd; he had to be to have stayed ahead of the game for so long, so he wasn't going to put his head in a noose just because Ethan asked him nicely. There had to be a way to tempt him out into the open. The memory of the world-class terrorist just letting that Brit go seriously troubled him. Anything that was outside an enemy's normal MO troubled him. Nothing to be done about that right now, though, but it would come back, he was sure of that.

Somewhere, somebody knew something, and he had all his contacts in all the federal agencies beating the bushes in the hope that something would jump up, though he knew that when it came down to it, it would be the same as always. An accident, a fluke, an error of judgement. Okay, he could wait for the fluke, or he could find a way to flush him out, which was easier to say than to do. He tapped his fingers on the windowsill and went round the loop again.

The door opened, and Leroy Lee entered. He was generally known as Bruce for two reasons, one being obvious and the other being his love of martial arts and winning the regimental cage-fighting champion three years in succession, which was no mean feat, considering the opposition. He hadn't knocked, he didn't salute, and he didn't wait to speak, which would have driven a regular NCO into a fit of apoplexy, but this team worked on mutual respect, and it worked well, without all that crap. "News, boss," he said and waited for Ethan to respond. He'd be waiting a long time. "Lupus has been spotted."

"Where?" Ethan said and strode back to his desk.

"Right where you left him," Bruce answered with no hint of criticism. "In Afghanistan, right outside Musa Qala. And don't we remember that shithole."

And Ethan did remember it, it being almost the last place any of them would remember. Intel said fifteen to twenty Taliban had been seen in the village, stirring up trouble, and Ethan's team had been sent in to neutralise them and grab couple of warm ones if possible. Intel was wrong, and they'd walked into a Taliban Red Square-type parade. Jesus! They got out of there with their tails so far between their legs, they were tickling their noses. Ethan had called in an air strike, which had successfully wrecked the market, shot up the buildings, set fire to everything flammable, and not hit a single Taliban, who had probably gone home to watch American football on television.

He headed for the door, leaving Bruce looking at the papers on his desk. He stopped and glanced back. "I thought I'd go to ops," he said with a thick topping of sarcasm. "Would you care to come along?"

Bruce jumped and strode after him, as if he was going to do that anyway.

Lieutenant Commander Jerome Patton — unsurprisingly known as George — like his namesake was a ferocious and brilliant leader, whose men would have followed him to the grave. A lean, hungry-looking man in his mid-thirties, his colouring and bones clearly advertised his Nordic ancestry, while his uniform showed him to be a Navy Seal, and he knew that pretty much made him the best of the best of the best, a fact never knowingly understated. Except Patton, and every member of his team, knew that the best of them was Navy Seal Team 6, who'd taken out Bin Laden and avenged the death of three thousand Americans in the Twin Towers. That more than twenty of these boys were lost when the helicopter was shot down by Taliban rocket fire was a loss felt by every member of Special Forces. The finest soldiers in the world, trained to the peak of perfection, taken out by a man's finger on a button. The anger burned so deep, Patton put it out of his mind and focused on the mission.

He checked his watch in the dark cabin of the Chinook, looked up at his number two sitting opposite, and nodded once. Senior Chief Nate Wilson could have been a professional basketball player, but let that slide so that he could serve his country in the most direct way possible. Yeah, of course, the promoters had told him the story of how being a rich and famous player would serve his country by giving the poor black kids from his neighbourhood a role model to follow out of poverty. If it looks like bullshit and smells like bullshit, it's probably bullshit. He joined the navy and fast-tracked to the Seals when his intelligence and phenomenal fitness were recognised, and from then on, it was a steady climb up through the ranks.

Nate looked around the darkened cabin at the twenty-five other Seals leaning back and trying to sleep or staring absently into space and rehearsing the mission they had practiced only briefly. They would do just fine, just as in other covert missions he had led them on. He knew there was a chance, a very real chance that some of them wouldn't be coming back, but that's the risk in war. Still, you'd think they would look a bit worried, wouldn't you? He smiled, not the Seals' style.

Patton went over the mission briefing for the hundredth time, and he'd go over it again in the next half hour before they reached their destination. It seemed straightforward enough. The helo would drop them at the LZ five klicks from the camp, and from there, they would double-time the rest of the way, overcome any resistance, grab the target, and get out without getting dead or captured. The satellite and drone surveillance photos had told him the strength of the opposition, which put them at a little over five to one against — so the odds were in the Seals' favour. There was a perimeter of sorts, but these rag-heads would be sleeping or screwing goats, or whatever it was they do when they're not blowing up women and kids, so that wouldn't be too much trouble. He knew that was just his bravado playing down the risk of what they were expected to do. These rag-heads, as he called them with a twinge of guilt, were not going to be the usual fanatical amateurs who got their throats cut while they were taking a leak or praying to Allah on their hands and knees instead of doing what the hell they were supposed to be doing. No, these men would have been chosen by Lupus, and that was a guy who'd been around the block a few times, had skills and intelligence, and the scalps of many Americans to prove it. So be careful, son, the voice in his head said quietly.

The Chinook touched down on the lee side of a hill away from the camp, and the team spread out and set up a defensive perimeter, while the swirling dust followed the helicopter out across the sand. Nobody spoke, and there was none of the "Move it! Go!" bullshit from the movies, they simply spread out and set off at a steady mile-devouring jog towards the camp and their target.

Ethan watched the ghost-images on the huge screen as the geo-stationary satellite relayed the position of every man in the team back to ops. The infrared images were overlaid on a map of the target zone showing the terrain and the distance to the camp.

Also in the room were the squadron commander, a couple of intelligence officers and some guys in suits that would have CIA as their designer labels. He wished he could be there on the ground instead of sipping coffee in the comfortable Virginian base, seven thousand miles from the action, but right now that action was running real-time like an episode of 24 right in front of his eyes.

He watched the team covering the ground to the camp at a steady six miles an hour, fast enough to get them there with limited exposure to the locals, but easy enough so they could still fight when they got where they were going. Truth is, they could have run that distance flat out and still kicked ass when they arrived, but in any fight, there are so many unknowns, so many imponderables that you control the ones you can, and handle the ones you can't. The pace they could control.

Patton stopped on the ridge a hundred metres or so from the camp perimeter and waited for the men to fan out on either side. A few moments later, the tail-enders caught up, and the rearguard took up defensive positions facing the way they'd come. Okay, everything was ready. He checked his G-Shock and watched the second hand glide towards twelve. Still nobody had spoken or made any sound, but no one even thought about that, it being the least that was expected. Two a.m. dead. He stood and moved forward over the ridge at a quick walk towards the fence posts silhouetted against the moonlit sky, posts that would support the barbed wire and mark the area where IEDs and regular mines would probably have been laid for idiots to step on.

When the team was within twenty metres, they flipped down their helmet-mounted enhanced night vision goggles and followed the five explosive technicians, who went ahead and scanned for the telltale scars and indentations in the sand. The insurgents didn't really expect anyone to be dumb enough to approach the camp so hadn't worked too hard on hiding the trips, but the disposal technicians took their time, assuming that what they saw was less than what there was to see.

The platoon crept forward in the shadow of the hill where the camp had been established so the lookouts could see far out into the desert — in daylight. The disposal team stopped at the two strands of wire hung between the posts and checked them carefully for little surprises. There was no sound, no clinking of gear or radio chatter, no thumbs up or any of that crap. The wire was clear, and the techies clipped it quietly and placed it on the ground, while the rest of the team moved past them like ghosts.

Patton and Nate switched on the helmet cameras in the night vision goggles to feed live infrared images up to the satellite and back to ops, and went forward slightly ahead of the team.

Ethan saw two mini screens appear above the map and the ghostly infrared smudges of the seals. The screens showed green images of scrub trees and orange thermal images of the rest of the team, rows of oil drums that were supposed to be cover, and a scattering of stone buildings in front of a mud-brick compound. Their objective.

He watched the images for a moment, saw the moonlight illuminate the compound through the image intensifiers to look as bright as day. The screen on the left panned slowly across the top of the compound wall, but all it reported was chipped brick.

Something was wrong, and Ethan's heart began to beat a little harder. "Abort the mission, now!" he barked.

The squadron commander turned to him sharply. "Master Sergeant?"

Ethan strode to the front of the room and pointed at the screen. "Can't you see? These are our boys..." He pointed at the images converging on the compound. "And these are the enemy." He pointed at the satellite images of the compound showing them lying down.

"What the hell is going on here?" one of the suits barked, showing who was really in charge of this op.

"Shut up!" Ethan said sharply and turned back to the commander. "There are only three men in the compound."

They all turned back to the screen to look again at what was now obvious.

"So what?" the suit said, clearly angry at having his superiority usurped by this... this... NCO.

Ethan ignored him. "It's a trap, sir," he said, stepping closer to the commander. "Abort the mission."

The squadron commander nodded once at the comms tech and turned back to the screen.

Patton also sensed something was wrong with the setup. They were almost at the compound gates now, and still no alarm, no tracers lighting up the night. They must be clearly visible to the guards now that they were no longer in the shade and standing out in clear moonlight like tourists on a sun-drenched beach. He hesitated for a moment, but his mission was to get in, get the package, and get out, and he would do just that.

Petty Officer Scott Calgrieve stopped at the double wooden gates, glanced back, and received the nod from Patton. The gates creaked eerily in the still night, but there was no shout, no commotion. Nothing.

This stank like a five-day-old fish, and everyone felt the tension ratchet up several notches. Patton moved up past Scott and stepped into the compound as the recall came over his comms link. He stopped and dropped to one knee and waited for the confirmation, and when it came through a moment later, he retreated through the gates and signalled the platoon to wrap up and withdraw. Then he vomited and fell to his hands and knees.

He raised his head against the massive weight pressing down on him and saw three men in dirty grey robes walk out through the gates, and even in his present state of distress, he recognised Lupus as he approached and put his hand on his shoulder.

"Die now, there's a good fellow," Lupus said, with a gentle nod of his head. "It's okay to go now."

Patton sank to his stomach and closed his eyes. Yes, it was okay to go now.

"Shit!" Ethan hissed as the infrared images showed the Seals' bodies littering the ground.

"What just happened?" the suit asked, his voice shaking with the shock of the images.

The squadron commander licked his lips and looked at Ethan. "Master Sergeant?" he said quietly.

Ethan tore his eyes off the three images moving through the fading seal infrareds. "Lupus knew we were coming," he said and clamped his jaw to suppress his rage.

"But they are all down," the suit said.

"Ya think?" Ethan said angrily.

"Master Sergeant," the commander said icily.

"Sorry, sir," Ethan said, not sorry at all. "We went to get Lupus for Uncle Sam and to get you your promotion. Right?"

The suit glared.

"Well, we found him."

The suit looked back at the screen and shook his head dumbly. "All of them?" he said to himself. "Air strike!" he added excitedly. "If we send in an air strike right now, we'll get Lupus out in the open, and that'll be an end to it."

Ethan fixed him with cold, blue eyes. "What we'll get... sir... is a whole lot of ordinance dropped on the bodies of our boys, while Lupus sits out in the hills watching the fireworks."

"Possibly," the suit said with a hard look at the marine, "but it's a chance I'm prepared to take."

The squadron commander shook his head. "I'll not send those brave boys home in sealed coffins," he said and left the ops room, his shoulders sagging, suddenly very tired.

"If he hasn't got the balls," the suit said angrily, "then I'll—"

"You'll what?" Ethan said quietly.

The suit looked hopefully at the comms tech, but he just looked back with pity and more than a hint of contempt.

"This cluster-fuck was your doing," Ethan said and pointed at the still images on the screen. "But you get to fly on home back to Langley in your business-class seat, while the families of those boys bury their dead." He put his face inches from the CIA agent. "But," he said slowly, so there was no mistake, "if you are still here in three seconds, your family will be burying you."

The agent glared at him for two of those seconds and then fled.

Ethan looked back at the screen, watched Lupus walk away from the compound and out of range of the satellite imaging, and made a silent promise to the men lying dead in the desert.

29

Harvey sat at the table and savoured the silence in his apartment, not that it was silent because all his guests had left, that would be just too much to hope for, it was silent because his guests were still in bed. He breathed a satisfied sigh and folded the newspaper so that he could read the editorial describing the wonderful Americans and how the Brits were their favourite third-world country, about to be saved by the life-changing accord. Well, there went the satisfied feeling. He picked up a triangle of toast and moved it towards his mouth in that slow-motion way of a man reading a gripping article that was making his blood boil.

Frank's bedroom door opened, and he emerged, wearing one of Harvey's monogrammed bathrobes, which Harvey clocked but decided life was too short.

"Morning," Frank said, crossing the room and taking Harvey's last piece of toast. "Got another cup?"

Harvey had an overwhelming feeling of deja vu as he lifted the phone. "Yes, thank you, Serge, and you too." He looked up to heaven, but God was taking a bath as cleanliness is... "Please bring another—"

Harry emerged into the lounge, wearing blue jeans and a wrinkled marine T-shirt. He looked like crap, but a bottle of recycled house white and a bottle of the good stuff, not to mention all that other stuff he'd drunk last night, is not famous for giving a man a good complexion. "Got any coffee?" he said through thick lips.

"Make that two breakfasts," Harvey said into the phone. "Oh, sod it, bring the kitchen," he added as Rocky's door opened.

"You boys have a good time last night?" Frank said, claiming one of the big chairs. "Heard you come home with the postman."

"Yeah, ta," Harry said, easing himself down gingerly into the other chair.

"Mmm," Frank said with a smile, "I can see that."

"We saw Mom," Harry said.

Frank raised his eyebrows and looked at Harvey, who was suddenly engrossed in a sheaf of court papers.

Harry smiled. "Stiffed us for the bill."

"Yeah, she would," Frank said and chuckled. "Follows your grandmother on that front." He pulled a face like he was chewing a wasp. "She say when she's coming home?" he asked Harvey, but got only a grunt in response, and winked at Harry. "Old place isn't the same without her. Quiet, you know?"

Harvey knew that.

The doorbell rang, and Frank got up when the other two showed no sign of moving. "It's okay," he said with a groan, "the old bloke will get that."

"Cheers, old bloke," Harry said.

Frank opened the door, expecting to see breakfast and Serge from Basildon, instead he saw Laura. He smiled and stepped aside to let her enter.

"Morning, Harvey," she said breezily, saw Harry, and stopped. "You used to be Harry, right?"

Harry put a hand to his head to confirm it was still there. "Yeah, morning, Laura."

"You look like shit, you know that?"

And Harry knew that.

"Harvey take you out on the town last night, then?" she asked, though her half-smile said she knew exactly where Harvey had taken him.

Harry followed her side look and sniffed. "That'll be a first. No, we went on a... recon."

"Oh yeah?" Laura said, still smiling. "Recon anybody we know?"

"Thank you, Laura," Harvey said, deciding enough was enough. "Is there something I can do for you?" He put the papers on the table. "Something life-threatening, I expect, to bring you to my apartment at this time in the morning."

Laura glanced at her watch pointedly. "This time in the morning for most people is coffee break."

"Quite, but they don't work into the evening," Harvey said, inventing a whole new working day.

Laura glanced at Harry, and he winked at her, and hey, she liked it. "Big case, remember Bob the Burglar?" she said quickly, bringing herself back to the business at hand. Still, he did clean up quite nicely.

"Yes," Harvey said, picking up his court papers again to move on to a technical issue less irritating. "He is to be arraigned tomorrow, I believe."

"He is."

"And?" Harvey asked, looking up, ready for the big moment.

Laura looked decidedly uneasy and stared out of the big window at the river, as if that would help.

"And?" Harvey repeated, though he'd been in this business long enough to know exactly what the "and" was. "He's disappeared, correct?"

"Well," Laura said, seeing something of vital interest on the river. "Not exactly disappeared."

"How exactly, then?" Harvey asked, raising an eyebrow.

"I think," Harry said, wanting to put the poor girl out of her misery, "what Laura means is the he hasn't disappeared, that would be a magic trick." He smiled at the girl. "He's scarpered." Well, that described it pretty well.

Frank chuckled from behind the sports pages. "Couldn't have put it better myself."

"You owe me fifty quid, then," Harvey said, reaching over the table to retrieve his coffee, swiped by Frank.

"What?" Laura turned from the window. "Is that it? Is that all you are going to do about it?"

Harvey looked up from the cold coffee. "I'm open to suggestions. Perhaps you would like us to form a posse."

Frank chuckled a little louder, and Laura scowled at the sports pages hiding his face.

"No, of course not!" she said, her hands on her hips.

Cute, Harry thought.

"But what if something has happened to him?"

"What?" Harry said, tearing his eyes off her body. "Like his gang have weighted him down and chucked him into the Thames for snitching about the theft of the mutt?"

"You know about Puccini?" she asked, turning and frowning at him.

Harry shrugged. "Yeah, it was a good story. Burglar saves mutt from watery grave." He framed a picture with his hands. "I can see it now. Hold the front page."

"This is not a laughing matter!"

Frank laughed, his paper moving up and down in time with his stomach.

"Laura," Harvey gently said, "the police will find him and bring him back to face the stern hand of justice. It's what they do."

She looked from one to the other, glaring a little longer at Harry, which was cool. "So that's it?" she said, angrier than she should have been. "We do nothing?"

"Precisely," Harvey said, sipping his cold coffee.

She stamped over to the door, opened it, and turned back to face the room. "My heroes," she said, strode out, and slammed the door behind her.

"That'll be you she meant, then," Frank said, looking at Harry.

Harry gave him a double take.

"Well, you're the only hero here, right?"

"Matter of opinion," Harry said, shaking his head and looking back at the closed door. Funny, though, he didn't remember her being that... well... nicely formed.

"Which reminds me," Harvey said, looking at the empty toast plate and then at Frank's newspaper, from behind which came distinct munching noises as his toast was finished off.

"What does?" Harry asked.

"Oh, Sir Richard wants to speak to you."

"Oh, does he?" Harry said with an edge.

"Mmmm... yes, something about a chap named Lucus, Lupid, or some such."

That got Harry's attention. "Lupus. Sir Richard wants to talk about Lupus?" Now that was odd. Nobody had believed his report of the firefight at the mosque, and now? Well, what was it Sherlock Holmes used to say? He couldn't remember, but it meant that's a bit of a turn-up.

30

Oscar's Pussy Club was a dive. Well, no surprise there. Tweetie Pie was seriously nervous and kept trying to hide behind Shaun, which was a bit optimistic, Shaun being only five eight and Tweetie standing six one in his socks. He'd hide — like a giraffe hides behind a barstool — and Shaun would pull him out and shove him ahead, until he tried to hide again. Jesus, what was there to hide from in this pink-painted, sticky-carpeted, gay bar?

Big Betty, that's what. If he'd wondered, even for a moment, why they called him Big Betty, well, his answer was right there in front of him. Betty was big enough to create his own gravity. Six seven if he was an inch and as wide as a fisherman's boast.

Shaun took an involuntary step back, but Danny was way ahead of him — going backwards. They mouthed, "Jesus!" at each other. Shaun waved Danny in first, but he shook his head and mouthed, "No way!" So the nation's finest police officers hid behind Tweetie Pie.

Big Betty took a step forward, and the earth moved. It was bad enough that he was huge, but he was wearing a dress, a flowery sleeveless thing with a narrow white patent leather belt. That outfit would have been expensive — if only for the amount of material.

Shaun closed his eyes. Come on, boy, do police things.

"Are you Big Betty?" Ah, that's why our policemen are the best in the world.

"Who wants to know?" Betty's voice sounded like a wrestler with a smoking habit.

Shaun had been a policeman for twenty years, and ten of those had been in the Ulster Constabulary, so it took a hell of a lot to scare him. He pointed at Danny. "He does."

It was just better if Danny handled it, that way he could observe and see any telltale signs etc. Yeah, etc.

Danny's mouth was open, and he was staring at Shaun like he'd tossed him an anaconda with toothache.

Oh, bugger it. Shaun stepped forward and looked up at the man-mountain. "Tweetie Pie here is an old friend, and he tells me—"

"You're cops, I can smell it."

So much for the sneaky approach.

"Nah, that's just fear," Danny said helpfully.

The tasteful bead curtain at the side of the bar rattled its little orange and red beads as Curly Sue swept in dramatically. Making her entrance.

God, what a horror! If she smiles at me, kill me quick, Shaun thought.

Since Curly Sue was dressed like a Parisian hooker, in a tight black skirt with a thigh-length split, striped pullover and high heels, Shaun decided he'd better call him, her, in case Big Betty got offended — and pulled his head off.

Curly Sue swept up to Big Betty and put a hand on his shoulder. She had to reach up to do that, being five seven tops, and as thin as a stick insect on a twenty-day fast. She had a nose like a pocketknife can opener. Was that rude? Well, if that wasn't, thinking she'd had her head flattened between two reversing vans surely was. Shaun couldn't take his eyes off her trowel-powdered face and bright red lips. And the reason he couldn't was that if he did, he might look down at her breasts. Sweet Mary mother of God, they were pointed. He thought of fries in a cone and instantly regretted it.

Big Betty was glaring at him, either for staring at Curly Sue's breasts, or because he wasn't staring enough.

Danny saved them. "Good day, ma'am," he said.

Shaun could hardly believe he'd said that and stared at him. Danny caught his look and shrugged.

"Yes, okay, we are cops," Danny said and raised his hands in surrender. "Hold on, we're not here to do anything stupid. We just need some information, that's all."

Big Betty seemed to relax a little and even managed a sort of smile at Curly Sue, who smiled right back. It was a warm and touching moment. Shaun wished he hadn't had chilli for lunch because it burns like hell on the way back up.

Curly Sue pointed at one of the little round tables with its thin brass lamp and pink flowery shade — it just got more and more tasteful. "Will you take a seat, gentlemen?" She had a voice like fingernails on a blackboard.

They sat at the little table, except Big Betty, who sat at several tables.

Curly Sue smiled a big, sexy smile that revealed the red lipstick lines on her teeth. "Now, gentlemen, what is it we can do to your good selves?"

You can stop smiling for one, Shaun thought. "We understand you were hired for a little job with our good friend Tweetie here."

They glared at Tweetie Pie, who decided crying was his best survival tactic. Big Betty grunted something that could have been sympathy or a promise of a painful death, while Curly Sue put a thin bony hand on Tweetie's arm and showed her red teeth. "There, there, Tweetie dear, don't fret your good self. We'll take care of you."

That didn't sound encouraging, and Tweetie blubbered quietly into a stained handkerchief.

Curly Sue turned back to Shaun. "As you can see, we run a legitimate business here." He waved nicotine-stained fingers at the brothel posing as a club. "So I'm sure I don't know what your good self is talking about."

Shaun leaned forward, caught a whiff of her breath, and leaned back. "Look, I don't give a shit about what you were doing in a warehouse full of dead Yardies, what I want to know is where is O'Conner?"

Curly glanced at Betty for a response, locked eyes, and played faces at each other. Shaun looked around, but there was no bucket. "Look, you just say an address, and we'll forget everything we know about twenty K's of H and a sack of money."

If he'd intended to shock them, he succeeded. They stopped playing coo-coo faces and glared at him. Curly tried to smile, but it collapsed like a soufflé in a stiff breeze.

"How did you..." She squinted at Tweetie Pie, who now looked like a turkey seeing December on the calendar. "There'll be words to be had with your good self, Tweetie," she promised.

"Look," Danny said, "you say a place, and we walk out of here."

They were considering it — or at least something was happening in Curly's head from the pain on her face. Big Betty just looked... well, vacant.

"Problem is," Curly Sue said, "if we tell you where Mr O'Conner is and then he finds out it was us give it to you, then our reputation will be besmirched."

Besmirched? He could shoot one of them, Shaun thought, and that would scare the other. No, that wouldn't work, they couldn't shoot Big Betty because they hadn't brought an elephant gun. "Look," he said, "Danny and—"

"Danny? That's a nice name," Curly Sue said, looking him up and down slowly. "I like the dark ones."

Danny's face said "help!"

"Hands off, sweetie," Shaun said sharply. "He's taken."

"Oh, I'm sorry, I'm sure," Curly said with a shrug. "Too skinny for my taste anyway. I prefer a girl I can get hold of." She smiled up at Big Betty.

God, it's a madhouse! Shaun wanted to run away. Here he was having a quiet chat with two screaming queens and a sobbing wuss, and had just said his partner was his special friend. "Nobody will know you told us," he said, trying to stop his mind running away and hiding. "You give us his address, and that's the end of it." There was an "or else" in there somewhere. "What do you say?"

Curly Sue was the brains, which spoke volumes. She thought about it with that pained expression and then nodded. "You're sure nobody will know we talked to your good selves?"

Shaun raised a hand. "Scout's honour." Oh, okay, that should swing it.

"Oooh, you were a boy scout?" Curly's eyes lit up.

He mentions my woggle, I'll... besmirch him, so help me. He took a shot in the dark. "I suspect you're no stranger to uniforms yourself." He raised an eyebrow.

Curly squeaked. "Oh, you are clever." God save us. "I was a soldier-boy." She brought her fists together in excitement. "Before I let the real me out into the light." She smiled and underlined it with her red lipstick teeth. "Oh, they were exciting times."

"I can imagine," Danny said with a shake of his head, but then caught Betty's eye. "All that soldiering and charging and stuff," he added quickly.

"I was in recon, like that nice Clint Eastwood. I like him," Curly said to stunned silence. "Would you believe that? Me, trained to sneak up on people and shoot them? Apparently I'm a natural, it's a gift."

Shaun had no trouble at all believing this dog's breakfast of a person was capable of killing people. He'd seen the bodies in the warehouse. The female of the species is the most ruthless, except for the pissed-off female stuck in a man's body.

Curly was going to expand on her soldier days, Shaun could see it and stood up quickly. "Look, we've got to go," he said, "we've people to shoot. We don't show up, who's going to shoot them?"

Curly seemed to understand the demands of business and nodded. "I would really like to help you," she said with another ghastly smile, "but I don't know exactly where the gentleman in question is at this moment." She raised a painted finger before Shaun could speak. "But I know a man who does."

Shaun wanted to slap her, but instead waited with a patience born out of the knowledge that he could empty his gun into Big Betty and he would still break him in half.

"The person who hired us on behalf of Mr O'Conner, so to speak, was an individual name of Junior Brown." She pulled a face. "Nasty little—" she glanced at Danny, "Jamaican."

"Where do we find this Jamaican?" Danny asked, letting the nationality error slip by.

"It's cool," Shaun said, "I know him." He stood up and nodded at Curly. "Thanks." He turned to go, but turned and looked back. "Like your hair."

Curly Sue fiddled with her straight black hair appreciatively. "Oh, really? I did it myself."

Really? Well, there you go, another surprise.

Danny followed Shaun to the door, and Tweetie stood up to follow, but Curly put a hand on his arm. "Can we keep him, Boy Scout?"

Shaun shrugged. "Yeah, we're done with him."

"We're not," Curly said with an edge.

"Wait! Wait!" Tweetie was desperate. "You can't leave me... I'm, err... in custody!"

Shaun shrugged and pushed open the door with his foot so he didn't have to touch anything.

Danny caught up with him on the pavement outside. "You're not really going to leave him with those two, are you?"

Shaun looked both ways down the street littered with food wrappers and old vomit. "Why not?"

"They'll kill him, that's why not."

"And?"

Danny seemed genuinely agitated. "I signed all that paperwork!"

Shaun smiled. "They won't kill him. They'll smack him around a bit, but they won't kill him. It's too messy."

Danny looked back at the door with just a hint of guilt.

"He had a machine gun to shoot some guys he'd never met," Shaun reminded him and walked to the car. "If he'd found the safety." He shook his head in despair. "He deserves a little slap."

Danny pulled the car keys from his pocket and turned sharply as a piecing scream came from the club. He looked at Shaun, who seemed more concerned by the dust on the car's roof.

Another scream came from behind the closed door, and Shaun shrugged. Screaming was good; at least Tweetie wasn't dead. Yet.

31

Harry had progressed from the elbow crutch to a regular walking cane, one with a big hooked handle like they have in the old movies, truly classy. He rolled it slowly between his fingers and watched the oak door across the marble reception area. There were magazines, there was coffee, and there was a very efficient and snooty receptionist. What there wasn't, was any sign of Sir Richard for the past — he looked at this watch — two hours. Not very respectful, except respect you have to earn. Well, what about getting killed for Queen and country? Two things, Harry boy. One, you weren't killed. Two, you don't have to be anybody special to get yourself shot; any grunt can do that. And three — well, there's always a three — you aren't rich or famous, so you don't count for squat. And amen to that.

He looked at the coffee station. What the hell was that all about? A coffee station — that being a steamer, a bunch of sachets of freeze-dried, taste-extracted dust and coffee grounds left over from the bottling plant. And anyway, if he was bothered to limp over there, he'd have to get the coffee back without spilling it, because that's so uncool, and then he'd have to sit. Well, then he'd probably need to go to the bathroom, because coffee is one of those diuretic things. Bit like anything good to drink—

"Sir Richard will see you now," the snooty receptionist said snootily.

Harry got up slowly, his leg having stiffened from all that sitting. He should really have got up and moved about a bit — perhaps got a coffee from the coffee station.

The snooty receptionist watched him limp slowly across in front of her desk to Sir Richard's door and wondered if he'd manage it with the stick. She could have got up and opened it for him, but why would she do that? That's a job for a porter, who had taken the day off, again. Just because he was old he just assumed... well, we would see about that.

Harry pushed down the silver handle of the heavy oak door and managed to shoulder it open without pitching head first into the office, though it was a close call.

Sir Richard was sitting behind an appropriately huge desk, reading something important. Harry could tell that because he didn't look up. He sat down in the Queen Anne winged armchair — having first made sure there were no hair-oil stains on the lace headrest cover, because this was just the kind of chair favoured by people with oily hair.

He would have crossed his legs, but Harvey Thorne's first born was not stupid... well, okay, he'd joined the marines, gone to a war zone, got blown up and shot, and gone back and got his two friends killed, along with two Americans, and nearly got himself waxed in a grubby little village in the middle of nowhere. But that didn't count.

After a few more minutes, Sir Richard put down the papers he'd been looking at just to piss Harry off and made one of those affected pyramids with his fingers. "Well, Harry, you have certainly stirred up a hornets' nest," he said quietly. And one thing was for certain, quiet usually meant bad. He tapped the papers with his finger.

So the papers were not just to piss Harry off, then. Strike two.

"I can explain, sir," Harry said, leaning forward on the stupidly inappropriate chair.

Sir Richard raised his eyebrows. "That would be an interesting and somewhat challenging feat."

Harry leaned back. Okay then, if he wasn't even going to give him a chance, then he could go screw himself.

Sir Richard waited for the required dramatic interval and then nodded. Now, in a situation like this one, nodding can be good or it can be bad. So, not much of a giveaway, then.

"Tell me, Harry," he said, tilting his head slightly. "This Taliban commander?"

Harry could have said, "Which Taliban commander?", but he wasn't stupid, as has been established, so instead, he shut up — which could have been a first.

Sir Richard picked up one of the papers and scanned it unnecessarily. "The commander who has subsequently been identified as the terrorist Mohammed Rahman Ali, and also known, though somewhat grandiosely, as Lupus." He glanced away for a moment. "Though also known as implies we know anything at all beyond his name."

Harry could see the life in prison and firing squad, dialling down to just a strong likelihood. At least someone believed he'd met this Taliban and had been allowed to walk away, so that was a start. "If you know about this terrorist, then the regimental CO knew about him when he was giving me all that grief in Helmand," he said, as the truth unfolded in his mind. "Which means..." He leaned forward. "It was all bullshit!"

Sir Richard shrugged. "Perhaps, but we had to keep it quiet, and if that meant showing you in rather less than a glowing light, then que sera, I'm afraid."

"That's big of you," Harry said bitterly. "You hung me out to dry and just left me there."

Sir Richard watched him without a flicker of emotion. "This is bigger than your reputation."

"Easy for you to say," Harry said, a little petulantly. "It's my reputation that says I'm a liar at best and at worst a coward who got his friends killed and ran away."

"Oh no," Sir Richard said, raising his hand. "It's much worse than that."

Worse? Shit.

Sir Richard watched him for a moment, as if weighing up the consequences of telling him versus those of not telling him. "The authorities think you are a collaborator who sold your friends out for money." Clearly the option to tell him won out — and if that was the best option, not telling him didn't bear thinking about.

Harry stood up angrily, but falling back into the chair in agony somewhat diminished its dramatic effect. After a few seconds he recovered his dignity. "But why?" he said through teeth gritted by anger and pain. "I've known you all my life, why would you let this happen?"

"Some things are bigger than patronage," he said and sighed heavily. "But this hasn't been easy for me."

"Oh, poor you!" Harry snapped. "What about me? I was going to get court martialed and probably shot."

"You may well yet."

Harry's jaw was hanging open. He snapped it shut. "This is nuts! You know I didn't collaborate with this... this... Lupus."

"Yes," Sir Richard said. "MI6 has known about him for some years, but we have never got anywhere near him." Now it was his turn to lean forward. "Until now, no one knew what he looks like."

And there it was.

Harry watched the man who had remained a larger-than-life figure throughout his childhood, never changing, and always scary. "You want me to help you catch Lupus?"

Sir Richard nodded. "In a way. We need you to identify him for us, so we can eliminate him."

"Okay," Harry said, "bring in your artist, and I'll draw you a picture."

Sir Richard laughed, which threw Harry completely because he'd never even seen him smile before.

"We have a whole gallery of drawings of the man."

"Then why do you need me? Just circulate the pictures in Afghanistan, offer a couple of dollars reward and sit back and wait."

"That won't work. Don't you think we would have done that if it would?" He shrugged resignedly. Good point. "His file is full of... different pictures. He will have already changed his appearance, he is a chameleon."

"Then what can I do? I only met him once."

"Yes," Sir Richard said, "and that is precisely the point."

"What, that I have met him?"

"Yes. Sketches, photofits, even pictures won't identify him, but you have met him. You have seen the way he moves, speaks, holds himself. You have met the *man*."

Harry didn't get it. "But if he's changed his appear— "

"You will know him," Sir Richard said.

And Harry knew he would. It was like reading a man through the rifle scope, knowing what he would do even before he did it. Instinct, training, and practice. He would recognise him. "Okay," he said, knowing when an argument was lost, even with himself. "What do you want me to do?"

"Nothing. Yet."

"He's coming here, isn't he?"

Sir Richard watched him steadily for several seconds. "We believe he is."

"In the village," Harry said slowly, reluctant even to form the words, "those dead marines." He took a moment to continue. "It wasn't some crude chemical attack to piss off the Americans, was it?"

Sir Richard didn't answer, and that was loud enough.

"A biological weapon?" Harry got the same response and drew the same conclusion. "But we've been waiting for some terrorist group to attempt a biological attack on London for years. What's changed?"

Sir Richard still didn't answer, wanting to see just how good the son of his best friend really was. And hoping.

Harry looked past Sir Richard, out through windows that distorted the light enough to show they were armoured. His frown deepened. "Why wasn't Lupus afraid to enter that village if there was biowarfare material there?" The question wasn't really expecting an answer. "It had dissipated." He thought it through. "Those bodies, the old men, the women and the kids. They were just to draw in the marines, to get them to send a patrol to check it out." He had it, but didn't want to believe it, but eventually he had to. "Unless... It was doctored to only attack the Americans." He shook his head. "But that's just science fiction."

Sir Richard watched him steadily for a moment. "Yes, it used to be." He closed his eyes for a second to ready himself for the enormity of what he was about to say. "What you are describing is an ethnobomb. Do you know what an ethnobomb is?"

"A weapon that kills a specific ethnic group, but that's— "

"The Israel Institute for Biological Research developed one back in the nineties, to target only Arabs, but it was too crude to be used. Only twenty-five percent effective, and as such, it would have killed a whole lot of Israelis too, so it was mothballed."

Harry closed his eyes. Oh God. "I remember reading about it. Caused a hell of a scare."

Sir Richard sniffed. "Well, you could say that. It certainly changed international law."

"But if Lupus has this ethnobomb, I don't get it? You said it was designed to kill Arabs and was only marginally better than regular bioweaponry."

"Yes," Sir Richard said. "It was." He looked out of the window while he collected his thoughts. "They changed it," he said at last. "Made it more effective. And now it targets anyone but Arabs."

Of course it did. The image of the marines dead in the market square came back to Harry as clear as a video replay. And all those villagers, just bait. He wanted to kill Lupus, and that was the first time he'd ever wanted to kill anyone.

"There is no way Lupus, or all of Al Qaeda together could do that," he said, pushing the hate away into a corner to be used later. "It would take state-of-the-art laboratories and the best biochemists in the world to produce bacteria that reacts only with Western DNA." He thought for a moment. "Syria? Yeah, they could afford it. But they have enough problems of their own right now. Saudi Arabia? But they have no reason."

Sir Richard watched him eliminate all the possible sponsors, until only the impossible remained.

"Russia?" Harry said as he reached his conclusion. "But they are our allies."

"In words, perhaps, but not in deeds. Many in Russia, even at the very top, long for the days when they were the big kids on the block. And helping Lupus indirectly helps their ambitions to that end."

Harry shook his head. "But a weapon like this could be used against them too. They're not Arabs, after all."

"They believe they can control Lupus for their own ends, harness him, as it were."

A light came on in Harry's head with almost an audible click. "Valentin Tal," he said, almost to himself.

Sir Richard jumped. "Valentin Tal? Where did you hear that name?"

"From Lupus," Harry said. "When we had our little chat on the rooftop."

Now it was Sir Richard's turn to frown. "Tell me exactly what he said about Tal."

"Not much to tell," Harry said. "Asked me if I'd heard of him, like I would have. He told me to get to know him."

Sir Richard stood up and walked to the armoured window overlooking the Thames. "Tal was good, back in the cold war days, better than just good." He clasped his hands behind his back. "But he retired years ago. When the Soviet Union fell, men like him were seen as dinosaurs, a throwback to a darker time, redundant and useless."

Harry knew he was talking about more than just Tal. The end of the cold war had changed everything. Given the bean counters a chance to cull those who were deemed unnecessary in the new enlightened age. Funny thing, irony.

"What I do not yet understand," Sir Richard said, returning to his desk and sitting, "is why Tal is providing Lupus with a bioweapon?"

"Like you said," Harry said, "he must think he can control him."

"Then he is a fool."

"Everybody gets to be one at least once," Harry said, wondering how many times in the last months that had applied to him.

"Perhaps," Sir Richard said, "but this foolishness may well exterminate us all."

Okay then, Harry decided to help find this elusive Lupus — call it a sense of duty, but its real name is honour.

Harry walked the couple of miles or so to his father's apartment, partly to exercise his leg, but mostly to have time to think in peace — which on the streets of central London at midday was a neat trick.

This Lupus guy, the terrorist, had let him go, which was a plus in anybody's book, but he'd also killed Tom and BJ. Okay, they'd killed a whole lot more of the Taliban, but the Taliban weren't his friends. He wasn't just going to stand by and wait for the suits to come up with something for him to look at. You're a trained recon expert, Harry, the only difference here is that this is a city, but terrain doesn't matter, behaviour remains the same regardless. Is that true? He stopped and looked into a shop window selling women's underwear. Does an enemy's behaviour remain the same regardless of terrain? It was a good point, and one that the trainers back in Plymouth would be able to answer, but they'd just ask a string of questions first — like, why did you sell out your friends. Cheers, Sir Richard, for that. Okay, think it through. Terrain and location must change the way an enemy behaves; it has to. He left the underwear shop window without seeing the suspicious glances from passers-by, and walked down to Victoria Embankment, with no thought of where he was going, it was just somewhere else.

What would you do? he asked himself and stopped and looked out across the river at the London Eye. First off, he wouldn't be operating in London. Don't be a prat; think it through. He'd want to make the biggest splash possible, as it was highly likely that he would be caught pretty soon after any atrocity on the scale that a bioweapon could deliver. But this is London, there are hundreds of places. Trafalgar

Square in the evening, or just about any time. But that wouldn't do it, okay, it would kill a bunch of people, and it might even be a place to start transmitting the germ — or whatever it was. But as big bangs go, it was a bit of a fizzle. He walked on, still ticking off the potential targets, but getting nowhere, they were all too small, and there were so many.

He glanced up as a low-flying jumbo coming into land at Heathrow roared overhead. If Lupus released a bioweapon in Terminal 1, it would not only spread the virus to the UK, but to every flight destination from Heathrow, and that was plenty. He stepped over a homeless drunk lying on the path. That had to be it, then, that's where he would deploy his bioweapon, if he had to.

So terrain does dictate tactics. But he knew that.

His subconscious snapped him out of his mental recon, and he recognised the tree-lined street. Home, or at least as much of a home as he'd seen in years. This time the concierge opened the door and smiled, which was an improvement.

The usual suspects were home, with Frank sitting in Harvey's big chair in front of the television watching football, and Rocky practicing what was probably a guitar in his room, though it could have been a violin. Harvey was at work because someone had to pay for all of this.

"Would you like some lunch?" Frank asked as Harry closed the door. "They have really good grub here, bit expensive, but worth every penny."

"I doubt it's a penny," Harry said. "No, thanks, I've had a crap day, and my leg is playing up." That'll be because you walked three miles. "I'll lie down for a bit."

"Okay," Frank said, "but I don't think you'll be doing much resting until Rocky has finished torturing the cat." He returned to the football, and his plate of sandwiches, and his beer, and... a table covered with plates of things delivered by the ever-grateful Serge.

The squealing stopped, and a moment later Rocky came into the sitting room. "Hey, bro, I thought I heard your dulcet tones." He was beaming, but what was not to beam at? "Get you a drink or something?"

"No, thanks," Harry said, "Gramps has already offered me Dad's hospitality.

Frank smiled at him and raised his beer in salute.

"Hey," Rocky said excitedly, "I've got a gig tonight! Want to come?"

You have got to be kidding. "Is that what you're practicing?"

Rocky glanced back at his room — maybe he expected to see the moggy escaping. "Nah, that's something new I'm working on."

Keep working, brother. "Sounds... err... experimental." Good catch. "Thanks for the offer, Warrington... Rocky," he continued, "but I'm too knackered to do any nightclubbing."

Rocky nodded. "Yeah, I can see that. You look like shit."

"It has been said." He headed for his room.

32

"Where the hell have you been?" Superintendent Baxter, clearly his usual happy self, was standing between the two desks in the small office as if he'd been waiting to pounce, but he hadn't, he'd been going through the papers to see if they were up to anything he should know about.

Shaun smiled at him. "Well, sir, this morning I received a very nice bravery award from the chief constable's ass-kisser." He patted his pockets. "Which I seem to have lost."

Danny pointed at his top pocket. "It's in there," he said, "with the mayo."

Shaun pulled a face and left the gong where it was. "And this afternoon we *proceeded*, as per your orders, to interview one Tweetie Pie." He smiled at the scowling super. "Who had been apprehended in possession of a shooter, to wit that being a Mini Uzi."

Superintendent Baxter stood with hands on hips and listened to the drivel that was supposed to be a report.

"After interrogating the suspect, aka Tweetie Pie," Shaun continued, "we *proceeded* to a club called Oscar's Pussy Club, where we— "

"Shut up, O'Conner. Just shut that Irish yapping!"

Shaun feigned a shocked expression and looked at Danny, who had suddenly discovered something of gripping interest in the cold-case notes he'd found on his desk.

"I'll have a full report, in writing," Baxter said as he headed for the door. "In one hour." He slammed the door behind him.

"That went well," Shaun said and tore open a sachet of Nescafe, tapped it into a mug with a 'World's Best Dad' logo, and poured in slightly warm water from the glass jug. No coffee stations here, just Nescafe and nuked milk in little foil cartons.

"Were you in the same bollocking as me?" Danny said, dumping the old notes into the trash.

"Well, we're both still employed," he said, tasting the coffee appreciatively and pointing at the jug. Danny nodded. "And hey, I'm still a sergeant."

"Yeah, and after only twenty years. Aren't you doing well?"

"Can I help it if my betters don't like me?" Shaun handed him a mug of something like coffee.

"You're not going to write the report, are you?"

Shaun shrugged. "Nah, he won't read it anyway."

"There you go."

Shaun looked puzzled. "What?"

"Teasing the pissed-off rattler, that's what?"

"He loves me, really." Shaun poured a slug of whiskey into his coffee and raised the hipflask, but Danny waved it away. Please yourself.

"So, what about this Junior Brown?" Danny asked, getting off the subject of their inevitable degrading dismissal from the boys in blue, the ultimate downward spiral to a booze-rotted brain and a lonely death in some homeless shelter after years living rough on the streets. He pulled himself out of that timeline before thinking it made it so.

"He's a gun dealer," Shaun said, tasting the coffee and adding another shot to sweeten it. "Sell anything to anybody. He'll sell your baby sister a Kalashnikov if she saves her lunch money."

"Charming."

"Not a word I would use to describe this piece of shit."

"But it's still just the word of a bunch of trannies," Danny said, waving away the flask again.

"Doesn't matter, I'm not after him on this trip," Shaun said.

"No, we both know who you're after, and we also know if Baxter finds out, he'll bounce us back to woodentops so fast we'll leave skid marks."

"You should stay out of this one. Truly."

"Yeah, right. And how does that work exactly?" Danny shrugged, "We're partners, right? Like Kurt Russell said, you go, we go."

"Those movies will rot your brain, you know that?"

"Not possible, man."

Shaun stood up, put the World's Best Dad mug back on the shelf, and started for the door. "Okay, your funeral." He stopped, turned round, and raised a finger. "Mayfair."

"Yeah," Danny said, "nice place to live, if you've got a few million."

Shaun came back to Danny's desk. "Those trannies said Patrick lives in Mayfair." He tapped the computer monitor. "Do computer things, and see if we have anything on a gun runner in Mayfair."

"Oh, right," Danny said, waking up the computer. "The place is a den of thieves and gun runners." He began to search the police database, grunting from time to time, and then stopped and shrugged. "Nope, the only vague connection is there's a guy got fined for having an unlicensed gun, but it was just a pocket pistol." He tapped the monitor with his finger, as if that would make everything clear. "Irish guy, apparently."

Shaun frowned. "What was his name?" Like it would be Patrick O'Conner.

"Err... Michael Collins." Danny shrugged. Not O'Conner, then.

"Ahh..." Shaun said, crouching beside the desk.

"What?" Danny asked.

"Your history's not too hot, is it?"

"I know about Henry the Eighth," Danny said. "Well, at least the stuff in the movies."

Shaun gave him a long sad look. "Michael Collins was a famous Irish revolutionary leader killed in the civil war."

"So you think—"

"I know," Shaun said. "That's just the sort of flash play Patrick would pull. Thinking he was giving the authorities the finger."

"Let's go get him, then?" Danny said, starting to get up.

"Now who's running into the burning building? No, not yet. I'm not going to tip my hand and let the bastard get away, not when I'm this close."

"Okay," Danny said. "Then we need to get enough proof to bury him."

Shaun got off the desk and headed for the door.

"Junior Brown?" Danny said, saving his search and logging out of the system.

Shaun nodded and opened the door a crack to check if Baxter was lurking. The hallway was clear, and he walked quickly and quietly to the stairs, followed by Danny on exaggerated tiptoe.

33

It was a classic London autumn, with the heavens having opened up and pretty much soaked any poor sod not indoors, which was good news for Oscar's Pussy Club because passers-by had mistaken it for an oasis and were now trapped by the torrential rain. Simple choice really, tranny bar or soaked to the skin. Well, okay, no choice at all. Pink drinks in long glasses and sticky carpet it is.

Not that the crowds intimidated Rocky and the Pebbles, they lived to perform... well, actually, they'd lived to perform for about four weeks, but who's counting? The drummer, the bass guitarist, and the keyboard player were playing more or less in tune with the singer, Shelly, a medical student in her final year. Rocky... well, he was doing his own thing; he just didn't know it. At last they got to the big finish, much to the relief of pretty well everyone in the club. Rocky took a bow to the person applauding and headed for the bar.

"Cool," he said as the others joined him. "We rocked the place."

They looked at him much the same way as they would an idiot child, but let him have his moment. God knew there wouldn't be any others. They ordered various drinks, and all got the same pink thing in long glasses. Same price as a bottle of wine, so a snip.

Rocky leaned on the bar and closed his eyes to let the adrenalin buzz fade. Man, this is the life. He opened them again to tell them exactly that, but he was now just Rocky — no Pebbles. Screw them, then, he'd be famous on his own.

It was too bright at the bar, and pretty soon crowds would be mobbing him for his autograph, so he took his pink drink and crossed the sticky carpet to an alcove table. It was occupied.

"Mind if I sit here for a mo?" he asked the occupier. "Was supposed to do another session, but the singer's taken ill. You know how it is with women's problems."

"Tell me about it," Tweetie Pie said, leaning on her elbows and snivelling.

"Hey," Rocky said, sliding onto the bench seat opposite the poor boy. "Man trouble?"

"If only," Tweetie said, blowing into the same handkerchief he'd blown into when that scary Irish policeman was talking to Curly Sue.

"Yeah," Rocky said, looking out at the clientele that was exiting the building as fast as they could. Clearly the rain had stopped.

"Why'd they have to go and kill Talcum?" Tweetie asked his handkerchief.

Rocky frowned. "Who killed what?" Might as well talk, there'd be no more playing tonight, which was a pity — for him, not the audience.

"Not what," Tweetie said, "who."

No, Rocky didn't get that. "Who what?" he tried.

"Talcum is a... was a boy. Oh, such a sweet, lovely boy." Tweetie blubbered again. It was a bit... well, messy and bordering on gross.

"Oh," Rocky said, wondering if he could just leave.

Tweetie reached over and took his arm. "He was my friend, did you know that?"

Rocky shook his head; he didn't know that.

"Yes, such a sweet—"

"Lovely boy?" Rocky suggested.

"Yes," Tweetie said, looking up with red-rimmed eyes. "Then you did know him?"

"I knew of him," Rocky said. As of two minutes ago, though it seemed longer.

"They killed him," Tweetie said, the sobs having subsided to a steady sniffle.

"Yes, I heard about that," Rocky said, looking around for an exit strategy, but none presented itself.

"Oh, I could tell you were sensitive, as soon as you sat down."

Oh, great. What the hell, though, he hadn't been paid yet. "So, Mr...?"

Tweetie frowned and looked over his shoulder at the burgundy flock wallpaper, looked back, and gave a little start. "Oh, you mean me." He shuddered for any number of reasons. "I'm not a Mr." He smiled — it was pretty grim. "I'm Tweetie Pie, but you can call me Tweetie."

Seemed sensible, that being his name. "So, okay, Mr Tweetie—"

"No," Tweetie said. "No Mr, just Tweetie. You know, like sweetie?"

Rocky wanted to run away screaming. "Okay then, Tweetie." He would have smiled, but he was already in it up to his neck. "How did... the lovely boy get killed?"

"Talcum," Tweetie corrected. "His name was Talcum, to his friends." There was that pathetic smile again. "And I think he would've liked you, so you can call him that too."

Okay, Rocky was back in the starting blocks again after three false starts. "So, how did Talcum get killed?" Though by now, he really didn't care.

"The Jamaicans shot him."

Okay, that got his attention. "Why?"

Tweetie shrugged, and the strap of his Chinese halter dress caught in his long blonde wig, pulling it to one side. Rocky looked out into the bar, not really to enjoy the sight of truckers with beer-guts in tight leather skirts, but anything was better than the view across the table.

"I keep asking myself that question you just asked myself," Tweetie said.

Rocky looked back, he couldn't help himself, but Tweetie had fixed the fashion faux pas and was looking as lovely as... well, a New Orleans hooker caught in arc lights. He looked away, but it was too late, the image was etched onto his retina like the circle of the sun.

Tweetie took a long drink of the awful pink stuff, illustrating that you can get used to anything, given time. He took a bottle out of an oversized white leather handbag and poured a long shot into his glass. "Medicinal," he said and held up the bottle to Rocky.

He was tempted, but the thought of getting drunk in this place killed the temptation pretty quick. Could you imagine waking up in the morning to find—

"I tell you what I fink," Tweetie said, leaning forward and looking both ways at the walls of the booth. "I think it was for those rifles." He touched the side of his nose... well, that was the intended target, but he put his finger in his eye. "Ow! Ooh! Shit!" Which pretty much covered it.

"Rifles?" Rocky said, mirroring Tweetie's lean forward. "What rifles?"

Tweetie's hand moved towards his nose, but he noticed it and dropped it while he still had one eye working. "They fink I'm fick," he said with the beginnings of a first-class slur.

God knows why anyone would think that. Rocky feigned shock. "No way," he said, shaking his head to add emphasis. "You point them out, and I'll give them a good kicking. Least I can do for my friend." And may God forgive the heinous lie.

Tweetie stared at him for several seconds and then began to cry.

"What?" Rocky said, showing genuine concern he didn't feel.

Tweetie took out the well-used handkerchief, found a dry spot, and blew his nose noisily. "No one has ever been so nice to me," he said, adding a second blow. "Not since my dear mother went away."

"Oh, I'm sorry to hear that," Rocky said, and just for once, he meant it.

Tweetie shook his head, and the wig moved independently. "No, she's not... you know?"

Rocky didn't know.

"She's gone to live in Spain," Tweetie said with a sigh. "Oh, she left me a note, so's I'd know she's all right." He nodded. "That's my mom, always finking of me and knowing how I'd worry if I didn't know what I know now that I know what she wanted me to know..." He lost his thread, but forty-proof gin, even watered down in cranberry and red wine, is good at that. "Where was I?" he asked with a quick shake to clear his head, and failing.

"You were telling me people think you're fick... thick," Rocky prompted.

"Oh, yeah." He looked around again. Same view. "They fink I fink the whole fing was about the drugs." His finger made the journey to his nose, very, very slowly, and hey, mission accomplished. The nose was touched. "But," he said with a midnight slur. "I seen the two big rifle boxes Curly Sue put in the van." He nodded to confirm he'd seen them.

"Rifles?" Rocky said. "How do you know they were rifles?"

Tweetie stared at him, but it was questionable as to whether or not he saw him. Eventually he gave a little start and did the looking around thing again. "Eashy," he said, taking his time to get the word formed. "They was in green cases what looked like rifle cases."

Rocky frowned, surprised. "You know what a rifle case looks like?" That was pretty damned amazing.

He thought about it for a moment. "I did when Curly Sue opened one when she fort I wasn't looking. So, yeah. Flash buggers, like you see in the movies, with telescopes and silencers and stuff."

Mystery solved.

Rocky knew exactly what sort of rifles they were — the dubious benefit of having a brother in the marines. "What the hell does Curly Sue want with rifles?"

Tweetie shrugged and took a moment to add more gin to the gin in his glass. He took a long drink and clearly felt better, or at least felt less. "We was supposed to be just nicking the drugs, see?"

Rocky didn't see, but also didn't care.

"But I fink Curly Sue was really after the rifles. She loves guns, you see, on account of her being in the army once."

Rocky's world wobbled a little, and he had to close his eyes to regain equilibrium. "Curly Sue was in the army?" No way. He looked along the bar on which Curly Sue was leaning and talking to a middle-aged man with close-cropped, dyed black hair, an orange tan, and an upper torso that told of many hours in the gym, focused solely on arms and chest. He looked like an orange tent peg, in a lacy blouse with a pussy-cat bow and skin-tight black patent leather trousers cut off just below the calf. He leant forward over the bar to listen closely to something Curly Sue was saying, and the leather stretched across his ass. Rocky snatched his head round so quickly he risked a dislocation.

The movement caught Curly Sue's eye, and she touched the face of the tent peg, careful not to smudge the carefully applied layers of makeup, and came swishing over.

"You still here?" she asked, arriving at the table in a cloud of Channel No 5.

"Another session," Rocky said, trying to smile and failing.

Curly Sue looked around. "Where's the rest of the band?"

"Taken sick," Rocky said.

"Not surprised, that bloody awful din was giving me one of my heads."

Not polite.

"I thought it was good," Rocky said, trying to talk it up.

"Yeah, you would," Curly said. "Now bugger off, you're frightening the customers."

Which was rich.

Rocky shifted uncomfortably, and not only because the plastic seat made his ass sweaty. "There hasn't been... err... any payment yet."

Curly stepped a little closer, excluding the last of the breathable oxygen. Rocky could see the sweat patches under the arms of the stripy French jumper and understood the reason for the hose-down with the perfume.

"I haven't got much change," Curly said. "How much money you got on you?"

Rocky fished out his wallet, opened it, and counted the notes. "About forty-five."

"Okay," Curly said, "that won't cover the losses from the customers you scared off, but it'll do." He put out his hand.

Rocky was totally confused. "Aren't you supposed to pay us?"

Curly reached down and took the notes out of the open wallet. "In your dreams," she said and walked off with his cash.

Rocky glanced at his wallet and at Curly Sue departing with his money and started to stand, but Tweetie leaned over and took his arm.

"Are you a nutter or somefink?" he said and pointed at Big Betty watching from the bar. "She hasn't been fed today, and you wouldn't even be a taster."

Rocky sat down and sighed. Well, the first and only Rocky and the Pebbles gig had gone down just great. And he hadn't got any cash for the taxi home. The day was as bad it could get.

"Hello, musical boy," a sultry deep voice said, as a huge, latex-clad biker sat down beside him, blocking his exit. "Do you take a dare?"

34

"How come I get to drive, again?" Danny said, as they made their way through the traffic along the A4 towards Kensington.

"Perks of the superior rank," Shaun said.

"Yeah, right, by one bloody week."

"That's all it takes," Shaun said, glancing at him. "Now give us a salute."

Danny gave him the finger instead.

Shaun smiled, opened the glove box, and chocolate wrappers, squashed drink cartons, and various junk tumbled into the footwell. He did the sensible thing and closed the glove box. He looked over to see Danny's disapproving look. "What?" he asked and looked down at the junk. "Rather this than yours. It's like nobody has ever used it."

"Tidy car, tidy mind," Danny said sagely.

"Bollocks, you don't have to be prissy to be sharp. Look at me."

Danny did exactly that, and what he saw was an expensive suit that looked like it had been carefully stored in a shopping bag, a tie that had never come close to his top button and a shirt that didn't need ironing — unless he wanted to get rid of the creases.

"What?" Shaun said, checking himself out and finding nothing amiss.

"If I've got to tell you..." Danny said in a superior tone.

"Ah, you look like a spiv," Shaun said, looking at his immaculate partner.

"I think you'll find the correct description is—"

"Get off here," Shaun said, pointing at the slip road ten feet ahead.

Danny chopped across the inside lane and made it onto the slip road with a good couple of inches to spare. He ignored the blaring horns behind them, followed Shaun's pointing finger, and took the first left. A few minutes later they turned right into a square with a railed garden in the middle. Shaun leaned forward for a better look and raised his hand for Danny to pull over.

"This it?" Danny said, also leaning forward and looking up at the four-storey houses. "Nice neighbourhood. These have to cost a bundle."

"What's a couple of mill to a scum-bag like Brown?" Shaun said, settling back for a bit of a rest.

Danny killed the engine and leaned back in the seat, slipping into an all-too-familiar routine. Waiting, surveillance, more waiting. It was what coppers did. Except this time they didn't get a chance to demonstrate the lost art of patience, but they did get to demonstrate the art of not paying attention. The car's back doors opened, and two men got in before they even realised what was happening.

Sad, truly sad.

"Ah-ah!" one of the men said as Shaun and Danny turned and reached into their jackets. "Leave the hardware where it is."

"Yanks!" Shaun pointed out unnecessarily.

"See, Greg, that's what I like about these Brit cops, they're so sharp."

"You know we're cops, then?" Shaun said. "Then you won't be doing any shooting."

"Why not?" said the man with the attitude.

"Call it our Special Arrangement," Shaun said without taking his eyes off the speaker. "You don't kill us, and we don't kill you."

"That'd be a neat trick," Rodriguez said with contempt.

Danny flashed them a smile, raised his hand slowly, and pointed towards the gap between the seats. They looked down and were rewarded with a fine view of Shaun's gun.

"That there's a Glock G36 45 automatic," Shaun said, reciting the advert to the stunned Americans. "Bit heavy, true, but worth it for the sheer bloody stopping power."

The Americans looked at the gun, at each other, and slowly back at Shaun, and for an eternal three seconds, nobody knew if he was crazy enough to shoot them. Not even Shaun. Finally he shrugged and put the gun back into its belt holster. The Americans relaxed, a little.

He nodded at Danny. "That's Danny Fouillade, and I'm—"

"Do we look like people who give a shit?" the man said.

"You're CIA, right?" Shaun said. "So that would make you Agent Black and Greg here Agent Green."

"I'm Special Agent Walker—"

"Hey, I thought you were a Texas Ranger!" Shaun said with mock excitement. "Can I call you Chuck?" Sure enough, he was getting right up Special Agent Walker's nose.

Tragic.

"And this is Special Agent Greg Rodriguez," Special Agent Walker said, ignoring the interruption.

Shaun flashed a hello smile for a microsecond. "I guess you want to talk?" Nod received. "Okay, let's go for a walk in the park. It's a lovely day."

It was cold, and it was raining. It was most certainly not a lovely day.

Danny started the car and moved off slowly, to avoid attracting the attention of the two black guys leaning on the railings across the gardens. They were Jamaicans, so were unlikely to be standing out in the rain for their health. Junior's boys, but no point telling everybody.

A few minutes later, Danny pulled into a space at Holland Park, turned off the engine, and opened the door, and he and the Americans followed Shaun through the drizzle down the deserted path into the park.

"So," Shaun said, "what's the mighty CIA want with a small-time gun dealer like Junior, Chuck?"

"Will you quit that Chuck shit?" Special Agent Walker said. "You can call me Special Agent Walker."

Shaun shrugged. "Then you can call me Detective Sergeant Shaun O'Conner Serious Organised Crime Agency Really Nasty Criminal Division."

Yes, truly getting up Walker's nose.

Walker glared at him for a full five seconds, then sighed and looked around as if he expected anyone to care what this bunch of suits was doing. "Okay, okay. Name's Steve Walker."

Shaun put out his hand. "Nice to meet you, Steve." The hell it was. "Now, Steve, why are you watching Junior Brown?"

"Who says we were?" Rodriguez said.

Shaun put his hand to his chin and looked at Danny. "What do you think, Danny? Coincidence?"

"Could be," Danny answered. "I once fell over twice on the same day and hadn't been drinking."

"Okay," Shaun said in a tone that said the Special Arrangement was over. "Now what, exactly, are you doing poking around on our patch without even the courtesy of a phone call?"

Walker took the tiniest step back, but it was enough. "It was decided, way up the chain of command, that we keep this op covert."

"Not very friendly."

"We don't need another fuckup," Agent Walker said, wiping the drizzle off his face with the back of his hand.

"Yeah, I can see how you might think you've had enough of those," Danny said, but kept an innocent expression.

Walker's hand froze mid-way from his face, and he glared at him. They could see he was trying to work out if it was an intentional dig. He couldn't, but it was.

"Don't take this personally, but this whole country is a fuckup, your air force and army are a fuckup, your security people are a fuckup," he squinted at them, "and your police are the mother and father of all fuckups."

There was no way anybody could take that personally.

Shaun shrugged, and Special Agent Rodriguez stared at him with a puzzled expression. Then looked at Danny with an air of expectancy. Whatever he was expecting, he didn't get.

Danny shrugged too. "Hey, we agree with you, man."

That threw them.

"Why not?" Shaun said. "I'm Irish, and Danny here is French-Algerian, okay, his folks are." He shrugged. "So why should we give a shit?"

Walker looked a little crestfallen now that his plan to unsettle the Brits had fallen on stony ground.

Shaun helped him out. "So your nice people have sent you over here to help out the poor fuckup Brits?" He shook his head slowly. "I don't think so."

Walker wiped the drizzle off his face again. "Can we get out of this shit? Jeez, this country is—"

"A fuckup?" Shaun smiled a totally insincere smile and pointed along the path to the mobile café.

A few minutes later, Walker put down the coffee, pulled a face like he'd been poisoned, and pushed it away.

"The way I see it," Shaun said and sipped his hot coffee as if it were nectar. "We either work together on whatever it is you're after Junior for, or..."

Walker squinted at him. "Or what?"

"Or me and Danny here stamp all over your surveillance and scare every bugger off."

"We could just shoot you," Rodriguez said.

"You tried that already," Danny said. "How'd that work out for you?"

"There's no way we're going to share intelligence with you—"

"Fuckups?" Shaun suggested.

Walker exercised a little common sense. "You're not secret service, you're just cops. There's no way I'd get authorisation to disclose intelligence to—"

"Fuckups?" Shaun suggested again and sipped more coffee.

"No! Jesus, will you stop doing that!"

Shaun gave up baiting the poor man, put down his coffee, and leaned across the table. "Look, this is really simple. You're after Junior for something, and so are we. Way I see it, this is our turf, so we get first dibs."

Walker's expression showed he understood that only too well. "What's he to you?"

Shaun shrugged. "Means to an end."

Walker frowned and chewed his lip — agent thinking here, nothing to see.

"So," Shaun continued, "we should work together and pool our resources." He raised his hand before Walker could speak. "No need for anybody else to know about it. It would be our little secret. And you'd get the brownie points."

Walker watched Shaun closely, continuing the agent-thinking pose.

"Man's got a point," Rodriguez said. "It would be easier if we had some on-the-ground helpers."

"Partners," Danny pointed out.

"Partners," Rodriguez corrected.

The decision was causing Walker some mental pain, so Shaun took a flyer. "It's no big deal. We've already got a pretty good idea what's going on."

Walker's eyebrows rose, and he threw Rodriguez a quick look.

"We know Junior has imported some exotic rifles, among other things. So I guess you boys are trying to find out who his customer is."

If that was a wild throw, it came up double six.

Walker's jaw dropped — not much, but it might as well have been cartoon-style.

Shaun nodded to confirm he knew all about it and drummed his fingers on the table, while Walker's mind went into overdrive.

Eventually Walker sighed and raised his hand as Rodriguez started to speak words of caution. "What the hell, they know the whole deal anyway. And like you said, we could use some local help... partners." He watched Rodriguez and got a slight nod. "Okay. You know there's a big pow-wow going on between our president, and your prime minister, and the German chancellor?"

Shaun shrugged, sure he'd heard something on the news, but couldn't really be arsed, it being politics.

Walker watched him for a few seconds before speaking. "Doesn't it strike you a bit strange this Jamaican importing top-notch rifles, right when they're about to sign an agreement to share... well, just about everything?"

Shaun and Danny exchanged glances. "Could be just a coincidence," Danny said, without much conviction.

Shaun was just thinking, what the hell does Patrick want with that kind of firepower, except he already knew the answer. Patrick used to be the armourer for the Boys, and it looked like he was still in that line of business. Question was—

"Who's the customer?" Walker said. "That's what we need to find out, if only to eliminate this as a threat."

"And if it is?" Shaun said.

Walker sipped his coffee and pulled a face. "If it is an assassination plot, then we either eliminate them or call off the signing."

"You can do that?" Danny asked, impressed.

"No," Walker said, raining on his parade. "But we sure as hell know a man who can."

"But it can't just be you two?" Danny said. "Not something this big."

Walker shook his head. "There are others." He shrugged to show he didn't know who or how many.

"Where are the rifles now?" Shaun said, knowing exactly where.

Walker looked at him steadily. He didn't know. But even if he did, he wouldn't be telling fuckup Brit cops.

"So, how are you planning to handle it?" Shaun asked.

"Sooner or later Junior is going to make contact with the buyers, and when he does—" Walker shrugged. "We'll take them and their rifles."

Danny sniffed. "Yeah, from their cold, dead fingers."

Walker nodded. "If he's planning to assassinate the president, then he doesn't walk away from this."

"Agreed," Shaun said. "You keep up your surveillance on Junior, and we'll sniff around."

Walker looked worried. "No leaks."

"No way. We tagged Junior on a drug deal, so we'll use that to ask around and find out who he's been talking to." Now that was a great way to start a new international relationship — lying.

They left the café and walked back to the car. Shaun pointed over his shoulder with his thumb at the rain-soaked café. "This is a good place to meet up." He took a card out of his pocket and gave it to Walker. "This is me. Call if you see anything starting to go down." He squinted. "You forget, and I'll blow the whistle, and every security man in the country will be looking for the two Yanks stamping all over our playpen. You got that?"

They got it. Walker took out a card, wrote his cell number on the back, and handed it to Shaun. "Same here, man."

A few minutes later, they dropped the CIA men off round the corner from Junior's place and headed back down the A4 to the office.

Agents Walker and Rodriguez watched the Brits' car turn onto the main road in the cold rain. "They don't know," Rodriguez said, and Walker shook his head.

"Fuckups," he said and spat. "Like their shitty weather." He turned up the collar of his thin coat and trudged off towards their hire car.

Danny glanced at Shaun several times, until it felt like an itch he couldn't scratch.

"What?" Shaun said.

"You know as well as I do that Junior isn't in that league."

Yes, he did. "I don't get you."

"Oh, come on," Danny said. "You know Junior is small time, he just supplies drugs to dealers and scum. Sniper rifles?" He shook his head. "I don't think so. I think the trannies have started a rumour with a life of its own."

"Okay," Shaun said. "What I think is that Junior got an offer he couldn't refuse. To use his sources in the US to get his hands on the rifles. They're not the kind of thing you can buy on eBay. He was just the personal shopper. The rifles have moved on now."

"Then why did Patrick get the trannies to off Junior's delivery boys?"

"Dunno, but my guess is he had to make sure it looked like a drug buy. We bought it, didn't we?"

Danny nodded. "Still, seems a bit excessive."

"It does," Shaun said. "Let's go and ask Junior."

The car twitched, and Danny steadied it. "What? You can't be serious? We just agreed with Bonnie and Clyde back there that we'd cooperate."

"You don't think for one second they intend to keep their part of the deal, do you?"

"Well, no, of course not. Okay, so how are you going to ask Junior?" He nodded back over his shoulder. "The goons outside his place aren't going to let us in without a warrant."

"According to his file, he's got some storage down on the docks," Shaun said. "I'm going down there and ring the bell."

"Storage?" Danny said. "Cool. Maybe the rifles are still there." Not likely. "We can wrap this up in time for supper." Even less likely.

Shaun shook his head.

"What?" Danny said, getting that old sinking feeling.

Shaun looked at him steadily. "Patrick's got the rifles."

35

"So how did you get away from Spanky the Hell's Angel?" Harry asked, barely able to suppress the laughter shaking his shoulders.

"Wasn't easy, I can tell you," Rocky said with a long sigh. "Told him I needed to piss, then climbed out of the bog window." He pointed at the greasy drag lines on his shirt. "Ruined my best gig shirt."

"Won't be needing it now, though," Frank said, looking up from the big jigsaw on the breakfast table.

"Didn't go too well, then?" Harry asked, feeling a lot calmer now the laughter had subsided.

"Nah," Rocky said, his shoulders sagging. "The rest of the band legged it in the intermission."

Harry lost it and laughed both the new and the stored laughter. He clapped his kid brother on the shoulder. "The hell with it... Rocky. That rock 'n' roll lifestyle is all sex, drugs, and parties. You wouldn't like it."

"I bloody would."

"Not something you have to worry about now, is it?" Frank said, fitting a piece into the jigsaw and thumping it with the edge of his hand.

Rocky tutted and began to slope off to his room for a good, well-earned sulk, but stopped and turned round. "Hey," he said to Harry, "something to interest you, though."

"Yeah?" Harry said, picking up the wrinkled newspaper with its loud headlines telling everyone how the economy was going to boom once the tripartite accord was in place. "What's that, then?" As if he actually cared.

"Tweetie Pie told me—"

"Tweetie Pie?" Harry and Frank said together.

"Yeah, Tweetie Pie told me his friend had been killed in a drug deal."

"Serves him bloody right," Frank said. "That stuff is poisoning our youth."

Harry glanced at him to see if he was kidding. Apparently he wasn't, which was weird, since he drank enough whisky to keep the Scottish economy going. He brought his attention back to Rocky for a moment before returning to the newspaper. "So what's that got to do with anything?"

Rocky sniffed. "Turns out it wasn't just drugs. They had sniper rifles in cases, with scopes and suppressors, the works."

As predicted, that got Harry's interest.

"What in God's name does a bunch of transvestites want with sniper rifles?"

"Dunno, just thought you'd be interested, that's all," Rocky said, resuming his slope off for the sulk over his lost stardom.

Harry watched him go and stood up, walked to the window, and looked out without seeing the Thames rolling by, as it does. It could be a coincidence, Lupus coming to town with his bioweapon and now these sniper rifles turning up. Yes, it could have been a coincidence, of course, but not in this universe. True. Experience had taught him there is no such thing as coincidence — when bad things could get worse, they usually did. But the significance of the rifles escaped him. If Lupus had the bioweapon, and he certainly did, then why would he want the guns?

He walked back and forth in front of the window, with Frank watching him quietly — which in itself was a novelty.

Eventually, he couldn't help himself. "Something on your mind, son?"

Harry stopped pacing and looked at Frank, but it took several seconds for him to register. Should he tell him? After all, it was an official secret, life in prison, off with his goolies, etc. "There's a terrorist coming to Britain — if he isn't here already."

Frank nodded, as if he knew that already. "Is that who you think the rifles are for?"

"No, this terrorist, Lupus, has something far worse than rifles." He closed his eyes, as if that might make it easier. "He has an ethnobomb."

"Oh," Frank said and was silent for a moment. "So what's that, then?"

"A biological weapon that only targets certain genetic types... ethnic types."

"Ah, right," Frank said. "That'll be us European types, then?" Proving that just because he was old, didn't make him slow. "Then why would he need rifles?" There you go.

"And that, Gramps, is the sixty-four thousand dollar question."

"Maybe there's another terrorist in town."

Harry thought about it for a moment. "I don't think so. I think Lupus and the guns are connected. I just don't know how."

"Why don't you go and ask this Treacle Pie bloke?"

"Tweetie Pie," Harry corrected absently. "If they're mixed up in it like Warrington says, then they're not about to tell me."

Frank gave up on the jigsaw and lost interest in the destruction of humanity in favour of the search for the TV remote.

Harry looked at the scissors on the table next to the jigsaw. No, don't be nuts.

"What?" Frank said, catching the look. "Oh, those. They're for the pieces that don't fit. It's a crap picture."

Harry stepped up and looked at the jigsaw picture of a sailboat on a stormy sea, almost complete, but do clouds have masts?

Frank saw the look coming his way and changed the subject. "These trannies, they're businessmen, right? Weird businessmen, but still businessmen who run a club?"

"Yes, so what?" Harry said, giving up on the kaleidoscope that was the jigsaw. "I don't think they'll take kindly to me offering them money for their terrorist secrets."

"They'll keep records," Frank said, finding the sports channel.

"Yeah, but they'll be locked away in a safe or something. And the marines don't do safe cracking, that's for the spooks."

Frank shrugged. "True, but Bob the Burglar cracks safes, or he's lying about his name."

"Bob the what?" Harry asked.

Frank looked back from the TV. "Burglar. Harvey's new client. Puccini the mutt saved from a watery grave?" He smiled to himself. "Laura's case. Might be worth you debriefing her."

Harry gave him a double take. Did he mean what he thought he meant? Of course the old bugger did. But hey, she was cute, and he wondered why he'd let the come-hither look sail by — must be all that being blown up and shot.

"There's a sight to make your eyes sore," Laura said as Harry limped into Harvey's office the next morning.

"I think the expression is for sore eyes," Harry said, flopping down into one of the armchairs opposite her desk.

"I'm a lawyer, remember? I don't make linguistic errors." She smiled, and it lit up her face.

Harry forgave her and looked at the way she filled out her white blouse. Yeah, cute.

Laura watched him checking her out without a flicker of expression. "Finished?" she said after a few seconds.

Harry jumped like a schoolboy caught looking out of the window. "Hadn't noticed how... cute you are before," he lied with a smile.

"And that's supposed to be a compliment, is it?" Laura said, tilting her head to one side.

"No, yes, I mean," Harry said eruditely.

"I know exactly what you mean," Laura said. "Men. Only one thing on your mind." Which, though not entirely true all the time, was right on the money at that moment.

"I'm looking for Bob the Burglar," Harry said quickly.

"Aren't we all," Laura said stiffly.

Harry's brow creased in a question. "Why, is he still missing?"

Laura nodded. "Yes, he's flown. Taken off. On the lam."

Harry guessed Bob was still missing, which justified his expensive education. "So the police haven't found him?" Scratch the previous justification.

She watched him for several seconds, waiting for him to join the dots. "He... has... run... away," she said, leaning forward to emphasise her words.

Harry went back to checking her out, now the view had changed. She let out her breath in a long, tired sigh and sat upright — just a little slower than she could have.

"Wasn't he supposed to be in court?"

Laura nodded. "We managed to get the court date moved."

"That couldn't have been easy," Harry said, smiling again. "Well done." No chance, mate, cheesy compliments will get—

"Thank you," Laura said with a smile. "Still, if he doesn't get back by the end of the month, they'll hunt him down like a rabid dog."

Bit colourful, but Harry got the gist. "Okay," he said, heaving himself up stiffly out of the low chair. "I'll find him."

"Ah," Laura said, "I'll believe that when I see it."

Harry half turned. "Wager?"

She squinted at him for a moment, then put out her hand. "Done." She shook Harry's hand. "What's the bet?"

Harry pretended to think about it. "Dinner?"

Laura pretended to think about it. "Okay, I suppose."

"Can I borrow his file?"

Laura thought about saying no, best chance of winning the bet, except winning was the last thing she wanted. She opened her desk drawer, pulled out the file, and dropped it on the desk. "Don't lose it."

Harry grinned and picked it up. "I'll use Harvey's office. He's not using it, is he?"

Laura shook her head. "In court. Knock yourself out." She inclined her head again. "But there's nothing of any use in there." Which just about said it all.

Harry sat at Harvey's desk and played with his letter opener as he went through Bob's file. He was puzzled as to why Bob had fled, as the evidence, even to him, was tissue thin. He was a burglar who just happened to have Lady Lucinda's dog on the night she was burgled, but that meant nothing. Yeah, right. He read on, but it was just a history of a burglar with only one conviction, until he got to the last page and thanked Harvey for being such a pedantic documenter. He read an almost verbatim transcript of Bob's visit, including the comments about the motorbike and a note that he was going to the local at nine thirty to meet friends.

Harry put the file back on Laura's desk as he passed and smiled, but all he got back was a frown. Until he'd walked away.

Bob's local was easy to find, it being local, and just up the street from his house. Harry leaned on the bar and took the head off his beer as he watched the four men around the pool table, taking it in turns to lose money to the barman, who seemed to know the pool table's angles and faults — odd that.

The barman put the black away with a flourish, picked up the notes, said thanks, and went back behind the bar. Harry nodded at him, and he strolled over.

"Same again?" he asked, looking at Harry's almost full glass.

"Yeah, and one for yourself," Harry said, taking a long pull on the beer. He waited until the barman put another in front of him, took his money, and kept the change, a whole lot of change. "You know Bob Doyle?"

The barman eyed him suspiciously, picked up a cloth, and began polishing a glass. "Who wants to know?"

Which was a good question, and one Harry wished he'd thought through. He could make something up, long lost friend from — yeah, that's the trouble when all you have is the facts from a crime sheet. Okay, what the hell. "I need somebody to get into a safe for me, and I hear Bob's the man to talk to."

The barman glanced around the bar, presently occupied by the three lads who now had less cash than when they came in, but it's always quiet at ten thirty in the morning. Also odd. "Never heard of him," he said helpfully.

Harry put a fifty on the bar — he'd seen the movies and knew how this worked.

The barman eyed the note for a moment. "That for me?"

Harry nodded and gave him a wink.

The barman took the fifty and put it in his pocket before returning to his polishing.

Harry waited a moment, but nothing happened. "So," he said in an unnecessary whisper, "where do I find Bob?"

The barman shrugged. "Never heard of him."

Harry blinked a few times to try and straighten things out, but that didn't work. "Give me back my fifty," he said through gritted teeth. "Or—"

"This here's Tony," the barman said, waving the towel at a point behind Harry.

Harry turned and looked up... at Tony.

"Tony hurts people," the barman explained. "I think he likes it."

"Hi, Tony," Harry said, slipping off the barstool and stepping back far enough to see all of the giant. "Hurt anybody today?"

Tony should have said, "Day ain't over yet," but that was way too many words, so he just grunted, and Harry took the hint and body swerved round the man-mountain. He passed the three failed pool players as he tried to reach the door without taking his eyes off Tony the Mangler.

"Hey," one of the three said.

Harry was otherwise engaged, mostly in running away. He could've taken the man, course he could, easy, bit of jujitsu, bit of karate maybe. Yeah, easy. But sometimes you just have to be kind, especially to those poor souls who don't know any better. So, okay, this time he'd just let it go. Walk away, as it were. No point—

"You looking for Bob Doyle?" the pool player said.

Harry stopped. "Yes," he said, switching between watching the man who liked to hurt people and the speaker, as he decided between fleeing the scene and engaging the pool player. He took a chance and stepped up to the pool table. "You know where I can find him?"

"Who wants to know?"

"I work for his lawyer," Harry said in a rare moment of brilliance. "I've come to tell him he's a free man."

"Cool," the pool player said and put down the cue. "I'll take you to him. Cost you fifty, though."

Harry sighed. "Does everything cost fifty in this place?" He picked up the pace now that he could see the Mangler had made up his mind and was lurching in his direction. "Let's go, then."

"Money first."

Harry took the man's arm and pulled him out of the bar. "The only way you'll get money off me before I see Bob is if we hang around here and Tony catches me, then you can take it off my broken body."

The pool player clearly understood that and led the way down the busy street, left and then right into a residential area, stopping at a house on the right. "Here we go," the boy said, his hand out. "Fifty, wasn't it?"

Harry looked at the house, then back at the boy. "Hey, I've already been here earlier, and there's nobody home."

"Nah," the boy said, "doesn't know you, see."

Harry took out his wallet and gave the boy his last fifty — as a penalty for his stupidity. Jesus, I hope nobody hears about this, I'll never live it down. He walked up the short driveway to the front door, past the cars that said 'someone home' as big as a billboard. What a bonehead.

Bob opened the door as he approached, a big smile on his face. "I saw you with Trevor, so I guess you're okay."

"I was," Harry said sadly, "but I was richer then."

Bob nodded, though he had no idea what he was talking about. "You look like you could use a drink."

"Not going to cost me fifty, is it?" Harry asked, glancing over his shoulder as if he expected to see a line of panhandlers with their hands out.

Bob chuckled, getting it. "You met Steve in the Nelson, then?"

"Yeah," Harry said, guessing that would be the helpful barman. "And Tony."

"Ah," Bob said, stepping aside for him to enter. "Big lad Tony."

"Apparently he hurts people."

"Not really," Bob said and saw Harry's puzzled look. "They're usually unconscious way before it starts to hurt."

Bob poured them both a tumbler of clear liquid from an unlabelled bottle and handed one to Harry. He took a pull on it and almost burned his throat out.

"Jesus Christ! What the hell is this stuff?"

Bob raised his glass in salute and swallowed half of its contents without even a twitch. "It's like vodka, but I distil it myself from potato and molasses." He licked his lips. "Good, eh?"

Harry nodded as a reflex and held up the glass to see if it had a chemical hazard symbol. It didn't, so he sipped it again, and this time the scorching heat was less, though that might have been because he had no taste buds left. "Smooth," he croaked.

"Yeah," Bob said, taking a seat on the sofa. "What can I do for you?"

"I'm Harry Thorne," Harry said, putting the glass of firewater on the floor beside the armchair he'd collapsed into. For later.

"Like Harvey Thorne?"

"Yeah, he's my dad."

"Cool," Bob said. "I like Harvey." Then he appeared to consider that, but clearly agreed with himself. "Bit... err... you know?"

Oh, Harry knew. "Eccentric? Yeah, that's one word for it."

"He really got a bike?"

Harry nodded. "Yeah, a Kawasaki ZX 10R."

"Bloody hell!" Bob said, with a whistle of admiration. "That'll get you there before you start out."

"So," Harry said, switching back to serious mode, "I'm in need of your particular... talents."

Bob waited and sipped his death juice.

Harry thought about telling him it was a job to catch terrorists and save the world, but decided a lower-key approach would cause less stress. "I need to see what's in the safe in a gay bar."

Bob watched him for a moment to see if he was truly nuts, but decided he wasn't. "Okay," he said.

"Just like that?" Harry said, stunned.

"You're Harvey's boy, right?"

"Yeah, one of them."

Bob shrugged. "There you go, then. Harvey helps me, I help you. Easy." He drained his glass, stood up, and pointed at it.

"No, thanks, I'm still working on the last one."

Bob chuckled. "It's an acquired taste." He poured himself another. "So, when do you want to look in this safe?"

Harry took a breath. "Tonight?" Yeah, like he'd agree to that. There'd be surveillance and planning and—

"Okay," Bob said. "I'll drive."

No, you bloody won't, Harry thought, looking at the bottle of firewater. "Tell you what, let's get a taxi, that way nobody can write down any license numbers."

Bob thought for a microsecond and nodded, and put down the hundred-proof vodka, for which Harry almost thanked him.

36

If Ethan hadn't read the two reports back to back, he probably would have missed the connection, even with his analytical skills, some things need to be in juxtaposition to be seen as connected. He put down the CIA report that had been routinely routed to him as part of the bullshit inter-agency cooperation forced on everyone by the Nine Eleven fiasco, took out three other reports from his desk, and read the one covering the progress on the search for the Silver Fox drone. The spooks in Afghanistan had heard a whisper that the drone had been shipped out of the country to destinations unknown. The pieces clicked together as he looked across the office and out onto the car park, as the questions popped up and were answered.

Why had Lupus used some of his valuable bioweapon to kill those civilians in the village? Well, it caused the navy to send in a Silver Fox sensor drone to pick up any traces of nerve gas or other nasty toxins. And it had disappeared, which got the attention of the top brass, and they sent in the patrol. And that's where Ethan frowned. Why? What was the point if they had the drone? What could killing a marine patrol add to the mix? He got up and crossed to the window, and as he walked, it came to him. A test? Of course, it was a test.

He returned quickly to the desk and flicked through the report on the villagers' deaths. Traces of Sarin had been found in the villagers, but not in the marines, they had died from an unknown and virulent disease. He put down the page. He knew Lupus had used the same biological agent that had killed Lieutenant Commander Jerome Patton and his patrol; it had to be. So, the attack on the village was all about testing the weapon. Lure the marines in and zap.

And the drone? Why had that triggered an alarm in his head? He picked up one of the documents and read the technical details. A UAV weighing no more than twenty pounds, with detachable wings that meant it could be packed into a modified golf bag, an endurance of two hundred and fifty miles, and a control radius of twenty miles. He nodded gently as the numbers added up. It was the ideal delivery system for a bioweapon. The payload was limited to five pounds, but that would be plenty for a biological weapon. He put down the spec and read the CIA report. They had traced the drone to London. He reached for the phone with one hand while scooping up the papers with the other.

An hour later he, Leroy Lee and Sam Ford were in an unmarked staff car heading for the airport.

"Commercial flight, I hope," Ethan said. "London's a hell of a long way to hang in the sky in a bone-shaker C130."

"No worries, boss. First class all the way," Leroy reassured him.

"Yeah, and I'll dance swan lake for the New York ballet," Ethan said with a shake of his head.

Leroy should have just let it go, but that that would have been a first. "Hey, boss, did you pack your tutu?" He grinned. "I think London's got a pretty good ballet troupe."

"I hear they're looking for some numb-nuts marine to guard the officer's latrine — in McMurdo."

Leroy decided to check the Virginia woodland for insurgents and stared out of the car window intently.

Later, Ethan reminded him of his words as they squeezed into economy seats. "First class all the way?"

Leroy shrugged. "Hey, just a latrine guard, here, boss, nothing to do with me."

"Nine hours and change," Sam said with a long sigh as he pulled his baseball cap over his eyes and fell asleep almost instantly, and minutes later the others were asleep too, applying the number one rule for soldiers everywhere: sleep when you can because it could be a long time before the chance comes round again. And a tired soldier pretty soon gets to sleep forever.

37

Mohammed Rahman Ali, known only to his enemies as Lupus, didn't sneak into the country through some ferry port, but flew first class into Heathrow. He was the son of a Saudi prince, and if he couldn't do something in style, then he didn't do it, and that included his brand of freedom fighting. Met at the airport by a functionary from the Saudi embassy, he was fast-tracked through immigration and was in a limo heading for London before most of the geese were off the plane.

"It is a pleasure to see you, my friend," said the immaculately dressed Saudi sitting opposite. "Would you like something?" He opened a cabinet to reveal spirits and wine.

Lupus fixed him with a hard stare, just to be sure the man got the message, and then shook his head. "This place has corrupted you, my friend," he said, using an address that had little meaning to him, few friends had survived the predators that struck without warning, and this man was not one of them. A petty official, and one who had strayed from the path. Allah would see to his education when the last day came.

The man squirmed under the intense gaze and sought to change the subject. It had been a stupid error to show this man alcohol, what had he been thinking? He hoped to live to rectify his mistake. "We shall arrive soon," he said. "Everything is as you requested."

"Good," Lupus said, giving the man a practiced smile. "You have done well."

The man seemed to brighten. "Thank you."

"And the package?"

"It has arrived and is being held by the armourer, as you requested."

Lupus nodded. "Good. And no one else knows of this?"

The man looked surprised. "No, you and I only. Those were your orders, were they not?"

Once again Lupus nodded. "You have done well. You will be rewarded."

The man licked his lips. "I do not seek reward. Only to know that my brother is safe."

"Your brother is safe," Lupus said.

Safe in the hands of Allah, almighty and glorious is He. He sat back and closed his eyes.

38

By the time Harry and Bob arrived at Oscar's, it was already buzzing, latex and rubber just about everywhere, it was like an audition for Village People - the Movie. A few horrors checked them out, but clearly thought they were a couple, which was a sort of good news, bad news result.

When they were finally alone in one of the sought-after booths they'd nipped in as it was vacated by two New York police officers — but only if NYPD wear bright blue cut-off latex shirts and rubber pants, which was possible, though unlikely. The cloying fog of God-knows-what perfume stung their eyes, and Bob tried to wave it away, only to attract the attention of a waiter in a full-length latex priest's cassock, complete with huge silver cross.

"Jesus!" Harry said in a stage whisper. "Cut out the bloody waving, you'll have an audience in a minute."

Bob wrinkled his nose. "Any chance of a drink? This perfume is gagging me."

"No, there isn't a chance of a drink, for Christ's sake. What sort of burglar are you? Are you always pissed up on a job?"

Bob shrugged. "Yeah, mostly. Helps to pass the time." He smiled. "Can get a bit boring otherwise, mostly waiting about."

"Well, wait about sober, right?"

"You're the boss," Bob said, watching an impossibly tall black guy stride past in a dazzling white zoot suit. He shook his head in disbelief. "Man, you couldn't make this up." He glanced at Harry, who was failing to respond, and saw him watching him steadily. "What?"

Harry leaned forward. "The safe, remember?"

"No hurry," Bob said. "Let them get used to us being here first."

Which kinda made sense, so he sat back and watched the sights getting used to him. His favourite so far had to be the peacock latex marine uniform. Man, he knew a couple of guys who would have loved that, even if they wouldn't admit it.

After a few minutes, Bob spoke to him out of the corner of his mouth. "You're having way too much fun."

"Why are you talking like Donald Duck?" Harry said in a normal voice.

"Being secret."

"Well, stop being secret because you look bloody strange, and you're attracting attention.

"Ten four," Bob said with a grin. "That's what special ops say, isn't it?"

"Yeah," Harry said resignedly. "That and code blue, which I think we might be hearing sometime soon."

"Okay," Bob said, clearly satisfied that they'd established communications, and also that they were fully integrated into this mad house. "We can go now."

"About bloody time," Harry said, sliding out of the booth, but stopped, suddenly realising that he was out of his league on this mission.

"Just do what I do," Bob said, seeing his hesitation.

"No way!" Harry hissed as Bob sashayed over to the bar. "I've got a bad leg," he added in desperation and limped after him.

Bob ordered two pink drinks and leaned on the bar, smiling. Happy gay people here, folks, nothing to worry about. He nodded almost imperceptibly at the door marked 'staff only', and Harry guessed it led to an area off limits to everyone except staff. Proving once again that our military training is second to none.

This should be good, he thought as he looked casually around at the door in full view of everyone in the busy room. He turned back to ask Bob how the hell he intended to do it, but he was gone. Harry looked quickly back at the door as it swung gently closed and shook his head in admiration. Timing like that isn't taught, it's just natural. He glanced around casually, but the clientele had eyes only for each other. Oh, and the single white male standing all forlorn and injured at the bar and clearly in need of tender loving care.

Bob arrived in the nick of time to save him from a really hairy guy in leather jodhpurs and waistcoat hanging open over his naked bony chest.

"Sharon," Harry said to the skinny guy, "this is Bob. Bob, this is Sharon. Say hello."

Bob looked from Harry to the jodhpurs-wearing advert for HIV and closed his eyes in dismay. "I leave you for five minutes," he said with a long sigh. "And what do you do? You hit on some unsuspecting sister without any thought for how it might hurt when the truth comes out. You, Trixie Belle, are a tart, you know that?"

Harry was having trouble breathing. "I know that," he said eventually. "But it's one of the things you love about me, right?"

Bob smacked his ass, just to add authenticity to the insanity. Take me now, Lord, nothing can top this weirdness.

"We could do a threesome," HIV guy said. "I'm not picky."

So it could get weirder, then.

"Love to," Harry said, "but we're on duty in an hour, and the sergeant is a real ball-breaker, you know what I mean?"

HIV guy had no idea what he meant, but he sure as hell knew what a sergeant did. He managed cops, and cops are really bad news. He fled.

"Come on, Trixie Belle," Bob said with a chuckle, "let's get the hell out of here before we catch something."

And that wasn't nice, but Harry unconsciously wiped his hands on his jacket as he followed him from the club.

Harry's love life might have taken a change from non-existent to totally bizarre, but Annie was working on a plan to get her mother and father's love life back on track and made her move while sharing the washing up with her mother. A totally selfless desire to see them reunited because she loved them both, she wanted only the best for them, they deserved happiness, their life together was worth one more try. And Margaret living in her apartment was severely cramping her social life. So, a mix of loving daughter and enlightened self-interest, but hey, that works.

"You are joking?" Margaret said, when Annie first broached the subject.

Annie shook her head. "Think about it, Mom, he strayed a little—"

"With a tart!" Margaret said through clenched teeth.

As if straying with, say a debutante, would have been just fine.

Annie pouted for a moment. "He swears it was a prank gone wrong."

"I'd say it went wrong. I found out, that's how it went wrong."

Not calmed down much, then. Annie tried a different tack. "Think about it for one moment—"

"No, thank you," Margaret said, bristling, "I have high blood pressure."

"And it won't get any lower bottling this up. But think about it. Can you honestly see any woman fancying Dad? I ask you."

Margaret glared at her. "What do you mean? Your father was a handsome man, and in many ways, still is."

Ah.

"I suppose," Annie said, sensing the opening. "You fell for him after all."

"Yes," Margaret said, absently checking a pan for washing-up quality. "He was quite the catch."

Annie frowned an exaggerated frown. "How exactly did you find out about Dad and the... tart?"

Margaret put down the pan and paddled the washing-up water with the mop. "Richard Coleman mentioned it at the conference we were attending."

"Mmm... Tricky Dickie," Annie said.

Margaret stopped fiddling with the washing-up water. "And what is that supposed to mean?"

"You tell me," Annie said. "You're the lawyer."

Margaret looked at her for several seconds. "If you are implying that Richard had some ulterior motive for mentioning it to me, then you are—"

"He asked you out, didn't he?"

"Well, yes, but not for several weeks after your father and I—"

"I think," Annie said with a firm nod, "that constitutes motive and opportunity."

Margaret closed her eyes and shook her head in mock despair. "You watch too many American police shows."

But...

Margaret licked her lips in a familiar tell. "But now you mention it, it was a shitty thing to do."

"Shitty little man," Annie said and shook her head knowingly. "You have to say Dick to say Dickie."

"True." Margaret wiped her hands on a towel and walked slowly out of the kitchen.

Annie smiled and followed her, sensing her apartment returning to its rightful owner. "Sounds to me like you were set up so you wouldn't believe Dad, no matter what his reasons—"

"Excuses," Margaret said, but the edge was missing.

"Whatever, but if the shitty little man hadn't mentioned it, maybe you would have heard it from Dad, and then been more inclined to believe his explanation."

Truth is like a landed fish; it's awkward and flaps about until something is done about it.

"It is just possible that I was—"

"Hoodwinked?" Annie suggested. "Set up. Fooled. Tricked. Made—"

"Thank you, you've made your point."

"Have I?" Annie said, hopeful.

"Perhaps I should give Harvey an opportunity to explain."

"Yes," Annie said, smiling, "you should. I'll fix it up." She reached for the phone.

"Whoa!" Margaret said, almost panicking. "Not so fast."

"There's no time like the present," Annie said. "Strike while the iron's hot, I always say."

"No, you don't," Margaret said. "You always say, I'll do it later."

39

Shaun squinted out through the car windscreen, but all he could see was darkness and his reflection looking back. Billie Holiday singing "Summertime" drifted quietly from the radio, and he leaned forward and turned up the volume a little. "How can she make a happy song so gut-wrenchingly sad?" he said, almost to himself.

"Dunno, but can't you find something a little less wrist slashing?" Danny said, shifting his feet among the cans and junk in the footwell. "Why couldn't we have used my nice clean car? Jesus, how can you live like this?"

"Like what?"

"Like a pig, for chrissakes, with crap all over the place, and why do you keep all this shit on the dash." He raked the rubbish with his fingertips. "Burger boxes, coke tins, last week's coffee." He pulled a face as his fingers touched something soggy. "And what the hell is this? No, stop, don't tell me. Some things are best left to die quietly."

Shaun looked up to heaven for guidance, but God was doing his nails. "Here," he said and swept the junk into the footwell to join the rest. On Danny's side.

"Oh, for Christ's sake!" Danny lifted his feet as cold coffee ran into his super-polished shoes and splashed his trousers. "Jesus, man, this is my best suit!"

"Nothing a dab of soda won't get out," Shaun said, leaning down into the footwell and retrieving a soda can. "Yeah, thought I'd left some." He offered it to Danny, but he was too busy swearing under his breath and dabbing at his trouser leg with a white handkerchief.

"Hey," Shaun said, "use that rag to clean the windscreen, we're all steamed up now with all that heavy breathing." He shook the soda can and downed the remains.

Danny's mouth was open as he gave him a long, hard look. His brain looked for somewhere to file the image, but failed and dumped it. "I mention that I hate stakeouts?" he said, wiping the misted windscreen with his handkerchief.

"Every time," Shaun said. "And this isn't a stakeout."

"No? Well, it feels like a stakeout, and it smells like a stakeout, so it's a stakeout."

"Nah, we're just waiting on ol' Mr Junior Brown to show up so we can say hi."

"Our luck, he's gone away for the weekend," Danny grumbled, as he was prone to.

"He'll be here."

"Says who?" Danny said, putting his feet back gingerly into the junk.

"Says me," Shaun said, leaning forward and wiping his patch of windscreen with his hand. "Because here he is."

Danny sat upright and squinted through the smeared windscreen into the darkness and saw headlights flash as a car bounced onto the wharf. He watched it come down onto the quay and pull up in front of Junior's storage unit, which turned out to be a badly converted boathouse. After a few seconds, two heavyset black guys got out of the front of the Range Rover and looked around slowly before one of them opened the back door while the other kept scanning the area for hidden foes.

Junior Brown got out of the car, his full-length leather coat billowing as it was designed to do. It was just so cheesy, Danny almost laughed, but Shaun interrupted his humour.

"Come on," he said, opening his door, "let's go ask him about the guns. Seems like a nice chap."

Danny looked over at him and wondered if they were looking at the same guy. He opened his door and swung his legs out. Sometimes he wondered if Shaun—

The empty coke cans cascaded onto the stone quay and rolled away with a clattering noise that sounded ten times louder than it actually was, but no matter, it did the trick.

Junior ducked back into the Range Rover, and the two bodyguards opened up with Steyr TMP machine pistols, without even waiting to see if it was friend or foe. Every window in Danny's car exploded, and the bodywork thumped with incoming rounds.

"Christ almighty!" Shaun shouted and rolled behind a pile of wooden cable reels. "Get down!" he called to Danny when he saw him crawling on hands and knees away from the car. Shaun stood up and emptied his gun at the two Jamaicans, but at fifty yards, they were right on the edge of the Glock's effective range, and that was a hell of a long way to shoot a handgun, particularly in the dark, but it did the trick. The shooters changed their target from Danny out in the open, to Shaun, now well out in the open, standing under a nice little streetlight erected by the thoughtful council. He got the message as rounds ripped into the wooden reels and dived back down out of sight, took a moment to snap in another magazine, and then stood up again, his legs spread, his left hand supporting his right, and sighted on the shooter on the left, who was marginally nearer. He thought about the wind from the right, the elevation to cover that much distance — and how stupid he was. He fired, switched targets, and fired again. The results were spectacularly underwhelming. The two shooters climbed calmly into the Range Rover and drove away.

So, not like the movies. Shaun swore in disgust and walked back to what was left of the car. "I think I worried them with those last—"

Danny was lying dead still on the ground, his beautifully ironed shirt marking the flow of the dark red blood. Shaun knelt down and ripped open the shirt to expose the wound above Danny's third rib on his right side, but the real problem was the sound of air being sucked into his chest. He placed his palm over the hole and sealed it, while he tried to get to his phone without moving his hand, and failing. The sound of approaching sirens fixed that dilemma, and he focused on releasing his hand a little in time with Danny's ragged breathing to let the air out of his chest.

He looked around urgently, but they were as alone as automatic gunfire on a river wharf can make someone. A helicopter suddenly appeared overhead and flooded the area with brilliant light from its Nightsun searchlight, while its rotors blew junk and paper all over Danny. Shaun swore loudly and covered his friend with his body, while the dickhead in the chopper started shouting at him through a loudspeaker. He had to wait only a few minutes for more heroes to arrive and also start shouting. What was it with these people? If he really was the shooter, would he still be here? Not bloody likely.

Three overweight police officers ran up to him and began grabbing him and pulling him away. He snatched his arm back and shouted over his shoulder, but the helicopter was making too much noise as it hovered there for the best view. One of the officers reached down, and Shaun took his hand and jerked the man to his knees.

"We're police officers, you dickheads!" he shouted into the sprawled man's ear. "Get that damned thing off my friend!"

The officer looked up as though it was the first time he'd seen the helicopter fifty feet above them and still showering everyone with crap. He finally found his wits, got to his feet, and waved the chopper away. It was obvious that the other officers wanted to beat someone with their sticks, or shoot witnesses, or however they got their kicks, but their demeanour changed visibly when they learned that the wounded man was a brother officer, albeit one with brains — and less body fat.

Shaun turned back to Danny and listened to his breathing, now shallow and painful. "Don't you do this to me," he said, leaning forward to make sure his hand was applying pressure to the wound. "Please," he said quietly. "Listen, God, I've never asked you for anything, you know that, but I'm asking you now. You let Danny here live, and I'll do anything." He closed his eyes. "You just say the word... anything." Danny's breath rattled noisily as he fought to get air into his collapsed lung. "I'll be a better man," he said as he released his grip to let the trapped air out through the wound. "I'll do stuff. Look, God, you let him live, and I'll clean myself up. Yeah, me, my place, the car, everything." Danny was dead still, and his breathing was fading.

The police officers looked at each other and shook their heads in response to the unasked question.

"Come on, God," Shaun said, looking up at the sky. It responded by beginning to rain. "Come on, don't be an arsehole!" The rain soaked his face and pattered onto Danny's bloody chest. "Please, God," Shaun said softly, "I'm promising. Please!"

An ambulance bumped onto the quay and rolled slowly towards them. Danny groaned, and Shaun looked up to heaven. "Thanks, I owe you."

As they loaded Danny into the ambulance, Shaun promised God one more thing. He was going to hunt down Junior Brown and kill him.

Jimmy Detroit nipped the filter off his Marlboro and lit the bare cigarette with a match that he struck on the wall he was leaning against. If it was some sort of subconscious rebellion against diktats from tree huggers and health freaks, he wasn't aware of it, but that's pretty much the way with subconscious rebellions.

He watched the ambulance bounce down onto the quay and roll up to where the stupid cops had got whacked. What kind of bonehead play was that? Forty-fives against machine pistols at that range? These people really were plain stupid, no wonder they lost every shitty war they'd got themselves into and had to be bailed out by the US every single time. Shit.

He tossed the cigarette and reached into his pocket for his cell. He had intended to wait for the Jamaicans to go inside, but the keystone cops had screwed that up. He pressed the speed dial and looked up in time to see the boathouse walls turn to blazing tinder and fly out in all directions, followed an instant later by the roof. He put the cell away and strolled back to the car. With a little luck, and no more incidents with this crap of driving on the wrong side of the road, he might get to see the ball game on satellite. And that would at least be a distant view of civilization.

He sat behind the wheel of the stupid little rental and watched the flames rising from the remains of the boathouse that was being ripped by secondary explosions every few minutes, as Junior's hidden armoury detonated. He felt nothing, no exhilaration, no sense of a job well done. Not like the early days. Maybe it was always like this at the end of a career, going out in a whimper after all those years of thinking you make a difference. He leaned back against the seat and closed his eyes. This was going to be his last job, he'd said that at the start, yet there had been a little voice, but that was silenced now. He recalled his days in Delta Force. And the men who'd become like brothers, yeah, all dead now, either in action or some bullshit illness from all the crap they'd been through. But he missed it, not the action, he'd had enough of that, all that stalking lowlifes through stinking mosquito-infested jungles, or lying in wait for hours in some hide in a shit hole

South American country just to blow some unknown dealer's stupid head off. He missed the... what? Too hard even to think it? Okay, he missed the feeling of belonging, yeah, belonging to a family. What he did now made more money than he would ever need, but it was just him, always just him. Sometimes he wanted somebody to bitch with, to blow off steam, get drunk, get laid — and still be safe. Last job for sure. Yeah, but then what? Whatever, but he was done with this shit, this—

He opened his eyes as two police cars raced past the stationary vehicle, but the voice in his head whispered on.

This... loneliness.

He gritted his teeth, irritated by his weakness, but knowing that his inner voice was right, as it always was, the only voice he trusted, because all the smilers and the back slappers and the way-to-goers were just out to promote their own agenda, to get whatever it was they really wanted. Yeah, this was the last job.

40

Harry had been summoned to MI5 by a polite female voice. He'd thought about telling the voice he'd got a bad back, or his granny was dead, but he'd been around authority long enough to know when a request wasn't a request at all.

He arrived at Thames House exactly on time, which puzzled him a little, being the last person in the world to give a stuff about orders from suits. Except these suits had the power to make his life very unpleasant indeed.

He was taken to an office by one of these suits who didn't speak and locked in. Now that was just rude. Yeah, write a letter to your MP.

A few minutes passed, and he was considering picking the lock to make his getaway. Problem being, he was in a secure building... and he couldn't pick locks, but other than that, it was a sound plan. Before he could put the plan into operation, a young woman in an immaculate grey suit came in, sat at the desk without speaking, and pressed something that switched on the wall monitor. And there was Lupus, as large as life, exiting Heathrow arrivals.

He glanced at the young woman. "So, you knew what he looks like all along?"

She spoke. "We had a tip that Mohammed Rahman Ali was arriving on this flight."

"So, why am I here?"

She watched him for a few moments, as if wondering the same thing. "We need you to confirm that this..." She pointed at the big screen. "This person is Mohammed Rahman Ali."

No, you don't, but okay, I'll play along. "Dunno, but I can confirm that this guy is the Taliban commander I met on the roof." He waited. "I can't say whether it's Ali or not."

She turned off the monitor, stood up and left, again without a word.

Okay, what was that about? Ah. They wanted to see if he blinked. So they still didn't trust his story about the roof meeting and Lupus letting him go. There was a lingering suspicion that he... what? He'd made a deal for his life? Well, that shows how little they knew him. Maybe they thought he was in on the plot. And what plot was that? Jesus, Harry, you're getting as paranoid as these spooks. Still, he'd past the test. Probably.

He stood and tried the door. It was locked. Well, doh!

The door opened before he returned to his seat, and the silent suit held it open for him to leave. And that was it. No thanks. No well done. Kiss my arse. Just here's a picture. Are you in it with him? Now bugger off.

He was back in the rain before his hair was dry from his arrival. He looked back up the steps at the imposing doorway. Who'd be a spook? What a shit way to make a living.

An hour later, he had the photos Bob had taken of the books from Curly Sue's safe spread out on Harvey's coffee table and was studying one carefully when Harvey came home, tired but happy with another day righting wrongs and putting bad people behind bars.

"What a shit day," he said, tossing his coat at the hanger and missing. "I swear I'm going to pack this in and become a missionary."

"But you think God's a figment of the uneducated man's flaccid imagination," Harry quoted, glancing over the top of the printed photograph.

"True," Harvey said, crossing to the table and looking down at the photographs of pages of journals and receipts. "But the poor uneducated natives wouldn't know that, would they?"

"And where're you going to find these poor uneducated natives?" Harry said, tilting his head questioningly. "They've all got internet now, even up the Orinoco."

Harvey grunted. Another plan down the toilet. Welcome to a truly shit day. He picked up a photograph and frowned. "Looks like someone's planning a computer game." He shrugged. "I don't really see the point, but hey-ho."

Harry's smile was intended to be supportive, but came out as just patronising. "It's a generation thing, Dad." He took the photo from Harvey and froze.

"Yes, quite realistic, if you like those futuristic weapons," Harvey said and headed for the drinks cabinet.

Harry stared at the photo and let his breath out slowly. "Holy... shit!" He turned the photo sideways, as if that might make it less scary.

Harvey came back with two scotches and ice and placed one in front of Harry. "Aren't you supposed to be looking for evidence, not admiring fantasy?"

Harry blew out his breath again, picked up the drink, and took a sip. "It's not fantasy, Pop, this is real." He pulled himself together. "These are CheyTac Intervention sniper rifles, deadly accurate up to two miles. The finest extreme long-range rifles in the world. They're the things of nightmares, but not fantasy."

Harvey shrugged, two miles didn't seem that far. "Oh," he said, and that would have to do on the shock-horror front.

"Okay," Harry said, seeing his father's indifference. "If a man set up this rifle on, say the London Eye, then he could kill you on the Embankment right outside here without any trouble."

Harvey stared at him. "But that's just impossible."

Harry shrugged. "I could do it, and with the ABC, I wouldn't have to be a particularly good shot."

"ABC?" Harvey asked, still trying to get his head around such a shot over a distance that would take him forty-five minutes to walk.

Harry shrugged and began re-examining the photos. "Advanced ballistic computer," he said absently. "Does all the calculations and takes the guesswork, and skill, out of the shot."

Harvey sat down heavily in his armchair. "What on earth would anyone want with a weapon like that in London?"

"Two weapons like that," Harry said and then caught his father's questioning look. "Two CheyTac M200 rifles."

Harvey tried to get his head round it. A new level of insanity in an increasingly insane world. But then it made sense, just like that. "The tripartite accord!"

Harry looked at him for several seconds, as his brain processed the enormity of it. It made absolute sense. An assassin would get off only one shot, maybe two, before the bodyguards smothered the target. Usually with their own bodies. And what kind of bloody insanity was that? Would he do that for some politician? No, but then he wouldn't pass the psych test.

"But two snipers?" Harvey said into the glass he held in front of his lips.

"There are three targets: the president, the German Chancellor, and our PM. There is no way a single sniper would be certain to hit all three before all hell broke loose, but two going for two shots each..." He raised an eyebrow.

Harvey reached for the phone.

"Who are you calling?" Harry said, putting his hand on the receiver.

"Sir Richard."

Harry held on to the phone for a moment. "Let's think it through first," he said.

Harvey took his hand off the phone and took a drink, as he thought about what they were saying. Minutes passed, and the mahogany Bramble wall clock ticked away their lives. Eventually he put his finger on his lip and let it circle his chin, as he reached a conclusion. "If this is true, and it's so awful it certainly is, then it is a career maker for the security service and for the person who breaks it."

Harry was ahead of him, but let him continue, partly out of respect for his father, but mostly out of his respect for the lawyer.

"There is no way they will be able to contain this, even with all the D notices in the world. The press will be all over it in hours. Then what?" It was a rhetorical question.

"Any chance we have of sneaking up on these bastards will be gone," Harry said, answering it anyway. "They'll go to ground."

"Until they emerge to kill the dignitaries." Harvey stood up and started pacing slowly and then stopped and pointed at the photos on the coffee table. "The shipping note on the photograph, does it have an address?"

Harry assumed it would be for a transient intermediary, but picked up the photo again anyway and examined the detail through his father's oversized magnifying glass. "Yes," he said, squinting one eye. "Junior Brown." He moved the photo back and forth to focus the tiny writing. "Holland Park."

Harvey raised his eyebrows. "Expensive."

"If he is supplying arms like these," Harry said, waving the photo, "then he can afford it." He glanced at his father. "I'd say somewhere around a million for this package with no questions asked."

Harvey nodded. "Okay, now we know who traded them, how are you going to find out to whom?"

Harry noted the switch in pronoun, but let it go and pointed at the photographs. "This tranny is a neatness freak, the kind I've seen a hundred times in the stores and supply depots around the world. You don't have the right paperwork, they'd let you go into combat without bullets. Somewhere in here is the info on the guy who took delivery of the rifles."

Harvey moved the piles of printed photographs about with his finger. "Lot of pages of very small print." He sighed and sat down next to his son. "Better get started, then."

Harry picked up a handful of pages and studied the photographed documents. They were in for a long, long night.

Five minutes later, his father handed him a page. "There you go."

Harry examined the photograph of a formal receipt for two 'boxed packages', complete with date, time, and an address in Mayfair. "This is it," he said, tapping the page.

"Really?" Harvey said in mock surprise. "Do you really think so?"

Harry smiled. "Okay, yeah, well done, Pop."

"Don't call me Pop," Harvey said, getting up for another well-deserved drink. "So now you know where it went, how are you going to find out who the end customer is?" he said, returning to the table and pointing at the page. "That... O'Connell is no more than a middleman."

"Chances are O'Conner has paperwork on this too. It's just business to him, and business means records."

"Be that as it may, it still doesn't get you his documents."

Harry thought for a moment and then snapped his fingers. "I'll ask Bob the Burglar, if I can find him again."

"Whoa!" Harvey said. "Cracking some transvestite's safe is a long way from taking on an international gun runner. Robert Doyle is just a small-time crook."

Harry shook his head. "I've seen him work, and trust me, he's anything but small time."

"Okay," Harvey said, "but I'm beginning to think we should bring Sir Richard into this."

"Not yet, let's see what we can find out from this O'Conner first. Then we will be in a better position to make a decision." He stood up. "We could just be jumping to conclusions and would look pretty stupid."

Harvey looked from him to the photos. "I don't believe that either. But I will talk to Richard anyway." He raised his hand before his son could protest. "Strictly off the record. He has to know. He started all this, after all. And I trust him."

Harry started to disagree and then put his hand on his father's arm — as near to a hug as either was going to get. "Okay," he said, disengaging from the non-hug and heading for the door. He stopped to take his coat from the rack and to put Harvey's in its place.

"And," Harvey said as the door was about to close.

Harry opened the door again.

"Tell Bob to be in my office by nine... okay, make that ten thirty tomorrow."

Harry nodded and closed the door behind him.

"If you're not both dead," Harvey said and immediately regretted it.

He reached for the phone. Two old friends going out for a drink, no harm in that, and who knows what topic the conversation might turn to. "Richard, it's been an age since we met at the club."

Neither man spoke for several seconds, both knowing that they'd met for lunch only yesterday.

"Yes," Sir Richard said, "ages. Shall we meet up later?"

"A fine idea. I'll be there in an hour, if that's convenient." He put down the phone.

Would anyone suspect there was more to it than what it appeared to be, friends having a drink and talking about politics, summit meetings, and family? No, a listener would have heard only that, if such a listener was listening. And he was certain that Sir Richard's phone was listened to. Paranoia is the norm for a spook, but it appeared to be contagious.

He said a quiet prayer, to the god who was a figment of the uneducated man's flaccid imagination, that his son would be safe.

41

Shaun stood in the doorway and looked at his friend lying in the hospital bed, strung with tubes and wired up to a rack of beeping machines, and looking like he was already dead.

"You decided to pay a visit, then?" a voice said from inside the room, and for a moment he thought it was Danny, but instantly knew better.

"Baxter," he said through gritted teeth. He entered the room and saw Baxter sitting with his chair tilted up against the wall.

"Superintendent Baxter, O'Conner, unless you want to be writing parking tickets for the rest of your career."

Die soon, and in great pain, you prick. "Superintendent Baxter," Shaun said with difficulty. He turned to face Danny, as much to get Baxter out of his face as any expectation that something might have changed in the last ten seconds. "Is he okay?"

"Depends on your definition of okay," Baxter said, keeping the sneer out of his voice with difficulty. "He had a bullet in him that should have killed him, and he is in a coma. If that's your definition of okay, then he's okay."

Shaun crossed to the bed, looked up at the monitors beeping quietly, and put his hand on his friend's shoulder. "Meant what I said," he said softly.

"What the hell were you thinking?" Baxter said.

Shaun barely glanced at him. "We had a tip-off."

"Bullshit!" Baxter said, crashing his chair back onto four legs. "You were looking for that scumbag brother of yours... again."

True. "Never crossed my mind," Shaun said, raising one eyebrow.

"Do you think I'm a fool, O'Conner?"

Shaun looked at him steadily and let the answer hang in the air.

Baxter flushed and stood up. "Take a good look at your friend," he said, pointing at Danny. "You don't get it, do you?" He squinted, and his cheekbones stood out as he clenched his teeth. "You did this to him."

Shaun took a small involuntary step back from the bed.

"Yes, you and your bloody unnatural obsession with killing your brother." Baxter caught his breath. "You ever heard of Kane and Abel?"

Ah, the educated man speaketh.

Shaun put his hand gently on Danny's shoulder and then walked to the door.

"Where the hell do you think you're going?" Baxter barked at his back.

Shaun half turned. "I'm going to find Abel, and when I do, I'm going to do unto others."

Baxter took a step closer, and for a wonderful moment Shaun thought he was going to throw a punch, but sadly the moment passed.

"You listen to me, O'Conner," he said, his voice shaking with anger, "and you listen to me like you haven't listened to anyone since your momma read you bedtime stories." He stepped up until his face was close enough for Shaun to feel the spittle as he spoke. "You are not to go within a mile of Patrick O'Conner." He spoke very slowly, as if talking to an idiot child. "If you're driving down the street and you see him coming the other way, you are to hang a U and speed away, even if this causes civilian casualties. Do I make I make myself clear, *Sergeant* O'Conner?"

"I hear you," Shaun said slowly. "And I can taste you." He wiped his face with his hand. "Now you listen to me, you jumped-up little prick." Baxter backed off, but Shaun matched his move. "I have the man who killed my father in my sights, and—" He poked a finger into Baxter's shoulder. "And if you stand in my way, or even stand close, I'll swat you like the irritating little insect you are." He poked him again. "Now are you hearing me, you piece-of-shit politician?"

Baxter sat back into the chair with a jolt as Shaun jabbed him one more time for good measure. "I'll have your job for this," he hissed, but stayed seated.

Shaun felt his heart thumping in his chest and waited a moment for the anger to subside a little. "You want my job?" he said slowly. "Then you run on back to your office and fill in the forms you love so much, you arsehole."

By the time Baxter had thought of a suitable riposte, the door had slammed shut. He sat there staring at the closed door for several minutes, thinking how much he wanted that man dead, and how he'd felt that way from the moment he'd met him. They said O'Conner was a street cop, admired by everyone for his skill and tenacity. Bullshit, the man was a drunk, but would anybody listen? No, they just kept telling him there are two kinds of cops, bureaucrats and doers, and every doer is worth a dozen of those who only occupy desk space and move paper. Well, this drunk do-good cop had pushed the wrong man. He was going to fall from so high it would make his nose bleed. Men like O'Conner made him sick, men who thought they could push everyone around, do what they want, be above the law. What God-given right did they think they had? He'd worked his ass off to get where he was, and did anybody say well done? The hell they did. It was all Sergeant O'Conner did this, Sergeant O'Conner did that. So, how did they think he did it? It was because of people like him, the paper movers, experts investigators who provided the foundation to make it happen. Of course it was. Nothing to do with all this street intel shit, getting drunk with criminals. If he had his way, these loose cannons would be thrown off the force and replaced by real cops.

He stood up. Well, now he had his chance. O'Conner had crossed the line. Now he was going to find out who he was dealing with, and he would find it he was a heavier hitter than he could imagine. He straightened his three-piece suit and licked his dry lips, but couldn't help looking around the small room in case someone had seen the confrontation. He'd planned that speech so well, rehearsed it in his mind, had seen O'Conner crumble and do his bidding, humbled at last.

He'd see him fall for this, so help him God.

42

"Are you waiting for your father, Debbie?" the doorman asked the little girl sitting on the bench seat in front of his desk in the foyer. He waited for a response, but none came. "Ah, I get it," he said with smile. "Don't talk to strangers, right?" She did exactly that. "Well, I'm not a stranger." Yes, you are. "I'm Derek, the concierge here." Oh, like she's going to get that. "That's just a posh name for the doorman. So that's me, Derek the doorman." He walked out from behind his desk and smiled at her. "Is he late?"

The girl was small and painfully thin, nine or ten, though she looked much younger, but a troubled life, even one so short, can affect kids in all sorts of ways.

She spoke without looking up. "No," she said, very softly.

"It's just that you've been sitting here a very long time, that's all." Derek smiled again, but she probably didn't see as she was still looking at the floor. "What time was he coming?"

"Four o'clock," she said, still not looking up.

Derek glanced at the wall clock, which was showing five fifteen. "Oh, I get it," he said with a quick smile. "He's always late, so if he's late as usual, then he's on time. Right?"

Debbie nodded.

"Smart kid," he said quietly. "Wish my kids was as smart." He sighed. "Or the missus, God bless her... and her sainted mother who's been staying with us for two years this Christmas."

If Debbie was supposed to respond, or even understand that, it failed to launch. She stood up.

Derek looked where she was looking and saw the heavy-set, short man get out of the Merc in front of the building. "Who's this, then?" he said almost to himself and walked closer to the windowed frontage. "Ah, O'Brian, isn't it?

Before Debbie could answer, even if she was going to, which she wasn't, the man pushed open the door and stepped into the foyer, along with a gust of early winter cold.

"Evenin', Mr O'Brian," Derek said. "Another cold one."

"Let's go, kid," O'Brian said without even acknowledging Derek.

"I'm not a kid," Debbie said. "I'm ten."

"Yeah, whatever," O'Brian said, opening the door and letting more cold air rush in. "Your father's waiting in the car." He glared at her as she turned to smile at Derek. "And he don't like to be kept waiting."

Derek almost said what about the kid waiting, but he caught it. No point letting his missus and her sainted mother get the house for free — after the funeral. "Give my regards to Mr O'Conner," he said to the closing door and took a step up to the windows to watch O'Brian walk to the car with Debbie trailing behind. "What is he doing?" He screened the reflection in the window with his hand. "Y'know, I think he's looking for kidnappers or hit men or something. Now there's a boy who thinks too much of himself." He sniffed and returned to his desk and the football match that was about to resume.

Patrick O'Conner was in the back seat of the Merc and reached over to move his papers off the seat as Debbie climbed in. "Hello, Debs," he said, scanning a paragraph that had caught his eye. "Is your mother well?"

Debbie nodded and struggled to get the seatbelt fastened. "Yes," she said, finally clicking the buckle home. "She's fine. She sends her love."

Patrick looked up. "Yes, I bet she does," he said, pulling a sour expression. "And you give her mine next time you see her."

"Okay," Debbie said, completely missing the razorblades in his voice.

Patrick figured it was worth a try. "Does she ever say anything about me?"

"Like what?" Debbie asked, straightening the seatbelt across her thin body.

"Oh, I don't know," he said, getting that old sinking feeling "Y'know, anything."

"Not really. Oh, I heard her tell the driver she's looking forward to your... your... moretopsey." She frowned. "Is that a party?"

"Depends on who's being moretopsied."

"Can I come?"

He gave a small shake of his head and almost smiled. "Look, love, I know I said we would go to the waxworks before dinner, but something's come up. It'll just take a few minutes. Okay?"

Debbie sighed and looked out of the window now that the car was moving.

"Don't worry," he added, a bit too earnestly, "we will go, I promise. Just a short stop at my place." He got no response. "Look, it's new, you'll like it. I've got lots of aquariums with coloured fish." Getting a little desperate now. "You like fish, right?"

Debbie glanced back from her reflection in the car window. "I like fish fingers," she said with a little shrug.

"I love that kid," O'Brian said from the front seat.

Debbie was still trailing behind when they reached Patrick's apartment and crossed the foyer to where O'Brian was holding the lift. Patrick looked back and almost told her to get a move on, but he owed her that one for ditching the trip to the waxworks that was closed for the day anyway, so he kept the false smile and waited for her to dawdle into the lift, her head full of whatever ten-year-old girls' heads are full of.

O'Brian opened the apartment door, and a rush of music and clinking glasses greeted them.

"G'day, Patrick," Grady said, one of the hired help slumped in the big armchair and clearly booze-brave. "Have a glass of champagne," he said, waving a bottle of Moet at Patrick. "It's my birthday."

"And it's my apartment," Patrick said, "and you call me Patrick again and you're fired."

"Sorry, Mr O'Conner," Grady said, quickly putting down the bottle. "It won't happen again."

Patrick glared at him for a nanosecond, but decided it was too much trouble to find a replacement.

Grady saw the look and read it correctly. "Thanks, Mr O'Conner." He grinned stupidly, which fitted his state just fine. "Good champagne, though, not that domestic stuff." He stood up and then sat down again quickly. "I'll get one of those penguins to serve it, if they haven't drunk it all themselves." He waved at the two waiters, who were... waiting. "Hey, you, what do I pay you for? Serve Mr O'Conner." He pointed out Patrick, in case they'd missed his arrival. "And the kid."

"Don't be stupid, Grady," O'Brian said, his feelings for the man clear from his tone.

"Sorry," Grady said, flushing a little. "Wasn't thinking."

"No friggin' change there, then," O'Brian said.

"That's enough!" Patrick snapped. "Can't you see my daughter, you retard?"

"Shit! Christ!" O'Brian said, digging a hole faster than a steam shovel. "Sorry, Mr O'Conner, I just—"

"Go and watch the fish, Debs," Patrick said, glaring at O'Brian.

"Hey," Grady said, "did you hear Junior Brown's warehouse got blowed up last night?"

Patrick looked at him for a moment as he processed the information and then shrugged. "What do I care? You got our merchandise, right?" The question was emphasised by a questioning squint.

"Yeah, yeah, I got it," Grady said. "And sent it on its way." He nodded to confirm the truth of what he was saying. "White van, so it could have been anything." He frowned. "Guy was weird, though."

Patrick took the glass of champagne from the waiter in the penguin suit without even noticing him. "Weird how?"

"Dunno really," Grady said, struggling with the effort of thinking. "Grunted a lot. Smelled like shit—" He looked quickly at Debbie, but she was tracking one of the brightly coloured fish with her finger on the glass. Patrick's expression was promising pain, so he went on quickly. "Carried one of those big boxes under each arm. Built like a brick sh—" He got the look again. "Outhouse, and stunk of aftershave. And he was one of those Eastern Europeans, I think." He shuddered. "Give me the creeps."

"What the hell you talking about, Grady?" O'Brian said. "How can an Eastern European give you the creeps? It's not like they're Chinese or nothin'."

Grady shrugged. "Dunno, it's the way they look at you."

"Oh, for Christ's sake," Patrick said, ending the idiocy. "So the packages have been delivered to the buyer?"

Grady nodded. "Yeah, like I said—"

"Eastern European," Patrick said with a sigh. "Good riddance, that stuff was dynamite with a sweat on." He downed the champagne in one gulp and pulled a face. "Get me a proper drink," he said to O'Brian.

O'Brian took the glass from his boss as he passed, handed it to the waiter. He stopped at the dresser and selected a whiskey from the array of bottles.

While O'Brian poured two large drinks, one of the waiters began packing away the champagne bottles and used glasses, taking care not to make any noise, both to avoid disturbing his clients, and so they wouldn't look and see him lifting his MP-5SD mini sub-machine gun from the cabinet under the serving trolley. This was Detroit's favourite weapon and formed a non-negotiable part of any contract outside the US. Heckler and Koch integration of the MP5's sound suppressor and the elimination of the butt stock kept the sub-machine gun's length to twenty-two inches and made it the ideal tool for a quiet kill. As usual, Detroit used the smaller fifteen-round magazine because if that didn't get the job done, a hundred-round drum wouldn't help — he'd be dead.

He flicked the trigger group off safe. O'Brian was behind him, so he killed him first, to get him out of the way. Set to a three-round burst, the nine-mil rounds slammed into O'Brian with barely more noise than a loud cough, hurling him into the dresser and scattering and smashing the bottles as his arms flailed in his death-dance. He coughed a plume of blood and slumped over the dresser as though his strings had been cut. Almost casually, Detroit turned and put three into Grady, shattering the champagne glass frozen halfway to his wide-open mouth. To his right, the other waiter recovered his wits and ran for the door. Detroit swung the gun round, fired once, and looked back at the room, without even waiting for the man to fall, but the way the man's legs stopped working in mid-stride was a pretty good indication of the effectiveness of the shot.

Patrick had been around assassinations most of his adult life and was way past being stunned by one in progress. As Detroit swung the silenced sub-machine gun in his direction, he bolted, dived through an open door, hit the floor, and slammed the door shut with his foot.

Detroit sighed heavily and walked across the apartment, stepping over the bloody remains of Grady as he went. He tapped the door with the gun's endplate and shook his head at the metallic sound. Panic room. Trust the man to have one of those. Okay, he'd just wait. He turned and crossed to the sofa, put the machine gun across his lap and sat back to wait it out. O'Conner was included in the contract, so he would wait patiently. There's no such thing as an impatient cleaner, not a live one, anyway.

A movement caught his eye, and he fired a burst left-handed on reflex. The aquariums fitted into the wall blew apart in a cascade of water and flapping fish. He stood up in a single move, caught the gun's barrel with his right hand, and held it steadily, pointing at the shattered glass. Another movement and he fired again, but he hadn't shot many kids, and his aim was high.

Debbie ran through the open door into the corridor without realising the sounds she could hear above her head were bullets meant for her, but she did know that there was a bad man in the room, and he was trying to hurt her, so she ran, and she was quick for a sickly looking kid. By the time Detroit reached the door, she was already at the end of the twenty-foot corridor and skidding to turn left in front of the city-view window. A long burst from the sub-machine gun blew the window out, and she threw her hands over her head as glass showered her. The movement did two things; it threw her out of the window, and it saved her life as Detroit emptied the magazine into the space she'd been using a moment before.

He ran down the corridor, replacing the mag as he went, put the gun through the window, and leaned out, but the kid was gone. He looked right and left and swore. The brat had fallen down the sloping tiles and off the roof, so now the cops would be all over the scene. He swore again, kids always screwed things up. He would have to make a second hit, an event so rare, he could only just recall the last time he'd had to do it. That time was because of some stupid kid, running across the front of the building like he was Spiderman or something. What was that all about? He'd run across the windowsill, right into the bullet that had been the endgame of weeks of work to get just the right building with a vacant room and a view of the courthouse. Okay, he'd tidied it up later, but it had been a messy, last-minute thing with explosives, and he hated explosives, with all that noise and shit.

He was still swearing quietly as he stepped into the elevator and stripped off the monkey suit, rolled it up, and stuffed it up through the roof access hatch along with the MP5, and that was a pity.

Harry and Bob the Burglar sat in Bob's decommissioned taxi and craned their necks to see the upper windows of the six-storey building that housed Patrick's apartment.

"Which one is it?" Bob asked, rubbing his neck.

Harry glanced at him for a moment. "The one with the Bad Man Lives Here sticker on the window."

Bob leaned forward and squinted up through the reflected streetlights at the top-floor windows, but couldn't see the sticker. Harry must be in a better position. "Shall I go and poke around?"

Harry looked at him quickly. "Poke around?"

"Yeah, y'know?"

Harry didn't know, but guessed ignorance was bliss in this case. "Come on, then," he said, opening the car door and flinching at the grinding hinges. "Bloody hell! What are you driving here?"

Bob grinned. "Cool, eh?" He opened his door, accompanied by the same sound effects. "I can drive down bus and taxi lanes, park wherever I like, and..." he winked, "nobody notices a taxi."

Harry warmed to the heap of rusting scrap and closed the door gently to avoid knocking any bits off it. He looked both ways down the quiet Mayfair street and walked towards the entrance to Patrick's building, staying close to the wall and in the shadows.

Bob stood in the road under the streetlight and watched him with his head tilted and a quizzical look on his face. "Harry," he said quietly. "Harry!" he repeated loudly, when he got no response.

Harry glared at him for breaking silence during a recon mission. "Shhh! For chrissakes, you'll wake up the whole street."

Bob strolled over to him. "The whole street is awake." He glanced at his watch. "It being eight o'clock and dinner time." He waited a moment. "And this being central London, not Afghanistan."

Ah, good point.

Harry came out of the shadows, avoided looking at Bob, and walked quickly to the wide, arched entrance. He expected to see a concierge, but the foyer was deserted. Odd, because any old street-bum could wander in and have the pictures and junk away. Maybe there's a camera—

"Can I help you... sir?" said a voice right behind him.

He jumped with shock and spun round to see a little old chap in a blue 'don't mess with me' uniform and a flat cap, standing a foot away, with Bob behind him grinning like a schoolboy in the girls' showers.

"Jesus!" Harry said and backed off another step.

"No, sir, I am the concierge," the old man said, without a flicker of expression.

Harry frowned. "How'd you do that?"

"Do what... sir?"

"Injun up on me like that?"

"I merely walked, sir, as one does."

"Well, don't do it," Harry said petulantly, "it's unnerving."

"Very well, sir," the concierge said. "I shall endeavour to make more noise in future, if it helps."

"Okay then," Harry said, satisfied that he'd won that exchange, and diverted attention from the fact that he, a highly trained sneaking-about specialist, had been out-sneaked by a creaky old guy.

The creaky old guy coughed. "Now... sir," he said, looking Harry over slowly and apparently not liking what he saw. "What can we do for you?"

Harry looked around in case the 'we' meant there was another one of these ninja doormen sneaking up on him. Satisfied that he was safe from sudden appearances of gnome people, he tried a smile. That didn't work; it was just scary. "We are here to see Patrick O'Conner," he said at last, having finished being a dickhead.

The old guy looked him up and down again for several awkward seconds. "I shall see if Mr O'Conner will see you." He walked to the highly polished mahogany reception desk in the corner of the foyer, stopped and looked over his shoulder as he heard Harry move. "Please wait... sir."

Harry waited, while Bob chuckled, and a moment later the concierge put down the phone. "It appears that Mr O'Conner is not at home. Good evening, sir."

That was like 'push off', right?

Harry felt like he'd been slapped with a rubber chicken – in church. "Try again, will you?" The word was coming, but sticking in his throat. "Please." There, not so hard.

The concierge blinked slowly to signal that he was thinking. "No, sir, I believe I have tried."

Not very helpful, but wearing a peaked cap causes that.

Bob took Harry's arm. "We'll come back tomorrow, okay?" He turned to the concierge and smiled. "Thanks for trying," he said, with a supporting nod. "And for scaring the life outa my friend," he added under his breath.

"Up yours," Harry said sulkily and followed him out into the cold night. "What now?" he asked as they went down the three wide steps back into the street.

"Give him a minute," Bob said, leading him off to one side of the entrance.

Harry frowned. "What for?" He looked over his shoulder quickly, just in case the old guy appeared again. "He's a ninja, you know that?"

Bob chuckled and glanced at his watch. "Almost eight."

"So what? Does he turn into a pumpkin at eight?" Harry said sulkily. He didn't like being made to look a dick by some old guy, when that was usually reserved for the women he met.

"No," Bob said, "but the racing results are on the radio at eight." He saw Harry's frown. "And he had a newspaper on his desk open to the racing section." He smiled again, happy chap, Bob. "He'll sneak off someplace to listen, in case the rich folks overhear him. And that just wouldn't do."

Harry was seriously impressed. "You're in the wrong business, you know?" He slapped Bob on the shoulder in admiration. "Recon scout, that'd be you."

Bob smiled. "No difference really between reconnoitring an enemy's position and scoping a gig." He leaned round the door pillar and looked inside the foyer. "Okay, we can go now."

Harry followed him into the foyer and across to the lift, keeping a lookout on all sides for another sudden appearance, but the lift doors closed without the geriatric ninja returning. "Okay," he said, regaining his composure. "O'Conner's place is on the top floor. Floor five."

Bob pointed to the floor indicators with number five lit. A few seconds later they stepped out into the small corridor that led to the two top-floor apartments. Harry pointed at the end one before Bob could beat him to it. He put his ear to the door, but it was silent, both because there was no movement inside and because it was soundproofed.

"Okay, do your stuff," he said, stepping aside so Bob could burgle the door.

Bob turned the handle, and the door swung open. He shrugged at Harry's expression and entered Patrick's sumptuous living room — except the luxury was somewhat marred by the copious amounts of blood splattered over just about everything. Bob stepped back out of the doorway as Harry entered. Time for the real difference between a marine and a burglar to come to the fore.

Harry stepped off to the side away from the door and wished he had his Sig, but the police frown on people walking about with handguns stuffed in their belts. He checked the room quickly and then relaxed. Whoever had killed the two men was long gone, unless he'd found a way of hiding in plain sight. He could've been in one of the other rooms, but the doors were closed, which would have been highly unlikely if a killer was wandering around the apartment. He signalled to Bob to come in.

Bob entered the room and blew his breath out in a low whistle, crossed to the panic room, pushed open the door, and looked back. "No bodies in here." He looked behind the door. "Do you think...?"

Harry nodded. "I'd say Patrick O'Conner locked himself in there while somebody killed his employees."

"Ideal employer," Bob said, crossing the room and moving the painting above the fireplace. "Welfare of his employees at the top of his list." He let the painting swing back. "Unless it inconveniences him in the least."

Harry watched Bob scan the room carefully before walking to the dresser with O'Brian's body slumped over it. "Okay," he said quietly, "give me a hand."

They lifted O'Brian's body off the dresser and lowered it to the floor with more care than a dead body really required. Bob opened the glass doors to the top bookcase and tapped the leather-bound books until the sound changed from bookish to hollow wood. He turned to Harry and smiled, despite standing astride O'Brian's bloody body, but he was dead so wouldn't mind. He felt across the top of the books until there was a click and the dummy books swung open to reveal a white wall safe with an oversized combination lock.

Harry sucked air in between his teeth and scratched his cheek. "Bugger, that looks like a real bitch."

Bob nodded. "It'll take a while," he said and started looking around again.

"Lost something?" Harry asked, also looking around, even though he didn't know what for.

"The combination," Bob said absently.

"Yeah, right. Maybe it's scratched on the woodwork," Harry said sarcastically.

"You'd be surprised. These locks can have a million or more combinations. People like O'Conner get a bit paranoid, so keep changing it, until they can't remember the latest one, so they leave themselves a clue."

"Kinda defeats the purpose of changing it, doesn't it?"

Bob shrugged absently and pointed at the books on the bottom shelf. "Ah!"

Harry looked at the leather-bound HG Wells' novels. So what? Bob saw his confusion and tapped each of the books in turn. Ah, the volumes were numbered, and more importantly, the numbering was out of sequence. That couldn't be it; it couldn't be that daft.

Bob turned the combination, leaned back to check the novels, spun the lock the other way, and after a few seconds, stepped back and waved Harry forward like a magician's assistant, but without the fanfare — or the sexy gear. Harry looked at him for a second, still doubtful. He pulled the safe door and was stunned when it swung open.

"Bob the Burglar, take a bow," Harry said, taking a sheaf of papers out of the safe.

"No, thanks," Bob said, reaching in and taking out a wad of cash that would have choked a horse. "I'll take this instead."

Harry nodded his approval, looked back in the safe in case they'd missed anything, and reached in to take out a revolver. He turned it in his hand and felt its weight. "Smith and Wesson M&P 340 CT," he said quietly. "Three fifty seven magnum. Nice piece."

"Cool," Bob said, pocketing the cash. "You keep it, and I'll keep this."

"You know in the movies, when the crooks are just about to leg it and they hear the police sirens?" Harry asked innocently.

"Yeah, bit clichéd if you ask me," Bob said, frowning. "So what?"

Harry tilted his ear towards the window and raised a finger. "Welcome to Hollywood."

"Hey, we should go."

"No shit? Maybe watch the game on the television first?" Harry said, but he was talking to Bob's back as he headed for the door.

Shaun heard the call as he was driving down The Mall on his way back from Saint Bart's hospital and knew at once that it had to be Patrick. Who else would be the cause of gunshots in Mayfair? He cut through Green Park, round Hyde Park Corner, bypassed Berkeley Square, and was outside Patrick's apartment in under ten minutes. Nice driving for Central London.

He parked halfway down the quiet street and looked up at the building where Michael Collins lived, except he'd been dead since 1922. He reached for the car door handle, just as three police cars passed him with their lights flashing and sirens blaring. Great, here come the boys in blue to totally screw things up. He released the handle and waited. There would be lots of running around and shouting first, so he might as well wait for them to make sure the shooters had gone, no point sticking his neck out unnecessarily when there were so many eager-beaver volunteers. Anyway, he needed a drink and pulled a bottle from beside the seat and unscrewed the top, but sat and looked at it in the flashing blue light as his promise replayed in his head. What the hell? It was a promise to a god that had dumped him decades before, stuff it. He lifted the bottle towards his lips and stopped. But what if? Right now Danny was hanging on, but it was close. The promise was made in the heat of the moment, with his best friend bleeding out in the rain. Sure, but he lived when he should've died. So maybe... bullshit, a promise to nobody under those conditions doesn't count. So okay, now promises and your word get measured by who was listening? He screwed the top on the bottle and got out of the car. Later would be soon enough for a drink, right now he needed his wits. Yeah, right.

He half expected to find DCI Gardener on the scene and still bleating on about the report that was supposed to be on his desk days ago, but he wasn't; it was just a clone.

"I know you," DCI Faulkner said as Shaun approached the entrance to the building and ignored him. "Hey, stop right there!"

Shaun stopped on the steps and even thought about turning round, but was just too tired to bother with all this crap. "Yeah, sir, and I know you too." You pompous little shit.

"O'Conner, isn't it?"

Shaun glanced over his shoulder at the police chief inspector standing under the entrance lights. He was wearing medals, for Christ's sake, what had he ever done to get medals? Probably hundred-metre backstroke. "Yeah, and you're DI Facker," he said with a little nod of welcome.

If Faulkner had flushed any redder, it would have merged nicely with the blue light to turn a lovely shade of purple. "Detective Chief Inspector Faulkner," the DCI said without moving his jaw. "What are you doing at my crime scene?"

Shaun could have explained that it was part of an on-going investigation, or that the gunfire was in his brother's apartment, but this DCI was a dick, and so were these ass-kissers in blue. He walked up the steps and into the foyer with Faulkner looking left and right as if he expected an apocalypse, or at least a horseman or two. By the time he recovered, Shaun was already pressing the button in the lift and had his eyes closed anyway, as he just couldn't watch any more of these histrionics.

He came out of the lift and walked slowly down the short corridor to Patrick's apartment door, which was open and guarded by a police officer, who nodded when Shaun showed him his ID. He stopped for a moment and looked back down the corridor at the door to the other apartment where Harry and Bob where hiding. Then he turned the other way towards the shattered window and tried to see what was causing the itch on the back of his neck. He should have had that drink, everything seemed clearer after a drink. He walked into the apartment and saw the bodies and the three police officers doing an impression of Hawaii Five-O as they checked the other rooms for gangs of armed assailants.

"Clear!" shouted one of them.

Sweet mother of God, he was getting too old for this shit.

He crossed to where Grady sat in the armchair, broken glass on his lap, three holes in his shirt and a look of surprise frozen on his face. He crossed to where O'Brian lay flat on his back next to the dresser, looked at the empty safe and frowned. If this was a robbery, then he was a hang-gliding nun from Budapest. It was a hit, except the intended target was not among the recently deceased, so Patrick had... had what? He looked to his right and saw the panic-room door open. Yeah, that would be Patrick's style, save himself and to hell with everyone else.

"I help you with anything, sir?" a sergeant said, who had finished his sweep of the three-roomed apartment and was now walking all over the physical evidence.

"No," Shaun said, heading for the door. "Looks like you guys can screw this up on your own." He closed the door behind him, but still heard the sergeant's response, and smiled.

He went to the end of the corridor and looked out of the shattered window. Nothing, just a steep slope over tiles to a rainspout and a low wall. So why was the window blown out?

Harry was also looking out at the sloping roof and the low parapet, but from the other apartment, and only in search of an escape route. From his angle he had a different view and saw the red coat hood hooked up on a bent metal bracket sticking out into a gap meant for a drainpipe. He didn't need to be a detective to realise that the coat was taut, and that meant something heavy was hanging from it.

He stared at the red hood for several seconds, as he tried to deny what his eyes were telling him. "There's a kid hanging off the bloody roof!"

Bob leaned past him. "I see it, a coat."

Harry pulled him back and started to climb out of the window, grimaced as his leg stretched over the sill, and fell back against Bob. "Help me over," he gasped against the pain.

"Why? So I can watch you fall right over the edge?" Bob said. "I don't bloody think so."

Harry leaned out and looked along the roof to the other window, turned and headed for the door.

"Whoa!" Bob said, catching his arm. "Have you forgotten the cops are swarming all over the place?"

Harry pulled his arm free. "That hood's not going to hold long, and when it goes, so does the kid."

Bob nodded. "Okay, but leave that," he said, pointing at the handgun. "The cops aren't going to ask questions if you start running around a murder scene with a gun sticking out of your belt."

Harry threw the gun onto the sofa and opened the door. "You stay here, no point us both getting banged up."

The officer guarding Patrick's apartment saw him come out of the apartment and watched him carefully as he strode past him and down to where Shaun was standing by the broken window. He had no trouble stepping over the low sill this time, but as soon as he braced himself on the treacherous tiles, he grunted in pain.

Shaun leaned on the window frame and watched the madman for a few seconds until he heard the cry of pain. Okay, enough. He caught Harry's arm and steered him back through the window with no more than token resistance. "What the hell are you doing?" he said, as Harry put his hand against the wall for support. "If you're trying to commit suicide, do it someplace else. Someplace I'm not."

Harry pointed down the roof. "There's a kid hanging off the roof."

He was going to say how, but Shaun was already climbing out onto the wet tiles.

"Say hi to the kid as you fly past," Harry said helpfully and then looked around for something to help the cop get down without killing himself. One of those fire hoses on a reel would have been just the job, but there's never a tidy red hose reel when you really need one.

Shaun felt his smooth-soled shoes start to slip and sat down quickly. Great, now he had a wet arse. He slid the remaining ten feet down the tiles until his feet hit the low parapet supporting the ornate brackets that had hooked the coat's hood. He looked across to where the kid had gone through the gap left for drainage down pipes. God, *I hate heights*, he thought. Why me? What have I done? Why couldn't it be one of those young woodentops doing all this hero shit? From all the creeping fear of heights, a strand of reasoning emerged. What was a kid doing up here in the first place? Patrick's apartment. Jesus! Holy Christ! Debbie!

He slid on his backside across the tiles, sidestepping against the parapet, moving as fast as this method would allow. "Hold on, kid," he called. The alternative being what, exactly? Okay, but he had to say something, while he braced his feet on either side of the two-foot drainage gap.

"Who's there?" a child's voice said from the darkness.

Shaun caught his balance, licked his lips, and leaned out over the six-storey drop to the pavement. "Hi, kid. Don't worry, I'm a good guy."

"Are you a policeman?"

"Kind of, yes." He thought about telling her he was her Uncle Shaun, but they'd never met, and he was sure she'd have been warned about creepy uncles, so decided to keep it professional.

"If you're a policeman, show me your badge."

"What?" He flinched as the strain of leaning out over his flexed legs began to tell on his thighs, put his hand on the parapet, and slid down until he was lying in the spouting. Great, icy water in his pants, lovely.

"Show me your badge," Debbie said from a distance.

"Or what? You're going to run away?"

"I'll scream."

"Jesus. Hang on." Shaun put his hand into his jacket, but ripped it out again as he started to fall towards the gap — which is what happens when your only support is used for something else. He braced his knee against the brickwork and finally got the process working. "Here's an ID," he said, thrusting his warrant card out into the darkness. "I don't have a badge. Satisfied?"

"How do I know it's not a fake?"

"Jesus, are you nuts?"

"You shouldn't keep swearing. I'm just a child," the distant voice said.

"Yeah, all right, sorry." He looked down to the pavement again, which was pretty stupid, being afraid of heights. "So, okay, why would I climb out here to fall to my death just to show you a fake ID?"

"I've seen it on TV. People have fake things."

Shaun was cold and wet, in places where cold and wet is far from pleasant. "Okay," he said irritably, "you've got me. I'm going home." He exaggerated the sounds of him moving, but went nowhere.

"All right," Debbie said, with more than a hint of alarm.

"So you believe me?"

"You hadn't gone, had you?"

"No," Shaun said with a shrug that was kinda wasted.

"Then that was a lie."

"A white lie," he said, as he slid along the gutter a little more so that he could reach through the gap.

"My mom says a lie is a lie and colour doesn't count."

"Bit of a smarty-pants, then, your mom?" he said, as a holding pattern while he set up to pull the kid in.

"I'll tell her you said that. She gets cross."

"Got to come up first."

"I want to see your badge."

"Jesus." Shaun sighed loudly. Fed up, cold, and embarrassingly wet. He began to wonder if the kid was worth saving. Okay, it was his niece, but hey, he'd never actually met her, so it's not like he'd miss her or anything. "Look, kid, you've already seen my ID."

"I mean, when I come up," Debbie said, with a slightly exasperated tone, which was a neat trick, bearing in mind her predicament.

"Oh, good," Shaun said, equally exasperated, "you're coming up, then?"

"If you like."

"How heavy are you, kid?"

"My name is Debbie."

Shaun shook his head. "Okay, how heavy are you... Debbie?"

"Don't know, haven't weighed myself for ages."

"I thought girls weighed themselves all the time?"

"Why? I don't."

"Pity," he said with another sigh. "So, okay, how much did you weigh... the last time you weighed yourself?"

"About thirty kilograms, I think."

"Oh, great, how much is that in English?" he said to himself. "Okay, two point two pounds to a kilogram..."

"About sixty-six pounds."

“Smart kid.”

“I’m not a kid, I’m ten.”

“Okay, you’re a smart ten-year-old, who weighs sixty-six pounds.”

“So what?”

“I don’t think I can lift sixty-six pounds with one arm.”

“You’re not very strong, are you?”

“Thanks. Look, kid...”

“I told you,” she said, her voice a little louder. “My name is Debbie.”

“Look, Debbie, I’m going to pull you up by your coat, but—”

“It’s a new coat,” Debbie said sharply.

“I’ll try not to rip it.” He leaned a little more over the drop. “If it rips, you won’t care,” he added quietly.

“Why not?”

Smart and good hearing, great. “Look, kid—”

“My name is Debbie.”

“You said. Look, Debbie, when I pull, you’re going to have to push with your feet against the wall. Can you do that?”

A scuffling sound came from below, and the coat’s hood made an ominous ripping noise.

“Whoa! Not yet!” The scuffling stopped. “Okay, I believe you can do it, but this time do it when I say. Are you ready?”

“I’m not doing anything else, am I?”

“How old did you say you are, kid?”

“I told you,” Debbie said, in that old exasperated tone. “I’m ten. And—”

“Yeah,” Shaun said tiredly, “your name is Debbie. So Debbie do you want to reach eleven?”

“Yes, of course, why?”

“Then stop making smart-arsed comments and push.”

“You talk a lot, don’t you?” Debbie said, not pushing. “Are you married?”

“I could just drop you, you know?” Shaun said, gripping the hood and jiggling it just a little.

“That would be murder, and they would hang you.”

“Maybe they would just think it took you a long time to land.”

“I’m not afraid of you,” Debbie said, a little afraid.

“Can’t say the feeling is mutual. Are you ready to come up now?”

“Yes, it’s cold.”

“On the count of three,” Shaun said, taking a strong grip on the coat hood. “One, two, three... push!”

He jammed his knees into the parapet and pulled with every ounce of his strength; the coat pulled back and began stripping his fingernails from the nail beds.

He could hear Debbie desperately pushing against the wall with her feet, but a part of his mind he wouldn't listen to told him it wasn't going to be enough, and he could feel his body tipping forward off the slope. They were going to go together because there was no way in hell he was going to let her go alone. His body rose a few more inches as the weight dragged him off the roof. Ah well, it was a shit life anyway.

Suddenly he was going the other way, back onto the roof at the very instant he passed the point of no return. An arm appeared under his and shared the grip on the coat, while another wrapped around his waist. One more pull and Shaun fell back onto the wet roof, his eyes closed and his breath coming in painful gasps, but the kid was still in the coat, and the coat still gripped in his fist.

He opened his eyes and saw Harry sitting just above him on the roof, his legs open and Shaun's head on his crotch. Motivation enough for him to sit up quickly. "Thanks," he said and pulled Debbie up to his side and away from the edge. "You all right, kid... Debbie?" His cramped arm muscles screamed at him, and he rubbed them with his other hand. "Are you sure you weigh only sixty-six pounds?"

"No," she said, trying to look at her hood. "I told you, I haven't weighed myself for ages."

"Weigh yourself soon, kid."

"Has the man with the gun gone?" Her voice betrayed real fear.

"Yeah," Shaun said, pushing himself up onto his knees, "come on, let's go."

"Go where?" Debbie said.

"Come on, kid," Harry said, using the experience he'd gained from having two sisters, "let's get off this roof."

"My name's not kid," Debbie said, glaring at him. "My name is Debbie."

Shaun laughed. "Welcome to my world."

"Yeah," Harry said, "I heard. Now can we go? I'm freezing my arse off."

Debbie shook her head and eased away a little. "I'm not supposed to go anywhere with strangers."

"Hi, Debbie, I'm Shaun, nice to meet you."

Harry chuckled. "And I'm Harry."

"That's silly, I still don't know you."

"Do you want to stay on the roof, then, until we all get to know each other?" Shaun asked, starting to shiver.

"No, not really. I'm cold."

"How did you get down here, anyway?" Shaun said, looking back up the slope.

Harry caught his eye and also looked up the slope. Yeah, that was a problem yet to be resolved. Slippery slope, little kid, and an injured hero.

"I slid," Debbie said.

"Well, yes, I see that," Shaun said. "I guess you slid down the roof after you fell out of the window."

Debbie glared at him, and the yellow light from the apartment made her look scary, even for a ten-year-old kid. "I certainly did no such thing!"

"Okay, then. How did you get down here?" Harry asked as a diversion while he tried to work out how the hell they were going to get back up. They could shout for help, but then they'd look like total twats.

"I ran through the window," Debbie said.

"That was careless, wasn't it?" Shaun said, also scouring the roof for a ladder, or a rope, or even a knotted sheet, but there's never a knotted sheet in real life.

"The bad man was shooting at me with a gun."

"Probably thought a bow and arrow would be too clumsy," Harry said. He patted Shaun on the arm and pointed up at Bob leaning out of the shattered window.

Bob hadn't got a ladder, rope, or knotted sheet, but he had stripped up the hallway carpet runner and was pushing it through the window. Cool. It rolled down the roof and stopped at the parapet a few feet from where they knelt. Just the job for a wet roof crawl.

"Okay," Shaun said, putting out his hand towards the kid. "Give me your hand, and I'll help you up—"

"You'll fall and pull me with you," she said, pulling her hand away as far as possible.

"Don't worry," Shaun said, in his best reassuring voice. "I got down here, so we'll get up the rug easy, right?"

"I will," Debbie said, "but you're old."

"Thanks, kid. Off you go, then," he said, pointing at the carpet. "You go first, and we'll stay here well out of the way."

"Why?" Debbie said suspiciously.

"So you'll miss us when you tumble past."

Harry laughed out loud before he could suppress it, and Debbie gave him a cold look.

"You go first," Debbie said, pointing at Harry.

Harry shrugged. "You think I'm younger, then?" he said and grinned at Shaun.

"No," Debbie said. "You're both old, but he's wet and will dribble on my new coat."

Harry's smile drifted away for lack of a reason to stay, and he began a very painful crawl up the carpet to the window, with Debbie following and Shaun staying back until she was safely at the window and being helped in by Bob.

Shaun climbed in, nodded at Bob, and turned to Harry, who was standing on one leg and leaning face-first against the wall, clearly in pain. Shaun put out his hand. "Thanks for that. For a second there, I thought we were going over."

"For a second there," Harry said, "you were."

Shaun smiled. "True." He shook Harry's hand firmly. "Shaun O'Conner."

Harry frowned and glanced pointedly at the apartment door and its guard, who was still watching, but showing no sign of offering assistance — policeman guarding will not desert his post, even if it means the death of a detective, a cripple, and a kid. A man with that moral compass should be an immigration official.

Shaun nodded. "He used to be my brother." And that phrase said all that needed to be said on the subject. "I owe you one..."

"Harry," Harry said, shaking the hand that still held his. "Harry Thorne, and this..." He nodded towards Bob. "Is Robert Doyle, a friend."

"Thanks, Robert," Shaun said. "I'll try to stop them billing you for the carpet."

Bob looked from him to the bare floor and back, a look of doubt on his face. "You don't think they'll—"

"Nah," Shaun said. "I'll tell them a sheikh nicked it and flew home." He chuckled and turned to Harry. "Okay, Harry. Let's go and get a drink. And you can tell me what you're doing here."

"What about the kid?" Bob asked.

"Her name's Debbie," Shaun and Harry said together.

"I'll leave her with the boys in blue," Shaun said. "They'll want to talk to her anyway, and it'll give me time to find somebody to look after her."

"I don't need looking after," Debbie said. "And you haven't shown me your badge."

43

Ethan and his team exited the same Heathrow terminal Jimmy Detroit had used to enter the country, except their mindset differed. Jimmy hated the country, while to Ethan and his team it was just another place to be instead of being someplace else.

They used the city link bus just like anyone else and arrived rested but jet-lagged at the Hilton in Green Park, not too grand, but no dump either, just a regular business hotel. They were to remain inconspicuous, and three Americans in a doss-house hotel was far from that.

"My room in ten," Ethan said as he slung his bag and exited the elevator on the second floor. Sam and Leroy followed with a groan, and Ethan spoke over his shoulder. "Second thoughts, take a shower first."

They exchanged glances, and Leroy made a show of lifting his arm and smelling his underarm. Not wise, and his expression said so.

There was a man sitting in the big armchair when Ethan entered his room. No big show, no grabbing his gun. No point. First, if the man was a bad guy, he wouldn't be sitting and reading the travel brochures, and second, Ethan's gun was en-route from the embassy. Not being the movies, carrying guns on commercial aircraft was a good way to raise a whole lot of fuss he didn't need.

The two men looked at each other for a while, each waiting for the other to speak. Ethan tossed his bag onto the bed and sat next to it.

"You're Master Sergeant Gill?" the man said with a smile.

"Last time I looked," Ethan said, hiding his surprise that the man was a Brit, but hey, he was sitting in a London hotel, so doh!

The man stood, crossed the room, and put out his hand. "Steven Priestly," he said with a white smile, which in itself was a surprise.

Ethan shook the offered hand once without getting up. "You're a spook?"

"That's a name for it, I suppose."

"What have you got for me?" The world bent a little as Ethan's brain told him to go to bed, yeah, if wishes were horses, the Lone Ranger would have a posse.

Steven took an envelope from his pocket and handed it to him. "Compliments of Her Majesty's government," he said and turned to leave.

"Be sure to say thanks next time you see the queen."

Steven chuckled quietly as he left. "Yes, she's coming for tea on Saturday." He closed the door behind him.

Ethan tossed the envelope on the bed and unzipped his bag.

He was showered and dressed in a well-worn shirt and jeans when the boys tapped gently on the door.

Leroy tossed him the gun the courier had delivered, and Ethan checked it over carefully. Colt M1911, the preferred sidearm for most Special Forces and S.W.A.T teams and the same as Sam and Leroy packed. It felt good to be dressed again.

Leroy handed Ethan a bottle of beer and shrugged. "Be rude not to come bearing gifts."

Ethan turned the cap and flinched, and caught the opener Leroy tossed him.

"Brits don't use twist tops," Leroy said with a grin. "I guess they wanna be bad-asses."

Ethan took a drink of the cold beer and waved Leroy and Sam to sit. "Okay," he said and leaned his arms on his knees. "Half the US federal agencies are here to look out for the president. And then there's us."

"So they can go home, then," Leroy said with a grin.

Ethan looked at him for a second and shut him up. "We're here because there is a clear threat to the president that these boys can't know about." He squinted. "Do I make myself clear?"

"Copy that," both men said in unison.

"The piece of shit rag-head Lupus is our only target." He took another sip of the beer. "If a bus load of terrorists roll up to the parade, we let them be." He waited a moment for effect. "That's the job of the suits."

"Copy that, boss," Leroy said. "I'm all for the easy life."

Jetlag caused Ethan's eyes to slip as he glanced at him. Easy life? The attrition rate for the unit was higher than any other Special Forces group in the US, and not through any carelessness, they were the vanguard and first to engage the worst the enemies of freedom could throw at them, and the cost was high, very high. He thought of Al Caponetto, Eddie Elward, and Manuel Alvarez, and the others before them, many, many others. And there would be more before the war was over. God, he felt tired, and not just from the jetlag. All those kids who'd stepped up to serve their country and were now gone, and for what? Did it make a difference? He couldn't say, nobody could, but they weren't just going to lie down and let their enemies strut their shit on American soil.

He opened his eyes and saw Leroy and Sam watching him quietly, and from their expressions he could tell that they knew, and that they felt it too. Three ordinary men standing in front of a hurricane of hate. Huffing and puffing and hoping to slow it down. He picked up the envelope the spook had left and tore it open, mostly to break the tension. It wouldn't contain anything he didn't already know. But he was wrong.

44

Valentin Tal had no idea what a lockup was, but he was in one. It was no bigger than a double garage, but it did what its name implied, it was lockable, and with two very expensive sniper rifles in their boxes laid out on the trestle table, locking was a pretty useful feature.

Patrick O'Conner was nervous because someone had tried to kill him the night before and because the quiet-spoken Russian scared the shit out of him. He was like something from a Cold War movie, and he felt that if he said the wrong thing, he might find himself in a gulag, or worse.

And he may very well have been right, Valentin didn't like this man who sold his country for money, he'd dealt with many such men in his long career, and he detested all of them. Where was their honour? Their love of country? This... this capitalism was like a cancer eating at the core of any nation that succumbed to its greed. When this was over, he would kill this man, when there was no more reason for him to live.

He smiled at Patrick. "Thank you for arranging these packages," he said, tapping the thin, wooden boxes on the trestle tables.

Patrick licked his lips. "No problem. It was a bit tough, but that's why you hired the best."

Valentin knew exactly how tough it had been to take delivery from the Jamaican shipper, but let it go, playing the game he'd played so many times. A grateful and stupid Russian spy. "You have received payment?" Of course he had, or he wouldn't be here.

"Yes, right on time. Thanks," Patrick said. "Now, if you'll excuse me, I have people to see."

Valentin raised a hand. "Of course, please," he said, waving the Irishman to the door. "And thank you. Perhaps we will meet again." Said the lion to the goat.

"Perhaps," Patrick said, leaving as quickly as he could, while maintaining what little dignity he could.

Valentin watched the man go, and his smile faded like a snowman's in the sun. Yes, they would meet again. He dismissed the man from his mind as he unclipped the catches on the nearest box and flipped up the lid to reveal the M200 rifle, its barrel removed and placed in its storage slot, and the rifle butt fully retracted to minimise its length and mask the case's contents. Below the rifle, tucked in their protective foam, were the rifle scope, the spotter scope, a box of one hundred .408 CheyTac rounds. And next to these was the advanced ballistics computer that did away with all the uncertainty of manual calculations.

It was an ugly little weapon in its cut-down form, but Valentin touched it gently, almost with awe. This was going to silence Russia's critics and change the financial dynamics of the West and open the door for the re-emergence of the Soviet Union. A lot to ask, even for the best rifle in the world, but it wasn't just the weapon, it was the people who would be using it, and the Brothers Vogel were the best. Veterans of half a century of struggle, who shared an astounding talent for killing at a distance, maestros of the long gun, as Valentin liked to call them.

The lockup door creaked open, and Valentin closed the lid of the rifle case, turned, and put his hand under his jacket as if scratching an itch.

"Perhaps if I gave you a chorus of Sing to the Motherland, you would not shoot me," Branislav said.

Valentin smiled. "If you sing, I probably will shoot you, if only to save my ears." He brought his hand from under his jacket and extended it to his friend. "It is good to see you again." He smiled as Jurgen stepped in behind his brother and closed the door. "Ah, and here is Jurgen."

They shook hands as if they hadn't seen each other for years. Valentin checked the street through a tiny hole he had drilled through the door, and when he was sure there was no one in the quiet industrial street, he walked back to the rifle cases and opened the second one.

"Take your pick. Choose as you would the woman who is to be your companion on a great journey," he said and waved his hand at the apparently identical rifles.

The brothers took one weapon each, assembling them with expert hands, setting them up on their bipods on top of the wooded cases, extending the collapsed stocks, squinting through the scopes and working the bolt actions, before finally examining them in minute detail.

Branislav lifted his rifle and held it across his chest like a trophy. "She will be my lover," he said with a wide grin. "Until the loving is done."

Then Jurgen lifted his rifle in one hand, as if weighing it, smiled and placed it carefully back on the case and patted it lovingly.

"Then," Valentin said, "we are ready to... how do the Americans say? Ah, to rock and to roll."

The brothers began to break down the weapons and repack them carefully in their cases. When the pleasant work was complete, Valentin looked out through the spy hole and turned back to face them. "Now take them somewhere quiet and make love with them until you know each other as you do your favourite whore," he said with a quick smile that just as quickly vanished. "There will be time for only two shots." He stepped a little closer to them. "If either of you miss, our mission fails and we betray the hopes of our Motherland. Do you understand this?"

They nodded.

"Very well, then," Valentin said, smiling again. "The next time we meet will be on the day of celebration." He waited for a moment. "Or the day of our death."

Valentin watched the East Germans cross the dirty yard, push the cases into the back of a hired Land Rover, and drive away without a backward glance. He closed the metal door, walked to the back of the unit, and pulled another case by its rope handle from behind a stack of empty cardboard boxes.

45

"I know what I was doing in Patrick's apartment, but the question is, what were you doing there," Shaun said, as they settled at a table in the window of the bar, from where they could watch the action further up the street. "Not that I'm not grateful," he added, raising his hands. "Okay, I would have got off the roof, but you helped some."

Harry chuckled, but let it go. "Just passing," he lied. "Lucky, I guess."

"Yeah, lucky that passing included a trip to the sixth floor," Shaun said and waved away Harry's protests. "And Bob here," he raised a finger towards Bob, who was busily downing a Guinness, "either he's got some sort of square growth on his gut, or he's got a wad of cash in his shirt."

Bob coughed and choked on the beer and started to formulate a plausible lie, which would have been a neat trick.

Shaun waved it away. "Look, I don't give a shit about Patrick's cash. You could've had his furniture as well for all I care." He leaned forward for emphasis and to make sure no one else in the busy bar overheard him. "You took a hell of a risk to break into his safe, and I want to know what it was you were after."

"Not really much of a risk, as it happens," Harry said, making no attempt to deny the undeniable. "What with everybody being dead."

"Except the worst one," Shaun added bitterly.

"Yeah," Bob said, "it looks like he ducked into a safe room and left everybody else to get massacred. Including that kid."

"That kid," Shaun said, "is his daughter."

Harry frowned. "Which makes you—"

"Yeah," Shaun said, "she's my niece."

"And the woman you called to fetch her?" Harry asked.

"Kaitlin," Shaun said and smiled. "Yeah, she is cute, but way out of my league. Met her at some lame ceremony. She came through, though, saying yes to taking the kid."

"Her name's Debbie," Bob said with a grin. "I believe she mentioned that."

They chuckled for a moment before relapsing into a serious mood.

"You were telling me what you were looking for in Patrick's safe," Shaun said.

"We weren't," Harry said and continued before Shaun could make the threat that hung in the air. "But no harm you knowing." He took a drink of his Guinness and arranged his thoughts. "My brother, the musician," he shook his head, "was at a gig in a tranny bar, and one of them told him he'd seen some guns. Nutty name..." He frowned as he recalled it. "Tweetie Pie," he said with a wry smile. "What sort of name is that?"

"Yeah," Shaun said, "and you should see him in the flesh." Now he wished he hadn't said it like that because now there was an image in his head that wouldn't flush.

"You know him?"

"Met him a while ago," Shaun said. "Him and a couple of his... girl friends were involved in a shootout. Nothing to hold them on that wouldn't put a dent in my day, so we cut Tweetie loose to see what he flushed out of the bushes."

"Well," Harry said, "what he flushed out was a couple of the finest extreme-range sniper rifles money can buy."

"Yeah," Shaun said. He looked around quickly, but nobody was reacting or listening, being far too engrossed in their own importance. "We met a couple of CIA types who told us all about them." He smiled. "Helpful of them. Must be this détente thing rubbing off." He smiled at the memory of the Americans in the rain. "I guessed Patrick was still up to his old tricks." He leaned on the round table and pointed at the papers. "So, do those tell you who they are for?"

"Yes. He's a businessman, and businessmen keep records." Harry tapped the sheaf of papers on the table.

"That's police evidence," Shaun said, making no attempt to do anything about it.

Harry glanced at the papers, then back at Shaun. "Yes, this is evidence," he said quietly. "So that raises two questions—"

"Why don't I take it, and why don't I arrest you for burglary and interfering with a crime scene?" Shaun said.

Bob coughed and spluttered his beer again. "I, err... have an appointment with my, err... Pilates instructor," he said, getting up quickly and pushing past the people milling around the bar.

Harry watched him go, smiled, and looked back at Shaun. "Yeah, it's a point. Why aren't we in handcuffs?"

Shaun picked up his whiskey and held it up to the light to see the amber liquid in its true glory and then put it back on the table. "You tell me?"

Harry thought about it for minute, while a waitress came over in response to Shaun's signal, took his order for another round, and left.

"Only one reason I can think of," Harry said. "Like me, you think something big is going down with these rifles, but you don't want to report it to your people. Am I warm?"

"Let's just keep it on a need to know," Shaun said, "and they don't need to know."

Harry frowned. "Why?" He saw Shaun's puzzled look. "Why wouldn't you tell SOCA about..." He picked up the page he'd been reading. "Gennady Lyachin—"

Shaun laughed.

"Did I say something funny?"

"Gennady Lyachin was a hero of the Soviet Union. Tried to save the crew of his nuclear submarine when it sank. Called the *Kursk*, if I recall."

"Wow, I'm impressed," Harry said.

Shaun smiled again, and his tired face lightened. "I saw the documentary about the sub, and it just stuck." He raised his eyebrows for an instant. "As things do."

"Okay, so that means Lyachin is probably a false name," Harry said, "which is a bit underhanded and sneaky."

Some spies can be like that.

Harry closed his eyes and let out a sigh. "What an idiot?"

"Who, me?" Shaun asked with a smile.

"Me," Harry said and tapped the papers. "Russian."

Shaun waited patiently, which was a change.

"Valentin Tal is Lyachin."

"And Valentin Tal is?"

"A Russian operative from the old days," Harry said. "A piece-of-shit spy who has given a biological weapon to an Al Qaeda nut-job named Lupus."

Shaun sat up. "What? Here?" He looked around quickly in case his raised voice had attracted attention, but nobody really cared. "Are you telling me there is a bioweapon on UK soil?"

Harry shrugged. "I don't know, but we think so."

"We think?" Shaun said, his voice suspicious.

Harry thought about it, but decided if this policeman couldn't be trusted, then the whole world really was in the toilet. "MI6," he said at last.

"MI6? Shit. That's all we need, spooks bollixing everything up."

Harry was surprised. "MI6 doesn't operate on home soil, just like the CIA doesn't operate in the US," he said quietly, still thinking that the loud and vain might give a stuff about two guys at a table talking.

"Yeah, right, course they don't," Shaun said. "So, okay, the Russian has provided Al Qaeda with a bioweapon to use here." He thought for a moment. "But that doesn't explain the rifles." He looked at Harry as he thought it through. "If this Valentin Tal is the end customer."

"Too much coincidence otherwise," Harry said.

"True. Still, if Tal is behind the bioattack—"

"What the hell does he want with the rifles?" Harry finished.

They were silent for several seconds while they waited for the waitress to deliver the drinks and place them on the table with the others. She gave them a puzzled look, but said nothing. People were odd.

"Maybe Tal is planning a diversion," Harry said.

Shaun shook his head. "You don't need a diversion to deploy a bioweapon, you just need an aerosol." He picked up the glass and swirled the whiskey gently. "What else does MI6 know?"

"About Lupus?" Harry shrugged. "Nothing, not even what he looks like. About Tal? Plenty."

"Well, yeah, they would if he was a Cold War spy," Shaun said. "We knew all of theirs, and they knew all of ours."

"Cosy," Harry said.

"Intelligence services everywhere leaked like a sieve back then."

"And things have changed?" Harry said, but his tone said otherwise.

"Yeah, maybe," Shaun said, putting down the still-full glass and looking around for the elusive waitress. "Lupus and his bioweapon are the real threat here." He signalled the waitress and pointed at the drinks lined up on the table. "But the Russian is the weak link. He's known, and he's old. Find him, and he'll lead us to Lupus."

Harry looked at the drinks forming a colourful grouping on the table, but let it go. "Finding Tal before he's picked up is easier said than done," he said. "MI6 will have brought all the other agencies into the loop by now. Somebody'll grab him."

"Maybe," Shaun said and pointed at the sheaf of papers, "but nobody knows there is a link."

"I told Sir Richard that Lupus had mentioned his name."

Shaun raised his eyebrows. "You've met Lupus?"

Harry nodded. "Yeah, we had a little chat last time I was in Afghanistan."

"And you didn't kill him?"

"No," Harry said, "seemed a bit rude at the time."

Shaun nodded. "Bit outnumbered?"

"A bit," Harry said. "Couple of hundred to... well, me."

"That'll do it," Shaun said. "Okay, but they don't know about the rifles." He considered that. "Unless the CIA told them, and I doubt that."

"I don't think they know. I only found out from the stuff in the trannies' safe."

Shaun started to ask the question, but let it go. One safe or two? What's the difference? "Okay," he said. "Let's keep it between us."

Now it was Harry's turn to be surprised. "I still don't get it," he said slowly. "Why not tell everybody what we know? Surely the more agencies looking for Tal, the better?"

Shaun shook his head. "You tell MI6 about Tal and the rifles, and it will automatically come down to SOCA."

"And that's good, right?"

"Usually, yeah," Shaun said, "but something stinks. Too many big fish have slipped off the hook, or not taken the bait at all." He dipped a finger into one of the glasses of whiskey and tasted it. "Some of them do slip the net, but I land pretty well all the ones I go after," he added, squeezing the last drop out of the fishing metaphor.

"And now?"

Shaun shrugged, as if that said it all.

"You have a mole in your department?"

Shaun watched him steadily, his silence saying it all.

"But why would anybody tip off Tal when there's a bioweapon knocking around London? It would be insane."

"Patriotically, that would be true," Shaun said, "but the bastard who's leaking information doesn't give a shit about patriotism or decency. Some of the scum he's tipped off are people traffickers and drug importers on an industrial scale. This bastard is doing it for money, simple as that. And I've got a knot in my gut telling me who that bastard might be. It's a racing certainty that Tal would pay big bucks to learn what we know about this operation."

"Makes sense," Harry said, "but MI6 will probably release what they know about Tal and a possible link to Lupus."

"I think they're sitting on that info," Shaun said, "or I would have heard."

"Why would they do that?"

"Dunno, these spooks don't think like the rest of us," Shaun said. "So this is how we work it. You stick with MI6 and give them a hundred percent on Lupus. Sir Richard is playing politics, and that's good for us. Don't tell anyone about the rifles for the moment. I'll dig into Tal on the QT and put out some BS story about a snitch mentioning a drug hit with a sniper rifle. That should cover my snooping. When either of us learns something, we share. This is my card." He took a business card from his top pocket and gave it to Harry. "Only use my cell, never give your name, and never mention any details. You got that?"

"Yes, no probs. You want my number?" Harry said.

"You're kidding, right? I'll know your shoe size and what you had for breakfast before you get home." Shaun smiled and got up to leave, but then leaned closer to Harry's ear. "Don't underestimate what you've got hold of here, son," he said slowly. "If you slip, it will kill you."

Harry shrugged. "Been tried before," he said and then saw Shaun's smile vanish. "Okay, I understand how dangerous this is. And I'll keep you in the loop."

"Son," Shaun said sternly, "you make sure I am the only person in the loop. Or we are both dead."

"Roger that," Harry said, and his leg began hurting again, as a subconscious reminder of what being dead is like. "Hey," he added as Shaun turned to leave. "What's with the drinks?"

Shaun glanced at the full glasses for a moment. "I made a promise." He turned and pushed his way through the crowd to the doors.

He stood outside and looked up the street to where the cop circus was in full swing, with blue 'keep the hell out' tape strung everywhere like bunting, and cops standing around looking important. Baxter came out of the arched doorway and looked up at the building, as if he expected to see King Kong swinging about up there.

"I see you, you bastard," Shaun said, stepping a little further back into the shadows next to the steps and glaring at Baxter. He pointed his finger like a gun and snapped his thumb down. Pow. He lowered his hand. "You'll get yours," he said quietly and walked slowly towards the apartment entrance.

The uniformed officer at the door eyed him suspiciously and examined his ID carefully before stepping aside and letting him in, but he still watched him all the way into the lift.

Shaun ignored the officer standing in the corridor leading to Patrick's apartment, and he ignored him right back. They'd met before, but even a blind man would have seen that.

He could hear Baxter mouthing off as usual as Shaun pushed open the door and stepped into the apartment. As entrances go, it was pretty impressive. The bustling room was suddenly silent, and the eyes of the five men in the room were fixed on him, except Baxter, who had his back to the door. He turned slowly, saw Shaun, and strode over, his cheeks taking on a touch of crimson that clashed with the blood on the furniture.

"O'Conner, what the hell are you doing at my crime scene?"

Not very welcoming for a member of the team.

"Thought this was DCI Facker's crime scene," Shaun said, stepping past Baxter and looking out of the window. "Yeah, nice view."

Baxter's cheeks reddened further, and he seemed to be having trouble breathing. "What part of stay away from O'Conner didn't you understand?' For a moment it looked like he might actually grab Shaun, and the rest of the cops watched with interest. Baxter felt the looks and pulled himself together, but only with a huge effort. "O'Conner, I asked you what you think you're playing at here?"

Shaun turned back from the window overlooking the sloping roof and the broken downpipe. 'I figured you could do with some help." He looked at the officers frozen in time. "Because, God knows, you look like you need it."

Baxter was shaking with contained fury. "Did your partner's shooting do something to your brain?" He squinted and leaned forward. "I know how close you two are."

It was supposed to be the ultimate insult. Shaun smiled.

"I can't believe you turn up at my crime scene after I explicitly ordered you to stay away from Patrick O'Conner."

Shaun stepped past him and crossed to where O'Brian was sprawled on the carpet. "Patrick's not here, right?" He looked around the apartment at the bodies and shook his head. "Pity."

Baxter put his hand on Shaun's shoulder, but snatched it back like it was burnt when Shaun looked back at him with ice-blue eyes.

"Get out! Do you hear me? Get out!" He was almost hysterical, and that was just too cool.

"Cold night," Shaun said with a little smile. "Nice and warm here."

"Taylor, Carter, escort O'Conner out of my crime scene!" Two of the men suddenly became unfrozen and crossed to stand next to Shaun. "And if he resists, even a little," Baxter said, leaning closer. "Shoot him."

That should have scared Shaun shitless, or at least that was the plan.

"You've been eating garlic," Shaun observed, then strolled out of the apartment.

The two detectives followed him from the room, and Carter took his arm to steer him to the lift.

Shaun stopped and turned to Taylor. "Saint Thomas' Hospital."

"What?" Taylor said. "What are you talking about, O'Conner?"

"He's been on the booze again," Carter said. "I can smell it."

"That's where they'll be taking your partner," Shaun said.

The two officers exchanged puzzled looks, and Shaun pointed casually at Carter's hand on his shoulder. Carter's lip turned up in a sneer, but he moved his hand.

"Get lost, O'Conner," Carter said, braver now he had stepped away. "Or I'll shoot you anyway and say you resisted."

Shaun smiled, but it wasn't pleasant. "Carter, you and I will talk some more on this."

"Yeah, whatever," Carter said, stepping up next to Taylor and putting his arm in front of the lift call button. "Take the stairs."

Shaun casually reached over and gripped Carter's radial nerve at the side of his forearm. It looked like he was just moving his arm away from the call button, but the effect was startling. Carter let out a girlie yelp and slumped forward in an unconscious attempt to ease the searing pain that crashed into his head.

"Thanks," Shaun said, pressing the call button, "but I'll take the lift." The lift doors slid shut as Carter clutched his arm and backed off. "Oh, that's Aikido." He smiled and pressed the lobby button. He made a quiet decision to go back to training now he had quit drinking. Apparently, it wasn't always appropriate just to shoot someone.

He was still smiling as the lift reached the lobby. Now why had he done that? Why had he gone out of his way to antagonise Baxter? He smiled. Because he could, that's why. One thing about quitting drinking, life had more fun moments.

Harry took a taxi back to Harvey's apartment, since Bob had taken the rust-bucket cab and almost sped away as soon as Shaun mentioned arresting them. Odd that. He leaned back in the hard seat and nursed his arching leg, while his mind went over the conversation in the pub. It was nuts, how the hell was he supposed to track down Tal when every agency in the UK was already looking? The rifles. Harry, you're a recon marine and a sniper, remember? This should be a walk in the park. Yeah, a walk in the park — Central Park, after midnight.

The concierge was clearly warming to him and pressed the front door release without making him wait for the privilege.

Frank was watching football on the over-the-top widescreen TV and waved hello without taking his eyes off the screen. "Good night out?" he said over his shoulder.

"Had better," Harry said distractedly. "Had worse."

Okay then, that described the night out, and the bodies.

Harry was planning to call it a day and turn in, but the TV decided that was the moment to break for the news, and Frank came back to life.

"Get you a drink?" Frank said, turning on the sofa and speaking over his shoulder. "Or some grub? I can get Serge to bring you a steak. He's a good lad."

"No, thanks, Gramps, I'm going to—" He stopped in mid stride and mid-sentence to stare at the image on the screen. The newsreader was telling the viewers about the Tripartite Accord signing and the river trip using the same barge as the Queen's Jubilee. Royalty by association — except putting shit next to roses doesn't make it smell any sweeter.

"You look like you've seen a ghost," Frank said.

Harry listened to the newsreader telling everyone that the signatories to the historic accord would travel by barge from Putney Bridge to Tower Bridge, also like the Queen, to celebrate the new détente. Security would be coordinated by the UK security services in close cooperation with its US and German counterparts. With Al Qaeda wanting another Nine Eleven and every nutcase in the world looking for immortality, no one would be allowed within a mile of the barge.

Harry sat down at the table and thought it through. That had to be it. The Russian was going to assassinate the signatories on the Thames, that's why he needed the extreme-long-range rifles. With all the variables of distance and movement, use anything less and at least one shot would probably miss.

Frank watched him and then looked back at the news and the pictures of the river Thames route the barge would take. He was old, but he wasn't stupid. He turned back to Harry. "You think somebody's going to take a shot at the barge with those fancy rifles?"

Harry frowned and let the newsreader get all excited without him. "What fancy rifles?" he said innocently.

Frank pointed at the table, and Harry looked down to see the pictures he'd left lying out in the open. "Oh, those."

"Yes," Frank said. "Those."

Harry came clean, sometimes it helps the thinking process to explain the problem. "Yes, I think somebody's going to take a shot at them," he said at last. "It's perfect. I couldn't have chosen a better place than the River Thames. Open, clean line of sight for miles." He thought about it for a moment. "Short of putting them behind bullet-proof glass, the security people won't have a snowball's hope in hell of preventing it." He looked down at the pictures of the CheyTac. "And even if they do put up some kind of Pope-mobile armoured glass, it won't stop a forty-cal round from one of those."

Frank turned off the TV as the football started again, showing how seriously he was taking this. "You've got to tell somebody," he said, standing up and joining Harry at the table.

Harry shook his head emphatically. "No, there's a leak. If I tell the authorities what I suspect, the snipers are going to know about it before I put the phone down."

"Then what are we going to do?"

Harry smiled. "We?"

"Yes, I'm not dead yet," Frank said. "If you're going to put yourself in harm's way, then I'm going to help."

That didn't come out quite as he intended, but Harry got the idea.

"That's great, Gramps, I'm going to take you up on that," he lied.

"Damn right!" Frank was flushed with excitement, and maybe a shot or two of single malt. "What's the plan?"

And that was a good question.

"Tomorrow I'm going to see if I can get a boat and follow the route the barge will take. Maybe I'll have an epiphany."

"Don't know about the epiphany," Frank said, "but I can get you a boat."

Harry was impressed. It was premature.

"You remember Cyril Shaw?"

Oh God, did he remember Shit-stain Shaw? "You don't mean that floating cesspit he uses to dump waste illegally in the river?" Of course he did.

"It's a boat," Frank said, "and you need a boat."

"I'd rather swim, but thanks. I think I'll hire a nice little runabout."

Frank shrugged. "Please yourself." He got up and returned to the sofa to resume watching football. "Some people have too much money," he added a little sulkily.

Harry smiled as he remembered Shit-stain Shaw's boat. He wouldn't get on that death trap even if he was wearing water wings and had a canoe strapped to his arse.

The next morning was cold and grey, and he thought about Shit-stain's boat with its warm if smelly cabin as he cast off the small motor launch he'd hired. It was the ideal craft for the recon mission, but the downside was it had no wheelhouse, no canvas cover, and no nothing of any kind to keep off the rain. He reminded himself it was perfect for recon, looked up at the dark sky, and asked God to hold off the downpour for a bit.

As he passed under Putney Bridge, it began to rain, but of course it did. But, he told himself as he wiped the cold rain off his face, no point being tucked away inside a nice warm cabin when you're supposed to be looking out for sniper positions. Within a few minutes, he'd found the perfect place. A high-rise apartment block a mile or so from the river, with an ideal angle and visibility. He was well into the process of congratulating himself, when he saw another perfect position, and another, and another. By the time he turned the launch round after Tower Bridge and passed HMS Belfast, he was soaked to the skin and totally demoralised. There were hundreds of places for a sniper within the optimum mile range of the CheyTac. *It was like looking for a needle in a haystack, or more accurately*, he thought *bitterly, a piece of straw in a field of haystacks*. He was fed up. He was wet. He hurt. And he'd skipped breakfast, eager to get to it. What an idiot.

By one of those twists of fate that happen in life more often than they should by sheer chance, Valentin Tal was also reconnoitring the river, but he was happy to find so many perfect positions. Spoilt for choice, he believed the expression to be. Standing on Tower Bridge, he was just another tourist, but unlike the rest of his fellow tourists, his interest was on the high-rise blocks to the south with stunning views of the Thames and the bridge. He smiled and went to find a taxi for a little trip up Jamaica Road.

46

Ethan was already forming the words to tell Leroy and Sam how they were going to capture or kill Lupus before he could release his toxin, when he scanned the documents he'd taken from the spook's envelope. He stopped, reread it, and put it on the bed.

"This shit job just got shittier," he said. "Not only do we have a bioweapon, now we have some Cold War Russian spook in the game." He closed his eyes and had to force them to open again, as the jetlag messed with his head.

"Don't those pricks know they lost," Leroy said angrily.

"Looks like they forgot," Ethan said bitterly.

"What have we got?" Sam asked, always the level-headed one.

Ethan got his shit together, got up from the bed, and paced to get his blood moving. "God knows, but we have at least one man on the ground looking to cause grief."

Leroy opened his mouth to sound off as usual, but Sam spoke first. "Spook's know what his game-plan is?"

"Not really, all they know is that a former Soviet Russian spy has imported two CheyTacs."

Sam sucked air in through his teeth. "Shit, that's a lot of firepower."

"Two?" Leroy said. "Then we can assume we have at least that many shooters."

Ethan nodded. "Anybody want to bet who the targets are."

"That's a sucker-bet," Sam said. "Question is, what are we supposed to do about it? The president's security is handled by Secret Service, and they're not going to buy us chocolates if we stamp all over their jurisdiction, post-Nine Eleven intel-sharing or not."

"Our mission hasn't changed. We're here to get the son of a bitch with the bioweapon," Ethan said. "If we trip over the Russian, well okay, we'll send him to Moscow in a body bag, otherwise, Sam's right. It's down to the Secret Service to sort that mess out."

"Roger that," Sam said. "How are we going to find Lupus in a city of ten million people?"

Ethan had been wondering the same thing, right up to the time he'd slept on the plane, but when he'd woken up, he knew. "I know how he plans to deploy the bioweapon," he said quietly.

"Okay," Leroy said, "now we're talking. How?"

"He's got the navy's Silver Fox drone," Ethan said.

"Shit!" Sam said, showing rare emotion. "Then he can launch that from twenty miles away!"

"Yeah, shit," Ethan echoed, sitting down heavily on the bed and fighting off a wave of dizziness. God knows what time it was in his head. "We need to get the navy boys to monitor its frequency and tell us where the hell it is. They lost the thing, so they can help us get it back."

"On it, boss," Sam said, taking out his satellite phone from his bag and ignoring the hotel landline on the desk.

Ethan thumbed through the papers the spook had left with renewed interest. "Looks like there're a couple of cops chasing down the rifles," he said, turning the page to a photograph of Shaun and Danny. "One of them got himself shot."

"Shall I send flowers?" Leroy said with his customary quality wit.

"I think I'll go talk to the other one," Ethan said, ignoring Leroy, as usual.

"I thought we were going to leave the rifles to the Secret Service," Sam said and then waved the response silent while he spoke into the sat-phone. He ended the call and put the phone back in his pack while they waited. "That was Lieutenant Command Lewis Druce, no less," he said, with no one any wiser. "The Lieutenant Commander was sleeping and was dischuffed to be disturbed. Dischuffed," he added with a grin.

"Never mind the poor man's broken sleep, is he going to play ball?" Ethan asked.

"He said, and I quote, 'If our commanding officer completes the necessary form and this is received in good order by his commanding officer, then he will follow his commanding officer's orders.'"

Ethan was going to swear, but so many suitable expletives rushed into his mind, by the time he'd selected one, the moment had passed, so he picked up his sat-phone from the night stand.

"Who you gonna call?" Sam asked.

Ethan let the obvious answer go. He was too pissed by the bureaucratic shit to bother. "Secnav," he said simply, and that had more impact than any wise-ass answer.

Sam and Leroy watched with undisguised pleasure as Ethan got straight through to the Secretary of the Navy. "Thank you, sir, I'm fine. How's the kids?" He went on to explain that they needed the navy to track the drone on the hurry-up, but were being stone-walled by a seat-polisher in Washington. He listened for a moment and then hung up.

They waited. He glanced at them casually. "Lieutenant Command Lewis Druce will be getting a call in a few seconds that will disturb his sleep and see him dischuffed for a very long time."

"Cool," Leroy said. "So you know Secnav? Didn't know you were so well connected."

"Did him a favour once," Ethan said non-committedly. "I guess he thinks he owes me one."

"Cool," Leroy said, not concerned about repetition.

"I'm going to talk to the cop." Shaun stood up. "Sam, you liaise with the navy on tracking the damn drone." He looked at Leroy. "Get a helicopter, and get tooled up. You are our fast-response force."

"Cool. Never been a force before," Leroy said with a smile.

If Shaun was surprised when the American marine turned up at his office, he didn't show it, he just shook his hand and took him to a first-floor conference room.

"I know about the rifles," Ethan said, taking the offered seat at the big table.

And if that was supposed to rattle Shaun into some sort of blurted disclosure, well, that failed to fly. He sat across the corner of the table from Ethan and offered him one of the many bottles of water in a neat collection.

Ethan shook his head and then changed his mind. Rehydration after a long flight is crucial for the well-being of the system, and it also gave him time to think of a new strategy because this shock 'n' awe wasn't working — though as military strategy it was pretty much a failure too, being mostly shock and really piss people off so they joined the rebels.

Shaun poured the water into a glass, having first blown out any dust. Ever the thoughtful host. "Yeah, that'll be Chuck and Chico," Shaun said.

Ethan took the water. "Chuck and Chico?"

"Spooks," Shaun said. "Though I've got to tell you, they're not very good spooks."

"Ah," Ethan said. "Walker and Rodriguez." He smiled, which actually rattled Shaun a little. "Agent Walker, Chuck Norris. Yes, I like." He frowned. "Don't get the Chico angle, though."

"You're too young, then," Shaun said, knowing that to be a flat lie.

"I wish," Ethan said, feeling every day of it in the damp British weather.

"Okay," Shaun said, leaning his elbows on the polished beech conference table. "Now that we're friends, do you want to tell me what this is about?"

Ethan smiled again. He was beginning to like this Irishman. "In three days, the president of the United States is going to stand out in the open and wave to the cameras, it being an election year. I now find out that not one, but two super-long-range rifles have suddenly arrived in this country."

Shaun watched him without a flicker of emotion. He should play poker, but hell, he had enough vices without adding that one.

"Agents... Chuck and Chico," Ethan said and smiled again, "tell me that you know about these guns." He waited. He waited in vain. Silence is the best weapon of an interrogator, nobody likes it, and sooner or later somebody needs to fill it. "I'm asking you," Ethan said, going first because he was asking so in the weaker position, "in the interest of shared intelligence, in the spirit of this BS agreement they're signing, for you to help me catch these bastards before they do something we will both regret."

Shaun spoke at last. "I won't lose any sleep over somebody killing politicians." He raised his hand before Ethan could tell him what he thought of that. "But," he said, nodding once, "I will help you." Which showed what a shrewd judge of character he was, for all the crap he projected.

"Okay," Ethan said. "Do you know who has the rifles?"

"Yes," Shaun said and then shut up.

Ethan was beginning to re-evaluate his liking for the man. He intended to say something diplomatic, but that failed in the delivery. "Will you stop jerking me around and tell me which lowlife shit has the rifles?"

Shaun smiled. "Okay then, that's better. It looks like a cold war Russian spy—"

"Valentin Tal," Ethan said.

"Yeah, so why the hell are you asking me?"

"Because," Ethan said gently, "I think you know more than you're saying."

"You show me yours first," Shaun said.

Ethan was clearly thinking it through. Done. "Something just doesn't add up here," he said at last. "We have a Russian with a bunch of rifles, and an Al Qaeda nut with a bioweapon, both turning up in London at the same time as the big pow-wow." He sipped some water. "It could be a coincidence, but—"

"You don't believe in coincidences," Shaun said with a nod. "I agree, coincidences are usually planned convergence."

"So," Ethan said, "they are in it — whatever *it* is, and I can guess — but they are in cahoots."

"I agree," Shaun said. "What I don't get is how? What have the two things got in common?"

"Maybe the bioweapon is the real weapon, and we're supposed to all run around after the snipers, who, let's face it, are a much more familiar and comfortable threat."

"Comfortable is not a word I'm used to hearing with sniper," Shaun said. "But what you're saying makes sense. We put all our resources in chasing down these rifles, which could well be just ghosts, and Lupus detonates his ethnobomb."

"My orders are to find this bastard Lupus and neutralize him, and that's just what I intend to do."

"Agreed," Shaun said. "Lupus is here, I have a contact who can ID him."

"I thought nobody has ever seen Lupus?"

"A marine had a face to face with him in Afghanistan," Shaun said.

Ethan looked surprised. "And this marine, is he named Harry?"

"That's the feller," Shaun said with a smile. "You know him?"

"Yeah, he saved my hide in some fly-blown village. Lost some good friends that day. And so did he."

"Well, we're one big happy family now," Shaun said, standing up to signal he was done. "So, we focus on the bioweapon and let the spooks take care of the diversion."

"That's how I'd play it," Ethan said.

And if Valentin had heard them, he would have smiled.

47

Harry held the striped shirt up under his chin, sighed, and tossed it on the bed with the others, unaware that he was truly his mother's son when it came to selecting an outfit for a date. He chose a blue shirt, because that was all that was left, and anyway, blue's good, probably. He held up his one tie and threw that back into the wardrobe. This was a date with Laura, not some special occasion.

The doorbell rang, and he heard Frank talking to the visitor. "I thought it was customary for the man to collect the woman for dinner?" Frank's muffled voice said.

Harry entered the living room just as Laura answered. "No guarantee he'd be able to find his way," she said, looking directly at Harry. "Remember the last and only time?"

Frank didn't and said so, but Harry did. "Hey, c'mon," he pleaded. "I was picked up by the MPs and sent on an urgent mission."

"So you say," Laura said slowly. "But I think you got cold feet and ran away to join the Foreign Legion."

"Maybe I saw myself as a latter-day Beau Geste, all dashing and romantic."

She looked him over, noting the creased blue shirt and the beige pants. "Yeah, dashing," she said and looked to heaven.

"Don't wait up," Harry said to Frank as he marched to the door, looking all dashing, and a right mess.

"Change of venue," Laura said, in pursuit. "We're going to the Chinese on the High Street." She winked at Frank. "They'll serve anyone there."

Frank grinned and returned to watching the game. "Young people. Thank God I was never one." He half turned on the sofa and looked back at the closing door. Still, it wouldn't hurt to give the missus a call, just to see how she is. Funny how you can miss someone, even when they're a real pain. And with love in the air, maybe he should get out of Harvey's way and let him... go on, then, let him what? He sighed, but maybe Margaret would rethink... nah, unlikely. He topped up his glass from the bottle secreted behind the cushions. Still, worth a bit of... y'know, matchmaking.

He'd call the missus, she was a dab hand at that sort of thing, and it would give him a reason for the call. He smiled. Two birds, one brick. He turned up the sound. Nice telly, though, he was going to miss it.

Laura caught up with Harry as the lift doors opened and he stepped inside.

"Hey, Prince Charming," she said, putting her hand on the door to stop it closing in her face. "Aren't you going to wait for your date?"

"I'd have to wait a long time," Harry said, pressing the lobby button. "I don't have one."

Laura decided she would have to do something about his dress sense if they were going to be an item.

The creased blue shirt played another starring role in their relationship later, when Laura leant over the table in the restaurant and dabbed a blob of sauce from the front. "Are you actually paying attention to what you are eating or trying to eat?" she said, with an exasperated tone.

He blinked twice and focused. "Oh, yeah, sorry." He looked down at the remaining stain. "Shit, this is my best shirt."

"Which is truly worrying," she said. Note to self, on-line clothes shopping as soon as poss. She looked him over and tried to guess his size, but all she got was fit and toned, which didn't help much and just made concentrating on her sweet and sour chicken more pressing. She changed the subject of the conversation that he wasn't involved in. "What exactly are you preoccupied with? You've hardly said a word all evening." Which, since they had been out only an hour, didn't amount to much.

He put the forkful of bean sprouts back on the plate. "It's military-type things," he said, and his man-brain thought that was an explanation.

"And do these military-type things have anything to do with sniper rifles?" She frowned, as if struggling to remember something she knew perfectly well. "Extreme-range sniper rifles?"

Harry's mouth was open, and not to receive a manly helping of gloop. "How the hell—"

She raised her hand. "Here's three words that I think will help you out," she said and leaned forward. "Harvey, Sir Richard, office door."

"That's five," Harry said absently, but he got the gist of it. "Okay, yes," he said and also leaned forward until their faces were just inches apart. Two young people with eyes only for each other. "I've been trying to work out where the snipers will set up to shoot the world leaders."

So, not romance.

She leaned back, sighed, and poured a glass of the liquid the restaurant called wine. "Tell me about it," she said disinterestedly. "It helps to bounce ideas off somebody."

Off somebody who isn't interested? Doubtful.

"They're going to use the Queen's jubilee barge," he began, and she nodded. "A bit of a flim-flam, but it will make the politicians feel important." He took the glass of wine she'd poured and swapped it for his empty one. "I took a launch along the whole route from Putney to Tower Bridge today."

"Clever you," she said, lifting the bottle of wine-ette to find it was empty. "And what did you find?" She raised her hand. "And I know it's a river, and that it rained, and that rain makes you wet. So you can just skip that."

Pity, it would have been so funny. He sighed. "Nothing." He saw her puzzled look. "Oh, sure, there are positions that offer a perfect shot at the river and anything on it. And that's the problem, there are hundreds of them."

"Then," Laura said, "we have to narrow the parameters."

Which made a hell of a lot of sense, but best not to mention it.

"Okay," Harry said, "like how?"

"Easy enough," she said, taking back her glass of wine. "Eliminate the impossible, the improbable, the unlikely, and the downright silly, and focus on what's left."

And that made total sense too, which was seriously worrying for Harry's male ego and Neanderthal expectations of a woman's logical thinking.

"Okay," she said, ignoring his look. "This sniper person—"

"Valentin Tal."

"Right, Valentin Tal. He'll want to make a splash." She raised her hand again and stopped that one. "So he'll want to shoot them in front of the world's cameras." She sipped the wine and quickly put it down. "So, it won't happen on the stretch between Putney and Waterloo Bridge. There's nothing there the cameras would be interested in. They'll want to see the great ones signing and shaking hands and waving to the fans who hate them."

"Okay, so far so good," Harry said, quietly impressed. "And the signing is right there at Tower Bridge." He sat upright. "The shooting's going to happen at Tower Bridge!"

Laura applauded slowly and quietly. "Give the boy a banana."

"All I have to do," he said, missing the implied comparison, "is work out the sightline from the bridge and I'll be able to select the best perches." He smiled, as if he'd worked it out himself, which of course he had — at least the last bit. He started to get up in eagerness to get it done.

"Where are you going?" Laura asked, knowing the answer already. "You know it's dark, don't you?"

He looked out of the window, and sure enough, it was still dark. He sat down again and poked at the oily meal that was rapidly cooling to a congealed mess on his plate.

"We could go," Laura said.

He looked up. "But it's dark," he said, puzzled.

"Yes," Laura said, "but there are things we could do in the dark that are more fun than standing on Tower Bridge." She stood up slowly. "And I'm in court in the morning, so I need to be up early."

He frowned as he tried to work out if she was saying what he thought she was saying. She raised an eyebrow at him, and her eyes twinkled. And there it was. A beautiful young woman inviting him in, without having to pay, or beat her insensible with a stick. He should stand up, hold her chair, help her on with her coat. And any of those things would have been better than what he was doing, that being sitting with his mouth open like an idiot.

"I'm going back to my place," she said. "You coming?"

He knocked his chair over in his haste and grinned foolishly at the half-dozen diners, who gave him no more than a passing glance. Idiots are everywhere.

They took a taxi back to her apartment, and all the way there, he was wondering why he hadn't even thought about sex with her before. She was stunning. He looked her over, and she watched him from the reflection in the taxi window.

He paid the driver and gave him too much tip, but what the hell? He followed her up the steps and into her apartment building. He was glad he'd taken a shower before she'd arrived. How stupid was it to think that at a time like this? He shook off the thought and replaced it with one just as stupid. Would the condoms in his wallet still be okay after all this time? She'd be on the pill, stupid. Yeah, but should he ask? Oh, great, that would go down well. 'Excuse me, Laura, but have you read the safe sex manual?' For God's sake, pull yourself together. What are you, twelve?

She held her apartment door open for him, like a gentleman role reversal, and he went in and closed his eyes for a moment while he got his head together.

He heard the clink of glasses and turned to find her holding out a half a glass of amber liquid and ice. He took the drink and sipped it, the ice clinking loudly in the silent room.

"I'll go and—"

"Slip into something more comfortable?" he said with a grin.

She gave him a long, long look and walked out of the sitting room without a glance back. Harry looked at the half-open door and shook his head. Something more comfortable? Oh God, take me now. Come on, Jesus! It's not like you haven't done it before. Yeah, but so long ago, it was like a black-and-white movie. It's like falling off a log. Ever tried getting onto a log with a gammy leg? He took another sip of whisky, but it didn't help, so he put the glass down before it screwed up what was left of his wits. Okay, time's up. Time to man-up. He needed to get his mind off being so nervous and stupid. He stepped into the bedroom and got exactly what he needed.

Laura was lying on the big bed, wearing nothing but the black judge's gown and tapping her naked thigh with the extra-wide pink leather spanking riding crop—the one that guaranteed to provide more slap and less sting.

Harry smiled. Which Laura read as approval, but was, in fact, relief. He crossed to the bed, took the spanking riding crop, and tossed it over his shoulder. "We won't be needing that," he said and put his finger on her lips before she could say whatever it was she was about to. He slipped the gown off her shoulders and started to toss it to join the whip, but changed his mind and put it carefully on the dresser. It might be the lawyer's outfit, and he wouldn't want her to look anything but her best in court.

He leaned forward and kissed her gently on the brow, straightened a little, and smoothed down her hair, then let his hand run down the side of her face to the top of the gown. It fell off her shoulders and back onto the bed. He looked down at her breasts, small but firm and with slightly oversized areola around her long nipples. He felt a kick as a shiver ran down his back and round to his groin.

She reached over and touched his belt, but he moved her hand. "There'll be plenty of time for that." He touched the tip of her nose. "You first."

She didn't get it. Was he gay?

He walked around the bed and sat down next to her, bent and kissed her lips, sucking her bottom lip and touching her tongue with the tip of his. She closed her eyes. Question answered. He leaned on his elbow and let his eyes run over her body, resting on her breasts for a moment before moving on.

She looked up at him, fully dressed, while she lay naked. It was erotic and felt a little naughty. She closed her eyes and let him look. When his fingertips touched her nipple, she jumped. It was nuts, what was this? Usually it was flip you over, wham-bam, thank you, ma'am, and d'ya fancy a beer? But this...

He kissed her gently on the forehead, swung off the bed, and began stripping off his clothes and dropping them over the arm of the chair next to the dresser, looking for all the world like he was getting ready for bed without any sense of hurry.

She watched him with pleasure as he took off his clothes, but when he pulled off his boxers, she gave a little cry. He looked over his shoulder and followed her eyes to the pinched and puckered bullet wound in his left buttock.

"Souvenir from the Taliban," he said with a shrug.

"Does it hurt?" she asked and was immediately aware of what a stupid question that was.

"Nah," he said. "Except when I do this." He poked the wound and made a show of staggering.

She sat bolt upright, instinctively reaching for him, only to see him grinning like a kid at her and standing just fine.

"You," she said with a slow shake of her head, "are a complete prick."

He looked down at his penis standing out hard and proud and took a little bow. "Well, thank you. We try to please." He stepped up and knelt on the bed. "Speaking of which." He took her face in his hands and kissed her, gently at first, but then growing in intensity as his tongue found hers.

It had been a while, a long while, and he could feel the first rapid thrusts begin. No. Not yet.

Okay, you want to shoot a duck on the river at three-hundred yards. What factors do you need to consider?

His mind flooded with the feel and the scent her.

Direction and angle to the target would have to be considered!

She pinched his nipples and swung her hips down and right and left.

And shooting down onto the river will reduce the bullet drop.

He cupped her left breast and stroked the nipple with His right hand, and her head kicked back in pleasure.

Then there's the wind, and wind over water is unpredictable!

"God, yes!" she screamed and rocked her hips as if riding a horse.

Assuming it's a scope shot, then using the mirage would be the best approach, but heat waves don't behave the same coming up off water.

He opened his eyes as Laura leaned over him, her hands on either side of his head, and her small breasts inches from his lips, bouncing in counter-time to her long, slow hip thrusts. Her eyes were tight shut, and her breath was ragged and sharp. His hips synched with hers, pushing, gyrating, becoming harder and deeper with each thrust...

Assume the wind is full value, that being right across the bullet's flight, from 3 o'clock, and fluttering the leaves, so around 10 mph.

Laura reached between her legs and raked his scrotum gently with her fingernails. His eyes snapped open as she sat up, slammed down on him and squeezed her breasts in both hands, screaming to God.

He would have to dope the scope by 10 clicks on the minute of angle scope. Then he could aim... who gives a shit about a duck!

He reached up and took over massaging her breasts as they crashed together. She cried out, almost in pain, and clenched her fists as her body shuddered and shook.

And a minute later she rolled off him and tried to catch her breath. "Jesus!" she gasped. "How did you do that?"

He blew out his breath, long and slow, and pushed himself up onto one elbow. He reached over and drew a slow figure-of-eight over her nipples. “I’m going to take a bit of a break now,” he said with a flashing smile. “So you’re up.” He stroked the inside of her thigh with his fingers. “But try to save some energy. You’re going to need it.”

48

Branislav and Jurgen had taken the train from London to Exeter, where they hired a car to travel out to the northern moors of Dartmoor, designated by the military as a live firing area, which, if you're going to test fire a couple of sniper rifles, speaks for itself. Sometimes it's better to hide in plain sight, providing there is nobody around to see you. Which is why the brothers had chosen this piece of real estate, long since fallen into disuse by the army, but kept on the books, just in case. Anyway, who wants civilians tramping around and probably getting themselves blown up? Causes a great deal of bother.

The Vogel brothers weren't tramping around, Branislav was standing on a windswept hillside in the middle of windswept nothing, and scanning the moor with binoculars for any sign of hikers, bikers, or idiots. After several minutes of meticulous inspection, he was satisfied that they were alone and turned and watched Jurgen trudging off across the peat towards a distant copse. He returned to the Land Rover and pulled one of the rifle cases from the back, taking his time because Jurgen was going to be a while. He pulled out a tarpaulin purchased from a camping shop on route, looked across the moor at the stunning landscape, and wondered why anyone in their right mind would want to spend a night out here in all this icy damp, though he knew a few German tourists who would probably be first into the freezing stream. He shook his head and wished he was American because at least they went to Florida for their vacation.

He crossed to the rocky outcrop they had selected as their base, laid the tarpaulin on the wet ground, and unpacked the rifle, refitted the barrel and the scope, slid the butt out to the required distance for his arm and extended the bipod onto a flat rock. Through the binoculars, he could see Jurgen just in front of the copse, busily erecting the target. A man-sized silhouette of a stag, as a man-sized silhouette of the president might have been a bit of a tell, should anyone see them out here in this bleak noplace.

After a few minutes, he saw Jurgen walk away to the right and stand next to the biggest tree available, this being a bent and crippled oak. A moment later, the phone in Branislav's pocket vibrated.

He wiped the fine rain from his face, lay on the wet tarpaulin, and felt the icy water creep onto his skin, having found every tiny gap in his waterproofs. On a moor, in the rain, lying on the ground, cold and wet. It was like a school holiday. Next time, they would shoot somebody in the sun.

He pushed the seven-round mag into the weapon, used the mil dot reticle on the scope to determine the range. The stag target was exactly two metres high. He multiplied this by a thousand and divided that by the mil dot indicator. One thousand eight hundred metres. He adjusted the scope gently, took a long slow breath, let it out, squeezed the trigger and, without looking at the result, stood and walked back to the Land Rover. He opened the tailgate and returned with the gear they would actually use on the day. The rock he'd chosen was ideal for the laser range-finder binoculars and the ballistic computer, which he plugged together before kneeling down to focus the laser on the stag's body. There would be no head shot on this mission, at this range that was just too risky, and unnecessary, as a hit anywhere on the target's body would produce a massive and fatal shock to the organs, as well as the loss of a huge chunk of flesh. When he was happy the target was set in the centre, he returned to the computer and read the elevation and windage results, which he used to make tiny adjustments to his manual settings. He lay down again on the wet tarpaulin, took slow breaths, and fired. The sound of the high velocity round was cushioned and swallowed by the sea of peat that covered the landscape from horizon to horizon. There would be no need for a suppressor on this mission, two shots were all that was required.

A moment later his phone vibrated, and this time he answered it. Jurgen had come out from the shelter of the oak, which could have been seen as a bit of an insult, it being ten metres from the target, but with a round one and half times bigger than the famous Dirty Harry .357 Magnum and travelling at supersonic speed, there wouldn't have been a second chance to say "oops".

Forty minutes later and twenty rounds fired, Branislav trudged out across the moor in the rain and worsening wind and passed his brother more or less halfway. "You know we have to do this again," he said, with a sad shake of his head, but Jurgen knew. There was no guarantee, even in this rain-soaked country, that the weather would be like this, so they would need to repeat the exercise on a dry, calm day. Great, but at least that meant it wouldn't be as grim.

By lunchtime, both rifles were fine-tuned and the values stored in the ballistic computer. With great relief, they packed the rifles away in the Land Rover, along with the range finder, scope, and the targets with closely grouped holes, and bounced away from that desolate place.

Branislav tuned the radio to the weather, and they listened to the promise that things were going to be dry and warmer tomorrow. He glanced at his brother, who was trying to pick the least rutted route off the moor, and received a nod. So they would be staying locally to repeat the exercise the next day. Then they would be ready for the main event. In a few days, they would be lying on a beach in South America, if things went well. If not, they would be lying on something a whole lot colder.

49

The courtroom was quiet and dignified, as courtrooms were supposed to be, and the judge was old, which was pretty much ditto. He rapped his gavel to silence the court that was already silent, and the case of the Crown versus Robert Doyle was underway.

Margaret was first up, being the prosecution, and gave Harvey and Laura a pitying look as befits the defenders of the indefensible. She looked over at Bob standing in the dock and looking smart and presentable in his new suit, purchased by Laura before the trial. She cut straight to the chase.

"Mr Doyle, did you break into number 23 Harlington Street Belgravia on the night of the nineteenth of July?"

"No, I didn't."

"Then can you tell the court what you were doing in Saint James' Park, less than five hundred yards from the home of Lady Druce-Wright on the evening in question?

Harvey stood up. "Objection, M'Lud. Five hundred yards is a long way from anywhere."

The judge shook his head. "Overruled. The defendant will answer the question."

Bob shrugged. "He's right, though, Your Majesty, five hundred yards will get you anywhere in London."

The judge tried to smother a smile and failed. "It is not necessary to address me as Your Majesty."

"Sorry, guv," Bob said.

"Or guv," the judge said, losing his smile. "You may address me as Your Honour. Now please answer the question."

"Okay, guv... Your Honour. I was in the park, true. I was rescuing a dog."

"Ah, the dog," Margaret said, raising her voice for dramatic effect. "If it pleases the court, I should like to present Crown Exhibit A, Lady Druce-Wright's dog."

"Objection, m'lud," Harvey said, standing up quickly. "Is my client charged with stealing a pet dog?"

"No, he is not," the judge said. "However, I am inclined to give counsel for the prosecution a little leeway, but only a little. Objection overruled. Have the bailiff bring in the dog."

With a great deal of crashing of metal against fine oak doors, the bailiff entered, carrying a crate containing a white dog.

"Have you seen this dog before, Mr Doyle?" Margaret asked, with a little smile as she mentally dangled the noose.

Bob leaned forward from the dock for a better look. "Looks like the one I found before the cops... excuse me, Your Majesty, before the police arrested me."

The judge smiled again and waved the proceeding on.

"You claim you found the dog?" Margaret asked loudly to squash the happy feelings the stupid judge was introducing to the courtroom.

Yeah," Bob said, wiggling his fingers at the mutt. "Rescued it, more like."

"You rescued it?" Margaret asked. "Please tell the court how you... rescued it."

"It was in the lake. In the park. In a sack," Bob said, succinctly.

"Yes, of course it was in a sack," Margaret said with that little smile again. Just put your head in this noose. "Because that's how you were carrying it. I put it to you that you stole this dog, Lady Druce-Wright's dog—"

Harvey stood up quickly. "Objection, there is no proof that this is Lady Druce-Wright's dog."

"Sustained," the judge said. "Can you furnish proof, Counsel?"

Margaret hadn't expected that and looked around for inspiration, and she saw it in Lady Lucinda. "Yes, m'lud. If the bailiff will open the cage, the dog will recognise Lady Druce-Wright, who is in court, and provide its own proof."

The judge signalled the bailiff. "Very well. Bailiff, release the dog."

Now that was a mistake.

As soon as the bailiff opened the crate, the dog jumped out, snarling. The bailiff just managed to grab it by the scruff of its neck, from where it continued to try to bite any bit of him it could reach.

Lady Lucinda jumped to her feet and leaned over the public gallery rail and clapped her hands in delight. "Oh, my little Puccini," she cried gleefully. "Come to Mommy."

The dog found something to bite, and the bailiff dropped it and clutched his groin in shock, and a great deal of hope. The dog, now free, made a beeline for Lord George, while the other spectators, smelling trouble, started to get out as quickly as possible. Little dogs, especially posh little dogs, can be particularly vicious.

The judge banged his gavel. "Order! Order or I shall clear the court."

Well, that didn't work, particularly since the court was clearing itself.

"Oh, Poochi-woochi," Lady Lucinda cried. "Come to Mommy." The dog ignored her completely, showing good sense. Instead it went straight for Lord George sitting next to her.

Lady Lucinda was stunned. "What is the matter, Poochi? Why are you growling at Uncle George? You love Uncle Georgy." She looked at the court officials and council and forced a frightening smile. "He does, you know."

The bailiff, now satisfied that everything was still where it was supposed to be, grabbed the dog by its collar and by its back, just to make sure its teeth stayed pointing forward.

Lady Lucinda leaned even further over the rail and reached for the dog, but the loveable little doggie just wanted to get its teeth into Lord George.

"I don't understand it," Lady Lucinda said, clearly stunned. "Poochi-woochi loves you, George. He's always following you around and doing that thing to your leg."

The bailiff decided to return the gnashing monster to its equally crazy owner and handed it up to Lady Lucinda, while George tried to squeeze his ample mass further back into the small seat, as the dog bared its pointed teeth and strained against Lady Lucinda's grip.

"Get that damned mutt away from me!" he shouted as it made a wild dive for his throat. "I thought I was damn well rid of it—" He shut up quickly, but it was already too late.

"What are you saying?" Lady Lucinda said, her face twisted in anger and suspicion, as only someone used to instant obedience can twist. "Did you throw Poochi into the lake?" She squinted at him and leaned forward. "You did, didn't you?"

George had managed to squirm out of his seat and was backing away towards the door.

"You monster!" Lady Lucinda screamed at him. "How could you?" She stood up and pointed a long, immaculately manicured finger at him. "Oh, I see now. You took Puccini, and you took my jewels." She took a step closer and pointed the finger at him like a dagger, while the mutt continued to struggle and gnash. "So that's how you paid for your gambling after I stopped your allowance," she hissed in a voice that could have cut glass. "You beast, you stole my jewellery!"

Lord George went for the Hail Mary defence of the hopelessly cornered. "It was insured, wasn't it?"

"How could you?" she snarled. "And you allowed this poor man to take the blame. You wait till we get home."

She either released the dog, or it escaped, either way, same result. George barely made it to the door before it was gnawing on his ankle — that being the only bit it could reach.

"M'lud," Harvey said above the bedlam in the courtroom. "I believe I rest my case."

The judge tore his eyes off the sight in the public gallery and banged his gavel. "Case dismissed."

Harvey got out of the court as fast as he could, a little unseemly for a barrister, but this case was bordering on the surreal, and he just wanted to return to his chambers and relative normality. As he reached the doors, he looked back to see Lord George trying to escape the enraged dog while being beaten on the shoulders by Lady Lucinda's umbrella.

To Harvey, it all seemed a return to his student days and a bad acid trip, and he tried to put it out of his mind, now that he was sitting quietly at his desk in his office and reading the lead in the *Times*. He looked up as Bob entered and walked up to his desk, his hand extended.

"Thanks for that, guv," he said with a big grin.

"Don't start that guv stuff again," Harvey said, standing and shaking the outstretched hand. "Anyway, it was the dog that got you acquitted, not me."

"Yeah, I suppose it was." Bob shrugged, still smiling. "Oh well, I saved it, it saved me. Fair enough. But thanks anyway."

Harvey sat back down, and Bob stayed on his feet, too wired to sit.

"I have just one question," Harvey said, inclining his head.

"Bet I can guess."

"Did you really rescue the dog?"

That wasn't the question Bob expected, but he took it anyway. "Oh yeah, it was in a sack."

Harvey's brow wrinkled in suspicion. "Strikes me as a little... err... coincidental that you were in that park on that night, at just the right moment."

"No coincidence, guv," Bob said, looking out of the window. "I followed old George and saw him throw the sack in the lake."

Harvey face said puzzled. "How did you see Lord George with the dog?"

Bob strolled to the window and looked down at the damp courtyard. Nice place. He turned back to face Harvey and smiled. "I saw him bag the mutt after he let me in and handed me the bag of jewels." He shrugged. "So I followed him."

"Lord George let you in? Into the house?" The wheels were turning at last. "So you followed him and rescued the dog? After you got the jewels?"

"Yeah, that's about it," Bob said.

Harvey was disappointed. "But you said you didn't do it."

"No, guv," Bob said, strolling back to the desk and smiling. "I said I didn't break in."

Harvey nodded an exaggerated nod. "Ah, because Lord George let you in." He sighed at the state of the world. "Rather tenuous, but nonetheless true."

Laura came in, put a cup of coffee on Harvey's desk, and watched him look from the coffee to her and back suspiciously.

"It's just a loan," she said and smiled at Bob. Happy memories.

"A loan?" Harvey said, afraid to touch the coffee in case he was agreeing to something he would regret.

"Yes," Laura said, "you get to make me one later." She looked back at him and his frown. "What? You think I'm the teaboy?"

"She's not a boy," Bob said, looking pointedly at her not-boy bits. "Count on it."

Harvey shook his head sadly, and his eyes closed. There was that old feeling coming back.

"Yeah, Lord George set it up," Bob said, continuing his statement. "I took the jewels from the old goat, as agreed. I followed him to the lake and saw him sling the mutt into the water, then go off to his club for an alibi."

"And he tipped off the police," Harvey said.

Bob frowned and then looked genuinely surprised. "Hey, I suppose he did. I never thought of that. What a rat." He tutted as it all became clear. "I wondered how come they turned up so fast."

"Never mind," Laura said, perching on the edge of Harvey's desk and ignoring his look. "He'll get his from Lucinda, and you're free."

Bob cheered up as quickly as a crying kid in a sweet shop. "Hey, right." His brow wrinkled as he thought about it. "Does that mean I get to keep the loot?"

Harvey's mouth opened, but then clicked shut. "What?" he said at last.

"If I'm innocent," Bob said, "can I keep the stuff?"

Laura laughed out loud. "You still have Lucinda's jewels?"

"Yeah," Bob said, "they're stashed under a flowerpot in the mad woman's garden."

Harvey groaned and put his head in his hands. Here comes another long day. "I don't want to hear this," he said, exasperated.

"Well, since the double jeopardy rule has been revoked," Laura said, exercising her legal expertise, "you could be tried again for stealing them."

"Good job I didn't steal them, then," Bob said.

Laura saw Harvey's confused expression and jumped in before he decided to bang his head on the desk. "I believe what Bob is saying is, he left the jewels on Lady LDW's property. So technically, they haven't been stolen."

"Cool," Bob said, "I get to keep the jewels."

"Go away, Bob," Harvey said, picking up his newspaper in the hope of returning to normality through the eyes of honest reporters.

Bob turned and headed for the door, stopped and winked at Laura, but she raised her hands and shook her head. Ah well, sometimes a fantasy works best when it's not overdone. He closed the door behind him, and Harvey looked over the top of his paper, glad it was all finally over. Yes, it had been truly surreal.

He took a sip of the coffee, which was awful and his expression said so. "So, lunch is on you today."

"That's hardly fair," Laura said, with a mock pout. "You didn't win the wager. He did it, just like I said."

"Actually, Lord George did it. Bob was just the... err... patsy."

"Ah," Laura said, surprised, "street-talk? Things are looking up." She got off the desk and smoothed down her grey suit. "Anyway, the dog caught the villain."

"Perhaps," Harvey said, "but the end justifies the means, particularly when the end is justice."

"Oh, please, give me a break. Nailing Lord Snooty is just the publicity you're looking for to support your push to become a Law Lord."

Harvey was shocked, truly shocked. "Nothing," he said, putting his hand on his heart, "could be further from my mind."

50

Unlike the shooters, Lupus didn't need the desolate expanse of Dartmoor to test his weapon. The Silver Fox drone, with a wingspan of only eight feet, was barely more than a large model plane, and although it might attract some envious looks, it wouldn't raise any alerts, so could be tested somewhere quiet but not necessarily remote. He chose Richmond Park, mostly because it was an easy drive, and he didn't drive well on the wrong side of the road, particularly in a hired panel van.

He parked at the top of a small car park next to the woods and sat in the van for several minutes, watching the few people who were visiting the park on this cold, wet Wednesday. He decided this place would do just fine, got out the van, opened the back, and lifted the eleven-kilogram drone out and placed it carefully on the gravel. A couple walking past with their dog stopped for a moment and watched, but got bored and continued on to the park. The catapult launcher was more trouble, weighing thirty kilos and two metres in length, it was awkward for one man to pull it out of the van, and Lupus was grateful for the kind assistance of a cyclist, who was clad head to foot in high viz wear and later peddled away with his ass in the air.

It took another ten minutes to assemble the drone and mount it on the catapult, during which time he had to field a few "watcha doing?" questions from people who should mind their own business. He told them it was a weather experiment, and that did the trick.

Finally, he slid the flight control console to the van's back door, opened the case, and powered it up. He was ready for the test and took a long look around to make sure there were no unwanted watchers. Satisfied he was as alone as it possible to be in the city, he released the bungee to send the Silver Fox into the air. The joystick felt alien in his fingers, but he managed to guide the drone out over the woods without crashing it into the trees. He watched the images on the console as it flew out to the edge of the park, executed a steep turn, dived, and hugged the ground across the deer park. With growing confidence, he put the plane through its paces for twenty minutes and felt perfectly at ease with the controls as he brought it down onto its belly skids in a near-perfect landing on the grassy clearing across the road.

He took his time packing the drone and its support equipment, careful not to damage anything through careless haste.

A couple of people had spoken to him, a couple more had watched the flight, but he'd tested the drone in the city of London without drawing any real attention. He was pleased with himself. But he shouldn't have been.

Sam took the call from the navy monitoring station and immediately called Ethan.

"We got a hit on the drone," he said, with as much excitement as he would have shown telling him it was raining.

"Okay," Ethan said, "he will have relocated by now, but get the data on the flight the bird made."

"Copy that," Sam said. "Distance, direction, radius. It's on the way to your phone."

"Thanks, Sam, and well done."

"Hey," Sam said, "don't thank me, it was those navy boys. Thank Lieutenant Command Lewis Druce. He was very cooperative." Sam was chuckling.

"Yeah, I bet he was," Ethan said and rang off. Maybe this was the first real break in the hunt for Lupus, and right on cue, as the signing was scheduled for noon tomorrow.

Harry stood at the base of the pillars at the road level of Tower Bridge with the cold wind off the river tugging at his thin jacket, but he was smiling. Turned out Laura wasn't just a lawyer, but had a cool analytical brain, among other things. Now focus, man, less than twenty-four hours to crunch time. He looked downriver past Saint Katherine's Pier, where the barge would turn after passing under the bridge for the world's cameras to make the most of the photo opportunity. And that's when Valentin would shoot, just as the barge started its turn, with the dignitaries waving to the world. He looked back upriver to Millennium Pier, where the signatories would disembark and swear undying mutual friendship and shake hands as another photo opportunity for the world press, before being taken on by car to the Palace for tea and bikkies. Unless Valentin and his crew had their way, in which case they'd be transported by meat wagon.

It had to be as the barge turned, or the bridge itself would block the shot. He looked west away from the bridge, towards Bermondsey and Southwark, and estimated the distance. That had to be it, the shooters would be in that direction, but anywhere in an arc up to two miles, and that still meant dozens of possible positions. Okay then, time for Sir Richard to do his thing and get the cops to do a search.

Sir Richard said no. Well, not the actual word, but being a civil servant, avoiding direct answers to a question is part of the regulation doublespeak. What he said was, "That's excellent work, Harry, and of course, I shall ensure that everything possible is done by the requisite services whose remit covers this particular aspect of the tripartite accord, within the parameters already ratified by multi-function enforcement agencies through their designated liaisons. However, within these boundaries, it would be unrealistic to expect parties not directly under the control or guidance and responsibility of this department to respond to a non-governmental operative's recommendations on a subject of such national and, indeed, international import."

"So that's a no, then?" Harry said, having learned long ago what BS smelled like, and this smelled like a herd had just passed by.

"That," Sir Richard said, bringing his fingers together in his hallmark pyramid, "is as it is."

"Then that's a no, then?" Harry said.

Sir Richard watched him for several seconds before speaking. "What I am trying to say," he said slowly for the idiot, "is that should I press the button on this and flood the skies with Black Hawks and Apaches searching for a gunman, or gunmen, as yet unknown, and it turns out to be, shall we say, unproductive." He raised his eyebrows as if he expected Harry to join right on in. "Well, we would all look rather silly, wouldn't we?"

"Not as silly as we're going to look when they're lifting the three top Western leaders off the barge in body bags," Harry said, in a remarkably calm voice.

"Be that as it may," Sir Richard said, which basically meant, argument heard and dismissed. "Can I ask you to do something for me?" he continued, getting up and walking round the huge desk and then taking Harry's arm and leading him to the door. "Would you employ those undoubted skills for which you are well regarded, and see if you can get a more... shall we say... accurate location and... if possible... a count of these foreign assassins?" He opened the door and practically threw Harry out.

Harry stood in the marble reception room and glared at the closed door. He couldn't understand what had just happened. Sir Richard was one of the good guys, so why had he waffled his way out of any action?

The snooty receptionist was watching him closely, maybe waiting for him to nick the oil paintings, the ones the public had paid for. He ignored her. Something else was going on here, something Sir Richard was keeping close to his vest. Okay, Sherlock, what?

He crossed the reception, with the snooty receptionist still watching him suspiciously, and sat in one of the oversized armchairs. Okay, two things: One, as soon as he'd told Sir Richard about the assassins, his whole demeanour had changed, which meant what? It meant, bonehead, that he thought you were nuts. And who wouldn't? First, there's this madman who'd sat on a rooftop and passed the time of day with him like old buddies, and suddenly there are two assassins in town, led by a Russian from the Cold War. Okay, kinda see his point of view on that. Probably thinks it's that post trauma shit. Yeah, probably, which is unlikely, because it all seemed so reasonable.

Harry stood up stiffly. There was a number two, but he couldn't remember what it was right then. One thing, though, Sir Richard had asked him to provide positions and a count of the assassins. Well, okay, that was a mission he would shove down his throat. He would deliver their bodies and dump them on the nice shiny marble floor. Screw him.

Harry kicked the lift door and heard the snooty receptionist gasp. And screw her too. He glanced over his shoulder. Nah, not even after a pitcher of beer and whiskey chasers.

51

Ethan sat at the small table in the hotel's executive conference suite and poured water from the free bottles they'd paid for with the room. Sam and Leroy sat across from him, Leroy spinning one of the glasses absently.

"So what we have," Ethan said, leaning over and taking the glass from Leroy, "is the drone's probable flight path."

"That's about it, boss," Sam said, pushing the bottles of water from the middle of the table and laying out a map of London with Richmond Par k circled, and the Silver Fox's flight path marked in red. "The drone flew southeast for two klicks, then circled north for one and a half klicks, before returning to its take-off point." He followed the lines with his finger as he described the route.

"That's not exactly pushing its range," Ethan said, turning the map a little.

"In London?" Sam said. "That would cover a hell of a lot of very sensitive real estate." He waited a moment. "And river."

"Okay," Ethan said, "let's assume he's going to hit the barge when the whole world is watching."

"Safe bet," Sam agreed.

Ethan stood up and leaned over the map. "He's going to want to fly it in from south of the river, away from the skyscrapers so he can keep it low. He turned the map slightly, put his finger on Tower Bridge, and traced the flight path back round and up to the river. 'That would put the launch site somewhere around... here." He put his finger on the Tate Modern Gallery.

"Be doing the world a favour if he does it the other way round," Sam said.

"You don't like art?" Ethan asked, a little surprised.

"Nah, I could never see the point of it. You want a picture of a flower, then take a photo, don't paint something that don't look anything like a daisy."

"You're a philistine, Sam, you know that?

"Yeah," Sam said with a smile, "it's been said."

"Well, you're going to get a chance to get educated," Ethan said, packing up the map. "We're going to check out the Tate and its area for a possible launch site."

"No problem," Sam said, "as long as we don't have to go in and look at stuff."

Lupus was also admiring London's sights, standing in a small crowd in front of the gates of Buckingham Palace. He smiled to himself as the guards marched out in all their finery and military precision. He turned and headed for Hyde Park, with it sports fields and other open areas, ideal for Frisbee, ball games, or launching of model aircraft, for example. He was still smiling as he sat in the restaurant by the lake and ordered a cappuccino from the polite waiter. What a friendly country.

"Yeah, that's where I'd launch," Sam said, looking down the open river bank running under Millennium Bridge.

Ethan stepped down off the path, and his boots sank a little into the muddy bank, but it was open and firm enough for a catapult launcher. Problem was, there was miles of the stuff, and it was still a bit of a stretch to extrapolate the drone satellite tracking route to exactly this spot.

"So what's the plan, boss?" Sam asked, having stayed out of the mud.

Ethan climbed back onto the path and stamped his boots. "I'll give the security boys a call, and they can stake this stretch of the river out. I don't want to be caught watching the ducks if we're wrong and he turns up someplace else."

"Amen to that."

52

Harry heard the doorbell ringing, but couldn't be arsed to get out of bed, he was still sulking over Sir Richard's strange behaviour the previous day. What was that expression? From hero to total shit, or something like that. So why should he give a shit if the government's top man didn't? No reason, that's what. Somebody was going to get shot today, and he was going to stay in bed and let them because if nobody else gave a shit... he'd been there already so reached over and took his wristwatch off the bedside cabinet. Five thirty. Who the bloody hell comes calling at five thirty? He threw the bedclothes off and stood up, slowly eased his stiff leg into operation, and limped off to tell the caller where to go.

He pulled open the door just as the bell rang again, opened his mouth to tell the caller to go screw himself, but closed it again and stared in surprise at the two military policemen standing in the hallway. Military policemen usually mean bad news, or a night in the cells, or... or he could just ask.

"Morning, gentlemen," he said, as calmly as he could manage.

"You Harry Thorne?" the sergeant said.

Harry thought about denying it and pointing at Frank's room, but that seemed a bit harsh on the old man, so he nodded.

The sergeant handed him an electronic signature getter, and he signed it as a reflex. The corporal stepped forward and handed him a large flat case, which Harry recognised instantly, it being part of his kit for the past eight years. He looked up at the sergeant and began to ask the obvious question.

"Don't ask," the sergeant said, turning to leave. "Nobody tells me nothing. Somebody says jump," he grumbled as he strode back to the open lift, "I jump, somebody says shit, I—" The lift door slid shut, but the comment kinda finished itself.

Harry looked down at the rifle case, and then both ways down the corridor, as if expecting the same police Harvey had looked for when Frank turned up. He closed the door behind him, took the rifle case to the table, and opened it. Who would send him a L115 sniper rifle? It wasn't like it was Christmas or anything. There was a brown envelope, and he took it out and emptied the contents onto the table. A single A4 page and a key. A moment later, the mystery was solved.

Sir Richard had arranged for the delivery, and the key was for the top floor of the north tower of Tower Bridge. He touched the rifle slowly, as if it was a religious artefact, and then re-read the note. He would be met at the tower at eight thirty, four hours before the signing ceremony, what he did with those four hours was entirely up to him. He smiled. So the old blow-hard was playing to the gallery with the big 'leave me out of it' speech.

He knew exactly what he would do with the four hours. He snapped the case shut and walked back to his bedroom, his leg no longer stiff and complaining. So, somebody gave a shit after all. He smiled. Okay then, so would he.

Shaun was even less impressed at being woken at six thirty than Harry had been, but the annoyance vanished the moment he heard Harry's voice.

"Fancy doing a bit of spotting for me?" Harry asked.

Shaun frowned for a moment and then got it. "Yeah, no probs," he said, swinging his legs out of bed. "Where? When?"

Harry chuckled. "Tower of London," he said, giving Shaun time to get the dig. "Okay, they haven't caught you yet. Tower Bridge, eight thirty. Bring hot coffee; it's going to be a cold morning."

"I'll be there," Shaun said, now totally awake. He was about to ring off when he had an idea. "Harry?" He waited for a response. "Are we all there is?"

Harry was silent for several seconds before answering quietly, and Shaun put down the phone. He thought for several minutes, weighing up the risk versus the possible reward, before picking up the phone again and calling Ethan.

"No can do," Ethan said in answer to Shaun's question. "My mission is to nail the son of a bitch Lupus before he launches a bioattack on the president."

"Problem is," Shaun said, "Tal and his death squad are planning to shoot your president's head off at high noon."

That should do the trick.

The line was silent for a moment. "That's your problem for now," Ethan said at last. "If we get Lupus before it goes down at your end, then the cavalry will come a boiling over the hill."

"Okay," Shaun said, "I can understand where you're coming from." One last throw. "Put my mobile... my cell number on speed dial."

"Now that I can do," Ethan said. "And good luck... to us both."

"Yeah, we're going to need it."

"What the hell," Ethan said, with a wry chuckle, "it's not like they're shooting at us."

"Maybe not, but tell that to the bioweapon," Shaun said. "Unless you've suddenly become Arab."

"There'll be no bioattack. Not on my watch," Ethan said, sounding a hell of a lot more confident than he felt.

"Okay then, and here I was worrying," Shaun said. "I'll put my sun chair on the roof and catch some rays."

Ethan was chuckling as he rang off.

53

Harry looked Shaun up and down and whistled. "Man, you look a hell of a lot smarter than the last time I saw you." He was going to say he'd looked like a hobo, but decided it might hurt his feelings.

Shaun brushed off his new three-piece mid grey suit. "Yeah, I made a promise." If there was more, it would have to wait.

Harry started up the spiral staircase, and Shaun looked up into the heavens and then back at the MI5 operative who would be guarding the entrance. "He's kidding, right?"

The spook looked at him steadily, but didn't speak — it's a spook thing.

Harry stopped and looked back. "Exercise will get the blood pumping."

"Yeah, pumping," Shaun said, starting up the stairs at a trot, which quickly slowed to a brisk walk, and finally to the pace he could actually manage.

Despite his stiff leg, Harry was already setting up the sniper rifle when Shaun made it over the top step, wheezed his way up to the battered old table, and leaned on it while he had his heart attack.

"Jesus!" he gasped eventually. "Is it me or is the air thinner at this altitude?"

Harry glanced up, smiled, and returned to assembling the rifle. He handed a spotter scope to Shaun, who looked at it like it was an alien device. "You look through it," Harry suggested.

Shaun looked through the scope.

"That way," Harry said, pointing at the window facing east.

Shaun changed direction from the blank wall and focused the single-eyepiece scope. "Whoa! I can see a pigeon taking a dump in Essex."

Harry chuckled again. "That's the plan," he said, sliding the rifle scope into place and tightening the clamp screws anchoring it to the rail.

"What am I looking for?" Shaun said and waved his hand to silence the response. "And don't say a bad man with a rifle because I can see one of those right here."

"Something that doesn't look right," Harry said.

Shaun lowered the scope and stared at him. "Something that doesn't look right? Here, in London? You've been in the hot sun too long, mate."

"Ain't that the truth," Harry said, walking over to the leaded windows and pointing east. "Check out the high rises."

Shaun joined him and looked out at the apartment blocks scattered across the East End. "Is that where you think they'll perch?"

"Yeah, it's where I would," Harry said, returning to the rifle and leaving Shaun to check each window of the apartment blocks. But there were dozens of high rises and hundreds of windows, and the reflected daylight made them impossible to see through.

"Man, this is hopeless," Shaun said lowering the scope. "I could be looking at him right now, and I wouldn't know it."

"No, they won't be there yet," Harry said, glancing at his watch. "Too early, too much of a risk they'll be seen. Give it till, say... eleven." He nodded to himself. "Yeah, an hour's set up, calm down, get comfortable. That'll do it."

"Then what the hell are we doing here at dawn?"

Harry looked out at the winter sun on the Thames and smiled. "Same thing. We get set up, scout everything in sight, and eliminate as much as possible. Then we get comfortable and calm down too. That way, the anticipation won't cloud our judgement or cause us to miss something subtle. It's standard operating procedure."

"Right, SOP," Shaun said with a sigh. "Yeah, and I could have had breakfast." And he'd forgotten the coffee. He turned the scope back onto the buildings and looked at blank windows. It was going to be a long morning.

Superintendent Baxter had intended to inform Sergeant O'Conner that he was suspended pending an inquiry that would finish his shitty career, but he was now looking at an empty desk in the squad room. He clamped his jaw and swore, furious that the revenge he'd been planning all through a sleepless night was thwarted. He turned and stamped out and almost knocked Carter over as he returned from the canteen with an extra-thick bacon and egg sandwich.

"Shit!" Carter said, juggling the sandwich back onto the paper plate. "Sorry, sir," he said quickly, seeing his commander's furious expression.

"O'Conner?" Baxter growled.

It took Carter a second to translate that into a question. "He's on a job," he said at last.

"Job? What job? I haven't authorised any case for that... that..."

"Cowboy?" Carter suggested, unconsciously rubbing his aching arm.

"Where is the soon-to-be-civilian slunk off to?"

Carter shrugged and did a rerun of saving his sandwich.

"Are you looking for O'Conner?" Taylor asked, having arrived with his coffee and croissant.

"Where is he?" Baxter asked, now getting even redder.

"I heard he's doing a job for the spooks," Taylor said with a shrug.

"What? Who the hell authorised that?"

"I think it came from..." Taylor pointed upwards.

"We'll see about that," Baxter said and stamped off down the corridor to do exactly that.

"O'Conner's in the shit," Carter said with a smile. "So, what's he doing for these spooks?"

Taylor followed him into the squad room. "He's down at Tower Bridge with some marine sniper." He put his coffee down and positioned his croissant for a bite. "There's a whisper that some dickhead is out to shoot the president. Good luck to him, I say."

"Yeah," Carter said, "I hear that."

54

Oscar's Pussy Club was closed, but it would be, there's not a lot of demand for a gay bar at ten o'clock in the morning. Jifmmy Detroit leaned against the ancient brick wall in the grubby little alley at the rear of the club, lit a cigarette, and watched the drayman rolling steel barrels of beer in through the roller door.

One more day in this dump and he'd be heading for Hawaii. Last time, so help me God. He looked blankly at the woman who glared at him and then pointedly at his cigarette. Some people are weird, y'know that? He turned his attention back to the delivery and waited until the guy had finished carrying crates of drinks into the storeroom, closed up his truck, and disappeared inside with a clipboard. He tossed the cigarette into the street, looked both ways, and strolled over to the roller door. One last look around and he slipped into the club and screwed up his nose at the stench of stale booze and piss. Sweet Jesus, there isn't enough money in the world to do this shit any more.

There was a pile of boxes of snacks on a palette, and he stepped behind them when he heard the drayman coming back. The roller door came down, its motor grinding for want of oil, and he waited until it clanged into the rusty base plate before he walked up the worn stone steps and into the club.

Curly Sue was behind the bar checking and replacing empty spirit bottles, and Big Betty was collecting the empties and dropping them noisily into plastic crates. There was some God-awful music playing, and Detroit flinched at the row. Neither Curly nor Betty saw him step in from the storeroom until he coughed.

Curly turned on the heel of his sensible shoes and glared at him. "How the hell did you get in here?" He stepped forward, the hem of his gingham dress catching on a crate.

Detroit brought the suppressed MAC-10 from under his overcoat. Not as good as his MP-5, but that was still lying on top of the elevator in Patrick's building, a testament to the thoroughness of Baxter's chosen men. But it would do, and he put three rounds into Big Betty before he could even register what was going on. Curly Sue screamed, but shut up instantly when Detroit swung the gun in his direction.

"Shut up!" he growled. "And turn that shit off."

Curly Sue was frozen to the spot. Detroit walked round to the front of the bar and put the gun down amongst the dirty glasses, leaned forward, and punched Curly Sue in the face, slamming him back against the shelves, smashing the spirit bottles and neat stacks of glasses. Curly put his hand to his broken nose and tried to stem the bleeding with his fingers.

"I said turn that shit off," Detroit said quietly.

Tweetie Pie skipped down the stairs from the upstairs flat. He was dressed almost normally, wearing tight black trousers, a slightly frilly white shirt, and slip-on white pumps. He was feeling happier than he'd felt since Talcum had been killed. Curly and Betty were his friends again, he'd got back his job as barman and customer services manager, and things were finally looking up.

"What is all that noise?" he scolded.

Detroit scooped the submachine gun off the bar in a single fluid movement and shot him twice, with no more than a thump from the gun.

Tweetie sat back onto the stairs, looked down, and tried to touch the holes in his chest, but his fingers wouldn't do as they were told. That was his favourite blouse, and now it was ruined. Suddenly very tired, he leaned back against the steps and died.

Curly Sue stood up from among the broken glass and stared in horror at the bodies. He froze, transfixed by the MAC-10, made even bigger by its oversized silencer pointing his way.

"Now," Detroit said in the same quiet tone, as if he was a friend over for tea. "Show me where you keep all your data."

Curly's brain wouldn't cooperate, and he stared open-mouthed at the gunman until the gun rapped on the bar and rattled the glasses. "What?" was all he could manage.

"Now," Detroit said, "I can understand how all this... tribulation... can throw you a curve, so I'm going to break a rule and ask you again." He raised the business end of the gun a fraction to make a point. Point made.

"Data?" Curly said quickly. "Do you mean the computer?"

Detroit nodded. "If that's where you keep all your business records, then yes."

Curly pointed at the stairs where Tweetie's body lay, and Detroit twitched the gun to encourage him to lead the way.

Despite his appearance, Curly Sue was as tough as a junkyard dog and at least as vicious, and had no intention of walking quietly to his death. He slowed his stride a fraction, as if overcome with grief at the sight of his friend's body, staggered as though in shock, spun on his heel, and went low and forward, his hand sweeping up and out and connecting with the machine gun. It was a desperate move that worked better than he could have hoped. He had the machine gun in his extended right hand and pulled it back to his body to give the guy a taste of his own medicine. But something was wrong, he felt it even as his left hand came round to grab the gun.

Something was wrong, fatally wrong. Detroit had simply released the sub-machine gun as soon as Curly touched it. Getting into a wrestling match over the weapon was fool's play and unnecessary. He shot Curly once in the head with the .22 he'd slid casually from under his left arm. Gun nuts always say a .22 has no stopping power, but in the hands of an expert, it is a gruesome weapon, powerful enough to put a round into the skull, but not enough power to punch through, so it just bounces around in there, tearing everything up.

He took the gun from Curly's hand, stepped over his body, and crossed to the stairs. People always did something desperate like that. And it always ended the same way.

He took a moment to wipe the blood from his shoe on Tweetie's shirt. A man has to have pride in his appearance.

55

Valentin's cell phone buzzed, and he put it to his ear slowly. Only two people knew his number. "Yes?"

"Tal, it's me," said one of the two. "There's a sniper team on Tower Bridge looking for your boys."

Valentin smiled quickly and then killed it in case it showed in his voice. "Thank you for letting me know. I will not forget."

"Make sure you don't," the speaker said.

"Mr Carter, have I not been prompt with your payments?"

"Yeah," Carter said in a hushed whisper, "but after this morning, you might forget. Don't." The line went dead.

Valentin allowed the smile to return. Sometimes unexpected developments improve an already detailed plan. He selected a number and pressed the call button.

56

The television crews had arrived and had set up across the bridge and on the piers for the big signing. Harry looked carefully downriver, but it was too early for anything dramatic, so he returned to scanning the buildings through the spotter scope. He looked back over his shoulder as Shaun wheezed onto the top step and stopped for a moment to catch his breath before he died from altitude sickness.

The bare wooden floor creaked and complained as Harry crossed to the stairs, took one of the take-out coffees from Shaun, and tasted it. "Ah, I wanted sugar," he said, offering the cup back to Shaun to return for the sweetener.

Shaun fixed him with his pale blue eyes, which narrowed as he began to visualise slowly strangling him.

"Second thoughts," Harry said with a quick smile, "I could do with losing some weight." He took the coffee back to the window, quickly.

Shaun put his cup on the shaky old table until the world stopped moving on its own, picked it up again, and took a sip. Not great, but coffee, though the price of delivery had been high. "Anything?" he asked, as much to get his head back to the action as any real expectation that the snipers had shot everyone and gone home.

"No," Harry said, glancing at his watch. "One hour ten. So if we're going to be the heroes, then we'd better do it damn soon."

"We're just going to be standing here with our dicks in our hands when the sky falls in," Shaun said without the slightest hint that he cared a jot.

The window in front of them exploded, showering the dusty room with glass. Instinctively Harry swung round the table and put his back against the thick wall, but then stepped out into the open, grabbed Shaun by his shoulder, and dragged him back with him.

"What the hell?" Shaun said, brushing the glass fragments off his jacket.

"That," Harry said, leaning forward and shaking glass from his hair, "is what a CheyTak .408 round sounds like... incoming."

"A what?" Shaun looked at the window and at the four-inch hole punched almost all the way through the opposite wall. He looked back at the window, and Harry could almost hear the coin drop. "The sniper is shooting... at us!"

"Well, there you go," Harry said. "That's why you're a detective, isn't it?"

Shaun gave him a dirty look. "Okay, hotshot. Shoot back."

Harry sniffed. "Yeah, sure. Point the way." He waved Shaun towards the window.

"Tell you what," Shaun said, not moving. "Let's wait till he gets fed up or goes for a piss."

Harry smiled, which seemed nuts under the circumstances, but that was the contempt folks talk about when they quote familiarity with war zones. "Let's take a peek out of the other window." He steered Shaun to the as yet unbroken window to the right. "He won't think to shoot at us through this one."

Shaun cleaned off the dust from the leaded pane and squinted through it, then jumped back. "Are you crazy?"

Harry laughed and tapped Shaun on the arm with the spotter scope. "Here, try this."

He took the scope from Harry, put it against the very edge of the glass and looked out, expecting to see a bullet heading his way. He focused on the high rises, starting again on the top floor windows of the nearest block. He raised the scope a little, tracked it across the roof, and stopped. There was a cardboard box on the roof, which was odd because it was windy, so physics should have had its way, and because it hadn't been there earlier. "Harry," he said quietly.

Harry was checking his rifle to make sure the glass and bits of window lead hadn't screwed it up. Keeping low, he stepped back up to the wall next to Shaun, took the offered scope, and pointed it at the high rise.

"Roof, right side."

Harry saw the box immediately and adjusted the focus a little. It was a hide, but it could just as easily be a dummy to draw out any counter snipers, like him. He could put a dozen rounds through the box and probably not hit anybody and just give away his position, except the sniper had already shown he knew where his targets were. He had to find a way to flush him out. He looked at his watch. And there wasn't much time to be dicking around trying to get a shot. One hour and it would be over, one way or another.

Shaun was looking over his shoulder and read his mind. "You take a shot and miss," he said quietly, "the sniper will put a round in your head. He can probably see your receding hairline right now."

Harry nodded. "That's what I'd do."

"Then we need to get him to pop his head up," Shaun said.

"I'm open to suggestions."

Shaun slapped him gently on the shoulder. "You're going to be glad you invited me along," he said, reaching into his pocket for his phone.

Harry lowered the scope, stepped away from the window, and watched with a puzzled expression. Okay, if Shaun was going to pull a rabbit out of his ass, it had better be damn soon.

"Get ready," Shaun said, putting the phone to his ear.

"I was born ready," Harry said, realized how cheesy that was, and turned back to the rifle sitting on its bipod on the old table, and ignored the thought of the massive round probably on its way to his favourite head right now. He took his time rechecking the rifle, to take his mind off... things. Yeah, it was ready, but it wouldn't hurt to give it another look. He checked the scope again for the distance to the high rise clearly visible through the hole made by the incoming round. It occurred to him that the shooter would just have to repeat the last shot and... yeah, okay, let's not go into that.

"Okay," Shaun said, interrupting the blood and guts movie running in Harry's head, "two minutes."

"For what?" Harry asked, checking his watch again. "And it's getting damned close."

Shaun nodded. "Yeah, and even if by some miracle you manage to hit him, it's just one of the bastards."

Harry gave him a shitty look, but it was wasted on a man for whom shitty looks were the norm.

Shaun sucked air in through his teeth. "Maybe if you get this one, the other will give up and leg it."

Harry looked at the cop with an expression that said it all.

"Right," Shaun said. "Professionals don't run."

"Not if they want to work again." Harry pulled a broken tubular steel chair up to the table behind the rifle, sat and looked at the high-rise roof through the scope. "I don't know what you're plotting, but now would be good."

"Don't worry," Shaun said, cleaning a small patch on the other window. "Here comes the cavalry."

"Okay," Harry said, putting down the scope and resting the rifle stock against his shoulder. "Let's rock and roll." He took a long slow breath and wished he'd remembered to bring his Tigger handkerchief. "And," he said in a voice muffled by the rifle, "if we pull this one off, I've got a wild-assed plan."

The barge carrying the US president, German chancellor, and the UK prime minister passed under Westminster Bridge and chugged slowly past the Houses of Parliament and on to the London Eye with the teeming mass of tourists. All the bridges were lined with well wishers, ill-wishers, and television crews. And police and security from the three nations — nobody was going to drop anything nasty on the great and the good. The small convoy of barge and police boats passed the Eye without incident, on schedule.

Valentin was cold and tired, having spent a long and cramped night in the small cabin cruiser tied up a little way downriver from Tower Bridge, near the retired frigate HMS *President*. An ideal spot, he had decided, and appropriate.

He stepped back from the dirty window and looked at the long canvas bag occupying most of the available surface space in the small cabin. He unzipped it slowly along its full length and lifted out the FGM-148 Javelin Missile launcher. It was heavy, but just about manageable for one man to handle, which was very thoughtful of its US designers. This was to be the instrument of assassination, while the noisy purchase of the sniper rifles had always been intended to draw intense interest from the security forces... what was it the Westerners called it? Ah yes, a red herring. And what of Branislav and Jurgen? It was sad, but they were expendable. Such is war.

He picked up his sat-phone and pressed the dial button. It was a risk, but calculated and very small at this late stage. A moment later it was answered in an immaculate English accent.

"Are you ready?" he asked.

There was silence for a moment. "Yes, I am ready. Are you?" Lupus said sharply.

"We are on schedule. The drone?"

"Why are you calling me now?" Lupus said, still angry at being questioned by this man.

"As I have said," Valentin said, "timing is everything." He let the man wait for a moment. "You go at eleven thirty exactly."

"Yes, yes, I know this. I am at a loss as to know why you feel it necessary to remind me."

Valentin smiled, amused at baiting the terrorist. "Everything hinges on you causing maximum disruption."

"At precisely eleven thirty, and on schedule, as planned," Lupus said slowly, "I shall fly the drone over the City of London and the palace, when all the tin soldiers are marching up and down. And then I shall detonate the ethnobomb, and—"

"Ethnobomb! Nobody told you to use a bioweapon!"

"Maximum disruption, remember?" Lupus said, now his turn to smile.

"Are you completely insane?" Valentin said slowly. "You will kill thousands of innocent people."

"There are no innocent people here," Lupus said.

"That is not your role in this operation," Valentin said angrily. "You are to create a diversion. That is all."

Lupus laughed. "You are a bigger fool than even I took you for." He let the Russian think about it for a moment. "You don't get it, do you? I am not the diversion. You are." The line was silent for a moment, while Lupus let it sink in. "While you are running around thinking you are striking a blow against Western decadence, your masters have entrusted me with the real mission. If you think killing these puppets will make any difference, then you truly are a fool. Yes, there will be a show of hand-wringing and crocodile tears, but in the end, they are just politicians and easily replaced. But when I turn the finance capital of the world into a graveyard, then you will see the West fall to its knees." He waited for a moment again. "But you will not see this, old man, you will be dead."

The terrorist ended the call.

Valentin's mouth was open, he could feel it, but his brain was recoiling from the horror of what he'd just heard. He closed his eyes and tried to think above the noise of a helicopter clattering downriver and over Tower Bridge.

Harry saw the police helicopter out of the corner of his eye, but kept his focus on the rooftop and the hide. The helicopter came in low across the roof, scattering the cardboard cover like confetti in a storm, and there lay Jurgen, his rifle resting on its bipod. All Harry could see through the scope was the top of Jurgen's head, and that was an impossible shot at over a mile. He needed more. And he got it.

Jurgen looked up and saw Sam in the helicopter, bringing his M14 into action. As the chopper flared and turned for another pass, he stood up and swung the sniper rifle up and round, sighted at near point-blank, and died with the message to fire already on its way to his trigger finger.

Harry's massive .338 round smashed into Jurgen's chest low and to the left, vaporised his organs, and blew out a hole on the other side the size of a fist. Jurgen's dead finger squeezed the trigger, but the rifle was already falling, and the bullet screamed out harmlessly across the city.

Valentin was on the launch's tiny deck and saw the helicopter suddenly change direction to the east and knew what it meant. They had found Jurgen. He hadn't really expected Jurgen to be able to take the snipers in the bridge, but it had been worth a try. It gave the authorities someone to play with. And part of his mind finished the thought. *It fitted into his plan.* He squashed the thought quickly, as to admit that would mean he had sacrificed one of his oldest friends—and not for the first time. And he would not be the last this day. He looked up at the pale sky and thought about the drone and its lethal cargo. He would be a casualty, and so would many others. The noble plans for a new Soviet Union had come to this. He was ashamed.

Shaun lowered the spotter scope, whistled, and slapped Harry on the shoulder. "Okay, you win a coconut. Now, time for your wild-assed plan."

"Can you ride a bike?" Harry said, abandoning the rifle and heading for the stairs.

"What, a cycle?" Shaun said, incredulous.

"No, you dickhead," Harry said, taking the stairs two at a time. "A motorbike."

"Yeah," Shaun said, bounding after him. "Wait up."

The barge approached Waterloo Bridge with a little over one and a half miles to go, and the trio of dignitaries waved at the crowds watching the big event, it being a quiet day with nothing much else to do. Smiling and waving done, the politicians returned to rubbishing the French for refusing to join the new entente.

Harry waited at the bottom of the spiral stairs for Shaun to recover enough to speak and then led the way through the main doors and onto the crowded bridge. Shaun told the spook guarding the entrance that the rifle was still upstairs and took off after Harry before he was lost in the crowds lining the rails and roadway.

Finding a bike was no problem, the police had dozens of them at the end of the bridge and in the hotel car parks. The owner of the one Shaun selected was a little reluctant to give up his wheels, until he saw Shaun's warrant card and stepped away from the machine, albeit still reluctantly.

They didn't waste time requisitioning crash helmets, and Harry climbed on the pillion behind Shaun, the siren blaring as they bullied their way through the crowd and crossed the bridge. Harry hung on as Shaun opened up the BMW R1200RT and weaved in and out of the traffic like a madman, which was so close to the truth, an onlooker wouldn't be able to squeeze a credit card into the difference.

Shaun manoeuvred the agile bike through the traffic and onto Jamaica Road, a fast A-road that would take them right to the shooter's position. He carefully jumped several sets of lights, avoiding crossing traffic and drivers who seemed to be deaf or indifferent to police lights and siren. But even with the siren, he wasn't stupid enough to shoot the lights at the first truly hairy junction and edged to the front, ready to go the instant an opportunity arose. And that opportunity arose when a truck left a few feet clearance from the car in front, and Shaun stood the bike on its back wheel and took off.

Harry clamped his eyes shut and wished he'd thought of a plan that didn't involve getting mashed. He hung onto Shaun, clamping his arms around his waist, grateful at least that none of the boys could see him hugging the policeman.

A few insane minutes later, the bike roared up to the front of the high rise, and Shaun waited for Harry to dismount before dropping it on its side and running for the doors. *Somebody's going to have a bunch of paperwork to do*, Harry thought crazily as he followed him into the building. The two men exchanged frustrated looks as the lift clunked upwards painfully slowly, as it is supposed to when its occupants are in a desperate hurry.

"Okay," Shaun said, punching the top floor button as if that would make it go faster. "I got you here, now what's the plan?"

Harry got his head together, took a breath, and let it out slowly. Okay. "I'm counting on the shooters setting up overlapping positions."

"Because you would," Shaun said before Harry could.

"I would," Harry said anyway.

"And if they have?"

"Then I'm hoping I'll be able to see the other shooter," Harry said.

Shaun shook his head and stared. "Is that it? Is that your ace-military plan?"

Harry shrugged. It was.

"You're *hoping* they'll be in overlapping positions. You're *hoping* you'll be able to see the other shooter?" Shaun sighed heavily. "Holy Mary, mother of God."

"Yeah," Harry said, "say one for me, we gonna need it."

And they truly were.

The chances of this half-arsed plan working were somewhere around those of him winning the lottery. The dignitaries were going to get shot, well, at least two of them. Shaun decided he'd try to save the US president, not because he liked him any better that the others, but he liked Ethan. He took out his phone and pressed Ethan's speed dial number.

Ethan and Sam were in the back seat of the SUV parked on the walkway of Westminster Bridge, watching the barge and its outriders disappearing slowly round the bend in the river. Ethan took the cell from his inside pocket and listened to Shaun tell him that one shooter was down, with the other one imminent — which he said with more optimism than he really felt.

"One down, one to go," Ethan said with a glance and a nod at Sam. "That's good to know."

"Listen," Shaun said quietly, as if afraid he'd be overheard. "None of these assholes is going to risk upsetting the big show on my say-so. The second shooter's going to get off two shots, tops. So you need to talk to your boys on the barge and make sure they know to keep your president out of harm's way."

Ethan was genuinely surprised, and that was a rare event these days. "Why are you giving me the heads up on this? Why not try to get the Brits to save your prime minister?"

If Ethan expected an intellectual discourse on the relative worth of the two men to Western civilization, he was going to be disappointed.

"He's not my prime minister,' Shaun said simply.

Ethan chuckled. "You're Irish, right?"

"Well, to be sure," Shaun said in an extra-broad Irish brogue.

"Okay, I'll warn the suits. If they'll pay me any more heed than your boys."

"At least you can say you tried."

"Yeah. All I have to do now is catch this mad terrorist, and I can take the rest of the day off," Ethan said.

"Piece of cake, then," Shaun said. "Shoot the bastard, then take in the sights." He wanted to say which sights to see, but had never seen any of them, so went with, "Go see the changing of the guard at the palace, it's spectacular."

Ethan put the cell back in his pocket and watched the last of the flotilla disappear past Waterloo Bridge. Suddenly he jumped as if he'd touched a live outlet and leaned forward. "Chris, get us to Hyde Park, now!"

The over-muscled British Secret Service agent put the SUV in drive without a moment's hesitation and pushed it through the crowds milling around, having watched the procession on the river. They swore, they dodged, and they almost got themselves killed, but they got the hell out of the way, like any sensible individual would with a truck-sized blacked-out SUV bearing down on them.

Sam waited and then could wait no longer. "Boss?"

"Shit! Shit! Shit!" Ethan said through clenched teeth. He turned to Sam. "How could I have been such a total bonehead?"

Sam's expression remained puzzled, and he just shrugged.

"Lupus isn't going to hit the barge," Ethan said, grimacing in anger. "He doesn't need to. He's got a bioweapon!"

Sam got it. "He's going to hit a high-value target that will drag everyone off the river or screw up the comms with panic chatter, while the shooters do their thing."

"To start with," Ethan said, getting his head in gear. "And I know what the high-value target is."

And Sam demonstrated a surprising knowledge of London. "Hyde Park is west of... Buckingham Palace." His expression hardened. "And it's the right distance. Shit!"

"Right," Ethan said. "Shit." He leaned forward again. "Floor it. Anybody gets in the way, run those civilians over."

Chris nodded once. Acceptable collateral damage came with the assignment.

Sam was checking the map and overlaying the drone's previous flight path. "After the palace, the flight plan will take the Silver Fox out over Westminster, as well as just about every government office worth mentioning. And over the City of London Financial District." Sam looked up. "And if that goes, it will bring down the whole financial house of cards."

Ethan nodded, but didn't reply. What was there to say?

Sam's phone buzzed in his pocket, and he put it to his ear and listened for a few moments. "Drone just activated," he said simply, putting the phone away.

Ethan looked out of the window for a moment while he thought about the logistics. When he turned back, his face showed emotion he rarely displayed. "Right," he said through dry lips, "console power-up is what just happened."

Sam nodded.

"Two minutes," Ethan said, counting on his fingers, and then steadied himself as the SUV lurched left past some unseen obstruction. "Set up the drone on the catapult." He continued counting on his fingers. "Three minutes?"

Sam inclined his head slightly. "Maybe for an experienced technician, probably more like five for Lupus."

"Okay," Ethan said, "five minutes, then. And to launch?"

"No time, he just has to fire it. Say one minute to be safe."

"And then flight time?"

Sam thought about it. "The Silver Fox has a top speed of sixty knots, but that kinda speed would draw all sort of attention, so I'd say half that."

"Then a couple of minutes flight time. That's ten minutes to ground zero, if we're lucky," Ethan said with an almost imperceptible shake of his head. "Less the time for the tracker to notify us." He looked at his watch. "How long to the park?" he asked Chris.

Without answering, Chris powered the SUV up the central paving, scattering the pedestrians and passing the stationary traffic backed up from the lights on Hyde Park Corner. He wrenched the SUV across in front of the traffic at the lights, clipping two tourists and sending them sprawling into the road, floored the gas, and went into the park through the arched exit gateway.

"Okay," Sam said, "we might make it."

Ethan looked at this watch. "No, we won't."

Shaun stepped onto the high-rise roof and crossed to what was left of Branislav. Harry took the spotter scope from his jacket and scoured the buildings up to the river, but saw nothing. He lowered the scope and bent down to check that the CheyTac was undamaged, and a .408 round screamed through the space he'd just vacated. It had been that close, but as Harry threw himself flat against the roof, it told him two things: that the shooter had to be at least eleven hundred metres away because it had taken a second for Harry to bend down, and the CheyTac round travels at eleven hundred metres per second. And the direction of the supersonic round told him where the shooter was.

He crawled up behind the rifle, now fully exposed with the loss of the non-bulletproof cardboard, and looked back to make sure Shaun wasn't still standing and admiring the view, and saw he was flattened against the roof and making himself as small a target as possible. Cool.

Harry took out the spotter scope, knelt, and scanned the direction of the shot for anything of interest. Another round screamed over his head, but it was at least a foot high, which most people would consider a good thing.

"Give me that," Shaun said, having crawled over from the nice safe spot on the flat, clear roof. "You do something with the big gun."

Harry raised an eyebrow. "Do something with the big gun?" He shook his head. "Is that how to address this fine weapon?"

Another round clipped the edge of the roof and tore a chunk of it away.

"Okay," Shaun said, focusing the scope. "Do something with the fine weapon."

"I would," Harry said, "if I knew where the little shit was hiding."

"He's on the top floor of those new warehouse apartments by the river." Shaun almost pointed, but common sense caught up. "Your two o'clock. Open window."

Harry lifted the rifle, shuffled round to face the river, and set it down, lay down prone behind it, and studied the buildings through the scope. Shaun was right, either the people in the top floor apartment were having a hot flush, or somebody needed the window wide open for nefarious purposes. He went for door B.

He adjusted the scope for the new range, as another round combed his hair. The shooter was compensating for the difference in the range he'd set for the barge to that required to blow Harry's head off, and he was getting close.

Shaun lay down against the roof. "For Christ's sake, shoot him!"

Harry continued to adjust the scope. He could have used the laser sight and the ballistic computer lying next to his elbow, but precise he might be, stupid he wasn't. This was going to have to be old-fashioned skill.

The next round ended any possibility of using the ballistic computer when it turned it to plastic dust.

"How many rounds has he got?" Shaun shouted, getting seriously nervous.

"Seven," Harry said quietly, sighting the rifle.

"Then—"

Harry fired. He put the rifle down and pushed himself up onto his elbows, while Shaun exercised good sense and stayed down. Harry stood up and watched him hiding under his hands for several seconds. "So," he said, "you think your wrinkly old mitts are going to stop a supersonic round weighing near on a pound?"

Shaun unhooked his fingers and looked up a little sheepishly. "You got him, then?"

"Does the pope shit in the woods?"

Shaun stood up slowly and looked at the sniper's position in the distance, at least twelve hundred yards away, as Harry had estimated. "That was a hell of a shot," he said and whistled.

"Not really," Harry said. "I normally shoot for the body, head shots are for show-offs and the movies."

"And?" Shaun said, taking the spotter scope off Harry.

"He moved," Harry said, heading for the door off the damned cold rooftop. "That's the problem with that distance, too much time."

"Still, you hit him."

"Yeah, but the apartment owner's going to be pissed. He took the round in the neck, and last I saw him, he was spraying the walls crimson." He shrugged at Shaun's questioning look. "Clashes with the carpet."

Shaun headed for the roof exit, swearing, but glad to be alive — which surprised him. He stopped at the doorway and looked back to see Harry had swung back and was standing at the edge of the roof, his spotter scope to his eye, scouring the sky to the northwest. Shaun walked back, a puzzled look on his face. "You looking for girls sunbathing?"

"Nah," Harry said, "too cold." He lowered the scope and shaded his eyes with his hand, still scouring the sky. "Not too cold for a UAV full of nasty bugs."

Shaun took the scope from Harry. "You set up the rifle, 'n' I'll do the injun thing." He focused on the river and swung out slowly over the city. "If I spot it, do you think you can hit it at this distance?"

Harry put the rifle back into position facing the city and looked up. "If the target is the barge at Tower Bridge, then yes. If it's the city, then..." He looked out at the city in the distance. "Well, that's about three thousand yards." He shook his head. "Even if it is in range, and that would be just about in range..." He was silent for a moment while he calculated the variables. "It's going to take a good four seconds for the bullet to reach the target. So— "

"So the drone has to fly straight and level for over four seconds for you to have a snowball's chance in hell of hitting it."

"That's about it," Harry said, "and that assumes I'll be able to judge its speed and direction at this distance." Harry made an adjustment to the scope. "Thing is," he said quietly, "it's not enough just to bring it down."

Shaun nodded. "Yeah, the bugs will still be released."

"I have to destroy the electronics."

"You'll do fine," Shaun lied. He gave a little start of surprise. "And here's your chance to shine." He pointed out at the city, as if Harry could see anything without the scope.

Harry turned the rifle to follow Shaun's pointing finger, swung it gently left and right, and saw the drone high above the Gherkin. He took a long slow breath and wished he had his Tigger handkerchief because he'd never needed it more. He squeezed the trigger, and the .408 Cheytac round started its supersonic flight.

Lupus was also swearing in a mix of Arabic and English. The drone was being a pain, and not doing what it was supposed to when he pushed the launch button. He wished he'd waited for the piston launcher that was lighter and more reliable, but the timing would have taken the mission right to the wire. He applied the Mechanical Realignment Principle and kicked the catapult. The drone wobbled dangerously on the flimsy structure, and was saved only when he ran forward and grabbed it, much to the amusement of a couple of kids watching and spreading ice cream over their faces.

He rechecked the bungee to make sure it wasn't caught up on anything and lifted the drone off the launcher, checked the running groove for dust or maybe rabbits, and put it back into its grooves, this time taking his time and placing it carefully in position. His nerves were still screaming at him to do it and get the hell out, but he shut that part of his mind down and concentrated on the job of getting the thing launched.

He stepped away, scowled at the kids, and pressed the switch. The Silver Fox shot off the launcher and into the sky, to gasps from the cherubs. He strode back to the console, took the joystick, and steadied the craft. Finally, he could get on with it. He looked back from the console as a black SUV skidded to a halt on the path and knew instantly what it meant.

Ethan and Sam bailed out of the car and ran the twenty metres or so to where Lupus stood behind his rental van.

"Turn around slowly, and let me see your hands," Ethan said, levelling his Colt with steady hands. "Now!"

Lupus did as he was told, turned slowly, and showed them his hands, one of which was holding a dead man's switch. He smiled, and it looked genuine. "I assume you are familiar with this kind of detonator?" he asked casually, showing no sign of any fear he might be feeling.

Ethan was very familiar with the trigger the terrorist was holding and could see that it was armed and would fire if it was released. "I'm going to count to three— "

"Count to as many as you feel you must," Lupus said, "but even if you shoot me, the trigger will engage and..." he shrugged, "the aerosol will be deployed right here, right now, and everybody dies. You, me..." He pointed at the kids standing over their dropped ice creams on the path. "Those kids, their mothers." He waved the switch for emphasis. "Everyone."

Point taken.

"Okay," Ethan said, raising his weapon a fraction, "let's negotiate. What do you want?"

Lupus smiled. "You see," he said with a real smile. "My little aeroplane, forgive me... your little aeroplane, after all you did lose it, did you not?" He waved his hand to silence the answer that wasn't coming. "Well, it's programmed to deposit most of its little cargo over the City of London and kill all those bankers, which I'm sure you'll agree, might not make me a bad person." The smile again. "It will, however, cause considerable damage to your economy. Now, how much do you think that is worth?" He waved again. "And," he said slowly, the smile disappearing, "I have saved the last drops of my little brew for the show at Buckingham Palace. A nice touch, don't you think?" No response, but none required. "So, how much will you pay to save the bankers? After all, your government has already given them seven hundred billion dollars."

"Boss," Sam said quietly.

Ethan took a quick sideways glance to see Sam was in position, his weapon steady and pointing at the terrorist's head.

"He's just yanking our chains."

"Copy that."

"I have the shot."

Ethan squeezed the trigger. "Take it."

"You need—" Lupus said, and the top of his head disappeared in a cloud of blood.

Ethan lowered his weapon to his side, and Sam stepped forward and picked up the detonator. It had fired. "Boss," he said quietly.

"Yeah, I see it," Ethan said and stepped forward, took the trigger, and examined it. "Ah."

Sam frowned and leaned forward for a closer look and smiled. "Jesus, it's a dummy."

Ethan turned and walked to the van. "Just a theatrical prop to keep us busy." He leaned in through the rear doors and swore a muffled curse.

"Shit!" Sam said, looking at the control joystick hanging off the console with its wires cut.

"Fix it," Ethan said, reaching for his satellite phone.

Sam turned the joystick over and shook his head. "Even if I had the tools, it's gonna take me at least ten minutes to splice that lot."

"Do it anyway," Ethan said, pressing the call button. He put the phone to his ear. "Leroy, what's your position?"

Leroy's voice came back over the phone, straining against the noise of the helicopter.

"Copy that," Ethan said. "Quick as you can." He ended the call and saw Sam's urgent look. "Refuelled and on route. Seven minutes."

"Might as well be seven days," Sam said, returning to his hopeless task.

Ethan punched another number and waited a moment. "The drone is loose," he said in a steady calm voice. "Pick it up, and put it into the river." He clamped his jaw at the response. "You just do your best. And, son..." he waited a moment, "if you know any good prayers, say them now." He put the phone beside the useless console.

Sam glanced at him with an expression that said all that there was to say. He returned to stripping the wires with his pocketknife. And Ethan looked at his watch.

Time up.

The barge passed under Millennium Bridge and headed downriver towards Tower Bridge and the big television event.

Valentin sat against the side of the launch, held the Javelin command and launch unit tight on his left shoulder, and squinted though the sight to locate the barge approaching slowly, with the politicians milking the watching crowds for every wave and shout. He placed the square cursor over the cabin surrounded by bomb-proof three-inch composite plastic, put his finger on the lock-on button, and stopped. In anti-tank mode, the missile would clear the launch, then climb almost vertically before powering straight down into the top of the cabin, where there was no need for protection against anything more than rocks dropped off the bridges. But he was early, too early for the world's press to catch the moment everything changed, but that madman Lupus was about to release a deadly virus above the city. He lowered the Javelin's launch unit and looked up at the ice-blue sky. Even launching early, he wouldn't make it. Nobody would make it.

To restore his beloved Russia was more important than life, but not more important than all these lives. The silent killer would spread itself on the wind, infecting everyone it touched, and they in turn would carry it out of the city and out of the country. The death toll would be unimaginable.

He set the viewer to four times magnification and switched the missile to direct mode intended for helicopter intercept. With one last look at the barge, he put the launcher back on his shoulder and swept the sky to the northwest. The day-sight thermal imaging unit picked up the tiny UAV almost immediately. *Call it luck, or call it God's intervention. Sometimes,* he thought, *a horror is too great for Him to look the other way.*

He positioned the square over the tiny dot in the distant sky and locked the missile on. Then he fired. The missile soft-launched from the unit to produce minimum shoulder recoil and rose fifty metres into the air before the rocket propellant fired, streaking the missile up towards the drone locked into its tracker.

Valentin put down the launcher and stepped off the boat onto the jetty without looking back. One day Soviet Russia would live again, but not rising from the ashes of Armageddon.

Ethan leaned forward and watched Sam struggling to reconnect the wires, but knew it was already too late, even without looking at the countdown nearing zero. Both men stepped back from the van as the Javelin detonated high above the city.

"Shit!" Sam said. "Is that what it looks like?"

Ethan couldn't help grinning like a loon. "It sure as hell is!" He slapped Sam on the shoulder. "Strike one ten-thousand-dollar model airplane!"

Harry was also being slapped on the shoulder, by Shaun. "Holy Mother of God, that was an amazing shot!"

Harry lowered the rifle and stood up slowly. "Much as I'd like to join in with you," he said, shielding his eyes against the bright winter sun, "I can't take credit for it. That was a surface-to-air missile."

"Christ, I didn't know we had air support," Shaun said.

"No, neither did I," Harry said and wondered why Sir Richard had kept that crucial fact from him. Probably more need-to-know bullshit.

57

Harry woke up, lay against his pillow, and thought about the previous day, which now seemed more and more like a crazy dream.

As he and Shaun had exited the high rise, Sir Richard's people had appeared as if by magic, bundled them into a non-descript little car with blacked-out windows, and whisked them away from the scene so that the event could be properly stage-managed.

He rolled out of bed and massaged his leg, which was finally giving up trying to drive him nuts. Dressed, but unshaven, he went in search of breakfast and found it on the table next to Frank, who looked at him over the top of the ever-present newspaper. He raised it so he could see the front page declaring that a new era of international security cooperation had thwarted an assassination attempt on the most important people in the world. Rah, Rah, go Good Guys.

"See you got the credit," Frank said, with a sniff. "International cooperation, my arse. They'll be shafting each other for the credit before the bodies are cold."

"They can have it," Harry said, buttering a piece of lightly burnt toast, that being all that was left. "Give me the quiet life."

"Yeah, right, for a week, then you'll be itching to shoot somebody."

Harry leaned over and tilted the newspaper. "Ah," he said quietly.

Frank turned the paper and read the story. "So what? Some twit launched a firework early." He shrugged. "Probably just a bit overeager."

"Yeah," Harry said, "overeager." He smiled to himself. That was a hell of a firework display, but hey, say it often enough and folks will believe anything.

"So," Frank said, "you planning to go back to creeping about and playing with big guns?"

Harry chuckled. "Bad men doing bad things must be brought to justice."

Frank stared at him in mock shock. "You know you're not dressed properly?"

Harry looked down at the faded blue jeans and carefully coordinated brown shirt.

"Your underpants aren't over your trousers," Frank said, returning to his newspaper.

Harvey came out of his room, immaculate in his pinstripe, looked at the empty plates, and picked up the phone, throwing a questioning look at Harry, who nodded and put down the burnt toast un-munched.

"Sir Richard tells me he's made you an offer," Harvey said.

"Really?" Harry said, surprised. "I thought it was supposed to be a big secret?"

"Richard and I go back a long way, so he thought he'd run it by me first."

"Like I was still a snotty-nosed kid?"

"Well, from where we stand," Harvey said with a smile, "you're not much more than that."

"So," Frank said, suddenly interested, "what's this big offer, then?"

"National security prevents me from disclosing the details of—"

"Bollocks," Frank said and fixed Harry with a look.

"Oh, okay then," Harry said. "Apparently, there's a need for someone with my particular skills to... what did he call it?"

"Work off the books," Harvey added.

"Right," Harry said. "Work off the books."

"What the hell does that mean, then?" Frank said, picking up Harry's burnt toast and completing its demise.

"It means," Harry said, "Sir Richard needs somebody to do his dirty work and not go bleating to the media when things get ugly."

"Strikes me," Frank said, "things start ugly and just get uglier."

"Now I can't argue with that," Harvey said, "but that being the nature of politics."

"So," Frank said, "you going to take up his offer and be a gun-for-hire?"

"Nah," Harry said. "Sooner or later we'll fall out, when he asks me to do something shitty."

"And that," Harvey added, "is the nature of that business."

"So, what you gonna do?" Frank asked, folding his newspaper and putting it between his leg and the arm of the chair for safekeeping. "Because you can't just sit on your arse all day around here."

Harvey stared at him in disbelief.

"I'm thinking of starting a private detective agency," Harry said.

"Yeah, right," Frank said. "What the hell do you know about detecting? You'll be out of business in a week."

"Thanks for that vote of confidence. But I'm going to have a partner, Irish guy I met recently."

They waited.

"Seems he's had it with the cop job." Harry smiled. "Too much politics. And he's suddenly got a kid, and probably a girlfriend." He smiled. "Cute too, apparently."

The doorbell rang, and Frank went to let Serge wheel in the breakfast trolley.

"Bonjour," Serge said.

"Oh, cut it out, George," Harvey said, "your secret's out."

Serge glanced at Frank, who just shrugged.

"Don't worry, son, it's between us," Harvey said, taking his breakfast off the trolley, as Serge seemed to have lost the use of his hands. "Provided you don't supply this old reprobate with any more single malt on my tab, that is."

"Not necessary," Frank said. "Your mother has graciously asked me to return to the family home."

Harvey didn't do cheering, but if he was ever going to, it would have been right then.

Shaun would soon feel like cheering, but didn't know it yet. He stood at the bottom of Danny's bed and listened to the steady beep of the monitors. This was his fault. If he hadn't been so dead set on killing Patrick, his friend wouldn't be lying here in a coma.

"You get better, Danny, you hear me?" he said quietly, as if afraid he might wake him. "Yeah, course you do. I'll be back every day, man. Until you're back on your feet, but don't forget I'm a busy man, so don't let's make it too many days, right?" He turned and started to leave.

"Wouldn't want to mess up your schedule," Danny said, his voice weak and dry.

Shaun spun on his heel and almost hugged his friend, but the mechanics of doing so defeated him. "Danny! Thank God!"

"Hey," Danny said, forcing a painful smile. "Don't I get any credit?"

"Nah. I always knew you were too bloody-minded to die off."

"Thanks, I think. Now, do you think you could give me some water?"

Shaun glanced over his shoulder as he considered calling a nurse and asking if it was okay, decided the hell with it, took the plastic bottle from the over-bed table, and put the tube into Danny's mouth for him to suck lukewarm water into his parched throat.

"That's better," Danny said, his voice slightly less painful.

"If you say so."

Danny raised his head an inch off the pillows and looked him up and down slowly, checking out his new suit and the striped yellow tie. "You going to a funeral?"

"Nah. Well, not anymore," Shaun said with a grin. "It's the new me."

"Jesus! What happened? You get married?"

Shaun smiled. "Nah. I made someone a promise."

Danny frowned. "Hell of a promise, but hey, I'm not knocking it."

"You ready for a trip to the pub, then?" Shaun said, changing the subject.

"Give me an hour to get ready," Danny said, grimacing at the pain as he moved a little. "Or maybe two."

"Okay, but first I think I'll go get one of those cute nurses."

"Hey," Danny said, and Shaun turned round. "Patrick?"

Shaun shook his head. "No. And you know what? I don't give a shit about him."

But he did give a shit about Baxter, the bastard who'd almost got their heads blown off in Tower Bridge. He'd sat by Danny's bed through the night, listening to the machines beep and working out the details of his revenge. One of Baxter's paymasters was going to get busted and would sorta find out it was Baxter who set him up. He'd had plenty of time to work through possible candidates and had finally settled on Tariq Abbas, the drug baron who'd walked away laughing when Shaun's two-year operation was blown by an insider tip-off. The man was an animal, a one-man morgue filler who'd hung one of his lieutenants from a bridge and butchered him like a side of beef as a warning to anyone who was dumb enough to need warning.

"What are you smiling about?" Danny asked.

"I was just thinking about Debbie." Shaun looked back from the door at his friend. "And a cute woodentop, who maybe isn't out of my league after all."

He stepped out of the ward, and the image of Patrick standing over his dead father snapped into his mind like a video freeze-frame. Could he really just let it go and walk away. He gritted his teeth. Yes, of course he could, and would. And that was a lie.

58

Jimmy Detroit was also thinking about Patrick O'Conner as he walked along the hotel corridor, looking for the maid's trolley left outside an open bedroom door. As always, he'd done his homework and knew about Patrick's place overlooking Cobh harbour in Ireland. He wasn't looking forward to that trip, it was always raining in Ireland, but that would be the end of it, no more countries like this shit-hole, with its cops who don't carry guns, and the stupid people and their obsession with tea. Hawaii was the next stop, with sun, surf, and good old Americans. Yeah, that and good ol' apple pie.

He glanced into the room, saw the maid busy straightening the bed, and took the key card from her trolley, slipping it into his pocket as he went to find the elevator. The room he wanted was only two flights up, but who uses stairs in a hotel?

He slid the key card through the lock and pushed the door open with his foot, his hands being used to hold the MAC-10 under the raincoat draped over his shoulders.

Valentin Tal had his back to him, leaning over the bed packing his small case, and heard a noise or felt the change in air pressure. Either way, he turned slowly, already knowing what he would find.

"Ah," he said in a steady voice. "You are the cleaner?"

Detroit nodded, but kept the gun steady as he pushed the door closed with the heel of his shoe. He walked slowly into the middle of the room. "If it makes you feel any better, I would have come for you even if you hadn't screwed up."

Valentin sighed heavily. "Of course, I should have realised." He shook his head at his stupidity. "Loose ends?"

"Not for me to know," Detroit said. "Too far down the food chain." Truth be told, he wasn't even in the food chain, just hired help. "Ironic, though, come to think of it."

Valentin raised his eyebrows. "How?" He saw the puzzled look. "How is it ironic?"

"Ah, didn't realise I'd said that out loud. But I was thinking it's ironic that this is my last job, and it's for the people who used to be the real bogey men." He shrugged. "Ironic, eh?"

A fleeting smile crossed Valentin's face. "Yes, I suppose it is... ironic." He pointed slowly at his case. "Do you mind if I write a note for my daughter? I can show you a photo, it is in my case."

"Sure," Detroit said, shrugging his shoulders. "Family is all a man really leaves behind."

Valentin turned back to the case and rummaged with his left hand, while his right found the gun he always had close by. In a fluid move that belied his age, he turned and fired twice.

But Detroit had moved two paces to his left, because people always did something desperate like that. And it always ended the same way.

BONUS: THE HELLFIRE LEGACY

HELLFIRE #2 - PREVIEW
Episode 1

THE CALL

Ethan felt the hairs on the back of his neck bristle and knew at once what it meant. He'd felt that warning many times before, first an uneasy sensation, then the increase in awareness to one side and suddenly heightened hearing. The marines call it the warrior sense, but whatever they call it, he never ignored it. He was walking past a furniture store that sold garish sofas to people with no taste, and he stopped to check the street in the window reflection. It was quiet, but at two a.m. it was going to be, in Chicago, in December with temperatures at minus 6, but feeling more like minus 60 in the moaning icy wind.

The warrior sense got worse, and then he saw the black BMW 5 with the smoked windows across the street. It was moving, but no more than walking speed, which was unlikely for a pimp-mobile like that. He walked on, turned as if to cross the street, and confirmed that the BMW was tracking him. He stepped back from the curb and walked on, checking the street for somewhere defensible. About twenty feet ahead was an alley, and he increased his pace a little. Ten feet from the entrance he heard the BMW screech as the driver put his foot down hard. He ran. The BMW wagged its ass, and the driver tried to keep it steady at maximum acceleration. Three more paces. He was going to make it.

Then he saw the kids. Two of them, boys. On skateboards. Right in front of the alley. What the hell were they doing out at this time of night? A stupid question at that precise moment.

He turned, dropped to one knee, and pulled his Sig. The BMW was right on him. An Uzi appeared in the rear window. Ethan put three rounds through the windscreen, right where the driver should be. Problem was, this was an import and the driver was in the right-hand seat. Maybe that was the whole point.

The Uzi opened up, and Ethan threw himself forward in a tight roll, came up onto his knees, and emptied the Sig into the side windows. The Uzi's barrel tilted up and sprayed the furniture store with 9 mm rounds, then fell out of the shattered window and bounced onto the street. The BMW wobbled and took off.

Ethan looked back at the kids and blew out his breath in relief when he saw them standing open-mouthed and clutching their boards as if their lives depended on it.

"Go home, kids," he said and got to his feet.

The kids didn't move. Couldn't move. They just stared at him and then at the submachine gun in the street. Ethan brushed the dirt off his battered suit. "Get!" he shouted.

His cell vibrated in his pocket, and he reached for it, wondering who the hell would be calling him at this time of night. Maybe the drive-by shooters wanted their gun back.

"Master Sergeant Ethan Gill?" It was a female voice, a voice with authority that was used to being answered.

"Who's asking?" said Ethan. He shooed the kids with his other hand, and they took off.

"Please hold for the secretary of the navy," said the voice.

He held. Not to do so would've been rude.

"Ethan?" said SecNav.

"Mister Secretary." Ethan realised he was almost standing to attention and relaxed. He looked up the street at the two black-and-whites screaming around the corner with their lights flashing, stepped back into the alley, and walked away.

"Can you talk?" said SecNav.

"Can now."

"Very well. Can you come to Washington? There's something I'd like you to do for me."

It wasn't a request.

General Prentice Davy didn't wear his uniform when travelling, there were just too many people who wanted to do the military harm, terrorists, fanatics, gun-nuts, and your everyday madmen. He did, however, wear a suit, an immaculate and very expensive suit, and he smoothed it down as he stood on the steps of the Pentagon and waited for his car to negotiate the security gate and pull up in front. He waited a moment for his driver to get out and open the door, but he seemed to be slow today, so he got in.

The Lincoln sedan moved off slowly while General Davy fastened his seatbelt and settled back into the soft leather.

"Is there a problem, Sam?"

The sedan stopped a little short of the exit onto the street, and the driver half twisted in the seat and looked back. "Sam's sick today."

General Davy opened his briefcase. "What's wrong with him?" He almost cared.

"Lead poisoning."

The general looked up and began to form the question, but froze when he saw the silenced gun pointing back from between the seats.

"Nothin' personal," said the driver.

Davy started to move, but it was pure instinct because there was just nowhere to go. The gun coughed twice, and he slumped sideways against the window. Asleep to anyone bothering to look. The driver eased the car slowly into traffic and headed for the airport—the general's original destination, but now just somewhere to dump his body.

A few hours later Ethan strode up the same steps that had been General Davy's last place on earth, and a few seconds after that he stepped through the metal detector in the reception hall, and it screamed. Of course. He sighed tiredly and walked up to the uniformed guard getting ready to pat him down with a wand. He waited patiently for him to find the Sig in his belt holster. The wand beeped rapidly. And, there you go.

The guard flipped open Ethan's jacket with the wand and looked at him like he was an idiot child. This is the Pentagon, and military types tend to forget that their hardware is in their pockets, under their armpits, or stuck in their belts. You'd think with all that training and expensive education—

Ethan took out his pistol and handed it to the guard with his thumb and forefinger, just in case. The guard took it, gave him a long, dirty look just because he could, and put the weapon on the security desk.

"Don't I get a receipt?" Ethan asked, just to press the little prick's button.

The guard looked from him to the gun, now being removed from sight by an overweight guy in a smart uniform. "Why? Don't you recognize your own weapon?"

"Yes, but now your boss has it." The fat guy wasn't his boss, he could see that, but—

"He is not my boss," the guard said, clearly irritated by this scruffy man.

"My mistake," said Ethan, smiling and heading off across the lobby to the elevators.

He stepped out of the elevator and was face to face with the woman who had told him to hold the phone in the middle of the night. Last night. So yet another day starts without sleep. He thought that was over when he retired from the marines, but here he was, jumping when ordered. And bad-tempered. He'd tried to sleep on the short flight down, but there were babies, and they were in the seat behind his. Of course they were.

"Please come this way, Mister Gill," the PA said and walked away towards the highly polished wooden doors. Closed.

Ethan thought about getting back into the elevator and finding a bar. He wasn't in the marines any more so didn't have to put up with being treated like hired help. He'd been shot at, caught a plane in the middle of the night, skipped his morning coffee, and here was this woman telling him to do this, do that—

She was watching him quietly and holding open one of the big doors. And there was SecNav, his eyebrows raised in a patient expression. Clearly forced.

Gill strode forward. Quickly.

"Mister Secretary," he said, extending his hand. "It's been a while."

"It has, Ethan." He looked him over. "Given up your uniform and started dressing like a bum, I see."

Now that was rude. Ethan looked down at his wrinkled blue raincoat and the off-the-peg suit that he'd been wearing when he'd rolled on the sidewalk. But that was to avoid some very annoying bullets.

"Disguise," he said.

"Trust me," SecNav said, "it's working." He waved him towards one of the ten chairs pushed under the oval, beech conference table and put down the folder he was holding. It didn't have *Top Secret* written on it, but in the Pentagon just about everything was top secret.

Ethan pulled out the chair and sat. He wondered why they were in a conference room instead of SecNav's office. But he didn't wonder much. He could wait.

SecNav pulled out the chair opposite Ethan, and they sat at the huge, empty table like two people who thought Christmas lunch was in April.

"Okay," said SecNav, leaning forward and resting his elbows on the table, "you'll be wondering why I asked you here."

Ethan shrugged. "Not really, I thought you were just missing me."

SecNav laughed, but cut it short. "What I am about to tell you doesn't leave this room."

Ethan said nothing.

"Three days ago, marine Brigadier General Tyrone D. Harper was shot dead as he left a diner in Atlanta." SecNav waited for a response.

"Met him a couple of times down in Fort Benning. Good officer," said Ethan, and that was enough to say it all.

"He was in civvies, so we thought it was just a mugging gone wrong." He reached over and took one of the bottles of water from the middle of the table and raised it at Ethan, who shook his head. He poured himself a glass and took a tiny sip. "It wasn't a mugging."

That was supposed to get a rise out of Ethan. It failed. He'd already come to that conclusion. Why else would he be here talking about it?

"Terrorist?"

SecNav put down his glass. "If it was, it was the sloppiest terrorist attack ever. Couple of street kids put two .38 rounds into his chest, stole his wallet, and ran in front of an APD patrol car. Still waving the pistol around." He shook his head. "The cops shot them to doll-rags. Which was a pity."

"Yes, it would have been nice to ask them why they shot the general."

SecNav looked at him steadily. He decided he was serious. "Yes, that would have been useful."

"But..." said Ethan.

SecNav raised his eyebrows.

"There's a *but*," said Ethan. "Otherwise you would have just put NCIS onto it. But I'm here. So there's a *but*."

SecNav smiled. "Yes, there's a but." He opened the folder, took out a white page, and slid it across the table.

Ethan turned it to face him and scanned the text. He looked up. "You believe this?"

"I don't know what I believe, but if it's true, and God knows it's scary enough to be. Well..." He shrugged.

Ethan read the page again. "Al Qaeda is going to kill ten generals to prove the Americans cannot even protect their own." He shook his head at the melodrama. Typical of the men he'd hunted. All mouth. He looked up. "Assuming it is true and an Al Qaeda terrorist is going on a killing spree of US generals, then you need to contact Homeland Security and bring in the FBI." It was pretty obvious.

"General Harper was one of ours, so it's my problem. And what if I'm wrong, and this note is just a hoax?" He shook his head slowly. "The other agencies will make sure everybody is looking at us. Like picking on the fat kid in the schoolyard, you know?"

Ethan knew. Make sure everybody is taunting the fat kid, and they'll leave you alone.

"So what can I do for you, sir?"

"I want you to poke around. See what you can find. Tell nobody about this, but determine if this threat is genuine." He pointed at the paper on the table.

"Why me?" Ethan brushed at his wrinkled jacket, conscious now of how shabby it was. "You've got a whole corps of people to call on."

"Nobody I can think of is better equipped for this than you." He waved Ethan silent. He wasn't going to speak. "Twelve years as a military policeman—exemplary record—then seven years Special Operations." He shrugged. "An extension of the police role, really. Examining evidence, following clues, finding people. Only difference being—"

"I shot them instead of arresting them." Ethan looked past SecNav at the framed photographs of warships. "Cuts down the paperwork."

"Quite. What I want is—"

The conference room door opened, and the PA walked quickly over and leaned close to SecNav and whispered. Ethan could hear her clearly; there was nothing wrong with his hearing, what was shot was his—

"Thank you, Collette." SecNav waited for her to leave and then took a long breath. "Air force General Davy has been shot."

Ethan had met the man. A bit of a prig, but as brave as a two-star general could get. "Looks like the threat is playing out." He pushed the paper back across the table. "Time to call the FBI."

SecNav nodded slowly as he thought about it. "Okay," he said quietly. "But I still want you to investigate this. On the QT."

Ethan tilted his head questioningly. "You're the boss, but I think the FBI will have something to say about me stamping all over their case."

"Don't stamp." SecNav put the paper back into the folder. "We need to move quickly on this. Federal agencies don't move quickly. It's not in their nature."

"Copy that."

SecNav stood and looked Ethan over. He didn't like what he saw, that was clear. "Buy some new clothes. And get a shave."

Ethan smiled. "Sounds like an order."

"That's because it is. Welcome back to the marines, Master Sergeant Gill."

Ethan swore under his breath. Two years out, and recalled. Great. Okay, he was overreacting, he knew that. This was a temporary call-up, just until the terrorist or terrorists got caught. Or all the generals got killed.

Back in the marines, but secretly he had to admit he liked the idea. And he'd get paid, which would be a novelty these days. He stood up and pushed the chair back under the table.

"I'll need everything you have on the assassinations."

"That won't be difficult," said SecNav, and dropped the file back onto the table. "One more thing." He started for the door, with a clear indication to follow.

Ethan picked up the file and followed him out of the conference room, down several corridors, a flight of stairs, and through more big doors. Then he was in SecNav's office. It wasn't what he'd expected, because it was smaller, much smaller. A round, inlaid coffee table occupied the middle of the office, and a stitched leather sofa and chairs the remainder. With just enough space for a polished teak desk and chair by the window. He looked around and thought if this was the best the head of the navy could look forward to, then a Master Sergeant was just going to get a hole in the ground. Which in Ethan's case was likely to be literally true. He shrugged it off. A man can only sit on one seat at a time, so this office was fine.

What was also fine was the woman sitting in one of the leather arm chairs. Mid-thirties, short auburn hair that said *military*, and a toned body beneath an immaculate grey business suit.

She waited for him to finish checking her out. It's what men always did. She returned the compliment and moved up from his scuffed tan desert boots to his blue suit pants, with the mud from the sidewalk still on the knees. An interesting colour combination. The jacket she just glanced at. A person can only take so much. She stopped at his face and raised an eyebrow. Not bad. A bit chipped from too much warfare, but good lines, and dark brown eyes that had wrinkles from laughter or from too much desert sun. His dark hair had a generous proportion of grey, but that was okay. Even if its length wasn't. He would probably be presentable when he got cleaned up.

"Kelsey Lyle, meet Ethan Gill." SecNav was smiling. He'd seen the way Kelsey had disapproved of his choice, until she met his eyes. If nothing else, he was a shrewd judge of character, and no mean matchmaker. Or so his wife would say, if she was still speaking to him. Water under the bridge.

Ethan stepped up to the armchair and extended a hand. "Pleased to meet you, Kelsey." And he was.

She looked at his hand for several seconds, to make sure it was cleaner than the rest of him. Satisfied by the spotless and well-manicured nails, she shook his hand.

"Kelsey is my NCIS special agent on this case," SecNav explained before Ethan asked. "She is also the liaison with the FBI." He smiled. "Yes, they have been informed and are on their way. Very efficient of them." The smile dropped. "And Kelsey will be your channel to me."

"I work alone."

"Not on this one you don't," said SecNav, and his tone showed he meant it. "This is too close to home and could just blow up in my face."

Ethan nodded. "Understood." He sat on the leather sofa and leaned back. "So, Kelsey, what do we know?"

She threw a quick glance at SecNav and got a nod in response. Ethan saw it and smiled.

"What we have," said Kelsey, sitting up and leaning forward a little, "are two dead generals. One marine brigadier and one army three-star." She pointed at the folder Ethan was holding. "And I see you've got the anonymous note."

Ethan opened the file and slid out the paper. "Not much. Al Qaeda says it's going to kill our generals." He put the note on top of the file. "Or that's what somebody would have us believe."

Kelsey frowned. "You think it's a hoax?"

"God, no. But I never believe anything anybody tells me until I see proof."

"Works for me."

He liked this woman with those deep green eyes. He liked anyone with good common sense.

"So far," Kelsey continued, "we have next to nothing. General Harper was gunned down outside a diner—"

"SecNav brought me up to speed on that one," Ethan interrupted. "What've we got on General Davy's killing?"

"Precious little," said Kelsey. "Uniforms found his body in his car at the airport. Right out in plain sight. Shot twice in the chest at close range. Probably from the driver's seat."

"And his driver?"

Kelsey was silent for a beat. "Missing. But we have to assume the worst."

"Safe assumption," said Ethan, a little callously, but combat will do that to a man. "So Al Qaeda—"

"Or someone pretending to be Al Qaeda," Kelsey interjected.

Ethan nodded slowly. "One marine, one army. I'm not a betting man, but I'd say they'll go after navy next. Probably an admiral. Just to keep things balanced."

"There are more than two hundred admirals serving in the navy right now," SecNav informed them.

"Then they have a lot to choose from," Kelsey added.

"We need to narrow down the field," said Ethan, standing and pacing the office. Two steps each way. He gave up and sat again. "They'll want a four-star to get the biggest buzz."

"How many?" Kelsey asked.

"Active? Nine," SecNav said. "But a terrorist is going to find it tough to get to them, really tough now that security is ramped up to maximum."

Ethan made a pyramid with his fingertips and put them on his lips. "We can't watch them all the time," he said after a moment. "Do the dead generals have anything in common?"

Kelsey shook her head. "Nothing that I can find, but Davy's assassination has only just been reported, so I haven't had time to check his history and contacts." She saw Ethan's look. "I'll get on that."

"Thanks," said Ethan. "Three days between hits, so far." He made the pyramid again. "But with a sample of two, that's not very telling."

"There's you," said SecNav.

Ethan frowned, then got it. "Yes, I did know them both. But I have an alibi." He stood up ready to leave. "I need to see Davy's car."

"The FBI will have it," said SecNav, caught Ethan's look and nodded. "I'll see what I can do."

"FBI have a lead," said Kelsey.

"And you were going to tell me this, when?" Ethan was irritated, but a night without sleep will do that.

She shrugged. "I was waiting to see if I can trust you."

"Thanks."

"You're welcome," she said with a smile. "First impressions aren't great, you know?"

He knew.

"There's a two-man terrorist team that fits the profile for this." She waited for him to react. He didn't. "Naser Alzesh and Mahmoud Faraj arrived in this country five weeks ago from Pakistan and then dropped off the grid. Alzesh is a person of interest in the assassination of a high-ranking Pakistani politician. Faraj ambushed an Afghan-led patrol in Helmand and killed a dozen Afghanis and four marines."

"And they walked in through JFK?" Ethan's tone showed he was not impressed.

"The FBI let them in," said SecNav, a little embarrassed but without reason. "They believed they could manage them and they would lead them to bigger fish."

"They were wrong," said Ethan.

"Evidently," said SecNav, a little testily.

"Okay, it's done," said Ethan. "Have we any idea where they are or what they're up to?"

SecNav shifted uncomfortably. "Homeland Security believe they're here to avenge Bin Laden's death."

"Oh, great." Ethan let it go. "I'll reach out to my contacts in Afghanistan and see if there's anything buzzing about these two or a whisper about a revenge attack." He crossed to the door, stopped and turned. "If you hear anything," he said to Kelsey, "you let me know. It doesn't matter how unimportant it might seem. Okay?"

"I've done this sort of work before." Her cheeks reddened just a little.

"Sorry," said Ethan. "I'm used to dealing with numb-nut... with marines."

"I'll keep you in the loop," she said, satisfied. "When there's a loop to keep you in."

"Okay, do that," said Ethan and left.

He collected his Sig from the security desk and smiled at the scowling security guard. It costs nothing to be nice.

Back on the steps, he stopped and looked up at the dark December sky that pretty much reflected how he felt. So, the first order of business was to get some food, get a hotel, and get some damned sleep before he smacked somebody for just looking at him.

Like so many great ideas, it came to him while he was sleeping. Give up this stupid mission and retire to Florida. He sat up in bed and leaned against the padded headboard. If only.

He was back in the marines. He'd accepted SecNav's offer, and even if it wasn't on paper, it was his word. So, no Florida.

He thought about calling room service for some coffee, but decided he'd head out and find a diner for lunch, or dinner, or whatever the hell meal time it was right then. And he'd get a haircut and some new clothes. Question was, would his cash stretch? He remembered the credit card that was tucked into the back of his wallet, unused. Maybe it was still valid, but it had been a while. Credit cards leave a paper trail, and seven years in Special Ops teaches a man to minimize his footprint.

He showered, shaved, and dressed in his shabby suit before leaving the hotel. It was late afternoon, and the city was busy with people heading out, or heading in. Whatever. First stop, coffee. A man can die from lack of coffee.

When he returned to his hotel two hours later, he was a different man. He'd bought a new dark grey suit that actually fitted him and a pale blue polo shirt and white vest. He'd been tempted by desert sand Nike Air Force sneakers—because he liked the irony—but went with sensible polished black lace-ups. With his hair clippered back to high and tight, he finally felt he was back in the world.

When he'd left the marines, he'd decided to see the country he'd been fighting for so took his '98 Chevy Tahoe and headed out of Camp Lejeune for the last time. West through Tennessee and the Mississippi Delta, the cradle of the Civil War. It was an amazing feeling to have nowhere to go, nobody expecting anything, and nobody to save. That was two years ago. And the novelty had worn off.

Twenty-three months ago. Trouble had found him quicker than a grizzly finds a beehive. He ran afoul of the New Orleans Police Department within a day of arriving. Some kid-cop resented him stepping in to stop him beating an old black guy with his baton. And to prove no good deed goes unpunished, it got him a night in the cells, and some bruises. The old black guy had said thanks, though. So that was okay. He didn't blame the NOPD, because some cops are just like that. Some people are just like that. And cops are people. Strange how many times something like that had happened in the last couple of years, though. Maybe he was just unlucky. Except he knew it was because he wouldn't just walk by and let something bad go down. What is it they say about all it takes for evil to triumph? He didn't see himself as a Good Man, but he wouldn't just stand by and do nothing; it wasn't in his nature. So he got into trouble. And that was in his nature.

He ate at a little Italian restaurant down the block from the hotel, because who eats in a hotel when they don't have to? The small, round tables were shoulder to shoulder, but at six o'clock, there were only two other people in the place. He ordered tomato and basil bruschetta, followed by spaghetti carbonara, cooked with just pancetta, garlic, olive oil, and Parmigiano cheese. He was a bit suspicious of the frugality of the meal, which lacked the usual mushrooms, chicken, onion, zucchini, and Canadian bacon that was a true American pasta dish. It was truly delicious, and he ate it hungrily. The waiter brought him an espresso coffee to finish, and that, by contrast, was truly gross. He remembered why he hated the thick, black stuff as soon as he sipped it and it strangled his taste buds.

He was about to order a real coffee in a mug when his cell phone intruded. He fished it out and raised a hand to cancel the signal to the waiter.

"We can see the car," Kelsey said. "But it has to be tonight. Now. Can you do that?"

He caught the waiter's eye and mimicked writing on his palm. With the bill on its way, he put the phone back to his ear. "Can you pick me up at my hotel in say—" He looked at his watch. "Twenty minutes?"

"Yes," she said, but sounded a little reticent. "Are you still wearing that suit?"

He smiled. "No, I bought a nice new one."

"Thank god for that or we'd be arrested at the FBI's door."

"We'll be fine. They'll love the electric blue jacket and burgundy pants." As he ended the call, he just caught the sound of Kelsey's gasp. And smiled.

She was ten minutes late. The cross-town traffic had been murder. He saw her black SUV pull up in front of the hotel, but stayed inside for a minute, just to worry her about being late, and his suit. He stepped out of the automatic doors and saw her look of relief by the dim interior light.

"You think that was funny, don't you?" she scolded as he climbed into the passenger seat. She looked at his smart suit. "Couldn't stretch to a tie, I see."

He straightened the polo shirt collar. "Don't want to overdo it."

She risked looking down at his feet and sighed in relief at the sight of the brogues.

He smiled at the thought of the Nike sneakers. Still, it was a pity because they were cool. And everybody knows khaki and blue go together stylishly. He looked ahead at the unchanging road. "Shouldn't we be moving? If we're going someplace."

She jumped a little and snapped out of whatever was in her head. "We're going. I was just waiting for you to put your seat belt on."

That was a lie, but he let it go and snapped the seat belt buckle with a flourish. "So, where is the car?"

"Well, it isn't here," she said with a flick of her head. "FBI lab on Pennsylvania Avenue."

"Hey, that's where the White House is. Cool, I've never seen it." He sounded like a kid on a school trip. "Is it far? I could do with a nap."

"Go ahead," she said, pushing into traffic. "It'll take us fifteen, twenty minutes."

"Thanks." He leaned on the side window.

She glanced at him and shook her head. "I was kidding, you know that?"

She was talking to herself; he'd gone to sleep instantly, even though he'd slept most of the day. It was a soldier thing to sleep when you can. She stared ahead into the traffic and smiled. He was okay, which surprised her, as she'd met a few ex-military men and mostly they were posturing bullies with an inflated idea of their own ability, both in life and in combat. She wondered if that was being a bit harsh, as the samples she'd met had come from Special Ops, and arrogance was pretty much a prerequisite for that role. She glanced at Ethan sleeping quietly. Maybe he'd revert when he settled in. She hoped not.

He woke up the moment she pulled into the visitors' parking and switched off the ignition. He stretched and flexed his shoulders as if he'd been sleeping for hours. "This it?"

She glanced at him. "No, I thought we'd stop off for a Big Mac en route. Keep the FBI waiting."

"You go ahead," he said with a suppressed smile. "I've eaten."

She sighed heavily, got out of the car, and slammed the door in a display of annoyance she didn't feel. She led the way out of the parking garage, down 9th Street and into the J. Edgar Hoover Building through the unimpressive revolving doors. They passed through the ubiquitous metal detector and handed over their weapons, as usual. Then they waited for the special agent in charge. And waited.

He let them sit for twenty minutes, to show how important he was. And how they weren't. The prick.

Ethan read a magazine and drank coffee from a plastic cup. After sitting in a hole in the Afghan desert, this was nothing. And it gave him time to think things through, now that he was no longer sleep-deprived.

Something didn't gel, but he couldn't get it to the surface, so decided to let it rise at its own speed. Something he'd done many times before. Push all the puzzles into his subconscious and let it work them out while he got on with his day job.

The special agent in charge arrived. Ethan could tell it was him because he spent time talking bullshit to the security guards. His opinion of the man hadn't changed. He finished his nonsense and strode over. His white shirt was immaculate. His tie was perfect. His shoes were shiny enough to be military. Yes, this would be the special agent in charge.

Kelsey stood. Ethan stayed seated and finished his coffee while the man glared at him. He folded the magazine and put it back on the table between the seats, stood up, and brushed down his suit. When he was ready, he looked at the agent and smiled.

"You must be the agent in charge?" he said, extending his hand.

The agent looked at the hand, then at Ethan, and back at the hand before taking it and shaking it once. "I am Special Agent Timothy Dryer. And yes, I am the agent in charge."

Well, good for you, Spanky, thought Ethan, but kept it to himself.

"This is Master Sergeant Ethan Gill," said Kelsey quickly, just in case. "And I am—"

"Yes," said Dryer sharply. "I know who you are. Follow me." He turned and strode off along the corridor.

Ethan looked at Kelsey, smiled and raised his eyebrows. He waved her ahead with a low swing of his hand. She sighed heavily and followed Dryer, who was holding open a security door and waiting, impatiently.

Ethan followed them into the elevator and then down another corridor and through several fire doors. He was just beginning to think the agent in charge was walking them round the building just to piss them off when he stopped and pushed open a door into a room with enough electronics to keep a geek happy for a lifetime.

"Lisa will show you what you need," said Dryer, ushering them into the room. "I'm late for a meeting." He left without a backward glance.

Lisa watched the door swing shut and shook her head sadly. "Dryer can be a..." She caught herself. "Now, you're here to see the analysis results from the general's assassination."

Ethan frowned. "No," he said. "We're here to see the car."

"Oh," said Lisa, and looked around as if she expected to see the car in the lab.

Kelsey picked it up without a pause. "That's okay, Lisa. You lead the way, and we'll follow."

They could see she was uncomfortable exceeding her orders but that she was thinking of doing it anyway.

Ethan opened the door and smiled nicely. "Ground floor, is it?" As if a car would be anywhere else—the roof maybe.

"Yes," said Lisa.

The grey Lincoln MKZ sedan was in the basement garage, as it should be. Lisa was over her indecision and led the way across the empty parking bays to the side of the vehicle. "The shooter fired between the seats."

"He would," said Ethan, leaning into the vehicle's nearside rear door. "Less risk of the weapon being seen from outside." He ignored the blood on the leatherwork and leaned forward to examine the two holes in the seat back. "Did you recover the bullets?"

Lisa shook her head, realised he couldn't see her, and spoke to Kelsey. "No. They passed straight through the victim and exited through the trunk, missing the real driver's body."

"The general's driver was in the trunk?" Kelsey said and walked round to the rear.

"Yes. Shot once in the heart. Looks like the same weapon."

Ethan pushed himself out of the car and joined Kelsey. He opened the trunk. "Did you find that slug?"

"No. It appears to be a through and through."

"Has Agent in Charge Dryer ordered a search?" he asked.

She looked a little uncomfortable again. Maybe because she didn't want to talk out of school. Though he suspected it was embarrassment. He was right.

"Special Agent Dryer said there's no way we're ever going to find the bullets, as the shooting could have occurred anywhere between the Pentagon and Dulles Airport."

Ethan and Kelsey exchanged looks but said nothing.

Ethan put his finger over the hole made by one of the bullets leaving the vehicle's trunk. "Nine mil."

Kelsey looked surprised. "A nine mil? It passed through the victim's body, the seat back, and the metal trunk. I don't think a nine mil would do that."

Ethan smiled and headed for the garage exit but stopped when the others stayed where they were. "Lisa is going to show us the results of her analysis. Right?"

Lisa gave a little start and walked towards the door. "Yes, of course. That was what Dryer—Special Agent Dryer asked me to do."

"Then let's do that," said Ethan, holding open the door for them to pass.

The analysis was thin. Powder burns on the sides of the sedan's front seats showed that the handgun had been fired from there. Two holes in the general and the seat specified the number of shots. And... and that was about it. No fingerprints, no DNA, no wallet accidentally dropped by the shooter. Nothing.

Lisa walked them back to the foyer, and they thanked her and crossed to the desk to hand in their ID badges.

"Have you got a metal detector among all that electronics?" Ethan called after her as she began to return to her bat-cave.

She stopped and looked back, frowning. "I think so, yes. Why?"

Ethan smiled. "Do yourself a favor and check the batteries," he said and headed for the revolving door, with Kelsey racing to catch up.

They walked back to the garage parking without speaking, as Kelsey thought through what they had seen. She waited until she pulled the car back onto the street before she asked the question.

Ethan glanced at her, and tried not to look at her body, but it was tough. He changed the subject in his head. "Can we go back to the Pentagon?"

She looked back, and tried not to look at his body, but it was tough. She didn't ask the question, because he would tell her when he was good and ready.

Back at the Pentagon, they went down to the security office and asked to see the surveillance tapes for the day. The security officer was polite and helpful, so was probably new, retiring soon, or sick. He did look past Ethan at Kelsey and mouthed the word, "Tapes?"

"Master Sergeant Gill hasn't caught up with the digital age, Tony," said Kelsey.

Ethan ignored the slight and pointed at the wall of monitors. "Can you rewind to the time General Davy left for the last time?"

"Yes," said Tony, sitting back at one of his keyboards. "Nine fifteen." Two seconds later, and no whirring tape reels, he froze the image. "There it is."

Ethan leaned towards the monitor and the image of the Lincoln waiting at the roadside. "Can you zoom in on the driver's window?"

"Can open it for you, if you like," said Tony, and the sedan's side window filled the monitor. "Tinted glass."

"Yes, I noticed back at the garage," said Ethan. "Just hoped he'd left it open. But that would have been too sloppy, even for this guy."

Kelsey caught the implication. "You think he was sloppy?"

Ethan pointed at the monitor and made winding movements with his hand. "Fast forward, but slowly," he asked.

Tony glanced at him, but decided a technical explanation of the CCTV system would be like teaching a monkey to type. He stepped the image forward frame by frame.

After a few seconds, Ethan saw what he needed. "Hold it there."

Tony looked back over his shoulder. "See something?"

Kelsey leaned forward towards the monitor and squinted, but could see only the sedan, stationary a little short of the road. "What is it?"

Ethan avoided the line from the *Airplane* movie and spoke to Tony. "Wind back a little and let it run at normal speed."

Tony did as he was asked, and the Lincoln ran backwards, stopped, and moved forward. Then it stopped. Ethan took a long breath, and Kelsey and Tony looked over their shoulders from the monitor. What?

The Lincoln moved off again at normal speed.

"Okay, wind it back to when it was stopped," said Ethan.

The sedan ran backwards and stopped.

"Make it bigger," said Ethan, leaning his hands on the back of Tony's chair. "There. Enlarge that." He pointed at the car's trunk.

A moment later they were staring at a single hole in the polished bodywork.

"Go forward," said Ethan. "Very slowly."

The image changed to another frame, and another. Then the third, and this one showed a hole where there hadn't been one before.

"Okay," said Ethan, straightening up. "We know where the general was shot." He looked at Kelsey. "And we know where the bullets are. Can you ask the agent in charge to get some crime scene investigators down there?" He winked. "They'll need a metal detector."

Kelsey grinned. "It will be my pleasure."

At nine thirty the next morning, after a restful night's sleep, Ethan and Kelsey were back at the FBI lab, and Special Agent Dryer was as nice as pie, wishing them good morning and offering them coffee and doughnuts. What a nice guy.

Ethan refused the doughnuts but took the coffee. Kelsey refused both, taking a bottle of mineral water instead. Coffee makes for bad breath. They followed Dryer past Lisa's lab and into a cramped but expensively furnished office. Dryer's office. Dryer sat in the ergo mesh seat, leaving Ethan and Kelsey to fight over the visitor's chair, leather and elegant, but too big for the small office. Ethan sat on the corner of Dryer's desk and watched him force a smile through gritted teeth.

Kelsey got down to it before the situation got any worse. "Did your people find the bullets?"

Of course they did.

"Yes, our agents found two rounds very quickly," Dryer said, a little smugly.

"Having their location pointed out must have helped a little," Ethan added, just to rattle his chain. He let it go at that. For now. Dryer was about to speak, but Ethan cut in. "Nine mil with a tempered steel core." He saw Dryer's look of surprise. "7N21 armour-piercing round. Probably from a Russian MP-443 Grach."

"Impressive," said Kelsey. "But how do you know?"

"He doesn't," said Dryer sourly. "He's just guessing."

Ethan shrugged. "The Grach Rook is the standard issue for the Russian military ınd law enforcement agencies, so you can pick one up for a bottle of vodka and a ollar."

"Still doesn't make it our murder weapon," said Dryer.

"Maybe not," said Ethan, finally getting off Dryer's desk. "But it makes it a contender and gets my vote."

"There are other handguns that use the 7N21 round," said Dryer.

"Yes," said Ethan, "the Russian GSh-18." He waited for Dryer to make some smart comment.

"You can't get one of those in the US," Dryer said with a slow shake of his head. "There's a BATF trade ban on their import."

"Oh, that's okay, then," said Ethan. "We can discount them, because they're illegal." He leaned on the back of Kelsey's chair and smiled nicely. "The point is," he said when Dryer had squirmed enough. "We have two dead generals. General Harper was shot by a couple of kids with a junk thirty-eight, and General Davy was executed by an expensive automatic firing armour-piercing ammo." He waited for some input.

"It could just be a coincidence," said Dryer. "It doesn't make sense that these two killings are linked."

"Hell of a coincidence," said Kelsey. "Two generals shot to death in the space of a week." She shook her head. "No, I agree with Ethan. Somebody is hiring gang-bangers to muddy up our investigation."

Dryer tapped his fingers on his desktop as he thought it through. "Then, if you're correct, and I'm not saying I agree with your conclusions, but if you are, then it has to be Naser Alzesh and Mahmoud Faraj hiring these shooters to do their dirty work."

"Not likely," said Ethan. He caught Dryer's puzzled look. "These boys do their own killing. They like it. Getting some idiots to do the fun part isn't their M.O."

"Then you're saying it is a coincidence?" said Dryer.

"What I'm saying is right now I don't know what the hell is going on," said Ethan.

"Then," said Dryer, "we finally agree on something."

Before Ethan could work out if that was a crack or not, Dryer stood and looked past him through the glass door. "Ah, I believe you've already met one of our senior analysts."

Ethan turned as the door opened. "Teddy!" he said, stepped forward and put out his hand.

The man smiled broadly and shook the offered hand. "Ethan, I thought you were dead."

Ethan chuckled. "I've come close a few times, but nobody has won the cuddly bunny."

"Yes, I heard about the drive-by in Chicago. It was that close?"

"Didn't need to shave that day," said Ethan. "And it wasn't a drive-by." He let i go at that and looked down at Kelsey. "You won't believe that this crinkly old gu served with me in Iraq. Teddy was the best intelligence analyst in the corps. Or so he said."

"That much is true," said Dryer. "It's why he now works for the FBI."

"Keeps him out of trouble," said Ethan. "And that was something I never managed to do. Him nor his boy." His smile faded.

"Your son is a marine too?" Kelsey asked, surprised.

"Yeah, he was the best," said Teddy. "Served with Master Sergeant Gill here in Special Ops."

"Wow!" said Kelsey. "Two generations ruined by one man."

Nobody smiled, which was a surprise. She got it. "I'm sorry."

"Don't be," said Teddy. "He died protecting the country he loved. I couldn't be more proud of him."

"He was a great marine," said Ethan. "And a better human being than I'll ever be. He saved us all that day." He put his hand on Teddy's shoulder. "I think about him every single day."

"Hey, lighten up," said Teddy. "He's up there laughing at us being all sorry and stupid."

"I stopped in at Arlington to pay my respects," said Ethan. "Everything was shipshape, just like Eli liked it."

"Hey, I think you've mixed him up with somebody else," Teddy said with a real grin. "Eli was a train wreck kept in shape by the marines. Nobody could accuse him of being tidy when he didn't have to be."

Ethan laughed. "Copy that."

"If we're done here," said Dryer, "I have a pile of paperwork to fill in on this case. Unless you'd like to stay and help?"

It was a textbook example of an orderly retreat, and the three of them exited the small office in perfect formation.

Christian Carter strode into the foyer of Senator Wakeman's congressional office and up the marble steps with a real spring in his step. This was it. This was the meeting that was going to put his company in the big league. Wakeman was on the military procurement subcommittee and a key supporter of the Christian Diem Corporation's bid to supply IED Early Detection Systems to the military.

Melissa Bates saw him heading down the wide corridor with a broad smile on his nned face, and her heart sank. She wanted him to get good news today, to keep the ile that lit up his face, but it wasn't going to be. He was gorgeous. Six-five, dark l slim, with overlong hair swept back in waves off his face. He had eyes that were lark, it was impossible to distinguish the pupils, but they flashed with laughter mischief, even when his face was serious. He had long legs and a spring in his walk that told of super-fitness. A happy, sporting man, with looks that a movie star would die for. Or so she saw him. Others might have seen something a little more sinister, more unnerving.

He stepped up to her desk, put his manicured hands flat on its surface, and leaned forward. "Good morning, Melissa. And how are you this fine day?"

She couldn't believe he knew her name, and had to check herself to make sure her mouth wasn't open like a stupid kid's. "I'm fine, thank you." Okay, her voice was steady, thank God.

Melissa wasn't comfortable with men, or women, or kids for that matter, which was odd as she was the senator's administrative assistant and her key role was interacting with people. And keeping the unsavory ones at arm's length. But that was her professional role, and she could hide behind her title. Personal relationships, well... what are they? She'd had relationships, of course, but that was when she was young, before her father died and her mother fell apart.

It had been a few days after her twentieth birthday when her father complained of feeling ill during dinner, fell off his chair and died. Just like that. People say that's the best way to go, no suffering. But going that way puts all the suffering on the people left behind. He was sixty-three when he died, and her life ended.

It didn't just stop. At first, she really believed they would get through it, but her mother just came apart over the next weeks. She stopped talking, she stopped eating, and would explode at the smallest thing, smashing crockery, kicking the fridge, and lashing out at Melissa. Until one day, maybe four weeks after her father died and two days after they put him in the ground on that Tuesday morning in the torrential rain, she came home from her job at the diner and found her mother sitting in the big armchair as still as death. The doctor said she'd shut down from the pain of loss and would recover in time. But she hadn't, and the shutdown had mutated into Alzheimer's or senility, which one she couldn't say, because the doctor had stopped coming around when she couldn't pay his bills.

Melissa stayed with the job at the diner that she'd taken temporarily while her mother had grieved for her husband. But now it was permanent, and any thought of moving to the city and starting her life was parked. And remained parked for sixteen years.

She washed clothes and bathed her angry mother while her friends settled down, got married, had kids, a house, and a life. They called her Poor Melissa, but were glad it wasn't them. It somehow made it easier that she'd been so popular at school, a sort of balancing of the books. But it was a shame, and they all said so.

Her mother would have what they ironically called 'lucid moments', when she would recognize her daughter enough to call her a tramp and a slut, and threaten to haunt her from hell if she even thought about putting her in a home. The people across the street would keep a lookout during the day and put her back in the house when she wandered outside. But at night she was Melissa's duty and burden. She'd loved her mother, but she no longer recognised this monster that slowly bled away her life.

On Christmas Eve, with *It's a Wonderful Life* playing on the TV, the old woman opened her eyes, smiled at her daughter, and died. Melissa wept for her mother, but also for the relief of it.

She buried her in the graveyard of the Catholic church she'd never attended. The priest had asked the Lord to unite them again as one family while Melissa begged the Lord to do no such thing. Then he'd walked away, and she was alone at the graveside, crying tears for her mother she had lost so many years ago, years that had not been kind to her. Thirty-six now, and tired. She'd taken everything life had thrown at her, but some of it had stuck. She was too thin, from the stress, but also because she hadn't had the energy to eat. Her superbly boned features that had turned so many boys' heads in high school now looked haggard and worn. And her once tanned and lovely skin was now pale and lined around eyes that had lost their light and become dead and dark-rimmed.

The bank took the house for the mortgage, and she threw everything else into the trash. Then bought a ticket on the first bus out of town, closed her eyes, and didn't open them again until the town was a memory.

The bus terminated in Washington, and she walked out of the bus station into a new life. It had been easy, though anything would have been easy compared with where she'd come from. She worked at another diner for a year and half while she got her degree in business studies. Long days at the counter and long nights with the books, but she'd loved every free moment of it. Without the weight of her mother dragging on her, she blossomed a little. Put on some weight in the right places, and got a little sun on her skin. But sun and a few good meals cannot undo the attrition of sixteen years. She would look at herself in the full-length mirror and cry a little while her mind overlaid the girl she had been on the prematurely middle-aged woman that looked back at her.

She'd got the first office job she'd applied for and never knew she'd been chosen above the other applicants because of the way she looked; since all she would have in her life was work, she was a good bet. And they'd been right, but she'd liked working at the congressional offices, and over the next five years, rose up the ranks until now she was chief of staff. So that was a fair exchange, a good job, big income, power. In exchange for a life. And love. Sometimes, in the small hours, the loneliness crashed over her like a black wave and her breath would catch in her throat, suffocating her. Filling the future with nothing but blackness, sadness, and a death that would leave not even a small hole in the lives of the people who smiled at her at work and pretended they knew her. But she could dream.

She stood up from the comfortable chair where she had been waiting for Christian Carter and led him to the senator's office, closing the door quietly after he'd entered. She was sorry it was going to be such bad news. She liked him, and that was unusual. She could have just returned to her desk and got on with the day, but instead sat back in one of the chairs arranged around the glass coffee table, and waited.

Christian Carter stepped up to the senator's desk and put out his hand. "Senator, it is good of you to see me."

Senator Wakeman was a big man. Well over six foot and his body filled out the white shirt under the red braces equally in all directions, straining the fine silk to its tolerance point. His hair was too perfect to be real and had a gloss that had gone out of fashion about the time Elvis died. But he had a good face that radiated sincerity and friendly charm—an absolute prerequisite for any politician.

He half rose from his big, leather seat and smiled the vote-winning smile. "Christian, so good to see you again." He sat back down and the smile vanished. "Bad news, I'm afraid," he said, getting to the spike as quickly as possible, as experience had taught him to do. "There's going to be a delay in the decision." He waved at the chair in front of his desk.

Christian sat down heavily and fought to mask his disappointment and anger. "That is bad news, Senator. Is there anything I can do?"

Wakeman shook his head, and his jowls wobbled gently. "I'm afraid not, Christian." He leaned forward, his man-breasts resting on the desktop. "You'll have heard about this business with General Davy?"

"Yes, assassinated by terrorists. Tragic affair."

"Quite. General Davy was providing expert military input into the decision, I'm afraid."

Christian saw light. "Oh, I see. So we're delayed until a suitable replacement can be found?"

Wakeman licked his bright red lips with a wet, pink tongue. "Well, yes and no."

Christian remained silent. But there wasn't much to say in response to that.

The senator did what most people do when there's a silence, he filled it. "However, General Davy was opposed to your company's solution."

Christian remained silent. The hole was dug, and the senator jumped in.

"He was one of three members who prefer the solution from General Dynamics."

So, thought Christian, four against. "Have I met the three members who oppose my company's bid?"

"I'm afraid it would be inappropriate of me to disclose their names."

Oh well, it was worth a try.

"Of course," said Christian. "I understand, and I wouldn't want to put you on the spot." Which was a lie. "But our bid has the majority vote?"

Wakeman was silent for a moment. A moment too long. "Once again, I can't discuss the bidding process until it's complete."

Christian considered offering to support his campaign for re-election, but couldn't think of a way of putting it that didn't sound like the attempted bribe it was. He stood up and put out his hand. "Thank you, Senator. I value your support." Which presupposed he was actually getting it.

The senator stood and shook the offered hand. "It's my pleasure, Christian. And if there's anything I can do, please just ask." The smile again.

"Thank you. I'll be sure to do just that."

Christian closed the door behind him and stood in the hallway while he replayed what had just happened. Today was to be the day, and now...

He saw Melissa starting to stand and smiled. The game wasn't over yet. Okay, she was on the wrong side of forty and dressed like an old maid, but in the right light, she could be pretty, and maybe was... once. But for eleven billion dollars, he'd smile at a rutting pig.

She crossed the hall and returned the smile. "Short meeting."

"Yes," said Christian with a shrug. "Delay in the process. Oh well, it's to be expected with so many people to be satisfied."

"It's a lot of money," said Melissa, and then realised what a lame thing that was to say. "Everybody is careful about being seen as spenders at a time like this."

He nodded. "Understandable." He smiled at her and pretended to start for the stairs, stopped and stepped back. "I've been coming to Washington for months now and have never seen the city. Perhaps I could buy you dinner and you could show me around."

She took an involuntary step back and was about to make an excuse and flee, but stopped. It would be nice to have someone to talk to, besides her cat. Yes, it would. "I'd love to show you around," she said and hoped she wasn't blushing on the outside like she was on the inside.

"Then it's a date," he said with a big smile. "Seven?"

"Yes, seven." She watched him stride back down the marble steps and almost ran after him to the top. "Where will we meet?" It was almost desperate.

He turned and winked. "Beautiful woman like you won't be hard to find. I'll send my driver for you." He turned and skipped down the stairs.

Melissa watched him go and then looked around in case someone had seen her making a damned fool of herself. The foyer was deserted, except for the security people, and they're paid not to notice.

Colonel Mitch Morgan walked slowly to his car from the terminal at Camp Pendleton Munn Field Airport. He was tired but glad to be back home on American soil after a year and a half in Okinawa. Not that Okinawa wasn't great; it was just having to leave Sarah and the girls for extended tours was wearing him down. Time to shoot for a desk job nearer home.

The grey SUV was right where he'd parked it, even though his brother, Tim, had been using it while he'd been away. Better than just letting it stand there and rot. He glanced at the scrape along the driver's door and shook his head. Maybe not. He smiled. Timmy was a bit of a speed freak, so having to use the SUV must have been tough on him. He opened the rear door and stepped back a little to let the stale hot air roll out. He threw in his suitcase and slammed the door. The air was just a little fresher as he climbed into the driver's seat, but only just. It smelled of wet dog and fish. Great. But he was still smiling.

He turned right onto Las Pulgas Road and put on the air-con and the radio—a country station. He wasn't a fan of country music, but nothing says home like it. A few minutes later he was on the canyon road heading for San Diego Freeway. He changed the radio channel to news. Somehow, listening to people crying about their lost love, or their dog, or some cattle drive wears thin real quick.

In less than two hours he'd be in Los Angeles. In time to take the girls to the beach for ice cream. Suzy loved ice cream. Sienna not so much, but she'd pretend for the sake of her little sister. She was ten, going on twenty. No, that was then, so now she was twelve. Two years of her life missed, and two years of Suzy's life was a third. This was no way for a man to live.

The traffic was light on Las Pulgas Canyon Road, and he settled back into the seat for a steady drive. He saw the Dodge Ram pickup in his rearview but thought nothing of it, except that he remembered somewhere that they were supposed to be the fastest pickups around. Which had struck him as odd. If you wanted to go fast, why buy a pickup?

The news reporter was telling him that financial turmoil in Europe was the cause of all America's ills. Which made him smile. The pickup closed the gap and overtook him like he was going backwards. Just showing off. Then it cut in suddenly and sideswiped the SUV, and Mitch had to fight the wheel to keep it on the road. The pickup driver must be blind not to see how close he was. He brought the car off the rough shoulder and eased off the gas while he settled down from the shock.

He was feeling almost relaxed again as he came around the long left curve. He glanced in his rearview as a movement caught his eye and saw the pickup coming out of a dirt side road. A fist closed in his stomach, and he realised it had been no accident. He floored the gas pedal, but knew the lumbering SUV would never outrun the Ram. He wished he'd taken the sidearm he'd been offered, but he was in logistics, not Special Forces. And local law enforcement take a dim view of people, even marines, carrying weapons in LA. Chances are it wouldn't have done him any good against a fast-moving truck from inside an SUV. Though he would've liked the chance.

The Ram came up alongside, and he looked across to see the passenger smiling at him and pointing at the rocky hill sloping down from the road. A second later the Ram hit the side of the SUV above the front wheel, and it started a slow left turn as Mitch fought the wheel. He was going to make it; he could feel the front end coming round. Then the Ram hit him again.

The SUV left the road and sailed ten feet over the rocks before crashing nose down into the boulders. It flipped almost in slow motion and slammed down on its roof, its momentum peeling it away like a can opener. But Mitch was already dead, with his head crushed by the compacted roof.

The Ram slowed a little and drove away slowly. No point being stupid. There was still a lot of Americans to kill.

* * *

...Ethan is back in the game. There's no decision to be made, no discussion. His country first. But maybe he wouldn't have stepped up if he'd known the hell awaiting him, any normal man would look away. But not Master Sergeant Ethan Gill.

ALL LEIGH BARKER'S BOOKS AT AMAZON

Jack Duggan

US Federal Marshals - Crime Thrillers

In Harm's Way (Book #1)
(Chapter 1 is free)
US Federal Marshal Jack Duggan: sometimes a man has to make a stand, no matter the odds.

A Warrant for Jimmy Detroit (#2)
(Chapter 1 is free)
Jack Duggan is the law. There is no exception. But sometimes there's only justice.

The Hellfire Series

All the roller-coaster Hellfire Crime Thrillers

A Whisper of Armageddon (Book #1)
(Chapter 1 is free)
Off-the-wall characters, edge-of-your-seat action and suspense

The Hellfire Legacy (#2)
(Episode 1 is free)
Action-packed Ethan Gill Thriller

The Orpheus Directive (#3)
(Episode 1 is free)
The Marine Squad is back in action

Clan Series

Historical Fiction: All of Calum Maclean's great adventures fighting English tyranny

Clan: Calum's Sword (Book #1)
(Episode 1 is free)
Rip-roaring Adventures during the Jacobite Rebellion

Clan: Calum's Exile (#2)
(Episode 1 is free)
Calum's adventures in The New World

Clan: Calum's Country (#3)
(Episode 1 is free)
Calum's Return to Scotland

Eden Series

Fantasy: All the adventures during the war in heaven

Eden's Last Hero (Book #1)
(Episode 1 is free)
Mad times with our reluctant hero

Winterwood (#2)
(Episode 1 is free)
A small town fights for its life

Requiem for Eden (#3)
(Episode 1 is free)
Four young knights take on Lucid's army and the Norsemen to save Eden

Soldiers

Historical Fiction: World War One

Regret's Mission
(Episode 1 is free)
Explosive Great War Adventures

10-Minute Escapes – The whole Short Story Collection

(First 5 Stories are free)
All 18 great stories – for when it's time just for you.

Leigh's website: www.LeighWBarker.com

Printed in Great Britain
by Amazon